Maureen McLean was born in London and worked for social services as a care assistant for the elderly for many years. She began writing in 2020 when she decided to do an online writing course. It helped her with her journey to becoming an author. *Jessica's Baby* will be her second novel.

To you, the many readers, thank you for reading my novel, especially the people of London, who provided me with the inspiration and support that I needed.

Maureen McLean

JESSICA'S BABY

AUSTIN MACAULEY PUBLISHERS
LONDON * CAMBRIDGE * NEW YORK * SHARJAH

Copyright © Maureen McLean 2025

The right of Maureen McLean to be identified as author of this work has been asserted by the author in accordance with sections 77 and 78 of the Copyright, Designs and Patents Act 1988.

All rights reserved. No part of this publication may be reproduced, stored in a retrieval system, or transmitted in any form or by any means, electronic, mechanical, photocopying, recording, or otherwise, without the prior permission of the publishers.

Any person who commits any unauthorised act in relation to this publication may be liable to criminal prosecution and civil claims for damages.

This is a work of fiction. Names, characters, businesses, places, events, locales, and incidents are either the products of the author's imagination or used in a fictitious manner. Any resemblance to actual persons, living or dead, or actual events is purely coincidental.

A CIP catalogue record for this title is available from the British Library.

ISBN 9781037108525 (Paperback)
ISBN 9781037108532 (ePub e-book)

www.austinmacauley.com

First Published 2025
Austin Macauley Publishers Ltd®
1 Canada Square
Canary Wharf
London
E14 5AA

Thank you to my family, who kept encouraging me to write; I couldn't have done it without you, and especially my dear friend Lucille, I'm grateful for your feedback and your support.

Table of Contents

Tianna	13
Rhys	22
Tianna	27
Kim	32
Drake	37
Tianna	39
Drake	46
Rhys	48
Tianna	52
Tamara	54
Tianna	56
Alex	64
Tianna	67
Renee, Melani, Kayleigh and Nyomi	74
Jess	76
Tianna	77
Rhys	82
Leah (Ex-Wife)	84
Tianna	86
Renee	88

Tianna	93
Rhys	101
Renee	108
Kim	110
Tianna	117
Melani	129
Rhys	133
Tianna	136
Drake	138
Renee	140
Tamara	145
Rhys	148
Tianna	152
Rhys	163
Kim	167
Drake	169
Tianna	171
Rhys	182
Tianna	186
Aubrey	192
Rhys	196
Sabrina	199
Melani	200
Tianna	201
Rhys	204
Sabrina	206
Tianna	208

Kayleigh and Nyomi	213
Drake	214
Renee	215
Jessica, Aka Jess	217
Alex Roberts	219
Kim	224
Drake	231
Tianna	233
Rhys	236
Aubrey	238
Renee and Tamara	239
Tianna	241
Kayleigh	246
Tianna	249
Rhys	253
Steve Brooks	258
Tianna	260
Tamara	265
Drake	268
Rhys	270
Clive	278
Tianna	280
Steve Brooks	282
Rhys	287
Steve Brooks	291
Drake	293
Tianna	295

Tianna

It was a beautiful morning, my face shone with a glowing smile, like a summer sunrise. I gazed through my bedroom window for a little while, listening to the birds, as if they were singing a beautiful love song. I closed my eyes, just for a few seconds, listening to the small birds singing softly. I felt a sense of joy, more focused, and alert. I certainly needed that mental boost.

I drank my coffee, quickly realising I forgot to add milk, yet again. Umm, it kind of tasted vibrant, and nutty, a bit like me.

Then, I looked at my watch, thinking, 'Oh no, I'm late for work again.'

As I was leaving, the postman handed me my letters.

"Hi, Andy. How are you this morning? It looks like another lovely day," I said, staring down at the four letters he just handed me.

He pretended not to be listening, as we walked side-by-side, for a short while. I continued to stare at my letters. Suddenly, I found myself walking behind him, trying unsuccessfully, to keep up with his long strides. Andy, he's kind of cute, but not really my cup of tea. What's my cup of tea, the wrong type of tea, that's for sure. Poor Andy, he's asked me out on a date, a few times now, my answer was always the same.

"Sorry, I'm not looking for a relationship at the moment."

Anyway, when I was 18, I found out that I was adopted as a baby. And I've been looking for my birth mother ever since.

No letters from the adoption agency today. Oh well, there's always tomorrow, and the day after, and the day after that.

I celebrated my 30th birthday two Saturdays ago. I had hoped that, by now, I would have made some progress in tracking down my birth mother.

Pausing at my normal bus stop, I debated, walking instead of waiting 10 minutes for the bus. But I made friends with a few people, waiting for the number 11 bus, and decided to stay put.

"Sorry, Martin, I'm late again."

He's my boss. The girls in the office, they all tell me that he has a soft spot for me. Hmm, I really can't see it though, as he stood, drinking a cup of tea, propped up against the office wall, as though he were stuck there.

As usual, he dipped his favourite biscuit, bourbon creams, into his tea. Which he just so happened to be drinking from. He takes any clean cup he finds in the staff room. Today, it was a blue cup with white spots. He glanced up at the clock on the wall, then stared in my direction, rolling his eyes.

I put my handbag down under my desk, then looked up at the office clock. It ticked 30 long seconds, then the silence was ripped by a ferocious growl. Hmm, only my boss Martin's empty stomach, no doubt. Seven biscuits were not enough to contain his hunger.

Later that day, a few of my work colleagues decided to go for drinks after work, but I didn't feel up to it. I just wanted to go home, lie curled up on my sofa, like I do most nights, and watch a movie. I guess I should be feeling sad, but I don't. Well, that's what I keep telling myself.

To be honest, I had a meltdown, crying uncontrollably. But my plan went straight through the window.

My best friend, Renee, had other plans.

"Sis, it's a Friday night. Girl, you can't stay in," she said, raising her voice slightly.

Before I knew it, she hung up the phone and headed straight to my house.

So, I called in reinforcements and invited a few of our other friends. We had a fantastic evening at my favourite club, dancing all night, singing romantic love songs. Then my friend, Tamara, had to go, and spoil the evening by reminding me that I am the only one out of the six of us who is not in a relationship.

"Okay, babe, I don't need reminding," I said.

Then I stood in silence, staring at my friend, until Kayleigh spoke, "Seriously, girl, the truth this time. What really happened between you and Troy?"

Troy, I thought, was the one, you know, that perfect guy you dream about marrying and having 2.5 children with. We were in a loving relationship for three years, a serious relationship. Then I found out he was married. Troy was a wolf, dressed as a sheep, speaking nothing but lies. I flung myself on my bed and cried until I had no more tears left. A little voice deep down inside cried. If I didn't let him go, he'll just continue to lie and hurt me. When I decided to dump his arse, he didn't sound broken up about it.

That's a day in the life of a cheating man, by the way. My heart was in pieces.

The emotions of love and hate are in everything. My friends don't know the truth about Troy, that he had a wife. Well, except Renee, she's my best friend. We tell each other everything.

Troy and I have been split up for six months, three weeks, four days, seven hours, forty-two minutes and one second. How sad is that!

He keeps on phoning, and leaving me sexy text messages, saying how he wants me back, and how he will leave his wife to be with me.

'I swear to you, babe, I never meant to hurt you. How can I hurt someone whom I love so much? Babe, I made idiot choices and idiot decisions.'

Those were his words, the last time I answered one of his many phone calls. I hung up the call, and cried, because every word that left his mouth was a damn lie.

My friend, Renee, doesn't play with her words. She's quite a feisty sort of woman.

"Look, block his number, tell him to stop calling you. If he loved you, truly loved you, he would have left his wife by now to be with you. Guys like Troy, they're just players, you deserve much better than him. He has a selfish mind. Dry your eyes, babe, and wipe your nose, girl." Renee said.

Anyway, Tamara, apologised, for upsetting me, but we're all friends, she meant no harm.

To tell you the truth, he's not the first guy whom I have dated, only to find out that he had a wife or a girlfriend. I often wonder why I am attracted to guys like that.

Renee, my best friend of almost seven years, was getting married in a few weeks' time to her boyfriend, Drake. She had been with him for almost five years.

It's quite a funny, or sad story, depending on how you want to look at it, of how Renee and I first met. About six or seven years ago, when I was about 23, I was dating this Asian guy called Tariq; he was lovely, the relationship was going well, or so I thought.

He was 25, generous to a fault. He worked for his parents. They have their own business. He never said what kind of company they owned, hmm.

Anyway, we dated for about two years. He swore how much he loved me, and if his parents agreed, we could get married.

You see, I am mixed-race, so his family were a bit hesitant, especially when they found out that I was adopted. They needed to know if I came from a good background, and would be a perfect wife for their only son.

Now, let me tell you how I met Renee.

I was in a supermarket car park, having just done my grocery shopping. I put my shopping in my car boot, and a familiar face was walking towards my direction.

At first, he didn't notice me. Well, why would he? It was Tariq; all googly-eyed and loved up, holding an Asian lady's hand, as though they were stuck together like some flipping crazy glue.

Glancing up, I found myself staring at his lady friend, wondering what's so special about her. Her light brown eyes were beautiful. The curves of her slender frame were complemented by the cut and shape of her dress. Okay, I see her beauty. So what do I do now?

The only thing that I could quickly think of was to give a half smile. My heart sank as they walked past me hand-in-hand. At that moment, I was certain that I saw something in his eyes.

His eyes overflowed with tears, and he fell on his knees before me. Err, no silly me, he dropped his wallet.

Tariq and his lady friend were laughing. I didn't understand what she was laughing at; he's not at all that funny, trust me.

To be honest, I felt angry and upset, but soon realised that I had been trying to work up the courage to break up with him for weeks. Well, that's the version I have decided to tell everyone, if they so happened to ask. I gave his lady friend an angry glance as I stood watching her stupid smile on her face, and swallowed down a throbbing heart.

I was fuming, you bet I was.

What the hell, Tariq, you liar. You're a bloody liar. This is what I told myself as the tears came flooding down my face.

It was as though he left a bad taste in my mouth. I realised that I had just fallen out of the reality tree.

I jumped into my car, pounding my fist hard on the steering wheel, and gave a blood-curdling scream.

"Why, why, why."

I started my car, something I shouldn't have done as I was still fuming. I hadn't noticed that I put my car into reverse and smashed into the car behind me.

The rear end of my car danced sideways, bouncing like a horse kicking up its heels.

"Oh my God, what the hell?" This is what I heard.

A lady was screaming at me, whose car I had accidentally hit.

She came out of her car, looking like a rabbit writhed in its claws, screaming in terror. Then she put a hand to her mouth and gasped.

She told me to, "Get out of the fucking car."

She asked me to have a look at what I had just done to her Mercedes. To tell you the honest truth, I was half listening while my gaze passed over the faces in the small crowd that had gathered in the car park. So, I did, it was bad, really bad. I felt so awful, I wished at that precise moment, that the ground would swallow me up.

She stood there with her hands on her hips, shaking her head. Her jaw tightened, as her frown quickly turned fierce, then she lowered her eyes, for a moment, assessing the damage to her car. I braced myself, thinking something awful was about to happen. But no, she kind of took pity on me, sensing I was a bit distressed, which I clearly was.

Tariq, once the love of my life, had shattered my carefully built world in a day. And he had done it without the brutal realisation that I stood there and let him do it.

We had to phone for a tow truck for both our cars.

It started to rain, literally, it started bucketing down with rain. We had to run for shelter, and decided to go for a coffee inside the supermarket cafe.

She introduced herself as Renee, and we chatted for a while. Then, we decided to have a slice of carrot cake while we waited for the tow truck. Since then, we have been inseparable. We just hit it off and became good friends. Despite me damaging her very expensive top of the range car.

As for Tariq, I never saw him again. I later found out that he went on to marry the lady I saw him with. I lost my man that day. But hey, I found a true friend in Renee.

Sunday afternoon, the sun was high in the sky as I made my way to my parents' house. Well, my adoptive parents' house. I go there every Sunday for lunch; it's just the three of us. My dad, Clive, is black, and my mum, Mitchelle, is white.

They met at college, got married at 20 years old, and have been together ever since.

They tried for a baby for almost 10 years before giving up.

That is where I fit into their lives. I am the only child that they have.

Mum and Dad, that is what I call them. Well, I got angry when I found out that I was adopted, and started to call them by their names, Clive and Michelle. That didn't last for very long; they are such good, loving parents.

I remember meeting up with Renee one Saturday afternoon. We had lunch or drinks, I can't really remember now. I told her about my trying to find my biological parents.

She frowned, with her glass of wine halfway to her lips, she said, "Do you really want to know?"

Anyway, for a while, my adoptive parents have been trying to help me find my birth mother.

At first, my mum, Mitchelle, got upset when I told her that I wanted to find her.

She said, "I'm your mum."

But I needed to know where I came from.

The urge was strong to find out if I had siblings, and do I look like them? Do they look like me?

Then there was the curiosity of why. Why did my birth mother chose to give me up for adoption in the first place? Didn't she loved me just a little bit, to keep me?

I cannot believe it's Thursday already. Here's Andy the postman, smiling, as he handed me a letter. Finally, a letter from the adoption agency, I braced myself, waiting for the rejection—that I knew would come—as my heart pounded hard. Above me was nothing but sky, the lofty sky, not clear, yet still, immeasurably lofty, with grey clouds sliding slowly across it. It's not good news. I stood to read the letter. Tears all welled up in my eyes.

The adoption agency finally tracked down my birth mother. In the letter, they explained that she has denied me all contact with her.

My eyes pinned to the letter, my chin trembled. I couldn't help the emotions spinning through me, as tears fell from my cheeks, onto the letter, smudging the handwritten words. I carefully folded the letter and placed it back in the envelope.

Feeling rather sad, and confused, as it didn't give a reason why, she has refused to see me.

My heart was wounded right now. It almost felt like a brick in my stomach, but I did not expect too much, as she had not even tried to find me in 30 long years.

I cried like a small child, but I have my mum and dad, who loved me unconditionally. I belong to them, into their family, as though I am blood related.

It's two weeks before my best friend, Renee's, wedding to her fiancé, Drake. All the bridesmaids, yes, all eight of us, have been paired up with a groomsman.

I've been paired up with a guy called Rhys. I think that I have seen him before. He was married for a while, then briefly dated someone.

It was time to practise with our groomsmen walking down the aisle, and finally, doing a dance for the happy couple with whom we've been paired.

I was introduced to Rhys. Wow, the first thing I noticed was his beautiful green/hazel eyes. The second thing was hmmm…he looked kind of cute—my future hubby's spitting image. He has a sexy smile, he appears to be so confident, and relaxed. So, now I practise the dance routine with Rhys.

Oh my God, the way he held me in his arms, I really didn't want him to let me go. The smell of his cologne, his soft hands touching my hand, and him holding me around my waist. I loved the feel of his warm body against mine and breathed in his scent deeply. I just didn't want him to let me go. Oh fudge, I've said that already.

Then the practice was over, he let me go. He walked away from me and glanced over his right shoulder to look back at me. I was staring right back at him.

So, I pretended for a slight second that I hadn't been staring, and quickly looked to the ground. Then moved my curls, that had fallen out of place, from my somewhat blushed face.

He went over to speak with Drake, and then they both stared at me. They stared at me for a long moment, then Drake shoved him towards my direction. But he turned around and walked back in the direction from which he came. Stopping suddenly, he glanced down at his phone in his hand.

Later that evening, I spoke with Renee about Rhys. She told me a little bit about him from what Drake had told her.

He's feeling a bit fragile, now. Having been in a relationship with someone called Kim, who truly broke his heart. He was having a difficult time getting over her.

Well, my response to my friend, Renee was, he hasn't really gotten to know me yet, I will surely make him forget about her.

But I had wondered why I had not seen or heard about Rhys until now.

A few days before the wedding, Renee told me that she and her soon-to-be husband, Drake, were discussing me and Rhys. Drake said he didn't know why he hadn't thought of it before, to introduce me and Rhys, as we're a perfect match.

He knew that Rhys had broken off with Kim because she could not leave her husband, and he has since moved on with his life.

"Okay, that sounds good to me, but where have you been hiding Rhys all this time? He's such a yummy," I said to my friend.

I really don't know Kim, but if she can walk away from a guy like Rhys, then her husband must be someone special. If Rhys were my man, I'm sorry, but there is no way I'd be giving him up so easily.

The day of Renee and Drake's wedding was finally here. My beautiful best friend is getting married and I get to see Rhys again. After the ceremony, we got to perform the wedding day dance for the happy couple. The one that all the groomsmen and us, bridesmaids, had been practising.

Finally, the moment I was looking forward to: being in Rhys' arms again.

My lips curved into a shy smile as I stepped eagerly forward into his embrace. He certainly didn't disappoint me with his touch, the sweet smell of his cologne, and his warm breath on the side of my neck. And then the dance was over.

He started to walk away from me, but I held onto his soft hand, and gave him a smile, which said, *don't go, come back to me, I so badly want you.*

He looked at me, just staring, as though he was lost. But what I saw was him looking at me, like he was seeing sunshine for the first time. He came back to me. Now I must figure out a way to make him stay, and to love me, like the way I think I'm in love with him, already.

We slow danced for most of the evening. Through his shirt sleeve, I could feel the swell of his biceps, my heart jumped into high gear.

He didn't ask for my mobile number. I was pretty disappointed, to say the least. He walked away from me. That's the second time in one day. Oh, wait a minute, he's coming back. He has two drinks in his hands.

Now, he's coming alive. He's chatting like the confident and relaxed guy I first was introduced to. Oh my God, so what just happened? He's asked for my number. He wants to see me. So, now I've gone all shy again, literally having butterflies in my stomach. My body started to shiver with excitement at the mad sexual tension. My cheeks have gone all red.

"Calm down," I told myself.

I'm blushing, something that I haven't done in years.

"So, Tianna, how are you getting home?" he asked.

His voice was warm and gentle.

He's staring at me with those beautiful green eyes—smiling, omg.

He drove me home that night. I so badly wanted to invite him in for coffee, but as I was thinking about it, he kissed me, on my right cheek, then told me goodnight.

"I'll phone you tomorrow," he said.

I closed my eyes, and was in a world of my own. If kissing me on my cheek made me weak at the knees, then, when we make love, what will he feel like? I'm going too fast. Okay. So, I'd slow down a little. I'm way ahead of myself in this relationship.

Rhys

Kim and I spent our last afternoon together. She cried. I cried. We both cried. Giving her up was one of the hardest things I've had to do. But I had to do it, for both of us.

Her husband, Alex, doesn't know how lucky he is to have a woman like Kim love him the way that she does.

I truly tried my hardest to get her to leave her husband, but she just couldn't do it. Looking back over these past few months, I don't blame her for staying with Alex. If it were the other way round, I'd want her to fight for our marriage.

But I must admit, every time I saw Kim, my face lit up with the biggest smile ever. She's a beautiful woman. I remember meeting her for coffee this one time. She came straight from the hair salon. She looked absolutely stunning with her new hairstyle.

Kim changed her hair colour from black to a dark brunette with a chocolate chestnut shade and had a side-parted ponytail, that bouncy blowout, and fresh-from-the-salon shine. Anyway, Kim's happy now. Alex has stopped the affair with her best friend, Chloe, supposedly. Although it must hurt Kim to know that her husband and her best friend slept together, and now have two children, Lucas and Finlay.

The reason why I'm telling you this is that I've met someone called Tianna. She's a beautiful young lady, a little younger than me. She's 30. I hope she doesn't mind me telling you her age, as I'm 34.

I phoned Kim a couple of weeks ago to let her know that I'm seeing someone and that I'm okay.

She was pleased that I'm not alone anymore.

"It's early days," I told her.

Nevertheless, she was genuinely happy for me. I also reminded Kim that if ever she needed me, I'm just a phone call away, night or day.

She told me that I always answer her phone calls, and that it wouldn't be right, if I'm in a new relationship, for her to phone me with her problems. I tried to convince her that it didn't matter, but she doesn't want to ruin any new relationships that I have.

Before I hung up the phone, I forgot, we weren't a couple anymore and told her that I loved her.

Surprisingly, she told me how she loved me too, and she will always have a place in her heart for me.

Like I said, I met Tianna, but wasn't sure about starting a new relationship at the time.

The reason being, two days before meeting Tianna, Kim phoned. She said that she needed to talk to me about something.

She came over to my house, it seemed like old times. I invited her in, kissed her on her cheek, she blushed, and asked me not to.

I just had to hold her, remembering how sweet she smelled, her vanilla scent. Then, as I leaned in to wrap my arms around her waist, I felt her baby bump.

"That's why I wanted to see you."

"Congratulations."

Kim stopped me before I could say anything further by putting her finger to my lip. She wanted to let me know that after having another baby scan, the sonographer realised that she was six weeks further into her pregnancy. She was having my baby.

The words fell from her lips as softly as the tears from her eyes.

After a few seconds of shocked silence, my heart pounding harder than before, I put my arms around Kim once again, then put my hand over her baby bump. I considered—smiling to myself, knowing the fact that—at least, she'll be in my life for some time, now that she's having my child.

Kim gently broke the embrace and stepped back before speaking again, as she wiped away the tears from her cheeks.

She went on to say that she and Alex discussed whether or not to keep the baby, and decided that they would.

Alex said that he would not stand in my way if I decided to be in my child's life.

I didn't know how I felt for a few seconds when Kim told me the news. Of course, I held her. At first, she didn't pull away, like I thought she would. Tears were still rolling down her cheeks.

"You're having my baby."

"Yes, I guess that I am."

"If only things were different, and I had met you first."

"I know, Kim."

"I do love you, Rhys."

She admitted silently. As I stood staring at her for a moment, her gaze lingered in my eyes, as her curls fell across her face, when she looked up at me. I leaned down and kissed her warm lips; she responded to me with raw hunger.

In truth, I'm guessing that she has never kissed her husband like that, and it troubled her, so that I might get the wrong impression of her true feelings for me. So, when she reached down into her pocket, retrieving a tissue, and slightly, only slightly, wiping away our kiss. It never bothered me.

I asked how her husband, Alex, was coping with the fact, she was having my baby. For a moment, she fell silent. Her eyes were filled with tears, her face flushed, as she searched her handbag for another tissue.

Kim's chin began trembling as she wiped the tears from her cheeks.

"He couldn't cope at first, knowing it's your baby," she told me.

Because he knew how difficult it was for her to let me go. And now, she will always have a part of me.

But their marriage is as strong as ever, they will survive this, as Kim survived knowing that he fathered two children with her best friend.

We went through to my kitchen. Kim poured herself a cup of coffee and sat down at the kitchen island. I sat next to her, staring into her brown eyes, as she continued to tell me about our baby.

For a slight second, I took my eyes off Kim, watching the small birds in my garden flitted about in the branches, chirping at each other, and battling over the best roosting sights. Kim smiled, turning her head to glance out of the window, then continued telling me about our baby.

She told me she's in her first trimester, 12 weeks pregnant, and due on 4 January. I asked if she knew the sex of the baby. She told me that she thinks we're having a boy, but would have to wait for the 20-week scan to confirm this.

Jumping from my chair, feeling an intense wave of emotions, I wished that I could be present when Kim goes for her 20-week scan. But soon came back to reality, like a whole stack of beer cans, comes crashing down. I quickly realised it would never happen, as long as her husband was around.

We don't exactly see eye to eye for obvious reasons.

"A boy, you're having my son."

Although initially shocked at the news, I wasn't about to freak out. After saying it out loud, she started to cry again.

"Don't cry, Kim."

"I'm sorry, Rhys, just give me a moment."

After a minute or two, Kim glanced up at me and then put her arms around my waist and leaned onto my chest. I held her as tight as I possibly could, and told her everything would be okay.

Our eyes met, and her smile came slowly, warming her eyes.

After sobbing for quite some time, she went on to tell me that, as she was married to Alex, our son or daughter would have his surname. A silent tear, a silent thought, before I spoke, because I could see the sadness in her eyes.

"I would never cause you or Alex any problems regarding my child's surname."

"Thank you for being so understanding."

"I love you, Kim, the same as the first day that I met you. I know it's Alex that you love more, I've accepted that now."

"Have you?"

"Yes."

She looked into my eyes, with one hundred per cent love for me, only. She wasn't willing to give herself to me.

"I love you so much, you do know that, Rhys. My heart is aching for you."

"I know, Kim."

We held each other, for what seemed like forever, then she said she had to go home. I kissed her. She kissed me back. I moved the hair from her face to look at her beautiful smile one last time. Our fingers interlocked as we held hands.

She held me again tight and whispered, "If only I had met you first." Then, she went home to her cheating husband.

I didn't want to let her go. All the feelings I had for Kim came flooding back. And now she's having my child.

Anyway, now you know why I was a bit slow to move to Tianna.

But my good friend, Drake, as always, talked some sense into me and said, "Let Kim go. Even though she's expecting your child, she won't leave Alex."

I guess the truth hurts when said out loud.

The next day, after my mate, Drake's wedding, I phoned Tianna. Like I said, I would. She said that she was on her way to her parents' house for lunch. I told Tianna that she should phone me later, only if she wanted to. Of course, she phoned later that evening. I picked her up from outside her house, and we went to a wine bar.

Tianna is a beautiful young lady of mixed-race, like me. With long brown curly hair and blue eyes.

Her high cheekbones and her ample lips invited a lingering smile. She looked absolutely gorgeous in a black leather skirt and off-the-shoulder top. Boy, she sure knew how to impress on a first date.

She smelled so sweet. I gave her a cheeky kiss on the lips. I could see the warmth of her blush as it crawled up her neck.

We've been dating for a few weeks now, and she is just out of this world. It's time to move our relationship to the next level. What's the next level, you all say, that's when I make sweet, passionate love to her. I can't wait to hear her call my name when she feels me inside of her.

Tianna

My best friend, Renee, is back from her honeymoon in Miami, Florida. She phoned and couldn't wait to tell me all about it.

Then she said, "I heard that you're dating Rhys. Girl, I'm so happy for you. Rhys is one of a kind. You're lucky to have him."

"Oh my God, Renee, he's the perfect gentleman."

She then asked if we've done it yet.

"Not yet, but hopefully soon," I replied.

I don't want to come over as desperate. Although I am so desperate for him to make love to me. I'm desperate, desperate, desperate, there I've said it now.

"Renee, when Rhys holds me in his arms, he sends warm shivers down my spine. I can't explain it. I crave his touch. When he speaks to me, his words are breathless. When he kissed me, he lingers for a few moments on my lips. His kiss is so soft and gentle. My whole body sparks with fire."

Renee could hear the smile in my voice. "Girl, stop right there, you're making me jealous. Seriously, Tianna, I'm pleased for you, don't let him go. Guys like Rhys, they don't come along too often."

"I know, I feel so lucky."

Rhys phoned, asking if I'd like to go out for a meal. We decided to go to an Italian restaurant near my home, then afterwards, to a nightclub. It was a great evening. The waiter commented that we looked like a lovely couple.

Then, during the main course of our meal, he fetched a small brown and beige box, with some Campari and white chocolate cannoli, as we happened to be guest number 100 at the restaurant that evening.

Rhys said nothing, but several times that evening, he caught me staring at him. He had that pleased smile on his lips again.

He leaned over, lowered his head, and brushed his lips lightly against mine.

After leaving the nightclub, there was a chill in the early morning air. Rhys took his jacket off and placed it over my shoulders.

We strolled along, hand-in-hand, back to his car, which was parked about five minutes away from the nightclub. We drove for an hour. Rhys is filling the time with engaging chatter about our perfect date.

Then the moment I've been so patiently waiting for. We went back to his place. He took me by the hand, and we went straight up to his bedroom.

Oh, before I get to that part of the story, we had a few glasses of wine, while I stared at the tv—which was not switched on by the way, as nerves got the better of me—then we went up to his bedroom.

He took the wine glass from my now-trembling hand, and placed it on the table in front of me.

Rhys stretched out his hand, switching off the lights in his living room, as I felt for his hand, and knew an instant warm rush, when I found it.

We walked along the hallway, then climbed the stairs to his bedroom. The thought of him without his shirt on, or better yet, naked…oh my God.

He shoved open the bedroom door with his right foot, showing his big bed. Yes, I noticed his bed first as the moonlight shone down through the open curtains. I flirted with him under long dark lashes, as he caressed my cheek softly with his thumb, then my bottom lip. I snuggled up close to him, delighting in the way his hands caressed my waist, then my hips.

He didn't disappoint me in any way. He held me with those soft hands of his. Stroking my arms gently.

He whispered in my ear, "Close your eyes, babe, relax."

He gently kissed my neck, breathing in my sweet scent, moving slowly to my lips.

I moaned softly, closing my eyes, and whispered, "I want you so much, Rhys."

He gently pulled me closer. I could feel his warm breath on my neck. He tucked my hair behind my ear and touched my face. Then, trailed a finger down my neck, between my breasts and rested his hands on my stomach.

With the feel of Rhys' touch, my body was tingling from his tease. His fingers trailed down my cheek to my lips, outlining the shape of my mouth.

He began with soft warm kisses, along my jaw line, and followed my neck, all the way down, to my first button on my blouse, before travelling back up again. Was he teasing me, hell yes.

Rhys started to undress me, slowly. I groaned softly as his fingers slowly removed my bra straps from my shoulders and slid them down my arms, as our eyes locked. His lips worked their way down the swell of my breast while he unhooked my bra. Then he slid his hand between my inner thigh, raising his hand slowly, and teasing me with every movement his hand made.

I'm in heaven, I thought.

I called his name several times, "Rhys, Rhys, oh Rhys, don't stop. Oh God, don't stop."

He looked at me, deep into my eyes, with his beautiful green eyes. I could literally see the pleasure he was about to give me, even more than he had already given me.

He held my hand, and we went over to his king-size bed. The light was dimmed, and bedroom music was playing in the background. I stood on tip-toes and wrapped my arms around his neck, while his arms went securely around my waist. I lay on my back, waiting for him to penetrate me, but he started to kiss me, gently on my lips, working his way down to my breast.

Rhys trailed hot kisses down my stomach. I was lost in a daze of heat and dark spices of his hot kisses, until. Oh, my God, did he just go there?

Oh boy, Rhys, my God, I screamed softly.

Closing my eyes, my mouth opened, as well as my legs, as he continued to kiss me between my inner thighs. Rhys' kisses continued, and his tongue flickered out, tasting my skin.

Then I felt him inside me.

"Oh, Rhys," I groaned as his lips captured mine again.

He just kept going, whining his body against mine. He gave me pure pleasure, and a rush of excitement ripped through my body. I feel him, all of him, pressed against me. I didn't want him to stop. I thought it was all over, but he wanted more of me. He wrapped his arms around me. He gently rolled us over until I was on top. He told me to give him all of me, all I had to offer.

Oh boy, did I whine my body against his. I showed him why he should be mine forever. I made love to him, as if I'd waited my whole life for the moment. He groaned out, in pure delight, as if he'd never been touched in a long time. Rhys held onto my waist, then raised his hands to caress my breast, all the while staring at me, while I made love to him, bouncing and moving my hips.

My God, he hasn't finished with me yet. He rolled us again. This time, he's on top; he raised both my legs over his shoulders, then, oh my, did he give it to me. Rhys went deep inside of me.

I could only scream out with pleasure. "My God, Rhys," I groaned softly.

He left me so exhausted. He asked me if I wanted more. How could I refuse? Afterwards, we both lay there, all hot and flustered. Wow, it was well worth waiting for. He lay on his side, with his body pressed against mine. He gently stroked my stomach, then gently kissed me on my lips.

He looked at me as though he wanted to say, *I love you*, but he just smiled. I pulled him gently towards me and held him tightly. I could feel his love for me, but now, I needed to hear him say it. I guarantee you, he'll say it soon.

A couple of days later, I couldn't wait to tell Renee.

"Oh my God, Renee, he's so fantastic, in every way possible."

As my excitement grew, I began to speak faster. Then it hit me, with all that sudden rush of excitement came, the realisation that I had gone an entire day without longing for Rhys. I asked her if Rhys had mentioned anything to her husband, Drake.

She told me that she could hear her husband speaking with Rhys. But she couldn't make out what was being said, as her husband started to whisper into his phone, but then suddenly started smiling, as he raised both eyebrows.

"His brows resumed their natural positions as he noticed me eavesdropping," she said. "Now laughing."

Hmm, now, why would my good friend be laughing? Well, as I continued telling her my news, I started to whisper. My body was shaking with yet more excitement as I spilt the beans on my steamy, passionate night with Rhys. Renee started giggling, like a schoolgirl, in a matter of minutes.

So, why, why is she laughing? Hmm, bear with me, I'm getting to that part of the story. It's just silly stuff that would be embarrassing to reveal, if you ask me. But, as we're all friends by now, I'm going to put my big girl pants on, remove my hidden face from my jumper, and tell you. But you have to promise not to laugh, like my good friend Renee did.

So, remember when I told you how Rhys switched off the lights, we went along the hallway, then up the stairs to his bedroom, in the dark. Yes, that's true, then I noticed his bed from the moonlight. Yes, that's also true. I also said how the lights were dimmed in his bedroom, and there was music playing in the background. Well, the music, yes. The dimmed lights, no, that wasn't true at first.

So, here it is, Rhys went to the bathroom, he came back, and jumped onto the bed.

At first, I thought it a little strange, but I thought, boy, he's eager. Anyway, I could hear him breathing really hard, more like panting. I rolled over to face him when he stuck his tongue in my mouth, then suddenly leapt off the bed, as if the house was on fire.

His breathing, well, his panting, disappeared somewhere in the room. I glanced around the dark room and did a double-take when I saw a dog huddled in the corner, staring at me. I foolishly gave a somewhat awkward scream. That's when Rhys came rushing into the bedroom, turning on the lights, then dimming it.

He, of course, laughed when I explained what happened. Apparently, it's his parents' dog, which he was taking care of for that weekend. He had forgotten to tell me that the dog usually likes to jump up onto his bed, and, of course, licks his face, to say hello. And there you have it, I had a dog's tongue down my throat, which I thought was Rhys'.

Anyway, let's forget about that, and I'd carry on telling you my story, as I told Renee.

Still laughing and talking. Well, Renee is the one laughing, while I'm the one talking.

I'm really falling for Rhys. I don't understand why any woman wouldn't want to be with him. He has it all. A good job, money and a big house in Finchley. And, oh boy, have you seen the car he drives—an Audi A8.

These are just material things. I mean, seriously, this guy, he's just sex on legs. He has the most amazing eye colour, green/hazel.

"Renee, when he held me in his arms, I never wanted him to let me go. And girl, we did it at last. He didn't disappoint; it was magic."

"Yes, girl, I feel your magic," she replied, still laughing. "Seriously, girl, you've got it really bad for Rhys, haven't you? But as a friend, just slow down a little. I'm not saying he will hurt you. I love you, you know that. I don't want to see you get hurt," Renee told me while still laughing about the funny dog story I told her a moment ago.

Kim

When I got home, Alex was waiting patiently for me to return, to hear all about what happened with Rhys. Yeah, *that dude*, that's how my husband refers to him.

He could tell that I had been crying because my mascara was smudged, and my eyes were all red and swollen.

"Come here, don't cry, babe," he whispered softly, as he handed me a tissue.

Alex held me so gently in his arms, then kissed my forehead.

He waited patiently for me to speak first.

"I love you, Mr Roberts," I whispered softly against the side of his cheek.

"I love you too, Mrs Roberts," he replied, staring down at a sad smile on my face.

So, I dried my tears and told him exactly what Rhys and I spoke about.

Alex held my hand, and we went through to the living room. He didn't sit, but stood staring down at me, as I patted the chair next to me.

"I prefer to stand, if you don't mind," he said, now putting both his hands into his pockets, looking as though he wanted to hear anything but me talk about my former lover, Rhys.

"He does want to be in his child's life. I told him what you said, about his child having your surname, and he seemed to be okay with that." I sobbed and wiped my eyes on the back of my hand.

I know that my husband is hurting deep down inside. I'm having Rhys' baby. It's killing him, I can see it in his eyes. But he keeps telling me that it's okay, and he's accepted it now.

A few minutes later, we headed for the kitchen, and Alex made a cup of coffee in silence, glancing over his shoulders at me a few times, as he wiped a tear from his eyes.

My ex-best friend, Chloe, has two boys with my husband. It broke me completely; the two most important people in my life, betraying my trust like that.

What kind of a woman would knowingly get involved with a married man? I really wanted to ask Chloe why get involved with a guy who lies and cheats on his wife? Why trust that kind of man?

But I also have to question myself for staying with my husband, when I knew he had broken my trust.

For a long time, it messed with my mental health. I often asked myself: How long do I keep coming home to someone who makes me feel like they don't love me anymore? The truth is that he does love me, and that's why I stayed.

I could tell that my best friend found my husband attractive. But I decided to keep fighting for our marriage.

My best friend, Chloe, had a front row seat to Alex lying and cheating on me. I remember, I drank too much one rainy afternoon, and drove to her house—something that I shouldn't have done—and confronted Chloe.

Standing on her doorstep, she clenched her phone in her hand and locked the screen, and just stared at me with a frown. A sudden gust of wind lashed rain against the back of my legs, causing my dress to ripple as if it had a will of its own, which prompted her to burst into laughter.

"You are soaking wet, and shaking like a leaf. If you're going to come out in the pouring rain, for God's sake, wear your coat," she said, watching rain water drip from my face.

My voice trembling and with heavy brows, I confronted her. I wanted to see what she would do when confronted about their affair. Of course, she denied being intimate with my husband.

Chloe stood on her doorstep and lied to my face.

"I know you are lying, Chloe. You need to look like you're in hell. I'm going to phone the police, because you are a thief," I blurted out.

She only laughed in my face, yet again, and asked me what the hell she had stolen from me.

"A thief, what the hell did I steal, Kim?" she shouts back at me, with her facetious attitude, which angered me more than I dared to admit.

Well, I yelled back, "My husband."

Chloe rolled her blue eyes and slammed the door shut, in my stunned and angry face.

That went well, yeah. It went fucking perfect, I'd say.

Anyway, Alex and I discussed our future as a family and decided to continue to have his eldest son, Lucas, every other weekend.

At first, I found it hard just to look at his son. I could see the resemblance between Lucas and my husband, it was plain to see, but I chose to ignore it, and be blind. When my husband, eventually, confessed to having an affair with my friend, Chloe, it turned my world upside down.

You have no idea the pain and lasting devastating effect that it had on me. I love my husband, so I had to love his child, Lucas.

Then he fathers another child with her, and my shock wore off, replaced by anger. What can I say?

Any woman in my position would have left her cheating husband by now. What Chloe had with my husband was stolen moments, drenched in lots of sex and little else.

But then I find out, they have both been seeing each other for the best part of five years. It was the same length of time that Alex and I have been together.

Well, for a moment, I was so shocked by his words. I wasn't able to move. At first, he denied ever being intimate with her.

"She's your friend, babe. I'd never cross that line," he said, shifting awkwardly, trying to avoid eye contact with me.

"Tell me, does your nose grow when you tell these lies?" I asked him, as he stood staring down at me, his cheeks flushed, and a shadow of guilt darkened his blue eyes.

The last straw was seeing them together, in that embrace, at his 35th birthday party, which I had organised for him. I must admit, I lost my temper, and viciously assaulted Chloe, that evening, knowing full well, she was pregnant, with my husband's second child. She pressed charges against me, which were later dropped. Seriously, I can't remember who asked police officer Sean Spencer, my husband's friend, to get the charge against me dismissed.

The realisation of what I did that night, my mind was like a thousand pieces of shattered glass, impossible to make whole, causing me to have a meltdown. That period of my life was absolutely the worst ever. Alex, although he and Chloe caused me such grief, he was there every step of the way and helped me recover to my old self. I'm still not one hundred per cent fully recovered; there are still the mental scars to heal.

That's when, I was introduced to Rhys. He came into my life, two years too late, for us to be together. I had already been with my husband, for five years, married for nearly three. I had recently given birth, to our second child, a girl, Maya, two months before meeting Rhys.

The love that I have for my husband, I stupidly gave some away to Rhys. I don't regret for one minute being with him. But I had no idea, at the time, that I would love him the way that I do. I know some people say it is impossible to love two different men at the same time. Let me tell you, they are wrong. I love them both equally—it's the same love, the same feeling.

The same heartache. It's all the same. I only turned to Rhys for comfort at first. Then my feelings for him went out of control. That's why in the end, he had to walk away from me, because I would have never walked away from him, never in a million years. Selfish, I know.

There is one more thing that I would like to share with you. When my husband and I split up, and I went to Rhys, I gave Rhys 99 per cent of my love. Rhys often told me that he knew I wasn't quite ready to give up on Alex.

Do you know, it was the one per cent of love that I held onto for my husband, Alex. Just one per cent that I couldn't give to Rhys, by holding on, clinging to one per cent only. That's what drove me back to my husband. Believe me, when I tell you that it's true. If ever you're not sure about giving up on someone you love, girl, I'm telling you, just hold on to one per cent like me.

I'm never going to leave my husband. As long as he wants me, I'm not going anywhere.

Don't ask me why, because in all honesty, I really don't know. All I know right now is that the love that we have for each other is stronger than ever.

The day I wore Chloe's necklace, our future—mine and Alex's—was sealed, and that's the way it's going to stay.

But, and it's a big but, I find myself pregnant, with my third child. Only recently had our daughter Maya, in February this year. On 14 July 14th I did a pregnancy test and it was positive.

Alex and I were happy. A little shocked at the timing, because of only just had our daughter five months ago. I felt something wasn't quite right about the pregnancy. So, I went for a private baby scan. The sonographer confirmed that I was further along in my pregnancy than we first thought.

Okay, so I saw the horrified look on my husband's face when he realised that the baby I'm carrying is not his, but Rhys'.

His eyes were heavy, his anger draining his last bit of energy. He said, okay I made a mistake, a huge mistake, and that we'll get through it no matter what. He has forgiven me for having an affair with Rhys, and he did turn a blind eye at times, knowing full well that I was with Rhys when I should have been at home with him and our two children.

Alex said it was payback for all the hurt he and Chloe have caused me for the past five years. It's so easy for Alex to say he's forgiven me, but I see all the hurt he's carrying inside of him. I see the pain in his eyes. I hear him cry sometimes at night, when he thinks I am asleep. He told me that he will love Rhys and my child, just like I love his and Chloe's children.

There is one small difference: my husband, Alex—the man I swore to love forever—will have to raise this baby as his own, give the baby his surname, feed it, cherish it, love it, and bond with it every day. I love my husband, but I can tell that he's not going to cope with doing that every day.

But knowing Alex, he's always full of surprises. That's why I love him so much. When it comes to Alex, always expect the unexpected.

Like I once said to my husband, "If I love you, I have to love your child."

Yesterday, he held me tight for the first time since we found out that the baby was Rhys'. He also realised that if he loves me, then he has to love mine, and Rhys' child also.

Drake

Where do I begin? I Spoke with Rhys, a couple of days before I got married. What did he tell me? Yeah, boy, oh boy, Kim, she's pregnant. What can I say?

This is some serious mess he finds himself in. Rhys, my man, he was just starting to get over Kim, now this.

Don't get me wrong, I spoke with her a few times. One of the last times was when we went for coffee, and she poured her heart out to me.

She is everything that my man Rhys desires in a lady. Unfortunately, she's married. They met too late, and she's never going to leave her husband. God knows why not, after the way he's treated her.

But I guess, you love who you want to love, just like my man, Rhys. When I tell you that he loves Kim, boy, he loves Kim.

Kim is a very nice lady. My man Rhys, I suppose, it's a small compensation that he gets to stay in her life now as she's having his child.

Then there's Tianna, my wife's best friend. She's also a lovely lady. I don't know why my wife, and I, didn't think to introduce Rhys and Tianna sooner. Oh well, he's with her now. Let's hope he doesn't mess her about, because he's still in love with his soon-to-be baby's mama, Kim.

Well, truth be told, he wasn't the type of guy to mess around with a lady. If he's with you, he's with you, one hundred per cent. That's until he met Kim. Now, his rules have changed. I gave him a good talking to, hopefully, he'll commit to his relationship with Tianna and see some sense.

I guess you can say the talk that I gave Rhys the other day—it worked. He's moved his relationship with Tianna to the next level. We all want to see my man Rhys happy.

My wife, Renee, suggested that we have a barbecue this weekend, and invite all our friends. So, I guess you're in for a treat, because when we do our garden parties, the whole neighbourhood wants to be on that guest list.

We have Hakeem to do the cooking. He's doing jerk chicken and flatbreads, jerk beef burgers and jerk-spiced goat shoulder.

Boy, when he cooks, it's out of this world. He owns his own Caribbean Restaurant called Mama Waveney's. Why that name? Waveney is his wife. She makes rum and raisin ice cream—the best I've ever tasted.

Then, you'll get to meet some of my other friends and my wife's friends. When we're all together, it's a nice atmosphere, trust me.

What day is it? Okay, so it's only Tuesday. Like they say, a lot can happen between now and then.

I've invited Mario and his girlfriend, Bethany. I haven't seen him since my school days. Boy, I'm laughing because I remember those days when no girl would look at me or Rhys. Those days are long gone. The days and nights that Rhys and I spent in the gym, just so we could get a girlfriend. I had Rhys cut off all my dreadlocks.

He got rid of his thick-rimmed glasses and braces. Now look at him.

All the ladies want him. Well, except for Kim. Well, to be honest, she did want him, but wouldn't leave her husband.

My wife, Renee, went grocery shopping with her friends, Melani and Nyomi. She did ask Tianna, but she's all loved up with my man Rhys at the moment, which is a good thing for them both.

My good friend, Deshawn, he's a DJ, and he's married to Renee's friend, Kayleigh. He's playing the music. He has some of the best playlists you can ask for.

I can guarantee, Saturday night is going to be a night to remember.

Tianna

A damp autumn morning was just dawning. A sudden, strange sound of a far-off whistling and thud was heard, followed by a boom of cannon, blending into a dull roar that set the windows rattling. It was windy, with blustery showers. A gust of wind blew through the window, causing the small stick used as a prop to drop to the floor, and the window closed with a bang.

My phone started ringing as I leaned down to pick up the stick from my bedroom floor.

"Hello," I spoke with a somewhat half-asleep voice.

"Hi, babe, just calling, to uh, say hi, I guess."

The rain continued to beat hard against the bedroom window, as I battled hard to hear the voice on the other end of the phone.

By now, the sky had grown darker, and the wind made queer sobbing sounds as it swept over the house. I put the phone back to my ear, still listening to the rain as it splattered hard against the window.

It was Rhys, calling at exactly 6:39 am on Tuesday, asking to come over later that day, because he wanted to tell me something. By the sound of his voice, it seems quite serious, a low and quiet tone.

My heart was racing when he said, "I want to tell you something."

My mind went into overdrive, thinking, what on earth could he possibly have to tell me? Well, except we're breaking up. I went straight over to Renee's house.

Well, not exactly, I had a cup of coffee first, to wake me up, then I braved the pouring rain. She advised me to stay calm and listen carefully to what he has to say.

To be precise, I left my house exactly one hour and ten seconds after Rhys had called.

The wind howled as I settled against the wall of the corner shop to wait out the blustery showers.

The breeze tossed my hair as I tied it up in a bun. Finally, I could see the blue street door of Renee's house. I hurriedly opened the front garden gate, as the wind blew it closed behind me. I was drenched, shaking from the cold, but happy to see my good friend when she unlocked the street door and opened it. She stood there, still half-asleep, yawning, and with a slouched posture, wiping the sleep from her eyes. I had not long ago spoken with her on the phone.

"I can't help how I'm feeling about him. I really do like him a lot," I blurted out, before I even stepped a foot in the hallway, all too aware that Renee hears the worry in my voice.

"Girlfriend, I'm sure it's nothing to worry about. I can honestly see how much Rhys is into you. So, stop worrying," she said, as rain water dripped off me, into a puddle at Renee's feet.

We walked towards the kitchen, and she turned around suddenly.

I was just about to let the worry out of my thoughts, when she asked, in a no-nonsense tone in her voice, "Does he have a secret wife, or a secret lover? Or, maybe he has no money, he's completely broke." Then she laughed.

Not exactly funny, Renee, I thought to myself.

"Don't worry," she whispered, smiling, with the kind of familiarity that grows between two friends. "It's probably nothing," she said, still yawning.

"Rhys—he's a good and honest guy. I've known him for as long as I've known my husband."

Later that evening, I sat nervously in my living room, drinking a very chilled glass of wine. I hadn't realised I was biting my nails until the doorbell rang, and silly me, I spilt the wine on my white top. I then saw my half-bitten nails, while wiping away the stain, that's when the doorbell rang again for the second time.

It was Rhys on the other side of the door. Okay, so he looked in a good mood, as I peeked through the window, looking at him holding a bottle of wine and flowers in his hands.

Just seeing him standing there, on my doorstep, my heart started beating like a hummingbird's wing.

The cologne that he wears, and just the sight of him alone—Oh God, whatever he told me, good or bad, I really don't care, I want him. I need him. Am I being silly or what? I don't care.

"Hi, beautiful," he said, smiling.

Well, that's a good start, I thought.

Whatever he has to tell me can't be that bad, right? I invited him in. He gave me a kiss on my lips, and I held him so tight, as though he was about to do a runner.

Renee told me to keep calm, so I let go of him.

He said, "Why did you let go? I was enjoying how tight you held me in your arms." Then he laughed.

So, let's get down to why he wanted to come over and talk.

He began telling me how much he cares for me. Okay. So, I can see where this conversation is heading, but I was wrong. He completely blew my mind—what a shock. Kim, it's about her. She's pregnant with his child. So now, I don't know what to say to him.

We both sat in silence, for about 10 to 15 minutes. After a few awkward minutes, I turned to look at him, and asked if he was okay, and did he need a drink, because believe me, I sure as hell needed one.

He gave me a smile, but I could see the hurt in his eyes. So, I gave him a hug. He wrapped his arm around my waist, and he rested his head on my shoulder.

His heart was beating fast. He looked at me and said that he was okay, and that he wanted to be honest with me about Kim having his baby.

He looked so downhearted, I could tell that it was tearing him apart, her having his child, and not being with her. So, I changed the subject and told him that I was adopted as a baby, and that I recently discovered that my birth mother has refused all contact with me, without giving a reason.

He asked how I felt about being rejected by her. Well, I told him that I have my adopted parents, so I was somewhat okay.

Rhys suggested, why not look for my biological dad, instead, if rejection wasn't going to bother me.

"Do you know, I hadn't given that a second thought about finding my real dad," I replied.

Rhys told me that, he'll support me in any way he could. He tore his gaze away from me and focused intently on the adoption letter, which was neatly laid out on the chair we both occupied. I had believed it was hidden away in my dresser, tucked beneath my bras and underwear.

We've both got issues in our lives. I'm glad that we have found each other, though. Rhys, he's a keeper, I'm not letting him go.

Before he left in the morning, he said that—as he was hoping our relationship would become more serious—that he'd like to introduce me to Kim, as she will also be in his life, because she's having his child. I raised an eyebrow in disbelief, then hugged him tightly, too emotional to speak.

It's Wednesday morning, and I'm late for work, yet again.

"Sorry, Martin," I said, looking at the clock on the wall, waiting for him to say something.

He's my boss, sorry, I know I've told you already.

The reason I'm telling you again is that I work in social media, and I had completely forgotten that my boss has a connection. And how he could find my dad. So, I asked him for help. He was only too pleased to help, on one condition, that I go for a drink with him after work. So, I grit my teeth and, unfortunately for me agreed.

Then, drinks after work it is. He wasn't too pleased when he realised that I also invited Sydney and Andre from the office.

Well, he's my boss, and I'm not quite sure what he was expecting in return for helping me find my dad. But I put any funny ideas—he thought he had—right out of that big old window. If you know what I mean.

It's Thursday evening, and Rhys came over. We went for drinks at a wine bar, then went to the cinema to watch a late-night movie.

We held hands on the way home with our fingers interlocked. He turned and looked me in my eyes, and said that he was glad we had met.

Finally, I think he's falling for me. His hands are so soft, the smell of his cologne, and his beautiful green eyes. I'm sorry, I know that I'm blabbing on about Rhys all the time. But I can't believe that he's with me, and we're holding hands. Well, I'm not bad myself in the looks department. But when you're walking hand-in-hand with a guy like him, you realise a lot of ladies—yes, I kid you not, a lot of ladies—just stare at him.

But he's mine. Oh yes, he's mine. I'm hoping it will stay that way, and that's why I have agreed to meet Kim.

Friday at last, nearly the weekend for Renee and Drake's barbecue. I suggested to Rhys that he could stay over at my house for the weekend, and then we could go together. He was happy that I asked.

I planned on having a takeaway meal, fish and chips, but he asked me if I was truly serious, and said, "Girl, I've got to teach you how to cook fried fish, the Caribbean way, my mum's recipe."

He then started to laugh, so I laughed too out of pure embarrassment.

I couldn't wait for him to come over. When he arrived, he had fried escovitch fish, marinated with a peppery vinegar-based dressing, with peppers, carrots and onions.

Wow, I just couldn't believe what a good cook he was. Okay, let's just skip past the good cook boyfriend. So, now what I've been waiting for—the sex. My, my, you must think that I'm crazy. Yes, crazy for his love.

Okay, should I tell you what we did, or if you like, we can just skip to the next person. Ahh, got you, you're all dying to know. So, I'm going to tell you, guess what, like me, you won't be disappointed.

The lights dimmed, and bedroom music from my playlist started to fill the room with love, pure love. I had scented candles burning.

The bed linen was already turned down for us to get straight into. And then, I heard a loud meow. Mr Kitty, that damn cat of mine, got in our way. I accidentally trod on my cat's tail. He's okay, I may add. No broken tail or anything.

But I had to go down to the kitchen, and give him some cat treats, and a cuddle, then he started to purr. He's okay, my Mr Kitty. But now, I had to get back upstairs to Rhys.

So, where was I? Oh yes, how could I forget? I left him in my bedroom waiting for me.

May I tell you, he was eager for me to get back to him, as I was eager to get back to him.

As soon as he saw me there, standing at the bedroom door, his beautiful eyes followed me straight into his open arms.

"Let me give you all my love tonight," he whispered.

He began by running his hands slightly through my hair. It sent tingles down my spine.

Rhys used his fingers to massage me, following the circles from my temples to my neck nape.

He started licking my breast, licking my inner thigh, and kissing my pelvis. I started to beg for more.

He sure made use of his hands and mouth to touch and kiss the insides of my thighs.

Rhys kissed me softly, gently biting my lip, then slowly put his tongue into my mouth, while still caressing my inner thighs.

He then raised his hand, all the way up, and used his fingers to please me, moving back and forth.

He whispered, "I love when you're so wet. God, you're so horny. Are you ready for me to please you even more?"

"Oh, Rhys, oh, Rhys," I kept calling his name.

I could feel him all of him, whining against my body, as he thrust me deep, slowly, and so passionately, enjoying each stroke, like he wanted to take forever, entering and leaving me.

Now and again, he'd slip out of me and used his fingers as he kissed me.

Rhys whispered, "You make me so happy."

He placed his hand on the small of my back. Wow, my arousal level just shot through the roof.

"This is heaven," I groaned softly.

He just kept going, pleasing me every way he could.

Rhys made a few gasps and took slow, deep breaths while penetrating me. Rhys made love to me with such tenderness and passion. It was slow, romantic love-making.

Our bodies did the talking and worked in sync with each other. I saw the hunger Rhys had for me in his beautiful green eyes. I felt his lust for me while he passionately ran his soft fingers against my back, then he gently held my hips. The way in which he touched me only aroused me more. Afterwards, I slid over, cuddling close to him with my head on his chest.

Rhys soon fell asleep with his arm across my waist, cuddling me close, without waking.

Saturday morning. Wow, I'm still thinking about last night with Rhys. He's still here with me. I'm looking at him asleep in my bed.

He opened his eyes and caught me staring at him.

"Morning, beautiful," he whispered, and kissed me on my lips.

"Morning, handsome," I replied.

We stayed in bed for the best part of the morning, making love.

Eventually, we had to get out of bed. It was Renee and Drake's barbecue later.

Their garden parties are really fun. The food is great, and there's plenty to drink. Well, that's what I understand, because I haven't actually been to one of their parties before. I was either away on holiday with my parents or too busy doing nothing.

That would explain why I hadn't met Rhys before. Then there's the party games. Oh yes, adults only, please.

Drake

Let's get this party started. Everyone is here except Terrell and Melani. They're always late.

The music's playing, the barbecue is on, everything is jerk. Yeah, my man Hakeem, just loves to jerk all his food. His favourite is jerk prawns.

Wow, we've got rum punch flowing all afternoon.

There goes the doorbell. Here he is, my man Terrell, and his wife, Melani. She's expecting their first child.

"Treyvon, go and help Terrell bring in the rest of the drinks," I said, as I sipped some rum punch, which definitely made my eyes pop out.

Here's my man Rhys, with Tianna. They make a lovely couple. They've gone straight over to love seat for two. They seem all loved up. I'm pleased for them both.

The early evening was fast approaching. Now it's time for the party games to begin. So, we start off with the naughty version of *Never Have I Ever*, the drinking game.

Time to play. We all sit in a circle, rolling the dice to make it more fun. It lands on me.

"Never have I ever looked at another woman while I am with my wife."

"Yeah, yeah," someone said.

All, us, guys take a drink. So now my wife, Renee, is looking at me all weird.

Rolling the dice again, it's somehow my turn again.

"Okay, so now it's my turn again. This game seems to be rigged," I said, laughing, as I threw the dice down.

"Never have I ever lied to my wife, saying she looks nice, when in actual fact she doesn't."

Okay, none of us guys took a drink. Roll the dice, my man Rhys.

"Never have I ever—"

Rhys shook his head, declining to speak, until he had sipped a glass of rum punch. His eyes crinkled. A smile played at the corners of his mouth when gazing at Tianna.

"Come on, Rhys, say something," I shouted at him, looking all confused as to why he had suddenly gone, all tongue-tied.

"I needed a drink," he answered.

"Okay, roll the dice."

"Lady luck, pretty lady, Tianna."

"Never have I ever locked my keys in my car." She giggles to herself.

"Really, Tianna, is that the best you can say? Try again," I said in a louder voice.

"Never have I ever stalked a crush," she shouts out.

So, now all the ladies took a drink, then Tianna started saying something that made us guys scream. I'm being dead serious.

"Woah, I think Rhys should start to worry a bit, Tianna. I think she's had too much rum punch. Let's stop this game, right now," my wife yelled.

That's when, my man Rhys, with his expression openly compassionate, as he reached out, drawing Tianna into his arms, and guiding her head to his shoulder. So, what did Tianna say…err…can't exactly remember.

The evening is going well, everyone is just chilling. The atmosphere is great. Deshawn, Kayleigh, Mario and Bethany are all dancing to the music.

"Where's my man Rhys. Oh, I see him."

He's all loved up with Tianna in the corner. She's sitting on his lap, her arms around his neck, and they're both laughing. He's whispering in her ears, sweet nonsense, I'm guessing. I'm pleased for both of them. To tell you the truth, when they first walked in, holding hands, I could feel the electricity. Even I was tingling with excitement for them both.

Rhys

I've had more than a few weeks, waking up to a lonely bed space. But not this morning. Here she is, Tianna, the girl of my dreams, staring right back at me.

She has the most beautiful blue eyes. I like her a lot, she's so sweet. She's what I would describe as my soulmate connection. We fit together like puzzle pieces.

My fingers touched her chin and slid down her throat, exploring their way down to her breast.

She took my face in her soft hands and traced my cheekbones and jawline with her fingers.

For a moment, she surrendered to my warm lips and embrace, clinging to me, as her heart stepped up a pace.

"I love you so much," she whispered.

I dwelt on her scent, the taste of her, and the kiss. I'm sure she'd never felt anything like my kiss or the warmth that flowed through her. Our kiss grew more passionate as Tianna melted into my embrace.

Well, until Mr Kitty jumped up onto the bed and started meowing.

"I think he's hungry. I'll be right back," she said, as she clutched the sheets to conceal her state of undress.

I grabbed her by the waist, causing her to fall back onto the bed. Her skin smelled of our love-making. She kissed my lips softly, stroked my hair, then kissed my forehead. She turned abruptly when Mr Kitty reached out with his paw and nudged her, trying to get her attention.

When that didn't work, he expelled all his energy by darting from the bedroom to the spare room. He started jumping up and down on the bedroom furniture, going a little bit crazy, knocking a photo frame off the bedside table, which just so happen to be of me.

Tianna went to feed him. I laid back in the bed, smiling, thinking of the day before.

She looked so stunning, the afternoon of the barbecue, wearing an off-the-shoulder cream-coloured dress and low-heeled sandals. I stood and whistled softly, my gaze taking in her dress and her hair appreciatively.

The way she blushed about me whistling was amusing and somewhat sweet as she grabbed her handbag from the dresser.

Sunday morning broke with a surge of nervous excitement. Tianna always goes for lunch at her parents' house, so I decided to go with her. Well, she asked, and I agreed.

Her parents, Clive and Mitchelle, are a lovely couple. They made me feel welcome in their home.

Her dad has grey hair, wrinkles, and looked somewhat tired.

He made a joke when shaking my hand, to which Tianna responded by saying, "Dad, I'm not a little girl anymore."

Her mum, Michelle, stood holding a plate, which she was about to put on the dining room table, when her gaze lifted slowly from the table and fixed on me.

She greeted us with a big smile, hugging Tianna, then me.

"Oops, I forgot the bottle of red wine in the car."

I made a dash for the street door, hearing footsteps behind me, to see Clive hot on my heels.

"I just wanted to apologise. My sense of humour is somewhat old-fashioned," he said, laughing.

I could tell by the look on his face, he'd probably had a drink or two earlier.

My eyebrows jerked up in surprise when he tried and failed to explain his little joke.

"My daughter is priceless, and I expect you to treat her as such."

That was fine by me. I'd say the same sort of thing to my daughter's boyfriend.

It was his joke:

"You treat her right, have fun, and if she drops her panties, use a rubber."

The words flew out of his mouth as he steadied himself, with his hands on his knees for a moment, panting.

To tell you the truth, I couldn't think of a polite response, so I kept my mouth shut and handed him the bottle of wine. Maybe this was all an act, trying to see how I would react. He was joking, of course, but his sense of humour is different.

After lunch, we headed for the garden, as the sun had been under a cloud all morning, and finally began to shine.

Tianna lifted a hand to shade her eyes from the sun.

Sitting down with a book, Clive propped his feet on the small table and relaxed. Michelle chatted away, saying how I seemed such a lovely young man. And thought that, I certainly drew the eye of every woman in a crowded room.

Clive caught my eye and winked while raising a glass.

Tianna took her hands in mine and rested them on my thigh, then whispered softly in my ear, "My parents love you."

Clive must have fallen asleep for a brief moment, and his loud snoring must have woken him up. Startled, dropping his wine over his favourite book, and then swearing under his breath, as he swung his legs over the table, staggered, stumbled. Then he landed flat on his backside.

Dazed, looking around, until his gaze finally fell on his wife. Michelle and Tianna stared at Clive, shaking their heads, then rolling their eyes. An awkward silence fell. Suppressing the urge to laugh wasn't easy, but I somehow managed it.

He rolled over and sat up, too embarrassed to speak. He placed a hand over his face, then, shaking his head, tried to stand up.

He smiled up at me as I stretched out my arm and yanked him to his feet.

Shaking the dust off his trousers, still looking embarrassed, he spoke, "Thanks, son."

After meeting her parents, I started going with her every Sunday for lunch and a laugh, now that our relationship is more serious.

I spoke with Kim last week. She told me the pregnancy is going well, and that Alex is okay so far.

Well, her words were, "He's coping at the moment. He's dealing with the whole situation in his own way."

She also said, it's their third wedding anniversary next week, and that he kept his promise to buy her a BMW 3 series.

Kim also mentioned that they are taking Mason and Maya to Disney World in the US.

I wanted to let her know about my relationship with Tianna, that I was being honest and open with her and told Tianna about our affair, and that Kim is pregnant with my child.

I suggested to Kim, if she would one day be willing to meet Tianna.

"Kim, I'd really like it if you'd meet Tianna. I'm hoping that the two of you will get along."

Kim was silent for a few seconds.

I could hear her breathing down the phone, then she spoke, "It's a good idea, but I need to speak with Alex first, to see what he thinks."

She wanted him there if she was to meet with Tianna, which I agreed—made more sense.

Kim being the type of person she is, I knew she would agree. She's still the same, beautiful person, always thinking of others before herself. I hope Tianna will agree to meet Kim. She'll feel at ease, knowing that her husband Alex will be there when they eventually meet.

Tianna

I met Rhys a few months ago now. He told me all about his relationship with his ex-girlfriend Kim and how they started dating. Although she was still married to her husband, they were separated at the time.

At first, I could see the hurt in his eyes when he was telling me about their affair. Well, he's with me now. All I can say is that Kim's husband must be some really special guy if she didn't choose Rhys.

Now I have Rhys in my life, I'm not letting him go.

At first, in our relationship, I realised that the feeling he had for Kim was still there. When he made love to me, he was only giving me half of his love. I guess that he was still holding onto her. My heart ached, and it hurts like crazy.

Now, he's arranged for us to meet up with Kim and her husband for lunch.

Should I? Shouldn't I? I really don't know. Oh God, I don't think I could do this, coming face-to-face with his ex and her husband.

Sitting on the edge of my bed, wiping the tears that fell down my cheeks. Mr Kitty jumped onto the bed, rubbing against my arm. Pausing to stroke him, it was as though he knew I needed cheering up. I bit my lips to keep them from quivering.

"What would you do, Mr Kitty?"

Fuck, I can't believe that I'm asking my cat for advice. Smiling down at Mr Kitty, only for him to meow, curl up, and fall asleep on my lap. So, I phoned my friend, Tamara, who's a bit more level-headed than Renee.

Tamara suggested that, if he's asking me to meet with Kim, and her husband, then he's serious about our relationship. Making sure that I know, even though Kim is having his baby, that she's no threat to our relationship.

"Girlfriend, think of it this way, if he didn't include you, and just had a baby with his ex, then how would it make you feel. He's being honest with you, not leaving you out. Babe, aren't you just a little curious to see what Kim looked like? If you do decide to go for lunch, to meet his ex, make damn sure you look stunning."

"Maybe wear that little black dress, the one with the lace, sleeveless halter neck, and your silver strap shoes. Oh, and I'd let you borrow my diamond stud earrings, the dainty chic ones. You know you love those earrings, babe. You've always wanted to wear them, now's your chance," she said, laughing.

But I wasn't sure whether I should be laughing or horrified.

What if, seeing Rhys again, Kim decides she wants him back? After all, the breakup is probably still fresh in his mind.

Tamara

My name is Tamara, and Tianna is like a sister to me. We've known each other for about two years now. We met at work, but I left to pursue a different line of career. We still keep in contact with each other.

Tianna is a good friend to have. I can honestly say she is one of the nicest friends I have met to date.

The only problem she has is falling in love with the wrong type of guys.

She has met Rhys. He seems nice enough. He treats her the way she deserves to be treated. Only now, she told me his ex-girlfriend is having his baby, even though she is married. Fucking crazy or what.

That Thursday evening, it rained a little, but I went over in the rain to comfort my good friend. Oh, and I bought a bottle of white wine. I just so happened to pick up the cheapest bottle, by mistake, as my eyes were a little blurry from the rain.

Tianna was already standing by the street door when I arrived. Her hair was messy, she had on jeans, a red t-shirt, and bare feet—not her usual look.

She grabbed the bottle out of my hand as I followed her down the hallway to the kitchen.

"It's just one big mess, don't you think?" she asked.

I've told Tianna to meet with Kim and her husband. What harm can it do?

"If Rhys is asking you to meet her, you're obviously important enough to him to have asked."

"I suppose so."

But my friend, Tianna, is scared of coming face-to-face with the woman who literally broke her man's heart. I have asked her what exactly she is scared of. She told me that his ex may think that she is not good enough for him, or she may want Rhys back, once she sees her.

"Tianna, I don't know Kim; she sounds like a nice lady, but if she wanted Rhys, she would be with him right now, not her husband."

Shit, that came out all wrong. I clamped a hand over my big, fat mouth as Tianna turned her face away from me, pouring herself a very large glass of wine.

"Anyway, we don't know her, so let's not jump to any conclusions. Babe, let Rhys introduce you, then hurry up, and tell me all the gossip, because I'm dying to know what she looks like, even if you don't."

Tianna raised her eyebrows and stared at me in mute silence. A single tear rolled down her cheek as she tried and failed not to cry.

"Don't cry, babe," I said, realising how sensitive my good friend can be.

"I'm sure it's nothing to worry about Rhys' ex. She's happily married, I'm assuming. Although she's having your boyfriend's baby, it's you whom he wants. So, girlfriend, stop worrying. You're going to make me cry, too."

My chin now trembling, my eyes filling with tears, as I stood looking at my friend.

We hugged, and that's when something dropped to the ground beside her, spilling its contents. It was the wine glass she somehow forgot that she was holding in her hand.

Tianna

It's a beautiful summer's morning. Staring out the bay window of my bedroom, I abandoned my coffee cup on the windowsill.

Right on time, every morning, I can hear the birds singing a beautiful song. I glance at my watch. Oh no, I'm late for work again. Only this time, I'm not alone, Rhys, he's here with me.

He held me tight in his arms, and kissed me on my lips. Gazing up into his beautiful green eyes, I tell him that I love him. He kissed me again, gently moving the hair from my face and smiles.

"Too soon," I ask him.

He shook his head, then said, "No."

Well, I've said it before, those three little words, not sure if he heard me.

Rhys gave me a lift to work. There was heavy traffic caused by a broken-down van. I'm only eight minutes late this time. I can see Martin, my boss, looking over in my direction, then he starts to wave me over.

Sydney, my work colleague, told me not to worry, as the boss has a soft spot for me.

Okay so, I think that I'm in trouble. I've been late twice this week already, and its only Tuesday morning.

"Come in, and close the door," Martin said.

He threw me a stern look as I made a face. My heart rate is a little fast right now.

He told me to sit down and not to look so worried. I sat on the chair, removing the empty biscuit packet, which he obviously forgot was there, as he sipped his cup of tea, looking around—I assumed for his biscuits.

"Good news, Tianna, I have a friend who can help find your dad, but he needs some background information first."

"Seriously," I screamed.

I got up from where I was seated, leaned over his desk, and flung my arms around Martin's neck, forgetting for a slight moment, he was my boss. I stepped back, after realising my mistake, only for Martin to smile; probably wishing I'd hug him more often.

You have no idea how relieved I was. For a moment, I assumed that I was in some kind of trouble for arriving at work late, yet again.

"Oh, okay, Martin, thank you. I'll get back to you with what I can find out," I said, gasping for air, with utter excitement.

Oh boy, I was so sure that I was in trouble. Now, finally, if I can find my biological dad, he may have the answers I so desperately need.

I'm seeing Rhys again this evening. He spends quite a lot of time at my place. He was happy for me when I told him that my boss has a friend who may be able to track down my dad. He held me in his arms and gave me a kiss. Deep down, I definitely knew he loved me. I could feel it in his soft kisses on my neck and the way he whispered my name.

Not only that, he listens to me without any distractions, and he never interrupts me. He remembers everything that I say, even the tiniest details. Rhys just can't help but take note of everything I say. That's why I love him so much.

We cuddled up on the sofa, watching a movie, then fell asleep. The sound of his phone ringing woke us both up, even though it wasn't very loud.

It was Kim. A long sigh escaped my lips as I stared at her name on his phone.

Okay, so I wasn't exactly happy about her phoning my boyfriend, but it is what it is. She's back from her holiday in the US and is phoning to make arrangements to meet me.

I started having palpitations. I guess that nerves got the better of me. Rhys moved his hand over my hair, smiled down at me, kissed my forehead, and told me not to be so nervous because Kim doesn't bite.

He held me around my waist as I leaned into his chest. Rhys said that I was letting out a long, shaking sigh. I think I was probably crying internally, and not showing it, or even aware of it externally. I wasn't aware of how sad I was really feeling.

He reassured me that I had nothing to be worried about.

"Babe, when you meet Kim, you'll laugh after and wonder why you were so nervous. She's a nice lady, just like you," he whispered in my ear, pulling me close and kissed my neck softly.

A nice lady like me, I thought.

Seriously, should I read into that statement, or just chill?

We all agreed in four days' time, that's when we'll all meet up. I'm a bag of nerves just thinking about it.

Three days before I met Kim and her husband, I had brunch with Renee and Tamara, just to get their opinion. I started to speak about my concerns, especially why Kim thought it a good idea to drag her husband along to meet me.

Maybe so, she wouldn't feel tempted to start their affair again, once she saw Rhys staring at her with his gorgeous green eyes.

But there was no telling by the blank stares on their faces, if they were shocked, disappointed, or just plain bored with me blabbering on about Kim. Or maybe the conversation was getting way too personal.

"Tianna, don't worry, there's absolutely nothing to worry about," they both said.

But I saw the face they both pulled.

They were lifting a brow and rolling their eyes to glance at each other, while filling their faces with apple pie and fresh cream. I tried to ignore the looks on their faces until Renee told me what her husband, Drake, knew of Kim, and it was mostly all nice things.

She told me about Kim's meltdown and chopping off all of her hair, because of the affair her husband had with her best friend, and how he went on to father two children with her friend Chloe.

I sat there stunned, and shifted in the chair, feeling like a fairy on a rosy cloud. Then, I stared at an iced carrot cake that sat on the counter. Tamara got up quickly, bumping her head against an older guy carrying a tray. I watched her as she filled two plates with the carrot cake I had been staring at moments ago, and sat down cross-legged between Renee and me.

Pushing one of the plates in front of me, Tamara pointed her fork at the plate and smiled.

"Eat, babe," she said, as Renee helped herself to a forkful of my carrot cake.

"She's been through a lot," I said to Renee, listening intently, swirling, and sipping a hot cup of green tea.

"Yeah, she has, and still, she refuses to leave her husband. If she really wanted to, the way that Rhys felt about her, she would've left her cheating husband, and be much happier with Rhys, don't you think? But she chose to stay with him for some strange reason."

"I mean, cheating is not an accident like you fell off a bike now, is it? If I was Kim, and thank God that I'm not, I would have dumped his arse so fast and ran off with Rhys." Renee said, rolling her eyes, then taking a bite of apple pie, which she had been moving around her plate for the best part of 30 minutes.

"Don't be silly, if she ran off with Rhys instead of staying with her cheating husband, then Tianna wouldn't have him," Tamara replied, rolling her eyes at Renee, who glanced down at the table.

"Oops, sorry, it was a foolish thing to say," Renee said, as she got up from her seat, leaned down with her hand covering her mouth, and then wrapped her arms around me and whispered, "I'm so sorry, Tianna, I really wasn't thinking straight, when I said that."

Two days before I met Kim, I spoke with my parents about getting as much information as they could to give to Martin, my boss.

Hopefully, his friend can help me find my biological dad, then maybe, one day, my biological mum.

I didn't have much information to give Martin, only the place where I was born and my date of birth. Apparently, the nurses called me Jessica's baby when my mother refused to name me.

So, my adopted parents came up with the name Tianna. Not much to go on really, but it's a start I suppose.

When I told my boss, Martin, he said not to worry, because his friend, Dave, is very good at tracking people down. Especially, people who don't want to be found, even people like my mum.

Martin did ask if I wanted Dave to find my mum. I thought about it for all of 60 seconds and decided against it.

"She doesn't wish to be in contact with me."

"Okay, hun, but if you change your mind, you know where I am."

"Thanks, Martin."

Before I met Kim, it had been an anxious and emotional day, to say the least. I covered my face with shaking hands and sobbed my heart out.

Why didn't my real dad want me either? Closing my eyes, rolling over on my side, I thought about why it hadn't bothered me until now. I imagined all kinds of reasons as to why he chose not to find me either.

The day before my 18th birthday, well, exactly five minutes before midnight, I overheard my dad, Clive, on the phone whispering to someone. I couldn't hear everything that he was saying. So, I crept closer.

He mentioned the day the adoption agency phoned Michelle at work and she came home crying two hours later.

She told him it was the happiest day of her life. They'd tried for a baby for many years without conceiving.

"Nobody wanted the little girl. She was abandoned at the hospital," he carried on whispering, knowing I was the baby my dad was speaking about.

When he said Tianna, I froze, then paced towards my dad, anger rippling through me.

Tears rolled down my cheeks, my heart pounded hard as I grabbed the phone from my dad's grasp. But whoever he was speaking to ended the call.

"What the hell, Tianna, what do you think you're doing, grabbing the phone like that?" he shouted at me, with fury on his face, but his words were lost to my mother's footsteps running down the stairs.

I started screaming, "Dad, who the hell were you talking to on the phone?"

Dad's gaze shifted to Mum. She walked towards me. Her hands gripped my shoulders and pulled me back, so that I could see her face. Then she kissed me on my forehead, dismissing whatever I overheard as utter nonsense. I leaned against my mum and burst into tears.

Mum dried my eyes with a tissue she found in her pocket, and smiled. Dad stood there, trying to take deep breaths, knowing what he was about to say next was a complete and utter lie.

As I turned to face my dad, his tone and expression stirred up an unwelcome truth that had long lain dormant, poised to emerge just minutes before my 18th birthday.

"I need to ask you something, and if you lie to me, we're done," I said, wiping my nose with the crumpled tissue.

"I wouldn't lie to you, love, well, not intentionally," Dad said, as he walked over to the dining chair, with me following him close behind.

I sat opposite, waiting for my dad to say something, anything.

The clock ticked away the minutes. I forgot it was my birthday. Rain splattered hard against the living room window, drawing Dad's gaze to the window, instead of me. Mum came and stood next to Dad.

"So," I asked, "are you…my biological parents?"

Mum ignored my question rather than lie to me. A tear trickled down her cheek as she stood there with her hands on Dad's shoulders.

"Mum, Dad, the truth," I shouted.

My heart fell, knowing that the truth, the whole truth, was about to hit me like a ton of bricks.

"Calm down, love," Dad shouted, trying to control the quiver in his voice. "I will tell you everything that you want to know. I promise, sweetheart."

That's when I knew for sure, without my parents uttering another word, that I was adopted.

That night, I wanted to pack my bags and leave, but instead, I crawled into my bed and cried. How long I lay there, and cried, I couldn't say, but gradually my sobs subsided.

The morning of my birthday, Mum brought me breakfast in bed, like nothing ever happened.

She sat on the edge of the bed, held my hand, and whispered, "Happy birthday, sweetheart." She kissed me on my cheek, handed me a card, and two birthday presents.

"Where's Dad?"

"He had to leave for work early, sweetheart, but he wishes you a happy birthday," she replied, as I stared into her big brown eyes, her long golden hair, and her rosy, pretty cheeks.

The complete opposite of my brown hair and blue eyes.

That was a complete lie. I always knew when my mum lied to me. Well, I thought I always knew, until last night.

Mum bit her lips, avoided eye contact, and started to talk way too quickly. Then there's the fidgeting.

My lips parted as I was about to ask mum not to lie to me. Her eyes were sad like mine. so, I decided to open my presents instead.

"I love you. You do know that, right?" Mum said, a smile started to tug at her trembling chin.

I hugged my mum, lying my head on her chest.

"Love you too, mum," I replied, hugging her tighter.

That was then, this is now.

Rhys handed me a cup of milky coffee and a slice of toast with strawberry jam. Kissing me on my lips, he picked up his phone from the kitchen island, glanced at it for a slight second, before shoving it into his jacket pocket, without answering the call.

"You okay, babe?" he asked.

I didn't ask him who was calling, he smiled, then asked about finding my real dad.

With a bit of luck, I'm hoping Dave can find my biological dad. Let's hope he's nothing like my birth mother and do not refuse to meet with me.

Rhys reassured me that he has a good feeling that Dave will find my dad, and he'll agree to meet me.

Then, there's Kim. Tomorrow I will come face-to-face with her. The woman who broke my boyfriend's heart.

She never loved him and probably told him, "I don't love you, Rhys."

The truth must have hurt him, but it's still the truth.

Well, I'm not sure what the hell she said to him. Whatever she did say must have stung like a bumble bee, don't you think? What do I even say to her?

How is Rhys going to react, seeing her with her husband? She's expecting his child. How is he going to feel? Am I going to have to pick up the pieces if he can't cope with seeing her? She used to be the love of his life.

How am I going to cope with all of this? But whatever happened, I will be there for him, no matter what.

That evening, we sat on my sofa kissing and cuddling each other. He kissed me with such passion, and I held him so tight.

I whispered softly in his ear, "I'm never going to let you go."

He moved my hair from my face and kissed me on my neck, breathing in my sweet scent.

"You're so beautiful," he said.

I told Rhys again, that I loved him, he kissed me softly, tugging at my lips, and gently bites my top lip. He closed his eyes. Oh, how I wished that, I knew what he was thinking at this precise moment.

He opened his eyes, just staring at me. My heart fluttered and began to pound when my gaze met his. His hands slid up my arms in a gentle caress. Rhys kissed me again on my neck, only this time, I can feel his warm breath. The smell of his cologne lingered in the cool air. He held me so tight that I could feel his heartbeat.

He touched my lips with his tongue, then gently put his tongue into my mouth. I groaned softly, then he kissed my earlobes.

Then, he whispered, "I love you."

I started to cry, at last…at last, he said that he loves me.

He took his thumb and gently wiped away my tears. He told me not to cry. His love for me was always there, but he had to be sure that I truly felt the same way about him as he felt about me.

We made love that night—all night.

"Never let me go," he said, his gaze wandered over my face.

"I'll never let go, Rhys, I promise you," I replied, staring up into his eyes.

You don't know how long I've waited to hear Rhys say those three words, that he loves me.

Oh boy, he's said it now. He's said it. He's mine, I love him so much.

It felt so good to wake up next to him every morning. Hmm, now I've got to get Mr Kitty, his own cat bed. He can't sleep on my bed with me anymore. Poor Mr Kitty.

Alex

Today, my wife, Kim, and me are meeting Rhys the moron, and his new girlfriend, Kianna, Brianna or whatever the fuck her name is.

Not really sure how I'm feeling about this, to be honest. What can I say, Rhys is the one who suggested it. What for, I can't see the point, to tell you the truth.

Any excuse to see my wife, I reckon. I really thought, that fucking dude was out of my wife's life for good, apparently not.

We were shocked when we realised that she was pregnant again, not long after giving birth to our second child.

Our daughter, Maya, she's only five months old. But hey, having two children under five, and one on the way, it's going to be a piece of cake.

My wife was at home on maternity leave, looking after our kids, for now, so another baby—no problem.

That's until we realised this baby…it's not mine. Yeah, it's that dude's baby. Disbelief surged through me. I clenched my eyes closed, wishing, hoping it wasn't true.

And now tomorrow, give me any excuse to knock this dude out, just one. If he dares to look at my wife, that's right, my wife, in the wrong way, I swear I'd swing for him. Why can't he be happy with his new girlfriend, and leave my wife the hell alone? I once had a quiet word, with the moron.

As a gentleman who prefers to maintain composure rather than resort to violence, I found myself listening to his absurd excuses for why he couldn't stay away from my wife after he dared to touch her.

He told me some bullshit story, which if I'm being brutally honest with you, I yawned in his ugly fucking face.

He kept banging on about his ex-wife, and had the audacity to compare my beautiful wife to his ex, Leah. Or did he say Tianna?

He then went on to say something else, to do with how gutted he was, when he and my wife broke up.

You got to be shitting me, right. I got angry, and told him to keep my wife's name out of his fucking mouth.

He looked at me, as though he was about to cry, then opened his mouth to utter some nonsense, but I shut him down and yelled at him instead.

"Rhys, you could have gone through a storm, who the fuck gives a shit."

Yeah, he didn't like my response for a second.

Do you know what, the dude had the nerve to look me straight in the eyes and yelled back.

"Ask your wife why she decided to have my baby."

He stood there with a big smirk on his face. Okay, so that shut me the hell up. Anyway, my wife is with me, not with that loser.

I'm only agreeing to this for my wife's sake; to give that dude's woman a piece of mind. I can't believe the mess we all find ourselves in.

Now, he's got an excuse to phone my wife and to see her whenever he feels like, because she's having his kid.

So, now, I'm not sure if I can pass this baby off as mine, especially if the baby has green eyes like his.

For fuck's sake, I can't deal with this shit. I am slowly losing it, knowing Rhys the moron is going to be my wife's baby's daddy.

Now, I understand that my wife made a huge mistake, having an affair with this dude, and getting pregnant by him. I'm not here to pass moral judgement, well, as you know, I cheated with her best friend, and lied about it for years. And yet, I can't understand why him? Why this dude?

Do you know, a lot of people don't like me because they all say I destroyed my wife. My wife forgave me. She's the love of my life, I will do anything for her, and she knows that. I really shouldn't say this, but I need to tell someone; I don't know if I can raise that dude's kid.

I'm trying to come to terms with my wife sleeping with him. That he had put his hands all over her naked body, caressed her breast and kissed her lips. It was more than sex. Sex and love-making are two separate things.

Fuck, I really can't deal with this shit. No, and no, it's nothing to do with the baby being black. My kids are mixed-race, my wife is black, and I love her honey brown skin. It's just this dude. I mean, he's mixed-race. It's just him, as a person that I hate. I think maybe I should just be quiet now.

Sorry, I don't mean to offend anyone. I am sorry, but that's how I found myself feeling at the moment.

My thoughts were not in a good place right now. Do yourselves a favour, and swiftly move on to the next person, as I've got a feeling you don't like me very much either. Yeah, I know, I'm the moron.

Tianna

"Morning, beautiful."

"Morning, handsome. Rhys laid on his side, stroking my stomach."

"Are you still nervous about meeting Kim later?"

"I'm not nervous anymore, babe."

"What's changed, since a couple of days ago, when you were freaking out."

"It's simple, now I know that you love me."

"You are very easy to love," he replied, then kissed me softly on my lips.

An hour before meeting Kim. I put my makeup on and combed my hair.

"Do you think I should wear the blue dress or the black?" I asked Rhys.

He told me that whatever I chose to wear, I would look stunning. But he thought the blue dress would do nicely.

He gave me a small jewellery box, which had a pair of diamond earrings inside.

"Oh my God, Rhys, they're beautiful."

"For a very beautiful lady."

He said how gorgeous I looked, then held me tight, and told me again that he loved me.

Five minutes before meeting Kim. We arrived at an expensive restaurant in Soho. It also had a heated patio for outdoor dining, but Rhys asked to be seated inside. I mean, it's clientele, treated champagne like water. I did see one of the waiters, with a dessert trolley, teeming with all sorts of cream cakes. I do believe it was at Alex's request that we came to this particular restaurant. I seriously hope he's picking up the bill.

We were led by the waiter to a secluded booth. Rhys asked if I was okay, then said that they were walking towards our table.

They were holding hands. Well, interlocking fingers, with their palms touching. I noticed her baby bump straight away.

Kim greeted me with a smile and said it was nice to finally meet me.

She was as beautiful as I imagined she would be. She has honey brown skin, wavy black hair, and looked about four months pregnant.

Rhys sat there, staring at her. Her husband, I guessed, didn't like that and gave Rhys a look of vexation on his face. Then, evidently, he tried to keep calm, with some difficulty. He turned away from Rhys to vent his frustration directly towards me. I could feel the colour draining from my face. I held onto Rhys', hand under the table, without speaking. I probably sensed there was little I could do to change the atmosphere or tension that was building up.

We sat in silence for about three minutes. Thank God, the waiter came over to take our drinks order.

Okay, so she's looking at me. What do I do, or say? She's just staring at me now. Her husband was also staring at me with his piercing blue eyes.

I leaned over and whispered. "Rhys, say something."

Okay, so it's down to me to start a conversation. But I decided to go to the lady's toilet, instead. Then Kim decided to come along with me.

This is weird.

She put her arms around my shoulders and said, "I'm glad that Rhys has you in his life."

She went on to tell me, when they broke up, they were both distraught and in a bad place. And she wanted to let me know that he left her, because she couldn't do it. It was selfish of her to want him, and her husband, at the same time.

She said, Rhys, made the right decision to break up with her.

But now she was pregnant again, and was quite shocked it was his. She apologised to me and said that she was no threat to my relationship with him.

Then she said, that we could become friends, but only if I felt comfortable with the idea. It was something that Rhys had suggested.

Hmm, I'm not sure, if that's such a good idea, I thought. But if she was willing to be friends, then maybe I should make the effort.

We walked back to the table, like we were best friends already. Rhys and Kim's husband, Alex, you could see that they were both uncomfortable at being left alone for so long.

Alex looked more uncomfortable. His gaze shifted absently to the floor. He sat very still for a moment, and it was evident from his face—which was flushed, and troubled—that a struggle was going on in his mind.

The four of us sat together at the restaurant, as though we were friends.

Not that it mattered, but no one mentioned that Kim's husband was a white guy. You love who you love.

Now, I saw why she was not giving him up. He was just so handsome, with golden brown hair and beautiful blue eyes.

And let me tell you, he has a physique most men would die for.

To be fair, both Rhys and Alex are evenly matched. They are both six feet two, both are sex on legs, and even I would find it difficult to choose between them. I saw why Kim wouldn't leave her husband. Yes, I saw it, ladies.

You can see the love he had for his wife when he looked at her.

Then there's Rhys. I saw the sparkle in his eyes when he looked at her. I knew he still had feelings for her. I can see it.

But right now, he was holding my hand under the table.

"You okay, babe?" he whispered, leaning towards me.

All I could do was smile at him.

The only one not smiling right now was Alex. He looked like he was ready for a fist fight with Rhys. Kim sensed her husband was not happy, and leaned over to kiss him on his lips.

That's when Alex looked directly at Rhys, as if saying, *she's my wife, you had your chance, now fuck off.*

Rhys turned his head, rolled his eyes, and gave a tut.

So, now what do we all do?

Everyone's just sat in complete silence. Alex's face, you could see he was just fuming. He looked a bit peeved, to be honest, fiddling with his wine glass, then occasionally looked at his wife, who was staring at my boyfriend. Rhys, on the other hand, I think he rubbed Alex up the wrong way, maybe not intentionally. But I'm guessing he enjoyed winding Alex up, just to see the look on his face.

Maybe this was a bad idea. Okay, now Kim was making light conversation, while Rhys and Alex stared each other out.

Then Rhys apologised to Alex for the mess that they all find themselves in.

All this tension between Rhys and Alex was ruining the evening for all of us.

Alex shook his head and blurted out, "You can keep your bloody apology, mate, we both know why you're really here."

"Oh, really, Alex, why's that then?"

"My wife, you flipping moron. Even a broken clock is right twice a day."

So, now I was looking at Rhys, who cut his eyes at Alex, then gave a smirk, laughed, then gave a tut sound, all the while side glancing at Kim.

That just made the tension in the restaurant ratchet up a notch.

What the hell is going on? I don't like being dragged along someone else's joyride. I mean, I tried and failed to ease the tension that bounded the room like a noose. I tried cracking a joke, which fell on deaf ears. I even tried smiling and making light conversation with enemy number one in the room, Alex, that is. Because he was hell bent on destroying the evening from the beginning.

After a few awkward minutes, Alex decided to stare up at the ceiling, yawned loudly, and then gave Rhys a cold stare. I don't know Alex, but it's hard to believe. Then, Kim finally decided to speak.

She asked both Rhys and Alex to grow up and stop acting like children in front of the both of us. I could only agree, both of them needed to calm down, and discuss whatever it was we met up for.

Rhys started to thank Kim for agreeing to meet me.

So, now Alex, I suppose he was looking for the same sort of thanks, but Rhys turned his head and gave me a wink.

I'm not sure who was worst right now. I don't really know Alex. He was definitely looking for a fight.

And I'm sure Alex was a really nice guy, but I guess Rhys was the one who was causing all the tension.

From where I was sitting, they were both fighting for her affection. I started to question the real reason why Rhys wanted me to meet with Kim.

Alex's tone was conversational after a while, but his body language indicated he was more furious with Rhys than anything else, as well as with me. I cursed myself for not saying something, anything.

My dad always said, "Sweetheart, don't ever let anyone love you less than you love yourself."

Rhys does love me. I can see it in his eyes.

But I also saw the love he still had for Kim when he looked at her. His heart ached badly for her.

That alone must kill her husband. I gave Rhys all of me, and look what I was getting in return.

I was sitting here, thinking, 'I don't even know who Rhys was anymore.'

He was showing her how he felt about her right in front of me and her husband. I would never have peace of mind, the wondering, does he still really love her? I was hurting right now. But was it better to try and fix a wound before amputating it? I sat back in the chair, and ate my meal, steak in mushroom sauce and salad, sipping on a glass of red wine. All the while, my eyes were glued on Rhys. Only for his eyes to be fixed on, the one and only…Kim.

The rest of the meal was taken up with light conversation about the weather. On the next table, the wine waiter was topping up glasses, humming a song. 'All I Could Do Was Cry', by Beyonce, you flipping kidding me. I stared over into the waiter's direction, as he jerked his head to stare right back at me, raised his brows, and smiled at me—seriously.

Alex placed his wine glass on the table and looked at Kim, his smile sad as hell. He probably felt exactly how I was feeling, my emotions were in turmoil.

He was hurting that much I could sense without him so much as uttering a single word. His wife was expecting a baby for my boyfriend. How should I be feeling, the truth? In that moment, there were screams echoing in my head. I wanted to scream and run, but my vocal cords were paralysed.

And, as for running, Rhys and I were still holding hands under the table.

The drinks kept flowing all night. In fact, it was the third round. Kim had orange juice. Then, Alex suggested going to a wine bar instead, because he needed to drown his sorrows.

Personally, I saw the look Alex gave when the bill was presented to him. He stared at Rhys and me, as though he was thinking, 'Why am I paying for this dude, and his Kim replacement?'

Rhys did offer to pay, but Alex refused, and said, "No, I'll pay the damn bill."

Kim nudged him, all the while, she kept smiling at Rhys.

She sat there, staring at him with her coy smile. Her head turned slightly away, while she gazed at him with a bloody, tight-lipped smile, looking as though she had a secret to tell.

We decided on a wine bar, a few streets away. Well, Alex decided, we just followed like sheep. I think that's what we all needed, because the atmosphere soon changed.

What a transformation. Both Rhys and Alex were being civil to each other. So, now the evening turned out to be more relaxed.

Before we went home, Rhys and Alex actually shook each other's hands. Not before Alex slid his hand around Kim's waist, pulling her back against him.

The drive home was mainly quiet, then Rhys asked me what I thought of Kim.

'Hmmm, honestly, I can see why he didn't want to give her up,' I quietly thought to myself.

"She's more beautiful than I imagined."

"No, that's not what I meant." He shook his head, then turned the volume down on the radio.

It was hard to look at the man whom I loved, knowing that he still had feelings for his ex.

"Do you think you could be friends with her?"

"Well, she did ask for my mobile number, I'll give her a chance."

I was fiddling with the straps of my handbag, looking through the car window, I plucked up the courage to ask him why it was so important for Kim and me to be friends.

He told me that our relationship, he sees it going far, and needed to know that, when Kim has his child, he wanted us both to get along, that's all.

"That's fine, but what about your relationship with Kim's husband?"

He then tutted and rolled his eyes.

"He'll never be civil to me. His wife is having my baby. I'll tell you something, I've been going to my gym for years, and I never noticed him before, until one day, he makes the point, of telling me to keep away from his wife, then sucker punched me. I haven't forgotten."

Rhys' voice was turning sour as he became more and more frustrated with each passing minute.

"Well, wouldn't you have done the same?"

"Yeah, when you look at it like that, especially if it was you, and we're fighting for your love."

So, now I was blushing. But this whole evening, it's been about Kim. Let's just say, I may have misjudged the deep love and attachment that Rhys had for her.

How does that make me feel? Sad. It's cruel and unbearably painful for almost any woman to admit that her guy loved another woman.

I was still staring through the car window, not wanting to cry. Rhys' fingers caressed my hand gently, as he quickly took his eyes off the road for a second, and smiled at me.

10 minutes later, we parked up outside his house. He opened his car door, and as I stepped out of the car, I felt his arms around my waist, and leaned into him.

Rhys cupped my face in his hands and leaned down, brushing my lips softly with his.

Then he whispered, "Tianna, if I had to choose someone, it will always be you."

Renee, Melani, Kayleigh and Nyomi

"It's Saturday night, let's go clubbing. Where's Tianna? Isn't she coming?" Melani said, glancing down at a text message on her phone.

"No, she's with Rhys. He's introducing her to Kim, remember?" Renee replied.

"Have you ever wondered what she's like? I mean why does he want Tianna to meet his ex-girlfriend so badly, yuk!" Nyomi replied, leaning over to read Melani's message.

"Well, I don't know about you, but I'd go, because I'm interested in what she actually looks like," Melani answered.

"I'm not sure if I'd go to be honest," replied Nyomi.

"Okay, but she's crazy about Rhys. So, Tianna will do anything to make him happy right now," Renee replied.

"Really anything? She's in love. Oh my girl Tianna is in love," Kayleigh said, staring at Melani, and Nyomi giggled at something on Melani's phone…hmm.

"Let's hope he doesn't cheat and mess her about like Troy and Tariq. Those two were the worst guys ever," Melani replied, texting with one hand, and reached for her handbag, next to Renee on the chair.

"Renee, didn't your husband know Rhys from school?" Kayleigh asked.

"Yes, he did, and Drake always speaks highly of Rhys. He's known as Mr 99 per cent."

We all started laughing, then asked why.

"Well, according to my husband, when Rhys is interested in a lady, he gets her 99 per cent of the time," replied Renee.

"Oh," said Melani, and Nyomi rolled her eyes, pulling a face.

"So, Kim, is his one per cent then," replied Nyomi.

"Well, technically, he did get her but couldn't hold onto her." replied Kayleigh, laughing.

"That's not strictly true. He gave her up, according to Drake," Renee answered with a raised eyebrow.

"Ouch, that must have hurt, poor Rhys. I mean if he was my man, there's no way I'd be giving him up…no way," Nyomi replied.

"Have you seen her husband? He's some gorgeous white guy." Renee said.

"Really…he's white," replied Kayleigh, spilling her drink.

"I mean, I'm white, but I do like the look of Rhys…he's a hottie," replied Melani.

"Okay, now you're being silly. Melani, isn't your husband, Terrell, black?" Renee replied.

"He's of Jamaican and Italian heritage," replied Melani.

"Yeap, he's still black," replied Renee, shaking her head, she rolled her eyes.

"There is one thing we've all overlooked," Renee said.

"And what's that then?" replied Nyomi and Melani.

"Why does Rhys want Tianna to meet Kim? What about his ex-wife? What about his daughter?" Renee said, looking rather confused.

"What ex-wife and daughter?" asked Melani.

"Okay, let's go clubbing girls, the Uber is here, because I seriously have no clue, where this conversation is going," Nyomi replied, looking rather bemused.

Jess

"Ladies, I see you're back again. I do hope you're all going to be on your best behaviour tonight, or you'll all have to leave," I said, with a half-baked smile.

I'm the nightclub manager of this wonderful club where these lively young ladies like to frequent.

"Jess, you know, we're always good. No getting drunk tonight…it's all good," replied Melani.

"One, two, three, aren't there usually five of you troublemakers, ladies?" I said, looking for one young troublemaker, in particular.

They all started staring at me.

"I don't know, the young lady, but I'm guessing, she's usually the life and soul of the party."

The young lady, in the navy-blue strapless dress, who stood closest to me, suddenly brushed past me and said, "Un-fucking believable."

"Oh yeah, our friend, Tianna, is not with us tonight," Kayleigh replied.

"Oh yes, I remember that one. She's the one who got you all thrown out last month, with her pole dancing antics."

"Well, you've got to hand it to Tianna. She's a lot better than some of your girls here," Melani said, smiling. She struck a pose and started taking selfies.

"Okay, so where's your friend tonight, then?"

"She's busy, not that it's any of your damn business, Jess," Renee replied.

"And your friend, the one who pushed past me, whose she then?"

They all stood there, like butter wouldn't melt in their flipping mouths.

"Go on then, go in, before I change my mind already," I told them, rolling my eyes and shaking my head.

Tianna

I met Kim yesterday. She was as beautiful as I imagined. Honey brown skin, black wavy hair, about four months pregnant, with my boyfriend's baby. I can't believe I've actually said it out loud.

The crushing emotions from last night were more tolerable today. Although a tear fell on my cheek, landing on my shaking hand, as I sipped on a cold cup of coffee.

In fact, this is my fourth cup of coffee, as I sat here, sobbing quietly, trying to contemplate what words were spoken last night. I could have kicked myself mentally for not asking Kim questions about how she really felt about Rhys. But I felt my timing was a little bit inappropriate.

A cold shiver went down my spine, just thinking about it.

The phone rang, causing me to jump out of the chair, spilling my coffee. It was Renee, I'd call her back later.

Anyway, I did as Rhys asked. I met her and her husband. So, her husband Alex was white and handsome. I have blue eyes. Alex's blue eyes are just, well, to be perfectly honest with you, he has an intimate gaze. But that's just between you and me.

Kim—I really don't blame her for staying with him. Rhys has these gorgeous green/hazel eyes. Oh, boy, he's just, what can I say? How can any woman choose between these two guys? It's too impossible. Really, it's too close to call.

I guess, with Rhys walking away from Kim, I now understand why she was so heartbroken. Now I get it because I couldn't either. But hey, he did, and now he's mine. Oh yes, he's all mine.

So, now, we all have to be friends, because she was having my boyfriend's baby.

Hmm, I've said that already, I think. Just thinking about it made my head hurt, believe me. My friends…they like Rhys, but think he's an arsehole.

I'm okay now with the idea of being friends with Kim. She's actually a nice lady. I could see that she was no threat to my relationship with Rhys.

But, then there's a big but. I could see the love he still had for her. What do they say, ahh yes, he was carrying a torch for her. I know he loved me, I can literally feel it, but it's nowhere near the love he had for her.

And I see the sparkle she had in her eyes for Rhys. When she looked at him, it was as though her eyes glowed like two big diamonds. However, I can see that she loved her husband more than words could ever say.

The way she held his hand, just her body language alone, could tell her story of pure love for him, which must hurt Rhys one hundred per cent. But he knew, when he started to pursue her, that she was married.

I'm so in love with Rhys. He has it all, a good job, money, a big house in Finchley, and ladies, have you seen his car? He drives an Audi A8, wow.

But these are just material things, seriously, this guy is a keeper, let me tell you. When he held me in his arms and looked at me with those eyes, I definitely didn't want him to let him go.

I've asked Rhys the question that we've all been dying to know. Why hasn't he spoken about his ex-wife, and why hasn't he asked me to meet with her, as well?

He bent his head back on the chair in the living room.

Then, shaking his head side to side, he closed his eyes, but didn't answer. The silence dragged on.

"Babe, are you tired?" I asked, watching him.

I waited patiently for an answer. Why is he so secretive all of a sudden?

"Babe, are you upset seeing Kim with Alex?" I asked, as my heart started to beat faster.

"You really need me to answer that question, Tianna," Rhys replied abruptly.

I was pretty sure the answer he wanted to give lingered at the forefront of his tongue, but for some unknown reason, he'd changed his mind. So I decided to leave it well alone for now.

The day couldn't get any worse when I looked in the mirror and saw this huge pimple on my nose.

It's Sunday. Rhys and I had to go for lunch every weekend to my parents' house. So, you'll have to wait until later for his answer. Because he apologised for his unusual behaviour, and explained, well, of course it did upset him seeing

Kim with her husband. It was a stupid question to ask. I know how Rhys felt about Kim. I cursed myself quietly for asking such a stupid question.

Then, I thought, what kind of a backward thinking was that, right?

Or maybe, I'm the one who's stupid, knowing my boyfriend still had feelings for his ex, who just happened to be having his baby.

We arrive about 30 minutes late at Mum and Dad's house. Rhys tried squeezing my pimple before heading out, but it hurt too much.

In the end, I had to use the concealer to cover up the pimple.

Dad opened the street door, smiled, then swiftly walked down the hallway, and entered the garden, yelling to Mum as he passed the living room door, "Michelle, your daughter, and her boyfriend's here."

All eyes turned to my dad, wondering why the hell he'd say such a thing, but my dad kept on walking.

We followed him into the garden. It was a bit chilly, but we decided to stay.

Mum brought a tray-out with tea and biscuits, although she knew Rhys only drank coffee. I must admit, Mum can be forgetful at times.

She sat next to Dad, shifting her bum side to side to get comfortable.

My mum asked how Martin's friend, Dave, was getting on with finding my biological dad. My dad nibbled on his lower lip and stared at his book, avoiding any eye contact with Rhys. I think my dad still felt a bit embarrassed about the other day, when he was drunk, and met Rhys for the first time.

He sat quietly in the corner, reading his favourite book as usual. He was sipping his cup of tea, now and again, agreeing with whatever Mum had said. Then, finally, he lifted his head up to ask Rhys one question in particular.

"So, what's all this I hear about you and Kim, then?"

My mouth dropped to the ground. I had spoken about Kim in complete confidence to my mum.

Rhys accidentally dropped the cup on the grass, spilling the tea—which he didn't want to drink anyway—all over his jeans. He turned and stared at me, raising his eyebrows.

There was an awkward pause, as he looked up at the sky, rolled his eyes, then said, "I hope you know that I would never do anything to hurt your daughter, Mr Hyde."

"Call me Clive," Dad replied, staring down at the cup that was lying on its side on the grass.

"Clive, as far as I'm concerned, there is no me and Kim," he replied, trying to wipe the spilt tea from his jeans with his hand.

Mum ran to the kitchen to get a tea-towel to dry the tea off Rhys' jeans. Her face was red as a tomato.

Dad carried on sipping his tea, staring at Rhys, as though he wasn't completely happy with his answer.

"I'm guessing you have some unfinished business with this young lady, now that she's expecting your kid. Do you still see her?" Dad blurted out, then rested the teacup he was holding on the edge of the small table in front of him, waiting for an answer that did not come.

"No, no, don't answer that," I replied, as I bit my lip.

Rhys didn't answer, unwilling to admit just how much Dad's question stung.

Another awkward silence fell, as mum asked, "Anyone for a slice of fruit cake?"

After about five minutes, Rhys gave up and answered Dad's question.

His answer *once in a while*, sounded more like *always*.

Mum and Dad sighed, not quite sure how to respond.

Me on the other hand, sat there quietly holding my boyfriend's hand. Near to tears, I turned my head so no one would notice.

Rhys smiled, pulled me close, whispered softly in my ear, "Love you."

Dad reached for the bottle of rum, hidden under the garden table, and drank straight from the bottle.

"The man with the green eyes is whispering, honey," Dad said, laughing.

His eyes sparkled with a devilish thought, as an expression of pure embarrassment, suddenly clouded Mum's face as she smiled slightly.

"Mum, what's up with Dad today? This is so not like him."

Then I changed the subject. I had to.

Touching a hand to my mouth, I stifled a feigned yawn out of boredom.

After a few minutes, brushing cake crumbs off her lap, Mum asked if there was any news on finding my biological dad, yet again.

"No, nothing. Hopefully, I'll have something to tell you both soon."

Dad raised an eyebrow, his words trailed off when he asked, "How are you going to feel, once he's been found, and if he doesn't want to meet you? How will you cope with being rejected by both of your biological parents?"

Then lifted the bottle of rum, which he had hidden under a cushion, and poured some into his cup.

"Well, let's cross that bridge when I get to it," I so bravely replied.

Rhys looked at me and said, "What father wouldn't want to meet his beautiful daughter?"

Rhys

The moment of truth, Tianna, and all her friends, everyone, literally everyone wants to know about my ex-wife.

What can I say, I'm quite a private person. A gentleman will never discuss his ex in a bad way. So, I'm going to give you the watered-down version of my marriage to my ex-wife Leah.

I met Leah at college. We'd been together for 16 years, and married for seven. We have a five-year-old daughter, Ella-Mai. My daughter means the world to me. I haven't really spoken about her too much, and there's a good reason for that. Yeah, I know, there's always a good reason.

My ex-wife uses my daughter as an excuse for me to visit her all the time. I made a simple mistake one night when I went to visit my daughter and ex-wife. I've been regretting it ever since.

But first, let me take you back to how I met my ex-wife, Leah.

Like I said, we met at college. She was one of those popular girls, you know, everyone wanted to be her friend. The life and soul of every party. She was my first true love. At secondary school, my friend, Drake and I couldn't get any girls to like us, until I got rid of my thick-rimmed glasses and braces.

The girls at school used to call me ugly Rhys. Yeah, those were the days. Drake had me cut off his dreadlocks, if you see him now.

We both started going to the gym, we had a six pack most men would die for.

Leah going out with me was my dream come true.

She was beautiful with blonde hair, blue/grey eyes and a lovely figure, and she was very intelligent. I was actually the second black guy she dated.

We lived together for a long time before getting married and starting a family. Not my choice, I can tell you that much.

Leah was very career-minded and put that first, before having children and getting married.

Finally, when she felt ready to settle down and have a baby, she found that she couldn't conceive. So she had IVF. We had our daughter Ella-Mai. Sadly, it was too much stress for Leah, so we decided not to try for another child.

Now you see why Kim, having my baby, means the world to me; if only she wanted me instead of Alex.

But I'm with Tianna now, and I hope they would both get along.

So, now let me tell you something else. My ex-wife had got it into her head that we're getting back together again. Why, because I fucked up. I'm holding my head down, right about now, with shame. I foolishly had sex with her.

Yeah, I'll hold my hand up and admit that I shouldn't have done it, especially when I knew she wanted me to come back home, to her and our daughter.

Ever since then, she had interfered in any new relationship she found out about and started making trouble.

She often phoned, late in the night, playing 2 am by ZSA.

Crying, she sang, "Come home, babes, Rhys, come home. I love you, come home, babes."

My ex-wife, I wouldn't say she's crazy, was very jealous.

Anyway, let's hear her version and see what she had to say. But remember, you know me, not her, and I've never lied to you.

Leah (Ex-Wife)

Rhys has told you a little bit about me. I thank him for not going into the real reason why we broke up. He's quite the gentleman, really, he is.

That is why I loved him so much. What I will tell you is that I broke his heart, no, not by cheating on him. Hell, no. What woman in her right mind would ever cheat on him? Come on, be serious now.

But I did something, no woman should do to their husband. For this reason, and this reason alone, I found myself without my husband. The man I've loved for 16 long, fantastic years.

We've been broken up for about 14 months now, not that long. And I found out from a mutual friend that he was in a relationship with a lady called Kim, and now he's with someone called Tianna.

Just so you all know, I was sitting here all alone, crying my eyes out, for a man who no longer wanted or loved me.

So, if it meant I go crazy, trying to get my husband back, I'd go crazy.

Rhys' girlfriend, well, especially this latest one, Tianna, seemed intent on driving me crazy, I'd say. Where would we be without crazy, right?

This was my version.

One afternoon, Rhys came to see his daughter. One thing led to another, and we made love. He'd tell you it was just sex.

I'm going to tell you something, don't be shocked. It was when he was seeing either Kim or his new girlfriend Tianna. He gave me false hope that we'd be back together again, as a family. If you knew Rhys, the way I do, you'd want him back too. At the moment, he's angry with me.

When I phoned him on the odd occasion, he hung up on me. I knew that you don't know me at all, but I want him back, so badly, because guys like him, you don't let go so easily.

One mistake, just one stupid mistake, and our marriage was over, just like that. He'd never forgive me. Once Rhys loved you, he truly loved you, one hundred per cent. But once that love had gone, it goes forever, there's no getting it back. But I'd try, anyway.

I guess you want to know what I did to make Rhys stop loving me. I'd tell you soon. Right now, I'm too upset to talk any more.

Tianna

It's Wednesday morning, and it's a beautiful day. The sun shone, and guess what, I was not late for work, thanks to Rhys.

So, I was sitting at my desk, and my manager, Martin, came over and gave me an envelope.

My heart just skipped a beat. I got up and went to the lady's toilet.

With shaking hands, my heart beating fast, I opened the envelope. Well, after I'd stared at it for all of 10 minutes. Inside the envelope was a name, my dad's name. Ainsley Gilmore. Oh my God, I'd found my dad. There was a mobile number on a piece of crumpled paper, written in red ink.

Tears came flowing down my cheeks, let me tell you. I was so emotional; I asked my boss for the rest of the day off.

Later that evening, with the help of Rhys, I picked up the courage to give him a call. As I sat nervously on the living room sofa, my body trembled, and my heart was hammering.

Sliding an arm under me, and gently taking my hand in his, Rhys leaned close and spoke softly in my ear, "Babe, you've dialled the number at least five times now, let it ring."

"I know, I'm just so nervous, babe."

So, that's what I did.

I let it ring until, a few seconds later, I heard my dad's voice, "Hello."

He sounded so nice over the phone that we arranged to meet up next Friday at 7:30 p.m.

Rhys explained that, although he's my dad, I shouldn't meet him alone, and suggested that he'd go with me. I totally agreed with him.

It was the middle of the afternoon on a Thursday, the skies were dark and grey. The day just dragged on.

It was only one more day before meeting my biological dad.

My parents were pleased for me, but wondered how they would fit into my life, now that my real dad had been found.

"You'll always be my real parents, no matter what."

"We know, sweetheart."

They both sounded thrilled about the news over the phone, but I spent 20 minutes trying to convince my dad that I'd never replace him as a father, no matter what.

Later that evening, around 8:23 pm, I climbed the stairs and headed for my bedroom. I sat on my bed, grabbed my phone from the bedside table. I lay on my stomach at first, then rolled over onto my back, staring up at the grey ceiling. I was smiling, just smiling, thinking about my biological dad. I wondered if I looked like him, just a little bit or my mum.

Who, I had no clue, as to where she'd been flipping hiding, all of these years. 30 to be exact, and phoned my good friend, Tamara.

She sounded ever so happy for me. I heard it in her voice. I couldn't even begin to tell you how much.

Like me, she too was adopted, but when she was four, her mother…well, let's just leave her story for her to tell.

Renee

I remember having a shower, after a hard day at work, and dragged my feet to the kitchen to make dinner.

There were half a dozen messages from Tianna. "Babe, I found my dad."

I read well the first message. The others, I couldn't tell you. I got straight on the phone and dialled her number.

My best friend, Tianna, had found her biological dad—at last.

Us, girls, were so pleased for her. She deserved happiness in her life. She is a very beautiful person both inside, and out.

She always put other people's feelings before hers. I guess that's why she always got hurt and betrayed by people.

A few of us, Kayleigh, Nyomi, and I, Meloni's not feeling well. So, we drove in the pouring rain to Tianna's house just to say good luck for tomorrow evening, when she finally gets to meet her dad, Ainsley.

We were not planning on staying too long. Well, because Rhys was there, he looked like he was ready for bed, if you know what I mean.

We gave her a bottle of champagne and flowers, because that's what we girls do when we're all happy—we all celebrate.

"Oh, before we all forget, what did Rhys tell you about his ex-wife?" Nyomi whispered.

"Tell you what, let's see how it goes tomorrow night with my dad, then we can all catch up on Saturday. Then maybe, maybe I might fill you in on all the gossip," replied Tianna, pointing to the street door, then waved her hands.

"Bye, girls."

Well, as you all are aware, my husband, and Rhys, were best friends. So, in reality, I should know about Rhys' ex-wife, his daughter, all the gossip.

But, it's not my story to tell, and it wouldn't be right, me telling all the gossip. In fact, to tell you the truth, in all the years that I have known Rhys, I can honestly say, come to think about it, I've only met his ex-wife maybe…twice.

His daughter's such a cutie. I'm pretty sure my husband told me that Rhys wanted me to be godmother to his daughter.

But his wife, Leah, apparently said, "Hell will freeze over first."

Hmm, seemed like his wife disliked me for all the wrong reasons. I did wonder why.

Apparently, because I questioned why, she hadn't had their baby christened, and waited for so long. I saw the horrid look on her face when I opened my stupid big mouth.

"Get out of here, you horrid thing!" is what she told me.

She stood there, staring me down, hands on her hips. Leah's attitude toward me did an about-face, so obvious that even my husband noticed.

That was the second time that I met Rhys' wife.

Let me just tell you quickly, the first time I met her, as the girls are about to leave.

We were invited to dinner, my husband and I, at their wonderful house, somewhere in North Finchley. A tree-lined road, with houses on that particular road, costing more money than I can count, that's for sure.

The lovely Leah opened her aluminium street door, her smile turned to a frown, as she suddenly noticed me, standing behind my husband.

Rhys stepped into the hallway. "Hi, come in," he said, with a big smile on his handsome face.

Well, it's kind of hard to come inside, with your wife standing in the doorway, looking as though I shouldn't be entering her home through the street door. I thought she got somewhat jealous with me standing there in my ripped jeans, and off-the-shoulder top, chewing gum, just being myself, in my opinion.

Her large blue-grey eyes took one look at the likes of me, not saying that there was anything wrong me—hell no. In fact, I screamed gorgeous, but she screamed, *one does not dress or act like a lady.*

The atmosphere felt stiff, and formal, as if this was not part of her normal routine. I remember, she stared at her husband's face, while handing me a cup of horrible coffee, in a tiny cup. A cup which seemed like it belonged in a dolls house. But he ignored her miserable expression. Good for him.

She did, after sometime, make light conversation. She looked bored out of her mind. But to be brutally honest, frankly, she bored me silly with her nonsense chit chat about this and that. I wasn't really paying too much attention to the words spoken out of her mouth, until she tried, and failed to insult…no, embarrass me, about where, I so happened, to buy my clothes.

Okay, so I can't exactly match her mega funds. But I certainly looked damn good, honey. Err, hmm, she was wearing a black Chanel dress, her hair was in a tousled lob hairstyle, also known as a long bob, with champagne blonde lowlights.

Okay, she did look nice. Anyway, like one does, I changed her boring conversation and spoke about how I met my husband.

She glanced over at me with amusement in the upturned corner of her lips.

Her mobile rang. "So sorry, I need to take this urgent call."

Thank goodness for that. My husband and Rhys had left the living room more than an hour ago to go to the kitchen, where the dinner Rhys was cooking. It smelt ever so nice.

Another 30 or so minutes later, it was dinner time. Thank God, for that, I was absolutely starving.

"Excuse me," I said to Leah as she got up from her cream leather corner sofa, and demanded that I follow her to the dining room.

So, I did just that, followed her down the hallway. The walls were painted white, and the floor had a stunning marble design in black, and white.

Not to mention the 22 pop ceiling designs, definitely attention-grabbing.

Well, I only knew the name because I so happened to have seen them in a home magazine with an eye-watering price.

There was also a console table with flowers and a lamp. Oh, did I mention the white and gold wooden bench in the hallway, where I had to perch, and take off my shoes. She handed me a pair of lovely white slippers, which I hoped that I got to keep.

I sat next to Leah. "Come, sit next to me," she said in a mocking voice.

I watched her as she held the fork to her lips, pecking away at the lamb chops and asparagus—her favourite meal, apparently.

She looked up at me in utter disgust as I reached over and helped myself to more lamb chops, which were the size of my thumbs.

"It's amazing how sneaky calories manage to gang up on you," she said, with venom in her voice.

No word of a lie, as she spoke, her voice came so near to me. I had to jump to my feet, just to get away from her, as she reached for the dish, containing the child-like portion of lamb chops, slapping my hand in the process. I was determined to give as much as she gave and blurt out some venom of my own. Then my husband and Rhys shook their heads, raising their brows, their eyes dark, as Leah's mood.

"Don't do it, don't you bloody do it," my husband yelled, then forgot his place at the dinner table, and thumped down hard, hurting his wrist.

"I'm sorry, but she's an uptight little princess who dared to invite the likes of me into her palace by mistake," I said, purposely eating a tiny lamb chop with my fingers.

I licked my lips and stared at her ugly face. She was staring right back at me in disgust.

Her lip plumper, which she so obviously used actually worked. Anyway, her freckles sprinkled over that upturned nose of hers gave her a youthful look, though I'm guessing she was closer to being 40.

"How dare you slap the lamb chops out of my hand? I'm starving, you bitch," I screamed at her.

Oh, she didn't like the tone of my voice, let me tell you. We had a fight, if only verbal, but a fight it was. Our husbands looked on in utter dismay, shaking their heads. What she did next was totally not called for.

She took the dish with the lamb chops, and threw them at me, one by one. So, I poured gravy all over her choppy bob, or was it lob, £210.00 hair style. Give me a pair of scissors, I could have done a better job.

"That's enough," Rhys shouted, with an annoyed shake of his head.

My husband, on the other hand, laughed when she took the mashed potatoes and slapped them on my hair, saying, "Now you look more like a lady."

As angry as we both were, I, for once, thought it was a fair fight. Especially when I had the last laugh by plastering a big, sloppy kiss on her husband's lips before leaving.

But no, she handed me back my cheap bottle of Merlot, according to her. She opened the street door and shoved me onto the cold pavement, then threw an insult my way.

"You're the most common—" she hooked her fingers, in quotation marks, "gold-digger bitch, I've ever met. What your husband ever sees in you is beyond thinking about."

She then proceeds to slam the street door shut in my face, leaving my husband stuck inside, with my shoes and, of course, her husband.

How Rhys put up with her and her little attitude is anyone's guess.

Okay, so I'm exaggerating just a little bit. Am I?

Just then, Kayleigh grabbed me by my arm and told me to keep my trap shut.

"I'm sorry, I was just having some fun," I said, laughing.

I knew nothing about Leah, even though she was married to Rhys, for quite a while. I did go to their house while they were married. However, she could never, let me repeat, never threw me out of her house. You crazy or what?

I gave Tianna a hug and a kiss and wished her good luck for tomorrow, when she finally gets to meet her biological dad. That was the whole point of us girls going over to her house, right?

Rhys wasn't too pleased with me, making fun of his ex-wife. He stood perfectly still in the hallway with a frown looming on his face, while his arms were folded across his chest. Well, she's his ex for a reason, dare I say it.

Now, my good friend, Tianna, was shaking her head. Her hand gently pushed me forward towards the street door, then motioned me to leave.

"See you tomorrow," she whispered, as a laugh bubbled up within me.

I suppressed the urge to laugh. Tianna obviously thought my story about Rhys' ex-wife was somewhat exaggerated.

Tianna

I'm so thankful to have friends who care for me so deeply. And there's my boyfriend, Rhys, who also cared for me. I'm so lucky to have such good people in my life right now, including my parents.

Even though one of my friends, not going to name which one, has a rather wicked sense of humour, don't you think?

Well, to be honest, I thought the story about Leah was in fact nonsense. But apparently, it's a true story. I asked Rhys about it, and he confirmed most of what Renee had said, but in a slightly different version.

A few days later, Rhys asked if I would like to go to Venice for a short break. Yes, and yes.

He wrapped an arm around me, securing my body close to his, while his breath was hot against my ear.

"Love you." His thumbs caressed my cheeks, his voice was soft.

"Love you too," I replied, as he handed me a white envelope, but said not to open it until after meeting with my dad.

Rhys cupped my cheeks in his hands and kissed me deeply. His warm lips kissed their way down my neck and across my shoulder. I unbuttoned the first few buttons on his shirt and slipped my arms around his neck. Then I heard the faint sound of his phone ringing downstairs.

He trotted down the stairs, leaving me staring after him. I followed him down the stairs, walking slowly towards the kitchen doorway, and hesitated. I did not want to pry. I was not sure if the conversation was supposed to end so abruptly.

I kissed him and asked, "Who was on the phone?"

Of course, it was Kim, who else.

His gleaming eyes were fixed intently on one spot—his phone.

The message Kim had just sent him, as he grinned to himself. I turned around and headed for my bedroom, tears welling up in my eyes. Rhys grabbed my right arm before I could back away and pulled me into his arms. I buried my face into his chest, sobbing.

"Babe, why are you crying?"

"Why can't she leave you the hell alone?"

"Who?"

"Your ex, Kim, that's who." I sobbed, my tears falling on his shirt.

"Look at me, Tianna. Babe, look at me."

So, I rubbed my sleeve across my eyes to dry them and looked up at him.

He stared down at me, smiling, with his beautiful green eyes.

"Tianna, you know how much I love you."

"Yes, I know you do."

My chin trembled, and I wiped my eyes and nose on the back of my hand. I stared up at Rhys.

"A moment ago, you asked me whom I was speaking to on the phone. I said Slim, but you heard Kim," he said, laughing.

I half laughed, half sobbed in response, before apologising for hearing what I wanted to hear.

Silly me, Rhys does indeed have a friend called Slim. Well, his name is actually Asher.

Friday evening, the day when I would meet my biological dad. Rhys was here holding my hand. I was so nervous, my heart was racing…boom, boom, boom. Beating like toy soldiers, banging their drums, all at once. I can hear it so clearly.

Okay, so he's late. I kept looking at my watch and paced back and forth, which didn't help. I was just a bag of nerves, and the waiting made me all the more anxious.

"Rhys, I think I can see him. He fits the description that Dave gave. Oh, hold on a minute, babe, Martin is calling me," I said, staring up a Rhys, looking a bit puzzled.

"Rhys, let's make a run for it, quickly."

Dave just phoned Martin. It looked like Dave did a bit more digging into my dad and this Ainsley Gilmore. He was not my dad. He was a con man, posing as women's long-lost dad, and had made quite a bit of money fleecing unsuspecting young ladies, pretending to be their daddy.

I could only turn and rest my head onto Rhys' chest and cry.

He held me, never imagining anything could feel so painful, despite the rain and cold.

"Don't cry, babe."

'How can someone be that cruel,' I thought.

"Dave made a mistake, but soon realised, before you got involved with him," Rhys said, wrapping his arms around me, then kissed me on my forehead.

We did make a hasty dash for it back to Rhys' car, parked on the fifth floor of the car park.

"So now what, do I keep looking?"

"Never give up looking for your biological dad. He's out there somewhere, and I'll be here with you, every step of the way."

I held him tight that my mascara smudged on his white shirt.

"What would I do without you, Rhys?" I said, as I gazed into his green eyes.

He stroked the side of my cheeks and kissed me so passionately that I somehow forgot about Ainsley Gilmore, not being my dad.

A few days later, Rhys said he'd like me to meet his mum and twin brothers. His mum, Marcia, and his brothers, Lewis and Kyle.

His dad, we know, was in prison, as well as a guy called Mark, for murdering Kim's dad. The whole situation was very sad.

Marcia was a lovely lady. She welcomed me with open arms into her family. And hoped that I'm going to stick around, much longer than the last lady her son introduced her to.

She then asked if I had a husband lurking somewhere in the background.

At first, I had no idea what she meant, then realised she was referring to Kim. Rhys slipped a protective arm around my waist as he listened on in silence to his mum talking non-stop about Kim.

With a vexed expression on her face, she wondered why she'd bothered being nice to her and why she wasted weeks trying to make her feel welcome in her home. I smiled and yawned, then my gaze shifted firmly onto Rhys.

"I must be boring you to death," she said, laughing.

She sipped her wine with eyes on me, clearly looking for a reaction that never came.

She got up and went over to the side cabinet, retrieving family photos and pointed out her other two sons and their families.

Lewis was married to Chantelle. They had two girls: Jacee was two and Evie was six months old.

Kyle was single, having recently broken up with his girlfriend. But they had a son, Jaxon. He was four.

Later that evening, we went to Rhys' house. We were cuddling up on the sofa, watching a movie, drinking wine—just chilling. That's when his phone kept ringing. He left it ringing when he saw who was calling, then decided to answer after a while.

At first, the conversation was quite pleasant, then Rhys began to tut left, right and centre. Oh dear, who on Earth could he be talking to?

It was his ex-wife, Leah, asking if he could come over because the sink was blocked, or something like that.

He told her politely to phone a plumber and to send him the receipt, as he would pay the bill. But no, she wasn't having any of that nonsense and demanded he come over immediately, or he won't be seeing his daughter, Ella-Mai, anytime soon.

So, that's what he did, went to fix her blocked sink. I stood on the doorstep, and waved him goodbye, watching him start his car, and sped down the road.

That's when our problem, mine, and Rhys' began, with her interference into our relationship, although at the time, I had no clue, what her real intentions were.

While he was gone, I remembered the envelope he gave me and said not to open it until after I had met my dad. I took a peek, then sealed the envelope back.

My eyes opened wide when I saw what was inside the envelope. Rhys was just so thoughtful and generous to a fault.

It was tickets for two for a West End musical show at the theatre, and a meal afterwards, at a very expensive restaurant. And a limousine was booked to take us there and bring us back home.

I assumed it was for me and my dad. Oh well, it won't go to waste. Rhys and I can go. What a lovely gesture it was of Rhys to think of such a gift.

Sometime later, in fact a lot later, when I woke up, it was 2:32 am, and Rhys had not returned from his ex-wife's house.

What should I do, should I phone him, or just wait? Then, I heard keys rattling in the street door.

I could hear him creeping up the stairs. He walked into the bedroom quietly and went into the shower.

No, no, no, Rhys, please don't tell me you had sex with her.

Some 22 minutes later, he slid into the bed next to me, hugged me tightly, then kissed me on my neck. But I pretended to be asleep. I lay there with my eyes closed, but the tears started to well up. I could almost smell the lingering scent of her perfume on him, or though he just stepped out from the shower.

"Tianna, babe," he whispered softly, but I kept pretending that I was asleep.

If you think for one second that you're going to touch me after sleeping with your ex, then think again, I thought silently to myself.

The feel of his warm, naked body pressed up so close against mine only made me want him. But, no, nothing. Definitely nothing was happening tonight or any other night, until he would tell me what the heck was going on with him and his ex-wife.

Later that morning, he apologised for getting home so late, and said that I was sleeping when he came home, and he didn't want to wake me up. I told him that it was okay, and not to worry, but deep down, I was hurting.

He said later, after work, we could do something nice together to make it up to me.

Just before he left for work, I thanked him for the tickets he had given me for my dad and me to spend some time together.

He kissed me and said, "Anything for you, babe."

I suggested that we should go, but he said to treat one of my friends instead.

Hmm, what should I do? He doesn't seem guilty of anything. I'd phone Tamara at lunchtime to see what she thinks.

I'm so used to looking through the window, in the mornings, listening to the birds singing, I always forget the time. Not today though as Rhys always got up very early. So, today, I'm actually early for work.

The view from his window was much nicer than mine. But the birds always sang the same beautiful song.

Today, I felt like singing along with the small birds, but silently smiled instead. Pain tugged at my heart once more.

"Morning, Martin," I said, smiling.

He looked at his watch, then tapped it, thinking it had stopped.

"I almost thought you were someone else. Good morning, Tianna. Go, and get yourself a cup of coffee, and come see me in my office," he replied.

Oh boy, what have I done now? I wondered.

Martin apologised for the mix-up with the man, who Dave thought was my dad.

"Oh, Martin, tell Dave it's not his fault. I don't blame him in any way," I quickly responded.

Then, Martin explained that Dave suggested finding my dad another way, by registering on the Ancestry website. Either my dad or a close relative could be a member there.

"Oh, wow, tell Dave thanks for the idea. I really haven't thought of that."

I discussed the idea with my parents, they agreed it would be a better way of finding my dad. So, that's what I did, let's see who turned up.

A couple of days later, Rhys and I went to Venice for a few days. He thought it would cheer me up.

We stayed in a swanky 4-star superior hotel, a few steps from St Mark's Square. We enjoyed a spectacular view from the large window, especially the church of San Giorgio Dei Greci, and its famous leaning bell tower.

In the evening, Rhys hired a private gondola for a romantic night time ride. In the morning, we went to Rialto Market, then stopped off for coffee, down a narrow-cobbled street.

On our last day, we took a day trip and went to the island of Murano.

Rhys bought me some glass beads and a bracelet. I too bought some glass beads and had a matching bracelet made for Rhys and me.

He smiled, then laughed when I gave it to him, and said, "I'll never take the bracelet off, even though it looks a bit girly."

He held me in his arms and said how much he loved me.

I didn't want the few days in Venice to come to an end, but it was time to go home.

Before we checked out, we surely made use of the hotel room. We made such passionate love that evening. I didn't want the evening to come to an end.

He looked me deep into my eyes, and told me that he hadn't been this happy in a long time.

I closed my eyes, held him so tight, and whispered softly, "Neither have I."

It's been a couple of days since our trip to Venice. I'm happy, Rhys was happy, we were so loved up. So, what could possibly go wrong? You guessed it—the ex-Mrs Brooks. What the hell, first the sink was blocked, now the downstairs toilet was blocked.

I was thinking of telling Rhys not to go. But he reassured me he wouldn't be long.

He kissed me and said not to worry, he'll be back soon. He said he knew she was taking the piss, and he was going to put a stop to her meddling, and ask her for a divorce.

My eyes opened as wide as my mouth as I stood there staring at him. He turned his back on me and slammed the street door on his way out.

Divorce, I thought.

I had no idea that he was still married to her.

While he was gone, I took the opportunity to phone my good friend, Tamara, and see what she thought of the whole situation.

Tamara's very level-headed.

The first question she asked, "Do you love him?" followed by, "Is he worth fighting for?"

"Yes, and yes," I told her.

"Then, girl, go fight for your man," she replied.

One thing I told Tamara, that he failed to mention, was that he was still married to her. Tamara asked if that was going to be a problem. I told her considering the relationship he had with Kim, why wouldn't he of seek a divorce then. The way he said he felt about her, why ask her to leave her husband, if he was still married. I really don't understand, because it doesn't make any sense to me.

Okay. So, now we're both baffled by the revelation that Rhys was still married.

Tamara said that I had two choices: either ask, or don't ask, about why he was not divorced yet.

"I'm thinking, hmmm, still thinking," I told her, hesitating. "Okay, maybe she refused to accept he wants a divorce, or maybe, maybe, hmmm…ahh…yes, I know, they're not really married," I said, laughing, but deep down I really wanted to scream.

"Girl, you're crazy. Just ask him when he gets in, to put your mind at rest, then phone me, because I'm dying to know too."

"Me too, babe, me too."

So, now I fell face-first onto my bed. No, actually, I sat down on the bed and sighed. Then lifted the blankets and crawled into bed, feeling rather disappointed with myself, thinking, here I go again—the married boyfriend. But somehow, this relationship felt different.

With nothing but my troubled thoughts, the cold rain beating against the window, and Mr Kitty for company, I slumped back onto the bed, staring up at the ceiling, watching shadows dancing, listening to, Confidently Lost by Sabrina Claudio—over and over again.

Rhys

"Seriously, Leah, this is the last time that I'm going to drop everything and come running. The toilet is not blocked. So, what the hell do you want?" I asked her, fuming.

The hostility in my voice and the expression on my face to my wife was unnerving. Even I was shocked.

But she stood there, on her doorstep, smiling with her big blue-grey eyes, long golden hair, which she flicked back over her shoulders.

For some reason, she was wearing her shortest skirt, funny enough that appeared to ride up her ample body, as if it were trying to get away, and her lowest cut blouse.

So now she started with her crocodile tears. "Please, babe, I want you to come home," she sobbed, and proceeded to put her arms around my neck loosely.

"Stop with your nonsense, Leah," I yelled, removing her arms and following her down the hallway.

"It's funny how you only want me back as soon as you find out I'm in a relationship." The words just came out of my mouth with even more hostility than before.

She said that it wasn't true, and that she still loved me. In fact, she had never stopped loving me. I asked her who was giving her the gossip about my relationships, but she stood there. Now, her arms are folded after I removed her hands from around my neck, for the second time. With her head tilted to one side, she showed me a little attitude and laughed. Leah refused to name someone, anyone.

"Leah, this crap…this crap stops right now, I've had it with you, and you're meddling. Leah, I'm filing for a divorce," I yelled, grabbing her arm, pulling her up close to me…my eyes were flashing fire.

She looked up at me as though I wasn't being totally serious and started laughing in my face.

"Yeah, right, babe, like that's ever going to happen, anytime soon," she said, and continued laughing.

This is when things started to get a bit ugly.

Hands on her hips, she yelled, cursed, screamed and shouted, "You can't divorce me. Daddy won't let you."

She carried on screaming and laughing so hard that she was in tears.

"Leah, I've had it up to here with you and your family controlling me and telling me what I can and can't do," I replied, then glanced down at my phone, vibrating in my hand.

She stupidly ran up those stairs, all 20 of them, grabbed a handful of clothes from the drawer in the bedroom. I headed for the street door, going down the steps, and about to walk down the front garden path, when she threw a handful of clothes out of the window at me.

One by one, the clothes fell onto my head. I looked and felt like a clown. all I needed was a red nose. Huh, by now I was shaking my head, rolling my eyes, still fuming.

"Take your fucking clothes," she screamed.

"They're not my fucking clothes. I don't live here anymore." I laughed.

She suddenly felt foolish, thinking that they were my clothes, somehow forgetting the fact that, I had taken all of my stuff, including my clothes, when I moved out.

She ran down the stairs, yelling and cursing. A few nasty words were spoken by her, which I took exception to, and then she grabbed my arm as I turned my back to her, heading towards my car. I removed her hand gently from my arm and told her my patience was hitting the wall. Her rosebud lips curved into a smile that never reached her eyes. She opened her mouth to speak, but no words came out, probably because of all the screaming she had done.

Leah slapped me across my face. When that didn't provoke the reaction that she had hoped for, she started hitting me in my chest and laughed through her crocodile tears. I stood there, like the gentleman that I am, trying to take deep breaths, knowing I'd lost my cool. But I wasn't going to give her the satisfaction of raising my hand at her.

As I opened my car door, a police car pulled up to the kerb, blocking my car in. It had its flashing blue lights on, as though a murder had been committed.

She pushed past me, waving her hands at the officers, and poked her head through the car window, whispering some sort of nonsense, with her fake tears running down her cheeks. I counted the seconds in tense silence, waiting for the police officers to arrest me.

"Until he does something to warrant police action, I'd say he has every right to be on his way," The officer told her, then looked at me.

She felt foolish for the second time tonight, thinking that she'd get me arrested for something I clearly didn't do.

Her face flamed, and tears were streaming down her red cheeks. Leah turned around and stormed off up the three steps, issuing a cry of frustration, when she realised the officer bluntly refused to arrest me.

Her erratic moods had grown more volatile over the past couple of days, and she knew better than to outsmart me. But outsmarting me is what she tried to do.

So, she changed tactics. Finally, she blurted out what was really on her mind. She stood in front of her street door, stomping her feet, yelling. Her eyes were large and wide.

"If you leave me, Rhys, I'm going to phone my dad and make sure he strips you of everything you own," she screamed at the top of her voice, which turned raw with emotion.

"Go ahead, Leah," I said, laughing at her stupidity.

She started to laugh, then cry again, remembering that her dad signed his entire company over to me six years ago, when he suffered a heart attack.

"I'm sorry, Rhys, I just didn't want you to leave me."

"Leah, I left you a long time ago, let's not go through all this shit again."

I shook my head in disbelief. She paused, sucked in a deep breath, and then threw her hands in the air in defeat.

"Rhys, I am so sorry, let's go back inside the house and talk," she said, raising her eyes through dark, full lashes, locked full on to mine.

I'm not a bad guy. She was still my wife, unfortunately. So, that's what I foolishly did.

We went through to the kitchen, and she leaned against the kitchen sink, staring up at me.

Before I could even contemplate her next move, Leah flung her arms around me and snuggled up close.

She loved my scent, the feel of my warm body against hers. I recall how soothing her hugs used to be.

The air between us shimmered with my body heat and her magic. I didn't flinch away like I should have.

The magic crept up through her legs, warming her body as it went. Leah leaned forward and stood on her toes, gripping my shoulders, and kissed me passionately on my lips.

"I love you," she whispered softly, and smiled sweetly up at me.

Her hands slid slowly around my waist, and worked their way up my back, moving gradually as she massaged every inch of either side of my spine, and eventually, caressing my inner thighs.

So, I grabbed her by the arm and pushed her away.

"Are you crazy? What the hell is wrong with you?" I yelled at her and accidentally shoved her.

She stumbled backwards, tearing her gaze from my lean, muscular thighs. Leah's untaught, unsatisfied hands destroyed whatever they touch, because they do not know what else to do with things. And because I didn't get aroused and respond to her, her mood flipped back and forth so fast. It was hard to know what she'd do next.

Tears collected on her lashes as she stared up at me with angry emotions. Whatever game she had in mind, it was a game I had no intention of playing.

The silence draped the kitchen, like a spring fog, until she finally spoke her nonsense.

Her high heels brought her up, almost to my height. She met my gaze and spoke inches away from my face.

"I expected better from you, Rhys. What you just did…it's dirty, unforgiving and cruel. You know what, you've thought about me every day, in your shitty little life, but guess what, babe, I haven't thought about you once. You're a fucking arsehole, fuck you very much."

And that's when she took her high heels off to throw at me, when she suddenly moved backwards, hesitated and cried instead.

It may seem a little harsh, the way I am with Leah, but you don't know what hell I'd been through with this woman.

She's nothing like Kim or Tianna, trust me. If any of you guys out there saw her, do yourself a favour and run for the hills. Trust me, you really didn't want to start any relationship with her. If you do, you'll need a get out of jail free card, and that's putting it lightly.

Anyway, I sat in my car, still fuming. The sound of my heart pounding was loud in my ears. I didn't want Tianna to see me like this. So, I gave her a quick phone call to let her know, that I'm just passing by to see Drake, and I wouldn't be too long.

The drive to his house was somewhat nerve-wrecking. As I swear, that bloody police officer was trailing me.

The clouds became dark, then it poured with rain. A gust of wind delivered the smell of raindrops on parched soil, coming from Drake's front garden, as I pulled up outside his house.

He stood staring at me, leaning against his front garden waist-high wall, holding a packet of cigarettes in one hand, and a beer bottle in the other.

Drake just shook his head and laughed.

"I told you man, not to marry that crazy psycho bitch. Well, you see, my man, 16 years later, and it's all come down to this shit."

He took a sip of his beer, then added, "If you're not careful, she'll definitely mess things up for you and Tianna…trust me on that."

I told Drake, someone was giving her all the gossip about my relationships and how she kept meddling. Drake takes a cigarette out of the packet and starts smoking.

"My man, you need to find out who's telling her your business before she costs you your relationship with Tianna. By the way, Rhys, why now? Why is she meddling now and not when you were seeing Kim? That's what I want to know. It seems as though you're stuck in a confusing breakup that has left Leah baffled. You keep running to her every time she calls, that shit has to stop, Rhys. This is some ugly situation that you have found yourself in, my friend."

"I've asked myself that many times, Drake, and I have no answer."

So, now Drake and I were just chilling and talking. My phone started ringing like there's no tomorrow. Of course, it was Leah, who else?

"Ignore her, she's crazy," Drake said, as he continued smoking.

"Seriously, she's doing my head in. I'm filing for a divorce," I said, still fuming with anger, just realising I was biting my fingernails.

"Only now," he said, looking at me with a frown. "I thought you cut her loose a long time ago, man, when you were seeing Kim," he replied, shaking his head, as his frown deepened.

Inside, I was burning with anger. I glanced over at Drake, smoking and helped myself to one of his cigarettes to calm my nerves. His lips drooped, a cigarette, curling a wisp of thin pale smoke. I wanted a cigarette, or at least, a swig of his beer.

I sometimes smoked when I felt sad, upset, or just to be smoking a cigarette, to have something to do, like people who play football, a pastime.

"I know, divorcing Leah should've been my number one priority, but I just got distracted with Kim," I said, and within two minutes, we were rushing into the house absolutely drenched.

"I'm going to get out of these wet clothes. I'll bring you down a towel," Drake said, running up the stairs to his bedroom.

My clothes were soaking wet, and my backside was numb with cold from sitting on the front garden wall. I stared at the kitchen wall, deep in thought for a few minutes. My thoughts tumbled in my head, making and breaking alliances like my wet clothes in the tumble dryer.

Drake laughed and dropped the towel across my shoulder. Fuck, I was standing butt-naked in his kitchen. That's how messed up in the head I was.

I changed the subject, because the more I thought about Leah, the more I became pissed off.

Drake asked how Kim was doing, especially after meeting with Tianna. And wanted to know how Tianna felt about meeting the woman who drove me crazy.

"Yeah, that's hard to describe, Drake. They seem to get along, but it was Alex who gave me a hard time. That dude just stared at me for most of the evening," I replied.

I was smoking and coughing with each puff, but I didn't care. I just kept on smoking like my mate, Drake.

He stood there. staring at me, then suddenly spoke. "Rhys, you were banging his misses, now she's having a little Rhys, that must hurt him, my man," Drake said, laughing, then gave me a fist bump.

"I love Tianna, but Kim, she's the one whom I'll never get over, and now, that baby she's having…it's mine."

"Rhys, man, Kim's not leaving her husband, just forget about her, and concentrate on Tianna."

"I know, but Kim, she's having my baby, we're having a baby together," I kept repeating.

Reining in my emotions, as I felt tears trickle down my face.

"Listen up, my man, her husband, that dude, I'm telling you now, Rhys, he hates you, like the sun doesn't shine. Trust me, he'll never, you get me, never, let you anywhere near that kid. Rhys, let's hope the baby has green eyes, like you. Boy, that will piss the dude off," Drake said as he threw his head back laughing out loud.

Well, he actually doubled over laughing, almost choking.

"Drake, you're too bad. Listen, I'm going to love you and leave you. Tianna's probably wondering where I am," I said, giving Drake a fist bump.

A gust of wind ruffled the leaves of the trees, creating a rustling sound, and that's when I spotted Renee. She was holding a rather large navy handbag over her head, her hair dripped around her shoulders.

Renee also came home drenched from the cold rain. She stopped and smiled, pulled her hair back from her face, and wiped the rainwater from her eyes.

"Hi, Rhys. Why are you and my husband standing outside in the rain? Come inside, come, and have a hot drink," she said, her lips trembling from the cold air.

"You're soaking wet and shivering like a leaf. Go inside, next time, I'm actually leaving now," I replied.

Tianna waited up for me, it was gone midnight by the time I returned home. You know, she's so sweet, I really don't want to hurt her, we're very happy together. You should see her gorgeous smile every time she saw me.

Right now, I was a total mess. My ex-wife was pathetic for trying to cling to me. We always argued in an emotionless voice. Well, I do. Can you blame me? I'm not putting crazy ideas into her head about us getting back together again. She was beyond upset, believe me.

Yet, I knew I should be thinking about Tianna, but I can't get Kim out of my thoughts.

Breathing raggedly, I tried hard to rein in the emotions that were close to landing me in trouble.

Kim's pregnancy has put my emotions into quite a fickle state, if I am being totally honest with myself.

But it's my wife who's doing the damage right now. I really don't want to lose Tianna. So, I'm going to file for a divorce and commit to her. Leah is not my headache anymore. I'd ask Tianna to move in and not forget Mr Kitty. I can't forget about her cat.

"Love me, love my cat," she said.

Somehow, that statement doesn't sound right.

Right now, I'm laughing, because believe it or not, Mr Kitty seemed to like me. I wonder if it has to do with me, giving him cat treats, probably.

Renee

Us, girls, are out on the town tonight. Yes, we were all out, all five of us. We were going to our favourite pole dancing club, Dare to Dance, it's a strip club, but I won't tell, if you don't.

I really hope Tianna's on her best behaviour because the manager, Jess, she thinks Tianna is nothing but trouble.

We're here, trying to cheer her up. She seemed okay though, considering what was going on in her personal life at the moment.

Tianna just loved pole dancing. She's really good at it, but needed a few drinks first to pluck up the courage to do it. Like I've said, she's really good, and like I expected, she had a few cocktails and headed straight for the pole, with manager Jess hot on her heels.

"You go, girl, shake that arse, go girl, go, girlfriend," I said, as we all clapped, danced and cheered her on.

The manager, Jess, disapproved of Tianna the first time we ever came to this nightclub. Jess took an instant dislike to her for no good reason at all.

She made a nasty comment about Tianna's pole dancing, something like, "Please, find an alternative way to disappoint your dad."

"Seriously," I yelled.

Tianna stared at me, too shocked to speak. I put my arms around my good friend and told her to ignore Jess' nasty comment. But Tianna got emotional, because you know, although she has a dad, he's not her biological dad. So that comment by Jess really hurt. Jess's as mean as a mama's wasp. She sure knew how to beat up Tianna's confidence.

But hey, we've been coming here for the best part of three years, give or take, and we'll keep on coming until we're barred, too old, or they stop inviting the public to take part in pole dancing—whichever comes first. And just ignore anything Jess has to say. As far as I am concerned, that Jess is a jealous fucking old cow.

On the way home, Tianna just happened to be checking her emails, and there it was a match on the Ancestry website.

At first, she looked surprised, and then her eyes lit up like two gems.

I flung my arms around her, held her tight, and said, "I'm so happy for you, babe."

So, okay, we were a little bit drunk and a bit too loud, to say the least.

I remembered staggering around, in six-inch-high heels, shouting at the top of my voice, "Tianna has a match. Tianna has a match."

Then I tripped over, falling on my bum. Ouch, that hurt. We were all just so happy for her.

Hopefully, now this would be the beginning of her finding her biological dad. And one day, maybe, just maybe, her birth mother. Even though her birth mother, a selfish woman, in my opinion, doesn't want any contact with her. If she knew Tianna, like we all do, she would love her as much, or even more, than her friends do.

Kim

It was such a lovely day. It was magnificent, and the cool morning air was as sharp as a knife. I spoke with Rhys about 15 minutes ago.

Anyway, he asked how I was doing, and asked how Alex was. Well, Rhys' not that kind of guy to hold grudges. I don't think. It's just that everyone had changed over the past few months, including myself, because of the situation that we all find ourselves in.

"We're all okay, Alex's coming to terms with me having your baby in his own way. I even overheard him telling Mason that he will soon have a baby brother."

"I'm glad to hear that, Kim."

Although I must admit, I got emotional. My heart was full of sadness. I fought back tears, not wanting him to hear me cry.

To tell you the truth, I wasn't feeling too good about myself right now. The sound of Rhys' voice, wrapped in emotional turbulence, of the kind that evokes the lump in the throat, knowing that he'll never get to raise our child.

It wasn't that long ago, whenever I spoke with Rhys, his voice held an upbeat note, and natural warmth, that I liked. But now, it is filled with pure sadness.

"Is it definitely a boy."

"Yes. I went for my 20-week pregnancy scan yesterday, and the sonographer confirmed it was a baby boy."

Rhys got very emotional over the phone. I could tell by the sound of his voice. He wanted to know if we had thought of any names yet. We've decided on Mikel Jordan Roberts. I told him that Jordan was Alex's middle name and asked what his middle name was.

He said, "Lyndsay."

Okay, so we both laughed, changing our mood slightly.

He told me not to ask about his middle name, as it was a joke. His parents gave it to him as they thought his mum was expecting a girl. So, they decided to keep the name.

Rhys went silent for a few seconds, then asked if we could catch up, and go for a coffee. I told him that I would have to discuss it with Alex first. He said that if Alex said no, then he would understand.

I said to Rhys, maybe tomorrow, or next Saturday in the afternoon, if Alex agreed. Rhys opted for tomorrow, as he was willing to finish work a little early to see me.

Alex wasn't too happy, but said if I had to, then it would be fine with him. I suggested to Rhys that it wouldn't be a problem if Tianna wanted to join us.

But he declined the offer and said, "No, just the two of us."

It wouldn't be fair to her. I let Rhys know that Alex and I were in the middle of moving house.

Unfortunately, when we planned on moving to Canada, the sale of our house went through before we had a chance to take it off the housing market. So, now we have bought a five-bedroom house in Highgate, not too far from my mother-in-law, Lyn's house.

That morning, when I did speak with my husband about meeting up with Rhys, I could see it in his eyes that he didn't want me to go anywhere near Rhys. However, in the end, he gave me his blessing, and said that Rhys was going to be in our lives, unfortunately, for the next 18 years or so, and it wouldn't be right for him to deny him from seeing his son.

After all, his friend, Charlie, it's kind of the same situation; Chloe had two children with Alex, yet my husband got to see his children whenever he wanted to. Charlie had never denied Alex from seeing his children. So he said, how could he turn around and be a hypocrite and deny Rhys the same opportunity of getting to know his child, when he'd be born?

Well, that's the version I tell myself, but in reality, it went more like this. Alex rolled his eyes and made a face, his lips clamped together firmly. Then suddenly, his chin trembled and he began to cry in the way full-blooded grown-up men cry. Though he was angry with himself for doing so. I could do no more than to put my arms around my husband and comfort him; we both cried that day.

It hurt me to watch my husband struggle this way, knowing that the baby I was expecting was for another man, and that man was Rhys, whom my husband loathed.

Alex felt betrayed because I'd promised after my and Rhys's affair, I'd cut him loose.

However, the situation has now changed. But that didn't stop my husband from saying, "You've stabbed me in my back, so you couldn't see my face."

I said nothing else to my husband, struggling to control my own scattered thoughts and emotions. I didn't need more emotions to hamper my decision making, whether to stay with Alex or leave, and be with Rhys.

Hormones and emotions kicked in at the same bloody time. My heart was breaking. The two most important men in my life, I did not know whom I loved more. My cheating husband, or the now, no longer single, Rhys.

Rhys and I met for coffee, the next day as planned. It was so nice to see his gorgeous smile and his green eyes. He seemed happy enough.

We stood staring at each other for a few seconds, until I blushed. I jokingly asked if it was because of Tianna, why he was so happy. He was silent for a few seconds, then said, it was because of seeing my beautiful smile again.

My blush brought a shy smile to his lips when he spoke. He held me in his arms and gave me a kiss on my left cheek. A part of me still longed for him, to smell him, and to feel his skin against mine.

Omg, I was still blushing. I stared at him, he stared right back at me.

This is a little bit awkward, don't you think? I know exactly what I was thinking right now, and I guess that I know what Rhys was thinking too. But it's only wishful thinking, no harm done, if we only think it, and not say it out loud. Do you agree?

He reached down, took my hands, pulled me into his arms, swallowing me in his warmth and scent.

Rhys whispered softly into my ear, "I've missed you," and breathed in my familiar scent.

I giggled like a naughty school girl, unable to help myself, and wrapped my arms around his muscular frame, breathing in his scent.

"You're looking so beautiful," he whispered, staring down into my eyes.

"Why, you're looking mighty handsome as ever," I replied, smiling then laughed at his latest attempt to hit on me, turning my head slightly.

Can it be possible, I thought, not daring to look at his face, but still felt his eyes gazing at me. The last thing I wanted to do was to tease him, knowing that I would be going home to my husband.

So, we sat in the corner, at a table for two, at the busy coffee shop, listening for a moment to strangers chatting amongst themselves. There was a guy sitting opposite us, who had a funny, prissy way of talking, old-fashioned, like…using big words, when he didn't have to.

As I gazed into Rhys' eyes, sipping my cappuccino and nibbling on a slice of lemon cake, I wondered whom the gentleman was trying to impress.

Breaking the silence between Rhys and me, he spoke, "You're having my son."

"Yes, I guess that I am." Then I held my head firmly, staring at my half-eaten cake.

"You okay, Kim?"

"Just feeling a bit overwhelmed, I guess."

"Kim, I'm glad that you and Alex have decided to keep our baby."

Rhys reached out and held my hand. Then he said he wanted to share something with me that he hadn't told anyone, not even his best friend, Drake or Tianna.

I asked Rhys if he really wanted to share his secret with me. He went on to say, once I'd heard what he was about to reveal, then, I'd understand why he chose to tell me, and no one else.

I would like to confide in all of you about what Rhys told me, but that would be breaking the trust he had in me. He has assured me that he was going to tell Tianna soon, as he had filed for a divorce, and was going to ask Tianna to move in with him.

"So, it's serious between the two of you," I asked him.

Rhys paused. "Yes," he said and gave me a smile.

"I'm pleased for you," I told him.

But in reality, my heart was broken. In fact, my emotions, at the moment, would better be described as uncomfortable, if not outright dread. At this point, I wasn't sure why I felt uncomfortable.

Why am I lying to myself? Of course, I knew the reason, it's Tianna. She was taking Rhys away from me, all his love, and now, he was flipping talking about getting a divorce.

He said that he knew I was pleased for him, but could see a hint of sadness in my eyes.

'You're damn right, I want you, I want you, God only knows how much. Let's run away together.' These were just stupid thoughts that entered my mind.

I closed my eyes, only for Rhys to hold my hand. Shit, he was already holding my hand, and reminded me that, if ever I needed him, he was only a phone call away. I know that I shouldn't have, but I wanted to. Our fingers began to interlock.

Both our eyes welled up. He took a tissue from his jacket pocket, which was draped over a chair, and wiped my tears, which started to trickle down my cheeks.

Rhys told me he didn't know why, but when I cried, I looked beautiful. I laughed and bit my lip, trying to stop.

I thought it was time to go, but Rhys asked me to stay just a little bit longer. We sat there in complete silence, holding hands for the next 10 minutes or so. Then, he leaned back in his chair and stretched his legs out. His piercing gaze sorted through my mind. I knew that I absolutely shouldn't have, but my lips teased him. He opened his mouth so he could taste me once more.

"This is crazy, Rhys. What are we doing?"

He replied by saying that we were not actually doing anything. We were just two friends who loved each other too much to go our own separate ways for too long. And that was a fact that everyone in the coffee shop had stopped what they were doing, and had now given us their complete unwanted attention. But that didn't stop us. Fallin' by Alicia Keys just so happened to be playing in the background.

We stared at each other, because what he just said is one hundred and ten per cent true.

"Kim," he paused, as his phone began to ring.

I turned my head, as to not hear the conversation, between him, and his new girlfriend, Tianna.

Turning to face him, once again, I fiddled with the coffee cup before taking a sip. Rhys' eyes scoured my face, then lingered on my lips, he had tasted moments before, while continuing to speak with his girlfriend. His fingers caressed my palm warmly, then brushed the hair from my cheek. He looked at me with pure love in his eyes.

He was hurting. I was hurting. But what can we do? I was not going to leave my husband. I can't do it. And now, he's found someone whom he loved. So, why did we feel the need to love each other the way that we do?

He shoved his phone into his jacket pocket and met my gaze, watching the emotions that crossed my face.

My heart was beating fast, and my chin trembled. I closed my eyes for a second, thinking about my husband, my Alex.

He moved the hair from my face, revealing a tear in my eye.

"Don't cry, Kim," he said.

With upturned lips that quickly turned into a closed-mouth smile.

"I know I'm being silly, Rhys, but I still love you."

"Silly, for loving me, the way that you do, never apologise. I love you just as much, so we're both silly." With him saying that, we both laughed.

He took his thumb and tried to wipe my smudged mascara, but accidentally poked me in my left eye instead. I choked on a half-laugh, half-sob, before reaching down into my handbag for a tissue.

He made an apologetic face that said, sorry.

He leaned over, kissed my cheek, and said, "I think we should go now."

He asked if we could see each other again soon. What do you all think?

We gave each other a hug, then a kiss, a hug, then again a kiss, with a bit more passion to it.

I closed my eyes and thought, 'My God, what are we both doing?'

In fact, I've never longed for anyone as much as I did for Rhys.

Rhys made a joke about my husband. "If he only knew what we felt about each other, he'd punch my lights out. Kim, I think Alex understands a lot about violence. He once threatened me, telling me that I had about eight seconds to decide my fate and to fuck off, or he'll fuck me up."

Rhys sat there, waiting for me to say something. Moving my hand away from Rhys' tight grasp, not wanting him to disrespect my husband any further, I just foolishly smiled.

Maybe we should stop, whatever this was, right now, because every time I saw him, it got more and more difficult for us to walk away from each other.

So, now I realised why my best friend, excuse me, my ex-best friend, Chloe, couldn't walk away from my husband, Alex, so easily.

This was just killing me inside. Now that I am having his baby, I'd always have a part of him.

My only wish is that our son, whom we were going to have together, does not have green/hazel eyes like Rhys. That alone would kill my husband; to see the baby every day, staring right back at him with those eyes. That's a big no, no.

"Let's go," he said.

We both didn't want to, but we had to let each other go. He went home to Tianna, and I went home to my husband and our two children, humming away to, Baby by Ashanti.

Tianna

Rhys came over to my place. I was in the kitchen, cooking dinner. His eyes were a little bit red, obviously, because he had been crying.

He had a large box of very expensive chocolates and a bouquet in his hand. Oh, and a bottle of Aslina Sauvignon Blanc. I gave him a hug and asked if he was okay. Of course, I knew that he went to see Kim. He told me that it was confirmed she was having a boy.

"I'm going to have a son."

"I'm pleased for you."

But wished it was me, having his baby, instead of her.

He leaned against the wall, sipping a glass of water silently, as he watched me mash the potatoes.

He told me that, after dinner, when he had composed himself, he wanted to talk about something.

Later that evening, as the clock struck nine, leaning back in the chair and lacing fingers behind his neck, he patted the spot beside him.

He met my gaze. His eyes warmed his lips, giving in to a smile.

Worry had prevented me from eating earlier, as he took the cup from my shaking hand and placed it next to his feet.

The way he kissed me and the way his gaze lingered on me every time we spoke was more than enough to convince me that he did love me and wanted me like never before.

He asked if Mr Kitty and I would like to move into his house, which I said yes to straight away. I snuggled against him, feeling the beat of his heart, or was that my own? Then he said he was filing for a divorce from his wife. So, I asked why he had waited so long to divorce her. He hesitated, stood, and turned away from me, staring out the window.

After some time, he sat back down on the arm of the leather sofa with a bottle of rum, not bothering to use a glass. Then finally, he spoke.

When he got married to Leah, her father insisted that they have a prenuptial agreement, a semi-binding contract, to protect his daughter's assets in case they divorced. His father-in-law's company was worth millions. If he had divorced Leah sooner, everything that he had worked hard to achieve in the company would have gone down the drain.

Unfortunately, her dad suffered a heart attack and signed the company over to him, as he had no sons and only four daughters, who had no interest in the company. I suppose at the time, it sounded like a good idea to Leah's dad.

Anyway, his ex-wife was worried that Rhys would abandon her and their daughter and leave them without any money, and the lifestyle that she was very accustomed to having. But he had reassured me, he would never do such a cruel act, even though she deserved to live like a pauper. I almost spoke, then stopped.

Rhys spoke in tear-filled gibberish, I didn't understand. I hugged him tightly, and spoke into his chest as he told me the real reason why he fell out of love with his wife.

When he first met Leah, all those years ago at college, what he loved about her was her drive and ambition to make something of herself, and to stand on her own two feet, not wanting to join her father's company.

She studied hard and then went to university. She was a well-respected barrister. It took her many years to qualify, and she put her career before marriage and having children. Although they eventually did get married, she said no to committing to having children.

He took a deep breath, then said, although the situation with Kim, having a child for him wasn't ideal, he was glad that she was having his baby.

After his wife's dad had a heart attack, she wanted to come clean about a secret she had been keeping from him. But then chose not to tell him.

A few years later, when she was settled into her career, that's when she decided to try for a baby. It took a couple of years trying before they had to eventually go for IVF, and that's when Rhys found out the real reason why his wife couldn't conceive naturally.

His wife terminated her pregnancy without discussing it with him first, all because she wanted her career. Now you see why he wanted Kim's baby so much. The son he never got to have with his wife.

He held me, I kissed him, and said, "What a cruel thing your wife had done to you."

He told me, if only he could go back in time, and had met me before Kim, that I would be having his child, and we'd be definitely married by now.

He wiped the tear away from my eye, held my hand, and said, "Tianna, whatever I do, I will never hurt you, or lie to you. I am going to be honest and tell you how I feel about Kim. If there were no Alex, we'd be together, one hundred per cent, I'm not going to lie."

"I still love her, and she will always have a place in my heart. Kim still loves me, you know that, right? But her having this baby, I promise you, if you decide to move in with me, it won't affect our relationship. Tianna, the more time that I spend with you, the more I love you. You know what that means, don't you?" he asked, holding my hand to his chest.

A little shocked at his confession, my heart slowed at the realisation that he was still madly in love with Kim. I shook my head, staring up at him, a little disappointed at his chosen words, as gloom tugged at my heart with a heavy hand.

Rhys said that it meant there was less love to give to Kim and more to give to me. My eyes filled with tears, and my face felt flushed.

Woah, woah, and woah. Wait a frigging minute. What did he just say? Did he just say that he loves Kim more than me? You all heard him say that, right?

Jumping out of my seat, with my hands on my hips, Rhys met my angry gaze as he stared up at me. Okay, so, I'm going to ask him to repeat what he just said, not all of it, just the last sentence.

Jumping up, and grabbing a hold of my arm, he said, "Tianna, I love you more today, and even more tomorrow." ("Jet'aime plus aujourd' hui dans encore plus demain.")

Oh, I thought that's what he said.

After calming down a little, I said, "I love you, too. Rhys, I, and Mr Kitty would love to move in. How's tomorrow looking?"

"Let's go and get your stuff now. Then we can celebrate tomorrow."

I'm not letting a little detail, of how he felt about Kim, stop me from being with him. Would you? Well, you're not me, and I am not letting him go, no frigging way.

Snuggling back down close, on the sofa, I lifted my face to accept his kiss. Then jumped up, knocking over the bottle he had placed on the floor earlier.

"Oh my God, Rhys, I almost forgot, I have a match on the Ancestry website."

I leaned forward, reaching for my phone.

"Let's have a look," Rhys replied, as he removed the phone gently from my grasp.

"Oh, wow, looks like you have a sister, look at your shared DNA," he replied, his eyes firmly fixed on my phone.

"Oh my God, you're right, I have a sister. Her name is Sabrina Hamilton."

My eyes were now firmly glued to my phone, as my heart raced.

"This is it, Rhys, I'm on my way to finding my real family. Should I contact her now, or wait for a few days?"

"Wait a couple of days, babe, until you've spoken with your mum and dad."

That night, I was so excited that I couldn't sleep. I lay on my side, watching Rhys asleep, wondering what dreams lived behind the smile on his face.

A few anxious days later, I made contact with my sister, Sabrina Hamilton, via text message. As I was so full of nerves, I kept calling her number, then, hanging up, shaking with excitement. She contacted me the very next day.

Sabrina sounded so nice over the phone with a sweet voice. I began to create a picture of what she looked like in my head. She mostly spoke, as I listened. I remember her saying she couldn't imagine an upbringing with no parents. I so badly wanted to correct her, saying, *err, excuse me, I do have parents,* but didn't want to get off on the wrong foot.

We've arranged to meet up on Saturday afternoon and go for lunch. She asked if it would be okay if her husband, Micheal, tagged along too. I didn't mind, as long as she didn't mind Rhys coming. Before I knew it, Saturday had arrived.

In the distance, I could see a couple was walking towards us. She glanced at her reflection as they passed by a shop window, then she looked down and plucked at a loose thread on her dress.

My heart was pounding as they stopped in front of us. Her husband's face was clean-shaven, but his dark curly hair was thick and unruly.

I turned my head slightly and whispered, "Rhys, oh my God, she's white. I thought she would be mixed-race, like me."

So now I'm a bit confused, to say the least.

Sabrina introduced herself and her husband. She wasn't surprised by my skin colour, not one bit.

Unlike me, I stood there wide-eyed, mouth dropping to the floor.

Rhys nudged me on my side and whispered, "Close your mouth, babe."

The restaurant was one that I had heard of, but couldn't afford to enjoy. We were led to a secluded booth near the back, where light poured in from the large window, and a fan overhead made the curtains flutter. We ordered our drinks, then her husband, Micheal, gave such a warm smile, then quickly picked up the menu, staring intently.

There were so many questions that needed answering. I hoped that she didn't mind. Rhys told me, just be patient, she'll answer all my questions, and to give her a chance, because it's probably a shock, for both of us, to finally meet.

The waiter brought us our wine, chosen by Micheal.

Sabrina cleared her throat, staring into the wine glass, then began to tell me her story. But, imagine every word you said was recorded by your personal recorder, and automatically, transcribed. That would definitely make life much easier for me to remember her every word.

She opened her mouth to speak, and I sat there watching her lips move, lost in my own thoughts, for a few minutes, staring without seeing.

She started off by saying, "Sorry," to which her husband, Micheal, repeated several times that his wife had nothing to be sorry about, and continued staring at the menu.

Sabrina began telling me her mum's story, every now and again, staring up at her husband, Micheal. It was hard to digest. Rhys held my hand as we listened.

Her mum had an affair, 34 years ago, with a black man called Aubrey. The affair lasted about four or five years, she wasn't quite sure.

Anyway, when her mum got pregnant with me, she wasn't sure if the baby would be her husband's or Aubrey's. So, she decided to take a chance and have the baby. It was a shock for both her mum and dad that I was born mixed-race. That's when her mum had to come clean and tell her dad about her affair.

"I'm so sorry, Tianna, my dad said to get rid of you, or he'll leave my mum."

So, that's what they did.

They gave me up for adoption and told everyone that I was a stillbirth.

"I'm so sorry that my parents did that to you, really I am," Sabrina said, wiping her eyes with a tissue handed to her by her husband, Micheal.

Okay, so now I was crying my eyes out as well. My whole body literally froze for two seconds, hands shaking, my thoughts were so scattered. I wasn't able to think for a moment.

Rhys rested a comforting hand on my shoulder as I locked eyes with Sabrina, demanding an answer.

The words just seemed to blurt out of my mouth, as Micheal sat with his hands firmly holding a glass of wine, his eyes straight ahead, like a statue chiselled in hell itself.

"Was I such a horrible baby, so awful, that my biological parents hated me enough to throw me away?" I asked, after a few deep breaths.

Sabrina, trying to control the quiver in her voice, said that they didn't throw me away. I told her that they might as well have thrown me away, as they thought of me as garbage.

That's what I said, in anger, and it upset Sabrina so much that she cried. She felt the full weight of a question that had no answer.

We sat in silence, after my outburst, for nearly five minutes, each with our own thoughts.

Do I really want to get to know a woman who would literally give me up for adoption, without a second thought, because I didn't look anything like the rest of her children?

After a few tears, and looking totally distraught, Sabrina placed her wine glass on the table, and looked at me. Her smile was sad as hell. A single tear fell down her cheek and rested on her right hand.

After 10 minutes, I apologised to her, "I'm sorry, Sabrina." I couldn't get the words out of my mouth fast enough.

Tucking a wayward strand of curly blonde hair back into her bun, she tucked her vibrating phone away and met my gaze, watching the emotions that crossed my face.

There were several women, around my birth mother's age, sitting and talking while choosing delicacies from large silver trays. I shrugged my shoulders as if I couldn't care less about our mother, who showed little to no interest in me over the years.

But what if Sabrina gave me her phone number? I could picture her sitting there, listening to the ringing telephone, but not wanting to answer it.

"Hi, Mum, it's me, Tianna, your long-lost daughter. You know, the daughter you threw out with the trash," I'd say, if she chose to answer.

Now, we were all still sitting there quietly. I really wasn't expecting a story like that. I shook my head to remove the cobwebs of imagination that I had about fitting into my own family.

This sort of thing happened to other people, not me. I closed my eyes and leaned my head against Rhys' shoulder. He put an arm around my waist and gave me a kiss on my cheek.

"Don't be upset, babe," he said, whispering in my ear. "Do you want to leave?"

"No, even though I'm upset, I want to hear the rest. I need to know if I have any brothers or sisters. I have to know, Rhys, I just have to know. And what about my mother? Has she ever given me a second thought, after all these years?"

"There's only one way to find out, babe, ask her."

Sabrina dried her eyes and carried on telling me what I so desperately wanted to know.

My questions and her answers fell into place, one after another, like a child's wooden puzzle.

I have two half-brother's Sam, 34, married to Andrea. They had twin boys, Codey and Corey.

Steven, but preferred to be known as Stevie, 28, engaged to Leyla-Marie, and they were expecting their first baby in a few months.

"Then there's me, as you know, this is my husband, Micheal. We've been married for nearly eight years. We have two girls, Maisie, she's seven, Esme, she's five, and a right little daddy's girl, and our son, Jayden, he's two."

So, I asked if both my brothers knew about me. Sabrina looked at her husband, Micheal, then bowed her head.

Eventually, she confessed that they knew nothing about me. A little surprised, I turned to look at a stunned Rhys, as he carried on staring at Micheal, who, for some strange reason, chose to be silent throughout the whole evening. He only looked up from his glass of wine to nod when his wife spoke. His lips twitched, as if he wanted to smile, as Rhys continued to stare. I then asked her why she was on the Ancestry website.

She told me that about two years ago, her mother was ill and had been admitted to the hospital. She went to get her some clean pyjamas and toiletries. Sabrina said that she wasn't snooping or anything, but in her mother's bedside table, she was just looking for her medication to bring to the hospital.

Tucked away under some papers, she saw an old, white handkerchief. So, she opened it up.

There was a small pink baby hat, a pair of pink baby socks, and a name tag, but with her mum's name on it. There were also two tiny baby name tags.

"I'm guessing they were yours," she said.

Then, about six or seven months later, when her mum was feeling much better, she asked her about what she had found. She broke down and confessed everything to her, but not to her two brothers.

"Mum asked me not to tell them, and made me promise never to breathe a word to anyone." Sabrina sobbed.

That's when she and Micheal agreed, a year ago, that they should try and find me. So, here we all were.

Her mum and dad had no idea that she was meeting me. That's why earlier, when her phone vibrated, she quickly put it away, thinking I hadn't noticed the caller—our mum.

It was certainly a lot to take in, but I had to ask her about our mum. She refused to tell me any information about my birth mother.

Overwhelmed and upset, I wasn't sure if I should get up, run and cry, or sit here with my heart breaking.

It was quite early, the sun had not been up very long, and the birds were just beginning to sing joyously.

"Mummy," I said.

It was the first time she had heard me call her that, and the tender smile on Mum's face made it clear that she was pleased. It was only a daydream, but I thought it was real. My heart sank within me.

Rhys brought his face to my ear and whispered softly, "Babe, are you okay?"

I turned to face him and smiled when Sabrina told me how to contact Aubrey, my biological dad, only if I wanted to.

Smiling, she gave her husband a don't-be-nosy look, as it seemed as though he would have wanted to hear my answer. At last, a reaction from him.

"Is your mum still in contact with Aubrey?" I asked, immediately realising the stupidity of the question.

For a long moment, Sabrina and Micheal stared at me. I suppose my question sounded enough like a statement, enough to earn me a frown from them both.

The best emotions are the ones that intuitively trigger the image, going along with the emotion. The smile, the frown, the pursed lips, or the widened eyes.

After meeting with my sister and her husband, I decided to just carry on as normal. Sabrina refused to tell me anything about our mum. Why? I'm totally clueless. It's like being abandoned all over again. I was disappointed, knowing she was out there somewhere.

For a long time, I struggled in silence, with negative feelings related to being adopted. Not feeling worthy of love, disconnected from a part of my identity, loss and grief. I built up a mental image of my birth parents, who were out there. I kept thinking of them, longed to have a relationship with them, and any siblings that I may or may not have.

Anyway, over the years, I've been emotionally prepared for any form of rejection. Well, like Rhys has stated, at least I got to meet my sister. Maybe, just maybe, she'll tell our mum how nice I am and she'll want to meet me after all.

On the drive home, Rhys asked me if I would like an ice cream to kind of cheer me up. I had vanilla ice cream with the most amazing chocolate pecan brownie. Rhys chose chocolate mint.

We were walking back to his car when he tripped on an uneven paving stone, and his ice cream fell to the ground.

He pushed up his lips, like a crying five-year-old child. So, I accidentally laughed.

He grabbed my ice cream, started to lick it all over, then gave it back to me, and said, "That will teach you not to laugh."

Okay, so Rhys licked my ice cream, but I ate it anyway. I told him that I wanted to do something very, very nice for him.

We drove back to my house. I held his hand and took him to my spare bedroom.

His eyes opened wide when he saw what was in there. Oh yes, my pole. I have my very own pole to do my pole dancing, ladies.

On my playlist, Earned It by The Weeknd started to play. This, ladies, is how to keep your man.

Here we go, I drove Rhys wild. Oh yes, I'd tell you later what he did to me, but first, let me tell you how dirty, downright dirty, I got for my man.

First, I changed into a skimpy outfit, you know, a very sexy bra, and g-string thongs, black stockings, and my six-inch-high heeled shoes. I could feel Rhys' intent gaze on me as he sat with his legs and mouth wide open.

Ready, first, I grabbed the pole, slowly, with my right hand, staring at him in a seductive manner, and did the simple wrap-around move first. I positioned my inside foot close to the base of the pole, and I hooked my leg with the pole. Then arched my body backwards.

I squeezed the pole with my legs, then began climbing up slowly. Then slid down the pole even slower. I started to spring up onto the pole, then spinning around, while watching Rhys' face, then repeated the whole dance again and again.

I slid down, all the while watching my man's face. Then shaking my butt, walking slowly towards him, sat on his lap, and performed a sexy lap dance to remember, moving my hips round and round.

Rhys started breathing heavily, caressing my arms gently, then wrapping his arms around my waist, and squeezing my bottom. I leaned into him, kissing his neck, breathing in his scent, as he caressed my breast.

Rhys sniffed my neck. I felt his warm breath, my whole body began to tingle, as he ran his fingers down my spine.

"God, I want you," he whispered softly in my ear.

Boy, did I drive him wild, you bet. His mouth was watering for more, his green eyes undressed me more than once. Ladies, don't try this at home if you have no experience. The pole, what else?

Let me just say, after my performance, Rhys couldn't wait to get to my bedroom. We walked the short distance hand-in-hand, from the spare bedroom, down the hallway to my bedroom.

He slipped his hands around my waist, pulling me closer to his body. Gazing into my eyes, he kissed me so passionately on my lips.

My heartbeat doubled in time, as a wave of passion surged over me. Rhys brought a soft moan to my lips. He lifted me into his strong arms and carried me to my bed. He sat on the bed beside me and gently pushed me onto my back.

Closing my eyes, quickly sucking in a breath, his thumb slid under my bra, gently up the curve of my breast, and surrounded my waist.

He trailed hot kisses down my neck, along my collarbone. I fluttered butterfly kisses across his face.

His warm hand caressed its way up my back and around to cradle my breast. Rhys' hands left my breast, caressing their way down my side, pausing briefly on my waist, and then continuing down my hips.

He went, full on, down and dirty on me.

"Open your legs, God, I love it when you're nice and wet," he whispered, gazing into my blue eyes.

I started to groan with pleasure, but it came out more as an eager whimper, which sent a rush of heat to my face.

"I love you so much," I whispered softly.

My hands held Rhys' head down between my inner thighs.

In a blink, I was pinned on top of his warm body, his arms locked around me, and his muscular legs wrapped around mine.

The feel of hot skin, his chest against mine, made me groan. I wrapped my arms around him and gasped into his mouth, my own desire matching his.

His reply was a soft groan, then he whispered, "You taste like honey," and revelled in the warmth of my body and my hot lips.

His gaze lingered, then went over my body. He took my arm with one of his hands that had explored every part of my body, not two weeks before. He pulled me down onto the soft bed, and now, his lean body was on top of mine.

My body entwined with his. I breathed in his scent as deeply as I could. Rhys eased into my body at first, then made love to me hungrily. He relentlessly pushed me deeper into the haze of pleasure and desire, until I arched beneath him. My body was on the verge of shattering.

The brief pain turned quickly into pleasure, intense enough that I began panting, and my hands roamed his body.

Afterwards, he wrapped an arm around me, pulled me into his body, and kissed me softly on my lips.

Rhys smoothed my hair from my face, and rested his warm hand against the soft of my exposed thigh, admiring my naked body. The warmth of my body made him not want to let go.

Aroused again, wrapped in his warm body, I couldn't move if I wanted to, but I whispered into his ear, something he just couldn't resist.

One of my favourite songs began to play. As exhausted as I was, I wanted to show the love of my life more pole dancing. Wild Side by Normani ft Cardi B from my playlist started to play. It was my favourite song when I was at the club, Dare to Dance. So, I got out of bed with Rhys hot on my tail and went on the pole for a second time to show him some more of my moves.

Ladies, let me tell you, mama mia, the look on his face, he was horny as hell.

Rhys kept saying, "Cette dame Est tellement sexy," over and over again.

And then explained it meant, "This lady is so sexy." Then he said, "Je t'aimerai pour toujours" (I will love you forever)

Who knew my boyfriend could speak such perfect French? When he spoke those words, oh God, he sounded so sexy, don't you think? Let's ask him to say, Will you marry me, in French.

He said, "Non, pas' encore." (No, not yet) And then said, "Veux-tu m'épouser?" (Will you marry me?)

Then threw the pillow at me, and said "Viens te coucher." (Come to bed).

Melani

It's a beautiful Saturday afternoon. The sun suddenly broke free from the clouds that had hidden it, casting brilliant rays—still partially veiled by wisps of cloud—across the rooftops of the street opposite.

I went into the garden, and made myself comfortable on the rattan garden chair, closed my eyes, and dozed in the warm sun, until my husband woke me up. Silly me, I'd half forgotten that, I invited a few of my friends and family to my baby shower/gender reveal party.

I was 30 weeks pregnant now, I'm really getting excited. It's mine, and my husband, Terrell's, first child.

He just popped down to the baker's. With all the excitement of having this baby, I forgot to pick up the cake that I had ordered. You know, to reveal the gender of our baby.

Here he is, oh, and some of the guests started to arrive.

Everyone was here, all the girls and their men. I glanced over my right shoulder and saw Rhys speaking with my husband.

Aww, look at my good friend, Tianna. She looked so happy, holding hands with Rhys, her eyes were fixed on him.

Not to be totally excluded from the party, the guys were joining in too. As the guests arrived, I asked them to guess the gender of our baby, then gave them a blue or pink drink, based on their answer.

We decided to give each winner a bottle of wine or a box of chocolates. They could choose which prize they preferred.

The afternoon was so perfect. We played games and tasted baby food. Then to make it more fun, all the husbands and boyfriends had to put a nappy on a doll, in under 10 seconds. Okay, so guess who won that game?

"The winner is Hakeem," I yelled.

Okay, so even though he won, we were all laughing because, somehow, don't ask, the nappy was inside out.

The time came to reveal the gender of our baby.

So, my husband did the honour of cutting the cake, his hands were a little bit shaky. Time to reveal, it's a…girl, pink sponge with vanilla icing.

"Oh, Terrell, we're having a girl," I said, and put a hand to my mouth.

My husband held me in his arms, and kissed me on my forehead, then said, "We are having a daughter, I love you."

Everyone was so pleased for us, but unfortunately, only Nyomi and Renee got it correct. Everyone else, including my husband and me. We also thought it would be a boy.

The day was so perfect, until Rhys got a phone call from his ex-wife, Leah, which upset my good friend, Tianna. She later left the party in floods of tears.

She accidentally bumped into me, nearly knocking me down, while I had a tray of food in my hand.

I'm no gossip, she's my friend, so I'd let her tell you what happened. But what I will tell you is, I've never seen Tianna so upset.

She rolled her eyes in response and crossed her arms when Rhys told her he had to pop by his ex-wife's house.

"Don't be upset, babe. I'll be back soon, I promise you," he said, then kissed her on her forehead, but Tianna shoved him in anger.

"Babe, I'm not upset for the reason you assume I am," Tianna said, then proceeded to walk away from Rhys, but he had a tight grip on her arm.

Now, I like Rhys, everyone does, but he can be a bit of an arsehole, sometimes.

He stupidly replied, "Tianna, I know you're upset, stop, and think about why you're having an outburst."

Rhys, for the second time today, made an arse of himself, and grabbed a hold of Tianna's arm. He pulled her in the opposite direction of where she so obviously wanted to go.

"Upset…upset. Do I look upset to you? Just go, just flipping go," she yelled, with tears now in the corner of her eyes.

Outburst, an outburst, Rhys. Your ex was making life difficult for your girlfriend.

It really isn't any of my business, and it would only upset Tianna more, if I said anything. Opps, I've told you most of what happened, me, and my big mouth. Anyway, where was I, oh yes.

Everyone stood there in complete shock at Rhys' stupid comment. Even his good friend, Drake, shook his head in disbelief.

But it was Drake's wife, Renee, who paced forward, grabbed Rhys aside, and raised her hand, pointing her fingers in Rhys' face.

At this point, her husband had to grab her quickly away from Rhys, before she said something. But too late, she spoke.

"Rhys, your life is shitty, and you have one good thing going for you."

And Rhys' response was. "Sometimes all we have are shitty choices."

Tianna grabbed her handbag and coat and rushed through the street door before Rhys had the chance to apologise.

Well, I think that was his intention, when he tried to grab Tianna by arm her, as she hurriedly walked past him crying.

Drake threw his cigarette to the ground, not bothering to stub it out. He went to his friend, Rhys and patted him on his back. I'm not sure exactly what that meant.

Anyway, he did say to Rhys, "That's fucked-up, man. Why are you disrespecting your woman like that?"

Rhys stood in silence, his emotions were getting high.

Drake put his arm around his friend and whispered in his ear. "You fucking idiot."

But we all heard him say it.

Eventually, Rhys did run to the street door, but unfortunately, Tianna had gone by then. I did phone her several times to check if she was okay, but her phone kept going to voice mail.

Someone, not sure who, shouted across the room, "If anyone wants to learn about how to be a complete idiot, just take a look a Rhys."

I thought that Rhys should have gone after Tianna. Instead, he just sat down with a bottle of rum, not bothering to use a glass. That is, until his friend, Drake, reached over and snatched the bottle from his hand, shook his head, and told him to go after his women.

"What's wrong with you?" Drake asked his friend, who, by the way, never bothered answering the question.

This left a few of us coming to our own conclusions.

What was it with Rhys lately? He had become a totally different person of late. Even Renee noticed the change in him and asked her husband about the reason behind his attitude.

"His cheerful demeanour had succumbed to the stress of his bad marriage," according to his friend, Drake.

Oh, so it's nothing to do with his friend Kim, who so happened to be expecting his baby. Just a thought. Yes, we all know about Rhys and his sweet little friend Kim. A friend? Certainly not.

Their relationship was romantic. So, calling her a friend doesn't seem like a good description. Anyway, I think that I have said far too much than I should have. You'll have to excuse me, and my big mouth. The girls all know me. Sometimes, I just don't know when to stop talking.

Rhys

"This shit has to fucking stop, Leah. You can't keep calling me for no reason," I shouted with an annoyed shake of the head and hung up the phone.

My blood tingled, my eyebrows raised, as I blew out a jet of air between flared nostrils.

A reminder of the strong emotions, that ranged from, feeling of being mildly irritated and annoyed, to being damn right pissed off. The effect that my ex-wife had on me.

This woman is doing my head in.

"Tianna, I am so sorry, babe, I have to go and see what she wants. I promise you, this is the last time I'll run to her when she calls."

As I stood there, arms folded across my chest, shaking my head. I was frustrated.

I could see the disappointed look on Tianna's face as I turned and walked away from her. I looked back at her standing there, she bit her lips to keep them from quivering, and blinked her eyes to get rid of the blur, as her eyes welled up with tears. Although I understood, there was a different version of what happened that night going around.

Come on now, do you really think I'd talk to the woman I love, like that, seriously? I mean, I might have said something a little harsh by mistake, as my ex-wife was doing my head in. I unintendedly took it out on the love of my life. Hence, it was the reason why she started crying. Because believe me, she wasn't crying before, when I mentioned having to leave because of Leah.

Please don't misunderstand me, but based on the cold, almost vacant stares I received that evening from the majority of the girls, it seemed clear that Tianna's friends had sown seeds of doubt and insecurity in her mind regarding my genuine feelings for her.

My sweet little friend called Kim. I heard them all gossiping over in the corner of the room, and every now and again, they turned around to stare at me.

It was so obvious their conversation was about me. Renee tried to smile as she looked at me over one shoulder.

For a long time, I just looked at her, my green eyes gave an indication, I could read her mind, as her voice turned to a whisper. Her tone and demeanour awoke an old, unwelcomed feeling; that I didn't actually like Renee, I just tolerated her, because she was married to Drake.

She carried on with her gossiping, turned to look at her husband, my good friend, the most open-minded among us. Then they all stared in my direction.

For the most part, the facial expressions of those ladies listening to her gossip might have been amusing under different circumstances. It was impossible to know what was going on in Renee's mind, most of the time. If I had just one wish, it would be that she gets her filthy little mind out of the gutter about my relationship with Tianna and my friendship with Kim.

Drake patted me on my back, gave me a glass of rum, then told me what I already knew—to chase after Tianna. She so abruptly left before me, without so much as saying goodbye.

After such a nice day, my ex-wife just phoned and ruined everything. What did she want? Nothing, as usual. She just turned into a scornful woman. She claimed to have sprained her ankle and needed me to drive her to the hospital.

In case you all think that I don't know what she's doing, I've noticed. She was just upping her game. She had a new haircut, wore new trendy clothes, and changed her perfume.

She was telling everyone that we were back together, and to look at the gifts I'd given her.

She asked me to do things with her, saying, *just the two of us*, as if we were a couple again.

She'd managed to drive a wedge between Tianna and me.

When I returned home that evening, Tianna had packed her bags. She was taking Mr Kitty with her.

I've tried calling her. I even went to her house, but she'd refused to speak to me.

My ex-wife, while I went to her house that evening, somehow got hold of Tianna's mobile number and texted her a pack of lies.

The message that she left was nothing short of jealousy on fire. She texted that we had been sleeping together the whole time that I'd been seeing Tianna.

That's why every time she phoned me, I came running to her for sex. All because she knew how to satisfy me, better than Tianna. This was a load of bullshit.

Like I said before, you guys know me, not my ex-wife.

Yeah, like I said, I did sleep with my ex-wife that one time, which was a big mistake. But believe me, when I tell you this, that I was not seeing Tianna at the time.

Let me be honest, I never lied, even though I could have, if I wanted to. Remember, when I broke it off with Kim? Yeah, you all remember that day. Well, I was heartbroken and so lonely, having lost the love of my life.

It's no excuse, I know. But my ex-wife phoned me as she did, and I foolishly went over there as I do. She saw the state that I was in and took advantage of the opportunity. Come on now, don't laugh. I'm being serious now.

We had a few drinks, and she cooked a lovely meal. I was just sitting on the sofa, chilling after having too much to drink. Then bam, she was on top of me. What should I have done? Push her off? Yeah, maybe, but I didn't. It just felt right at the time. I could sit here, and lie and say, I thought it was Kim, but why lie? I don't see the sense in doing that. I knew it was Leah, and that's that.

From that day, she claimed that we were back together again. And I don't know who exactly was giving her information on my love life, but it had to stop.

After breaking up with Kim, I didn't expect to find love again so soon, until I met Tianna. And now, she'd left me, all because of Leah's lies.

What I can't understand is why you, women, always believe each other's lies? Why not believe your man for once? Believe me, when I tell you this, we're not all liars.

I'm not giving up on Tianna. I'd phone her every day if I had to, until she'd be mine again. Believe me, I am not ready to give her up, not just yet. Although I won't lie, I still have strong feelings for Kim. But I'd not act on them.

Tianna

I can't believe that Rhys went running to his ex-wife again. So, while he was on his way over to her house, she texted me. This is what she said:

'Hi bitch, you don't know me, but I sure as hell know all about you. Forgive me, but I'm not about to let you take my husband from me without a fight. Oh, yes, honey, we've been having sex behind your back. Ask him if you don't believe me. Good luck trying to keep hold of him. Why would he want you when he has me?

'Oh, look here, bitch, where do you think he is now. That's right in our bed, where he belongs, and we're about to make sweet love. Oh, by the way, I've heard you're quite pretty, but a pretty face is nothing if you have an ugly attitude, which you do. So get over yourself. Beauty fades, dumb lasts forever.'

The tears rolled down my cheeks, I screamed, throwing my phone to the ground, and unfortunately, it broke into tiny pieces. Well, the screen broke. I collapsed on my bed and started to cry quietly this time. No, I threw myself on the bed and sobbed myself free of tears. I felt sick to my stomach. I dried my eyes, then pulled my suitcase from under the bed and packed up all my clothes.

I held my breath and waited for Rhys to return home. I sat in complete silence, going over and over what Leah had said. I listened for his keys to turn in the keyhole, which never did. I sat there in the dark, waiting patiently for 30 minutes, before I decided to leave, taking Mr Kitty with me.

I didn't really know if what she was saying had an ounce of truth to it. But right now, I just can't cope with him running off to fix something in her house every time she phones. And that's the story of my life; always getting involved with men who were married or were already in a relationship with someone else.

So, I'm here in my house, alone, night after night. I lay sleepless in my bed, crying. Well, what really happened was, I hauled myself to bed. I shook out a pillow from its case and draped the pillowcase over my head like a hood. And why would I do something so ridiculous? So, I wouldn't have to stare at the photo of Rhys and me on my dresser.

Even Mr Kitty looked sad. Oh, damn how silly of me. I've only gone and forgotten Mr Kitty's cat food at Rhys' house.

It's past midnight. I'd have to drag myself to the shop.

My face was flushed from exertion, and anger, yet I found the strength to crawl out of bed, to wander off down the road to buy some cat food.

Strolling along, veins of light, threaded through dark, low clouds. I was startled by the ringing of my phone. Looking down at my broken screen, I had about four missed calls and numerous text messages from Rhys. But for now, I have chosen to ignore them. Looking at my messages, I realised that I also missed a couple from my biological dad, Aubrey.

Right now, I'm not in the right frame of mind to contact my dad. So, I'd text him later and make up some excuse. Sad, I know. But right now, I was so broken-hearted, about my relationship with Rhys that I'm not even going to go to my parents' house for lunch tomorrow.

It's Monday morning, and I could hear the birds singing a beautiful song. I'd leave the singing to you. I'd not look through the window, as usual. I'd stay in bed. I'd not even go to the office, I'm too depressed right now. My phone kept pinging, but I cared not to look.

I'm crying, I'm silently screaming. I heard my doorbell ringing, and my phone rang. Right now, my heart was in pieces.

Rhys, I love him so much, I can't believe that I found myself in the same situation again. Right now, I just want to be left alone.

Drake

Oh boy, oh man. I can't believe the mayhem that Rhys' ex-wife had created. How many times have I told Rhys to cut that crazy psycho ex-wife off, just cut her loose? But my brother wouldn't listen.

First, he lost Kim, but that's another story. Now, he's found another nice lady, who has no husband, and loves him as much as he loves her, now look what's happened.

Rhys, my man, you're too kind, that's your problem. I'd spoken to my wife, to see if she can talk some sense into Tianna about Rhys' ex-wife making up that bullshit story. But sorry, my man, her phone just kept going to voicemail, all day, every day.

Tianna's friends were all getting worried about her; no one seemed to be able to get in contact with her.

Rhys, my man, I knew you'd been phoning and going to her house. Hey, how come you never had spare keys to her place then? Oh well, it's a little too late to ask you that now, I suppose.

Rhys my man, just keep trying. She can't stay mad at you forever. I mean what lady can?

Listen up, my man, because I have a word of advice. "Don't you dare go phoning Kim. I know you too well, my brother."

You mean no harm but if it's Tianna whom you really want, concentrate on getting her back. Kim, I knew she gave you a lot of comfort, but don't side track once you start with Kim, I knew you definitely won't try hard enough to find your way back to Tianna, even though you wanted her back.

Rhys, my brother, I'm going to try again and ask my wife to contact her. Even though I knew my wife was as mad as hell with you. I think she'd get through to Tianna, eventually.

You know these women? They never stay away from each other for too long. Oh, by the way, who's been telling your ex-wife all your business? I've been racking my brain on that one, because Leah, my man, it seemed as though she knew your every move.

Rhys my man, when you do eventually find that person, let me know, because I'd deal with them, trust me.

Renee

It's been a few days now, and Tianna has not answered her phone. I've been to her house too, no answer either. I know how she gets when she'd broken up with a boyfriend.

I met up with Nyomi and we went to Kayleigh's house to ask if she had heard from Tianna.

"I'm really worried too," Nyomi replied, as she looked back at the last text message on her phone from Tianna.

"My husband said that Rhys is really upset about the whole thing. His ex-wife is hell bent on causing trouble," I told my friends.

Sharing a bottle of red wine, I nibbled on a bit of undercooked biscuits that Kayleigh had baked. Bless her for trying. I turned to face Kayleigh, who was brushing the biscuit crumbs from her dress, then put a few crumbs in her mouth when she thought no one was looking. Yuk!

"Guys, why would Tianna believe that crazy ex-wife, instead of her man? I really don't get it, unless there is something Tianna hasn't told us," she said, with a worrying frown.

Opps, sorry. That's what Kayleigh said in between eating her undercooked biscuits.

"If only she told us what was really going on. Oh heck, how did that crazy bitch, get her mobile number, in the first place?" Nyomi replied.

"Oh, do you know, I never thought of that," I replied, with a finger to my lip, thinking.

"Do you know, guys, it has to be someone close to either the ex-wife or Tianna, because that ex-wife knows way too much information," Kayleigh answered, still brushing biscuit crumbs from her dress, and gave me a side-glance.

Yeah, I see you, not only with crumbs on your dress, but all over the floor. Girl, there must be a dustpan in your cupboard somewhere.

"Don't look at me, I would never do that to my best friend," I blurted out, rolling my eyes.

"No, no, don't look at me either, I'm as loyal as you can get. What about Tianna's friend, Tamara?" Nyomi suddenly replied.

So, sure as hell. I've turned my frigging head, swiftly, to stare at Nyomi with her ridiculous accusation.

"No way, not Tamara. She would never do that to Tianna. Those two share a special bond. I'm not sure if you're aware, but Tamara was adopted too, like Tianna. Although their stories about their birth mothers are completely different to each other."

"I'm sure Tamara is in contact with her birth mother; she was adopted when she was four, I think. Hey, I forgot that Tamara has the spare key to Tianna's house. That's right, she has," I said, with a frown, thinking, why I hadn't remembered.

"Renee, if you're Tianna's best friend, how come you don't have a spare key?" Nyomi blurts out, staring at me.

Hmm…I raised my eyebrows, folded my arms in annoyance at my friend, and let her know that, in fact, I did have a spare key.

"The key that Tamara has is my key. I forgot to take it back. Remember, when Tianna went to Venice for a few days with Rhys? She asked me to feed Mr Kitty, but I couldn't do it. So she asked Tamara, instead. Oh my God, what's Tamara's mobile number?" I asked.

"Oh my God," Nyomi screamed, as anger crossed through her eyes, as green as spring buds.

"What?" Both Kayleigh and I screamed with such a high-pitched voice.

I seriously thought that all Kayleigh's windows were going to shatter.

"What the hell? I know who's been giving Rhys' ex-wife all the gossip, that fucking bitch," Nyomi blurted out.

She spilt red wine on the floor as she abruptly stood up.

Fuming, pacing back and forth, I could hardly contain my anger.

"Who? Cos I'm going to kill whoever it is," I screamed.

Kayleigh also screamed, "Yeah me too. Who is this bitch? Do tell, cos I'm in the mood for a flipping fight tonight."

Nyomi's response was, "No, bloody hell, it can't be, but it all adds up."

"Look, Nyomi, just tell us, cos right now, my blood is boiling," I said, my tone of voice spit more and more anger.

"Renee, promise me, you're not going to go to her house, and do something stupid," replied Nyomi, pleading with me to calm the fuck down.

Kayleigh turned to Nyomi, and said, "Just call the bitch's name already."

Nyomi replied, shaking her head, her lips all quivering as she spoke. "Okay, but you're not going to like it," She blurted out.

"Nyomi, for fuck's sake," I remember shouting.

Kayleigh told Nyomi, "Stop stalling."

Nyomi, after taking a couple of deep breaths, forced out. "It's…it's…err…err…it's…, please, no. I hope I'm wrong, but it could only be…Melani."

Both Kayleigh and I stared—with wide-opened eyes and mouth on the flipping floor—at stupid Nyomi. We were unable to believe our ears.

Then, we screamed, "You what, no frigging way. Are you crazy?"

Then, without thinking, I replied. "That's it. Where's my frigging car keys? That bitch…that fucking bitch."

However, Kayleigh jumped up from where she was seated, and stood in front of me, more like she blocked me from ever reaching the street door, and said, "Hold up, Renee. Why would Melani do that? Come on, think…think. Nyomi, maybe you're the one telling all the gossip."

All hell broke loose.

Now, an upset and angry Nyomi glanced up at Kayleigh and rolled her eyes as she replied, "Who? Me? Why on Earth would I do that, honestly?"

An argument broke out.

Kayleigh shouted at the top of her voice, "Because you're a jealous bitch yourself."

I mean, what the hell was going on here?

Nyomi now jumped up, as though she wanted to slap Kayleigh, but chose to be more subtle.

Instead, she asked, "Hold on a minute, love. Where's all this hate coming from?"

So now, I had to jump between the two of them.

"You two, stop with all your crap," I said, with my arms stretched, keeping them apart for their own good.

Nyomi, not backing down, said, "Okay, girl, bring it up then. Come on you, bitch."

Again, I shouted, "Stop with your crap, you two, for crying out loud."

Nyomi said, looking all flustered, "No, no that bitch, has something to say, so let her say it then."

Kayleigh, upset, and now had tears welled up in her eyes, replied, "That's right, Nyomi, it's always about you. Piss off...why don't you?"

I grabbed the pair of them by their arms and said, "Look, you two, I thought you sorted out your differences a long time ago."

Kayleigh asked, sobbed, and wiped her eyes. Her mascara blackened her face, but I won't tell if you don't.

"So, Renee, what would you do if you found out your friend slept with your husband?"

Wide-eyed and looking a bit confused, my mouth almost touched the hardwood flooring.

Yet again, I asked, "What? Who slept with whose husband? You two, you're so stupid. You know what, I really don't want to hear this crap anymore."

Kayleigh, mad as hell, rolled her eyes and replied. "Really, if she slept with Drake, would you be happy?"

You all know me. My response was something like this:

"Girl, you're crazy if any of you had sex with my man. Seriously, you both would be six feet under. But you know what, that is what happens when you go to a swinger's party. I don't go to parties like that. Well, not anymore. And as you remember, I did tell you two fools not to go."

Both their anger turned to embarrassment.

So, now Nyomi replied, "I'm sorry, Kayleigh, I thought you were doing it with my husband. So, wait a minute, who did my husband go with, then?"

Kayleigh looked a bit bemused and then replied, "Girl, so, who did your husband go with that night?"

I just had to ask, "Excuse me, Kayleigh, if Nyomi did it with your husband, and your husband did it with someone else, who did you do it with?"

Kayleigh blushed, took a deep breath and then answered, "I'd rather not say."

Hmm...she looked away from my stare rather sharply.

"We're all sensible adults here. So, what is this argument really about, then? You both thought you were banging each other's husbands. So, why get upset? Secrets and lies. So, Kayleigh, if you didn't sleep with Treyvon, is it someone we all know?"

Kayleigh hesitated, held her head to the ground, still brushing biscuits crumbs from her dress, then she whispered, "Yes."

Walking swiftly in the direction of the kitchen, with me hot on her heels, she opened the fridge door and stared into it absently.

Looking rather stunned, everyone expected her to reveal her dark secret.

"Who?" I demanded to know, grabbing her by her right arm.

Just then, my mobile rang. "It's Tamara. This conversation…it's not over," I told her.

I've always had my suspicions, but wanted to hear it from her. Fucking my husband, and keeping quiet about it? I don't think so.

Tamara

"Hi, Renee, it's Tamara. I'm at Tianna's house, just to let you all know, she's okay, so don't worry. I'm just making her something to eat, and feeding Mr Kitty. She sends apologies for making you all worry about her."

I made the short drive to Tianna's house, swallowed by torrential rain and a cloak of darkness. I let myself in, and all I could hear were cries, which pierced the silence along the hallway, and up the stairs into her bedroom.

I stood in the doorway of her bedroom, my eyes held a depth of emotion, as I watched Tianna, lying motionless, in her bed.

"Right, Tianna, I've let everyone know you're okay. Well, it's not strictly true, but come on, get yourself up and into the shower, girl, because you stink."

I'm sorry, but it had to be said.

So, I am here with my beautiful friend, Tianna. We'd all been worried about her. She'd been in bed for days; I had to immediately open the window for fresh air.

Not exactly sure if it was my good friend or Mr Kitty who made the room smell somewhat awful.

Mr Kitty was curled up next to Tianna on her bed, then ran off down the stairs as soon as he caught eyes on me.

"You think Rhys has hurt you by sleeping with his ex-wife behind your back. Come on now, you're not the first, and definitely won't be the last woman, to be hurt by their boyfriend. Did you even talk to him about it? Do you even know his ex-wife? Why believe her? Come on, Tianna, don't cry, babes. I know you're hurting."

But she just stared up at me and won't respond to my conversations.

When I first walked into her bedroom, she was all curled up into a ball with a white pillowcase over her head. I simply didn't have the heart to tell her how ridiculous she looked.

"Tianna, get yourself out of that bed, now. You really do smell awful," I screamed.

Cruel, I know, but it had to be said.

As I walked towards the window to open it for some much-needed fresh air, I looked at my friend. I felt guilty for hurting her feelings, despite her need to return to her own world.

"Okay, give me Rhys' mobile number, let me talk to him," I yelled at her, until she looked in my direction.

That's when Tianna leapt out of bed, knocking me off balance, in her haste to grab her phone, which was next to Mr Kitty, on the floor.

Oh, I thought he had run down the stairs.

Anyway, before I had a chance to grab the phone, yet again, I found myself yelling at her.

"Don't you dare phone him," she screams.

"Oh, so now you can speak, then," I replied.

She picked her phone up, then tossed it onto her bed.

"Tianna, come on, babes, don't cry, stop crying. If I were you, I'd go see him and hear what he has to say for himself. You may feel miserable, like crying, but crying is not allowed. Babes, look what I've got, yes, girlfriend, your favourite ice cream, yummy—cookies and cream flavour."

Well, it was her favourite last month.

She glanced up at me, while wiping her eyes, on the back of her hand, as she forced a smile on her face.

"I don't feel embarrassed about crying, as it helps when I release these intense emotions," she said and sobbed.

"Tianna, babe, I never thought I would see your beautiful smile. Here, babes, eat your ice cream before it melts."

"Thanks, Tamara, what would I do without you?"

Even though we sat and ate two tubs of her favourite ice cream, deep down, I knew she was hurting. So, I put my tub down and wrapped my arms around my friend, which only made her cry again.

Mr Kitty, he's such a clever cat. He sensed Tianna was sad. He went and jumped up onto her lap, knocking her tub of ice cream onto the floor. The cheeky cat jumped down, licking the ice cream, then ran off, leaving his pawprints, for, guess who to mop up.

I stayed the night with my good friend. Well, I couldn't leave her in the state that she had found herself in. I slept next to my friend, with my arm firmly wrapped around her waist, all night.

Would you believe it, if I told you Mr Kitty slept all curled up next to Tianna, even though I was in the bed too. In the morning, I found his cat bed at the bottom of the stairs. Now, that's the God's honest truth.

Rhys

I'm gutted. Tianna still was not answering any of my calls. I'm sitting on the edge of my bed, listening to the birds singing a beautiful song.

Tianna loved staring through the window every morning, listening and humming to their song. I am so lonely here without her.

You know that empty feeling you get when someone you love is not there anymore. Several times during the day, that empty feeling returned. I find myself just staring at a photo of her on my phone.

Sadness had wrapped itself around my heart, leaving me breathless in its suffocating embrace. And we all knew where the blame lay. I got used to waking up next to her in the mornings. Now, there's just an empty bed space.

Her sweet smile, as she gazed into my eyes, her touch, with her soft hands. The way she kissed me, lingering her lips on my mouth. Her taste, her scent, now…she's gone.

My ex-wife…who was filling her head with gossip. I really wanted this person to stop, like yesterday.

Drake told me that his wife and her friends thought it could have been Melani. I didn't think so. My ex-wife doesn't know Melani, as far as I know. Boy, it could be anyone.

I've been sending flowers to Tianna's house every day. I phoned her first thing in the morning, and last thing at night, but nothing. I texted, and she hadn't replied. So, I would go to her house this evening and ring her doorbell until she answers the street door.

Well, that was my intention, until my phone started ringing. It was Alex, yeah, that dude. Huh, why's he ringing me?

Kim's been admitted to hospital and she was asking for me. A feeling of helplessness and panic welled up in me.

Oh fuck, what should I do? I was still sitting on the edge of my bed, listening to the birds, thinking about Tianna. The two most important women in my life;

whom do I go to first? I was a wreck just thinking about it. If I phoned Drake, I knew what he'd say, but what the hell, I'd phone him anyway.

He surprised me and said, "Go to Kim first."

I put my foot down, drove to the hospital, weaving in and out of the traffic, going through a few red lights. A journey that should have taken at least 45 minutes, but ended up somehow, only taking 16.

My walk turned to a trot, then a run, until I eventually found the right ward, she was in. I stupidly took the wrong lift to the wrong floor. I guessed that must have been Alex's fault, or maybe it was mine, being a bag of nerves, I misheard him. I watched him sitting by her bedside, stroking her cheeks with one hand, then brushing her hair behind her ear, until he glanced up, and noticed me.

Alex sighed and walked over to the door with a worried look on his face and deep concern in his eyes.

As he spoke quietly, his tone was less than friendly. He kept glancing over at his wife. Yeah, that dude was talking to me as though. I wasn't really welcomed here. I asked how Kim was really doing. I thought Alex was pondering, to tell you the truth, until he spoke.

We only exchanged words for a few minutes before Alex bowed his head, staring down at the floor, and walked away.

Kim's not doing so well with this pregnancy. Alex explained as best as he could that she had severe, persistent nausea and vomiting.

He also said she needed to stay in the hospital for at least a few days. Then he told me to go and sit with her for a while, as she was asking for me.

So, I thought he was being civil to me for once in his life, but as I sat there holding her hand, speaking to her, with a big fat grin on my face, it couldn't be helped, you know how I feel about his wife. I could see his face going all red as he leaned one shoulder against the wall, listening to our conversation. Alex was getting more and more frustrated as the minutes ticked away.

For a few seconds, he merely stared at me, and his expression became sour. He left the room finally and began to pace up and down the hospital corridor, just watching me. Alex rolled his eyes, drew his brows down to feign a stern expression. His jaw tightened, and his penetrating gaze prowled over my face and pounced on my eyes. He resisted for a moment longer, until he just couldn't bear me being alone with his wife any longer and entered the room.

Okay, so holding her hand wasn't such a good idea, but she reached out for my hand first. No matter what, I was not going to pull my hand away from her just to make Alex happy.

I could hear Alex mumbling curse words to himself. He cut his eye at me, with a deep furrow running across his forehead, and sat down on a chair near the window. He couldn't remain still; as he observed me observing him, he paced back and forth across the room several times, casting me a stern glare. Suddenly, his intense gaze transitioned to the clock on the wall.

He left the room once more, then suddenly did a U-turn, shaking his head. Boy, okay, now he was coming back into the room.

Kim didn't even utter more than a few words to me. Alex told me that it was time for me to sling my hook, as his eyes mocked me.

Well, what could I say? What? I'm grateful that he rang me at least. I gave Kim a cheeky little kiss on her left cheek and whispered in her ear, breathing in her sweet scent once more. And I told her that I'd phone in a couple of days to see how she and our baby were doing.

Of course, her husband hated the idea of me whispering in his wife's ear and made a beeline for me.

He grabbed a hold of my arm and basically told me to, *fuck off*, because, I was neither wanted nor needed.

"Come on now, Alex, there's no need to get physical," I said, looking down at his tight grip on my arm.

The dude responded with words that I didn't want to hear. His angry words were spat through clenched teeth.

Can you believe this idiot, two seconds later, he head butted me. We stood inches apart. He was really close to my face, staring deep into my eyes, and spat fire, never mincing his words.

"Maybe, you didn't hear me the first time, fuck off. Seriously, do you think that you can fuck my wife? What was it like fucking her? No, don't answer that. My wife may have opened the door, but I am fucking closing it. Sorry to tell you this, but you're dumped. Go on, sling your fucking hook, before I lose my cool," he shouted, standing his ground, fist clenched, and with utter hostility in his voice.

Woah, this dude was totally out of control. I guess I forgot myself for a slight moment and reminded him, "Your wife, but my baby."

He didn't like my response one bit. It was the midwife entering the room, as to why Alex didn't throw that first punch. His face went red as a tomato, bloody idiot. Still clenching his fist, trying as hard as he possibly could, holding in all his built-up anger.

Shaking her head and looking as if about to cry, Kim spoke. "Alex, for God's sake, calm down. Rhys, I think you should leave now. Thanks for coming."

Yeah, okay, whether I wanted to admit it or not, I knew that I wound him up, slept with his gorgeous wife, destroyed his marriage, or so he said. It was almost as though I could hear his every thought running through his mind as he stood watching me leave.

"My marriage was a haven of love and happiness, shared with dreams, and yet, it was tethered with an unfulfilled yearning for Rhys."

The magic had obviously gone from their marriage, otherwise, Kim would have never turned to me, looking for that something her husband wasn't giving her.

This dude—he took no responsibility for his actions, none whatsoever. All that said and done, it didn't excuse me, having an affair with his wife. If I could turn the clock back, knowing what I know, would I do it all again, you fucking bet, I would.

Tianna

It's been a few days since Rhys and I broke up.

Tossing my head to throw the hair from my face, I rolled over in bed.

Drunk and crying, I didn't bother opening my eyes when I thought I could hear a noise coming from downstairs. Then, I heard footsteps coming up the stairs.

My heart started pounding, as I took a peek from under the duvet, when I heard my bedroom door swung open. I got such a fright, first it was Mr Kitty, and a welcomed familiar face, came smiling towards me.

"Tamara, what a relief. You almost gave me a heart attack. I completely forgot that you had a spare key," I said, as I raised the pillowcase over one eye.

Tamara gave me a hug and told me that everyone was so worried about me.

"I'm okay," I said.

It was not completely true, but hey, she knew me well enough to know when I'm telling a little white lie.

She fed Mr Kitty and showed me the ice cream, cookies and cream flavour—my absolute favourite.

Then told me to get out of bed and into the shower, because I apparently didn't smell very nice.

"My heart is broken." I sobbed, my chin trembling, I wiped my tears away with the back of my hand.

"I know babe," she said, hugging me, and proceeded to tell me to go in the shower with my broken heart, regardless.

While I was in the shower, Tamara told me that my dad, Aubrey, had messaged me again.

"Babes, you've been looking for your biological dad for a while, and now you're going to ignore him?"

I told Tamara that I really wasn't in the right frame of mind to meet him at the moment.

So, now I'm freaking out. Tamara messaged Aubrey back, and we were meeting tomorrow afternoon for coffee.

"Don't worry, I'm going with you."

"Tamara…I can't meet him. I'm a total mess right now."

Staring at me, her eyes almost as sad as mine, Tamara asked me to remove the pillowcase from my head, as I looked completely ridiculous.

She meant no harm. Tamara then handed me a cup of coffee, with two sugars, yuck—one sugar was enough—and a slice of burnt toast with a bit of strawberry jam on it.

She sat next to me on the edge of my bed, as we continued to chat about the reason why Rhys and I broke up.

"You know why."

"No, not really, Tianna," she said, biting into the toast she had made earlier for me, and took a finger to scrape a bit of jam off the toast and proceeded to wipe it on the small plate beside me.

"You've given up on Rhys too easily. Give him a chance to explain himself."

"I want to, but every time his ex-wife phones, he goes running to her. It begins to wear thin with my patience to tell you the truth," I replied, staring down at the half-eaten cold toast.

Tamara suggested meeting up with Rhys and hearing him out. "He's a good guy. I can't imagine him hurting you," she replied.

But first, I've got to put my happy face on to meet my dad, Aubrey, tomorrow. Thanks to Tamara.

Later that evening, I decided to get out of bed. Well, I was dragged out of my bed kicking and screaming by my friend. But let's just say, she helped me out of bed.

We went down the stairs in the dark, as to why, I was not completely sure, and headed to the living room and watch a movie.

We were eating ice cream, just chilling, having a girlie night in. I'd finally stopped crying and burst into such a ringing fit of laughter at something stupid on the TV when there was a loud knock at the street door. Hmm, a loud continuous banging at the street door.

Turning my head to my friend, she said, "What the hell, who is that, knocking on the door like that?"

I got up from the sofa and peeped through the window. It was a lady, smartly dressed in a navy trousers suit, obviously in some distress as she was crying, visibly shaking.

So, stupid me, I opened the street door without asking who she was first.

Really, it's Mrs Brooks. That's right, Rhys' ex-wife. So, what does she want with me? She stood there smiling, but silent at first.

My heart leapt as I stood very still and waited for her to speak. Her sharp look reminded me that she wasn't someone I wanted to get into an argument with.

Within a few seconds, she completely changed, looking as though she would explode any minute.

The woman was absolutely deranged, she was breathless with anger, as she stood there on my doorstep. I could clearly see the anger stirred within her, she was about to explode with rage. Tamara came running down the hallway, and closed the door in her face.

My heart rate increased by the second, and my mouth suddenly became dry.

"What the hell, Tamara? Why has she come to my house?" I said, all shaken up.

But Tamara pointed out the fact that she knew where I lived in the first place.

She was still there, ranting and raving like a madwoman.

The neighbours started to gather on the pavement, wondering what the hell was going on, until someone phoned the police.

That's when I noticed Alice, almost 100 years old, a sweet elderly lady, partially deaf, answering questions no one had asked.

She stood across the road with her grandson, pointing in my flipping direction.

"She's having an affair with my husband," Leah started screaming, for all the neighbours to hear.

"He's my husband…he's my husband, you can't have him," she yelled, when a neighbour approached her, asking if she was okay, and gave her a tissue to wipe her eyes.

Tamara wasn't standing for Rhys' ex-wife, disgracing my name to my neighbours like that.

She opened the street door, glanced back at me, smiled and said, "I'll try to be nice, but find tardiness to be such a pea in the shoe."

To which I replied, "Rhys' wife is as common as an old shoe. She's totally making an arse of herself."

That's when all hell broke loose. Tamara and Leah had an almighty screaming frenzy on my doorstep. I just couldn't stand there and leave them to it.

So, I went inside, got a large bucket of ice-cold water, and threw it all over Leah.

Her long hair hung loose, and dripped around her shoulders, and the water dripped onto her lovely expensive navy suit, oops.

Oh no, that was a very bad move on my part. Now the police have arrived, and you guessed it, Leah knows them all too well.

Unfortunately, Tamara and I were arrested that evening for breach of the peace, or something like that.

As far as I am aware, you cannot be legally arrested for breach of the peace, but I'd have to get back to you on that.

So, now the arresting police officer. He was quite a handsome guy, dare I say it.

He said, "Hey, pretty lady, why are you looking so sad?"

I'm not really sure what happened, but he asked for my phone number, to which I replied, "You're not supposed to be chatting me up on duty."

His response was to start counting backwards. "Five, four, three, two…okay, so I'm officially off duty. How about I take you out for a drink, or a nice meal, then?"

I stood there a bit stunned, confused, or amused, not sure how I was feeling, still holding the bucket in my hand, with Tamara's feet frozen to the pavement. I glanced over at her, and saw the bewildered look on her face.

Oh, wait, I think the other officer was deadly serious about arresting us, until Officer Eddie whispered something into his ear. It angered the lovely Mrs Brooks when she realised no arrests were going to be made that evening.

It really was only meant to have been a joke, at first, agreeing to go out for a drink, to get myself and Tamara out of trouble. But hey, who knew he'd be quite a catch?

Anyway, I soon perked the hell up and went for a meal, two days later.

Oh, by the way, I haven't forgotten about meeting up with my dad, Aubrey, or Rhys for that matter.

But let me just tell you about my fling with Officer Eddie Marshall first. Crazy, I know, but what the heck, right?

A warm late spring breeze held just a dash of chill as I stood on my doorstep staring up at Eddie.

My body was doing funny things, like growing warm in places it shouldn't, and scattering my unclean thoughts like confetti in a stiff breeze.

On our first date, we went to an all-you-can-eat buffet…hmm.

The red vinyl booths worked well to complete the vintage feel in the cosy restaurant. He seemed to know the owners well enough, two brothers.

The wine kept flowing all night, free of charge, I may add.

Eddie's…hmm…friendly and nice, very charming. He had a magic effect that made people like him. Until they realised that he was a police officer, their attitudes changed slightly. But hey, it didn't bother me in the slightest. Eddie was open and honest with me from the beginning.

He let me know that he wasn't interested in a serious relationship at the moment because of work commitments.

He found that with his previous relationships, they broke down rather quickly, because of his work. So, he decided it was better to just have a bit of fun, rather than commit, which suited me just fine.

He was quite the gentleman too. He never kissed me on our first date, but made up for it on our third. Oh yes, there was a second, and third date and a few more after that.

On our second date, we went for a drink at an exclusive wine bar—members only. Sliding an arm across the back of my chair, he leaned close, kissed my neck, then my earlobe, and began whispering softly, telling me all kinds of naughty things.

"Such as?" I heard you ask.

Eddie asked me what I really thought of men in certain uniforms, and that he had a spare set of handcuffs at home. And would I like to play cops and robbers with him? I mean, I'm not really sure how you play that game, so I declined.

Okay, so he laughed. "Tianna, Tianna, have you been bad today at all?" he asked.

To that, I replied, "Yes, Officer Eddie Marshall."

That's all he needed to hear, because he then invited me back to his place.

Seriously, I mean, did I really just go back to Eddie's flat already? You bet, I did.

He put some music on with the volume on low.

The lights were dim. He asked if I would like to dance, so we did. Slow dance, I may add. He was very good at slow dancing. Thinkin' Bout You by Frank Ocean.

His warm hands slid around my waist, pulling me close against him.

My heart was beating fast, my hands trembled with excitement, as I wrapped my arms around his neck, breathing in his scent, and rested my head on his shoulders.

The muscles in his arms and shoulders were straining against his shirt as he held me closer against his lean body.

His fingers lifted my chin so that I was forced to look at his handsome face. Maybe, just maybe, I came over as a little shy.

His hair was tied back, his jaw and chin were scruffy from a couple of days of hair growth, but, boy, did he drip sex appeal? I gazed into his eyes and traced his jaw line, from temple to chin with my index finger. I smiled up at him sweetly. He smiled back at me mischievously, then suggested that we play a game called Our Moments; a card game for couples.

Hmm…seriously? Not sure if I would play this game again, it asked some really deep, provoking questions, which I really wasn't prepared to answer. So, we stopped playing before we really got started.

So, now, Eddie asked me what I would fancy doing instead. Hmm, I know what I had in mind, but he said he'd like to ask me a few questions, nothing too personal. If he didn't like my answer, then I would have to take an item of clothing off.

Okay, hmm…I like this game better. Seriously, come on now, what if he loses? I get to see his sexy body.

Unfortunately for me, I'm down to my bra and knickers. I'm beginning to blush, covering myself with my shaking hands, giggling, definitely a naughty girl vibe.

Eddie watched me smiling, as he stared at me, trying to cover my boobs. I'm not going to say…I laughed.

"But you did," he said, smiling to himself.

He was very good at this game, not sure if he'd ever lost before.

Anyway, Eddie was looking at me. I was looking at his manly, peppered stubble, flashing my eyelashes at him. Hmm, not quite sure what he was thinking right about now. Out of nowhere, he produced his handcuffs and placed them around my wrist.

He said, "I'm arresting you, there is something deliciously naughty about sporting bad girl lashes." His voice was full of humour, then his phone started ringing.

Oh boy, his workplace has called him in to do an extra shift, and he cannot refuse to go in. I closed my eyes as he leaned in towards me and started to kiss me.

His velvety tongue was hot against my neck and my lips, as he pleased me in ways I'd never experienced before.

Then he caressed my breast, I tried to raise my arms to put them loosely around his neck, then remembered that I was still in his handcuff, which he eventually released me from.

"Tianna, Tianna," he kept whispering softly. "I wish that I could spend more time with you."

He asked if he could see me tomorrow, to which I whispered softly in his ear, "Yes."

So, now my mobile phone starts ringing. Oh God, I think I'm going to go crazy sometime soon. I screamed to myself. It was Rhys. I completely forgot he phoned every morning and last thing at night. But for now, I have decided to decline all of his calls. Let's see what would happen with Eddie.

He's one hell of a sexy police officer, and I'm not exactly sure if I liked him, but I think it'd be fun finding out.

Over the next few days, I thought about Eddie several times with mixed feelings. So, I drove to my best friend, Renee's, house.

As much as Renee can be blunt, hurtful, with her outspoken harsh words, without realising, of course, she gets to the point rather sharply.

She's made me cry a few times. She's my best friend, and I value her honest opinion.

Anyway, I spoke with Renee about Eddie. She told me that I am crazy, and to ditch that police officer, and get back with Rhys.

"Get your act together," she yelled at me.

I agreed, but said that I needed some time away from Rhys and his crazy, psycho ex-wife. She gave me a stern look and then made a face.

"Girl, if you don't go, and get your man back, I know plenty of women, who'll take him from you," she bellowed out, as she stood there, hands on her hips, a big frown on her face, then rolling her eyes.

Renee leaned back with a triumphant look on her face, as if she had made a point. I frowned and lowered my eyes for a slight moment, but pushed back any feelings I once had for Rhys.

Handing me another glass of wine, we carried on chatting about my love life, as she listened to me pouring my heart out.

My best friend sat there. She would often turn her head, smile, and act as though she had heard what was said, especially when Eddie's name was mentioned.

Renee lifted her wine glass, and took two gulps, staring at me, with me laughing one minute and then crying the next. My thoughts often rose and beat up like birds against the wind.

Renee was too occupied with my problems. She obviously forgot about the peppered chicken tartlet on a bed of rocket leaves, which she had just prepared for her husband.

The smell still hung in the air as he yelled, at the top of his lungs, to his wife, "Where's my dinner, babe? I'm starving."

By the end of the evening, Renee appeared as confused as I felt about my feelings for sex bomb Rhys, whose eyes lit up when he saw me, and the way his voice cut through my heart, and stopped me in my tracks. And Officer Eddie Marshall, who was easy on the eyes.

Remembering that evening, when we strolled along the embankment, with not a care in the world, and he began laughing at a silly joke that I had made, causing him to walk ahead of me.

Eddie walked with a tiger like tread, and normally the one to crack a joke or two, but I thought I'd give it a go, and show my humorous side.

He seemed moulded from a different cast than most of the men I had previously dated. Well, except for Rhys.

His eyes were brown and bright and bewitched me every time I fell under his steady gaze.

Eddie took my hand in his, and my stomach did a backflip. He smiled at me, winked, and my heart definitely spread through my whole body.

Eddie reached down, and took my hands, pulling me into his arms, and when I gazed up at him, he leaned down and kissed me with his warm lips.

As promised by my police officer boyfriend, Eddie, we spent the following evening together.

He was a very good cook indeed. He made stir-fried garlic prawns. As much as I hated to admit it, it tasted good, much better than anything I could have prepared.

Eddie slowly picked up his fork, never taking his eyes off me, as I ate the prawns and sipped the white wine.

I tucked the fallen strand of my hair behind my ear and blushed as Eddie continued to smile at me from across the table. I may just point out that he was doing something rather naughty with his tongue.

Later that evening, like we usually did, we went for a stroll in the spring sun.

We held hands, he made me laugh, and whispered naughty jokes in my ear. Oh wow, who knew that a police officer could be this humorous?

Afterwards, we went back to his flat I plopped down on one end of the sofa, taking my heels off, as he joined me, wrapping his strong arms around me.

We began to kiss. Oh, Officer Eddie, he sure knew how to use his tongue. His fingers slowly removed the straps from my shoulders and slid them down my arms, as he started to lick my body all over, slowly. This sent tingling all over my whole body. And gently started biting me.

Oh boy, he slid his hand between my legs, stroking me gently there, then he caressed my breast.

Closing my eyes, I leaned back, quickly sucking in a breath, as his warm hands surrounded my waist.

Eddie asked if I wanted to go to his bedroom, or if he could do it to me right there on his sofa.

I asked him to stop. He must have sensed the cause of my sudden change of mind. Eddie kissed my neck and released his tight grip around my waist, getting off the sofa.

He stepped away as he spoke. "Tianna, I have a lot of pleasure to give to you."

The reason I asked him to stop, my phone began to ring. I knew it was Rhys. He always phoned at the exact same time every evening. I really didn't want Eddie to stop. Oh boy, really, I didn't. But I began to think about Rhys, what Renee had said to me, and how much he meant to me.

So, I made an excuse and told Eddie that I wasn't quite ready to give myself to him just yet.

My gaze took in his masculine chin, the square cut lower lip, and his piercing brown eyes, only right now, they weren't piercing.

He stood, stared down at me, rubbed his forehead and ran his finger through his hair. Eddie, understood, right?

He zipped up his jeans, then, sitting back down beside me, he asked me to tell him a little bit about myself. Hmm, what's with all the questions? Have you noticed too?

So, I told him that I was adopted as a baby, and have since found my biological dad, whom I'm yet to meet.

He asked, "Why haven't you met up with him yet?"

So, I told him about my brief relationship with Rhys and his ex-wife, Leah, who destroyed our romance before it had any chance to progress. So, I really wasn't up to meeting him just yet. I managed a smile, too overwhelmed by my emotions to continue speaking.

A touch of humour came into his eyes as he turned his head to look me full on in the face.

He said, "Oh, Leah, the barrister."

I could tell by the look on his face that he thought it amusing.

"A barrister, you flipping kidding me," I fumed.

"Yeah, I know her, don't mess with her, she's an iron lady." He laughed, shaking his head.

I almost laughed, thinking it must be some kind of terrible joke, until I realised he was deadly serious.

Eddie nudged closer to me, with a comforting arm around my shoulders, as I caught my breath, and sat up sharply.

"Do you want some wine? You look as though you need a drink," he asked, still laughing.

He poured me a large glass of white wine, sat back down on the sofa next to me, and took my hand in his.

After the shock wore off a little, and I was able to think more clearly, Eddie started with his questions again.

"So, you were dating her ex-husband then, what's his name again?" Eddie asked.

I reminded him, "Rhys."

Eddie joked, "Rhys, Rhys, what's this guy's surname?"

So, I told him, "Brooks."

At first, he was silent thinking, and said, "I know this guy, well not know him to talk to, but my work colleague, Sean, has a mate called Alex, his misses had a fling with Rhys Brooks."

Sinking back into Eddie's sofa, I gently removed his hand from mine, thinking over and over. What the hell?

My heart leapt, then dropped to my feet, when I realised who and what Rhys' ex-wife happened to be. A barrister, a flipping barrister, an airhead with a face of a bitch.

Somehow, the fact that Rhys and Kim's affair was well-known and talked about at the police station. A few awkward moments went by before I asked Eddie to take me home. Which he did, in a car very similar to Rhys' black Audi.

Rhys

I phoned Kim, just to see how she was doing after being in the hospital. She asked if I wanted to go for a coffee. How could I refuse that offer? So, we arranged to meet up tomorrow morning.

Later that evening, on my way home from work, who did I see? Boy, oh boy, Tianna was holding hands with some guy.

They were strolling along without a care in the world.

Well, in fact, she looked so happy with this guy. They were both laughing. They kept stopping, then walking, as he whispered nonsense into her ear to make her laugh. Seriously, come on now, Tianna, he's whispering foolishness into your ears.

He pulls her in close, then kissed her. She responded to his kiss and draped both her arms around his neck, gazed up into his eyes and smiled.

Smiling, seriously, what the hell has she got to smile about, with this guy?

I just stood there watching them both for a few painful moments. I couldn't take it, seeing her with some other guy.

It was with a heavy heart and a cold burning in my soul that I turned around and started to walk in the opposite direction. And who did I see, my PA, Kyla, whom I was about to call out to, until I saw her with my ex-wife, Leah.

What the fuck, is going on this evening? I had no idea that my ex-wife knew Kyla. Then it all started to make sense. Kyla's the person giving Leah all the gossip about my love life.

I'm a bit confused at the moment as to why Kyla would tell Leah anything. But let's not jump to any conclusions. I'd simply ask her tomorrow.

The next morning, the air was crisp and cool. I was looking forward to meeting up with Kim for coffee, although I didn't sleep very well last night, thinking about Tianna and her friend, holding hands and laughing.

Walking towards me, she tucked her hair behind her ear and smiled as she caught a glimpse of me. Kim looked so radiant, and her baby bump was getting much bigger. I gave her a kiss on her cheek, she smiled and asked how I was.

I just shook my head, side to side, and said that I was okay.

She looked at me as though she knew that I was lying.

"Rhys, you know that you can tell me anything. You've always been there for me in the past, haven't you? Let me be there for you now."

Before I got a chance to respond, a sudden gust of wind circled us and whispered words in her mind, which made her blush and giggle.

She held my hand and smiled up at me sweetly, her lips curved, and her cheeks glowed. I told her everything there was to tell, about my ex-wife destroying my relationship with Tianna, and how I saw her with some guy, holding hands, all loved up.

Kim stared at me, surprised for a few moments, her eyebrows raised, her mouth hung open loosely.

Then she said, "Are you serious? I don't believe it? Why would any woman want to leave you?"

Again, she touched my hand, our fingers began to interlock, as we stared at each other for quite a while.

Okay, so we eventually pulled our hands away from each other. Kim asked if I still wanted Tianna. If so, then I wouldn't let her go so easily.

"Remember, how you put up a fight for me?" she said.

Then reminded me that I may have lost that fight, but never give up hope, when it came to Tianna. I responded by telling her, although I may have lost her to Alex, I'd always love her, and would forever have a place in my heart for her. And this baby, that we were having together, will only make the love, we have for each other, even stronger, than before.

We strolled along, taking in the sweet-smelling flowers from the florist next door to the coffee shop.

Once seated, Kim was recognised by a work colleague, seated alone in a cramped corner, looking sad, dressed in a summery yellow and white dress, unsmiling, but nodded in acknowledgement to her greeting.

Kim—I love her as much, if not more, than she obviously loved me. But Tianna was the one breaking my heart right now.

"What do I do, Kim, to win her back? Tell me what."

Kim looked at me, held my hand, and told me not to worry.

She told me that as soon as we had finished drinking our coffee, she was going to phone Tianna and speak with her.

"I guarantee you, Rhys, by the time I'm finished with Tianna, she'll be begging you to take her back."

I looked at Kim and asked, "What are you planning to do?"

"Trust me, it's best if you didn't know. Do you trust me, Rhys?"

"With every bone in my body."

As we left the coffee shop, Kim held my hand. I walked her to the car, which had a parking ticket slapped on the windscreen.

"Rhys, whenever you think there is nothing left, trust me, there is always hope," she said in a sweet, soft voice, which only melted my heart.

Changing the subject, well, I just had to. Believe me, Kim and I were definitely not done yet, you know that right.

I looked at her, she always knew how to make me smile. I asked her how Mason and Maya were, then I had to ask about Alex, her idiot of a husband. Yeah, him, that loser.

"Everyone is fine."

But I saw the smile in her beautiful brown eyes, as though she was reading my mind, laughing perhaps, at my unkind thoughts of her husband.

I wanted to know if Alex knew where she was. She replied by telling me, in all of their five years of being together, that she has never lied to him or had hidden the truth from him.

"Of course, he knows I'm with you, it's only coffee." She laughed, rolling her eyes, and rummaged around in her handbag for her car keys.

She held me around my waist and whispered in my ear, "Rhys, I do love you, not being able to be with you when I want is killing me."

"Kim, I love you more than words could ever say. It's killing me too that we cannot be together."

I cupped her face in my hands and leaned down, brushing her lips softly with mine.

"If I asked you to leave Alex, what would your answer be?"

She slipped her arms around my neck and whispered against my lips, "Yes, I mean no."

I'm not sure what just happened between Kim and me, but I'm not giving up the love that I have for her, and neither would she give up the love that she had for me, either. One day, maybe one day, we may just get to be together, but for now, she's with her husband, the idiot, and I'm trying to get Tianna back, with the help of Kim, whatever that entails.

I had to let Kim know, if Tianna does come back to me, she has to come first.

Kim just smiled and whispered in my ear, "I know, but it's when, not if, she comes back, right?"

Taking in her scent, breathing in slowly, I closed my eyes, savouring every last moment of her, as my lips gently found her neck.

"When the deed is done, I will text you with a smiley face," she replied.

That is what I love about Kim so much, always putting others before herself, and willing to do whatever she had to do, just to help me. I do hope she was not going to destroy her marriage with Alex just to help me.

It was time for Kim to go, she left Maya with her mum, and said that Mason is thriving at nursery.

She also let me know that our baby was doing well, and that she felt much better and thanked me for visiting her in the hospital, although we didn't really get to talk to each other much.

"Rhys, don't worry about giving whatever love you have for me to Tianna."

"Kim, you sure?"

"Yes, I'm sure, Rhys."

We hugged, we kissed, then hugged for a little bit longer, then kissed.

The sweet smell of her perfume, her warm breath against my lips, I really didn't want to let her go, but in reality, I had to.

"One day soon, your love for Tianna will be greater than it is for me," she said, as she removed the parking ticket from her windscreen and shoved it into my pocket.

Kim

I met Rhys this morning. I could see the hurt in his eyes when he spoke about Tianna. I knew what you're all thinking: how can he love Tianna if he loved me so much?

Well, our love for each other is just love, nothing more, nothing less.

We have what some people would call an unbreakable bond. Let me put it another way. Have you ever known what it was to love someone? Well, it is from the power of love which was in our own hearts.

However, the time to act on our feelings, for each other, has since passed, as you all know, that I can never leave my husband Alex, no matter what.

Rhys, I do love him as much as I love my husband. It did hurt me to see him so sad, let me tell you that.

So, what I'm about to do for him is out of pure love for Rhys to see him as happy, if not happier, than I am.

I phoned Tianna after meeting up for coffee with Rhys. You bet I dared to call her. As promised, I told him that I would have Tianna running back to him.

What I'd do is tell her my true feelings for him, but I would never act on them.

Believe me when I tell you, it's only to make her go back to Rhys. I don't want to see him hurt or lonely.

Trust me, it will work. Remember, what I was about to say or do was only for Rhys, no other guy, would get me telling such a damn lie or to stoop so low.

When I called her, she seemed a bit taken aback to hear my voice on the other end. Initially speechless, she quickly warmed to the idea of us getting together.

So, we'd meet up on Saturday evening in a wine bar.

Sure enough, Saturday came along in the blink of an eye. I sat near the entrance on a table for two, so that I could see her before she noticed me. Clever, don't you think? She was attached to the arm of a good-looking man, wearing a dark coloured suit. Anyway, what's so terrible about thinking she was cheating on Rhys?

Err, sorry, it was only my wicked sense of humour running wild, or was it baby brain, you chose.

We started off with a friendly girly chat. She asked how my pregnancy was going, and said she had heard I was in the hospital, and hoped that my baby and I were doing okay now. I looked at Tianna, and thought how lovely she was, and thought about the pain I was about to send her way was not intended.

I looked at her face, took a deep breath, and went full speed, like a high-speed train about to crash, and made Tianna cry. I'd never seen anyone cry as hard as she did. You know me, I'd just do whatever it took to send her running back to Rhys.

I'm sorry, I hate to disappoint you all, but it's best if Tianna would tell you in her own words what happened between us on that Saturday evening.

It's only fair, as this love story is about Rhys and Tianna, unfortunately.

Oh fuck, really, seriously, I can't believe I just said that, unfortunately or fuck. Seriously, do I have a baby brain, or what?

Drake

It's been a while since I'd actually spoken. I just wanted to say a few words about my man Rhys and his ex-wife, and soon-to-be-back-together girlfriend, Tianna, according to Kim.

He told me what happened with Tianna, and his ex-wife, the day the police were called. Also, now Tianna had a new man in her life. Boy, she moved on quickly to find a man already.

Rhys' really cut up about the whole situation. He even went crying to Kim. Those two, Rhys and Kim, would never leave each other's side.

Boy, I really don't know what kind of glue held them together. The love they had for each other, but they were apart, I just don't get it. I'd never get it.

Oh man, so where do I start? Rhys told me about the conversation he had with Kim. That must be some true love if she was willing to jeopardise her marriage to get Tianna, running back to Rhys.

But to be honest, we had no idea what she'd planned, but it can only go one of two ways.

The only way that I could see a woman running back to her ex was only when another woman declared war over that man. Kim, I really hope that you know what you're doing to help my man Rhys.

But what I know about her husband Alex, whatever Kim does, he's never going to leave her, trust me on that.

So, just in case Kim's plan didn't work, my wife and I had come up with plan B. Sunday afternoon, we'd be having a barbecue and invite everyone, including Rhys and Tianna.

Let's hope that whatever Kim did to help Rhys doesn't backfire.

Have you ever thought maybe she was doing it, so they could be together? No, I didn't think so either, if she wanted Rhys, trust me, she'd just take him. And knowing my man Rhys, he wouldn't hesitate to be with Kim.

To tell you the truth, I quite like Kim. I've spoken to her on many occasions, and I asked her, "Why are you with your husband, when he's cheated on you with your best friend?"

He fathered both of her children behind his best mate's back. What kind of messed up shit is that.

Anyway, she sat there, sobbed her little heart out, thinking, I guess, to come up with some plausible reason, excuse, or whatever.

Before she came up with a story that I could believe, I asked her another question, "Why don't you want my man Rhys?" Believe me when I tell you her face lit up when I mentioned his name. "He has everything that your husband has, if not more."

She only looked at me with her big brown eyes, which were red and swollen and cried, bawling her eyes out. I had to offer her my only tissue. I had it on me that day.

This was her answer to my second question. "If only I had met Rhys first, we'd definitely be together."

My reply to her, "Kim, you met Rhys at secondary school, but I guess you were one of those girls who ran in the opposite direction when you saw ugly Rhys coming."

She stared at me in mute horror. I'd say no more.

Tianna

It's Monday morning, I was looking through my bedroom window, the birds were singing as usual, as I sipped my coffee. Oh, wow, I haven't forgotten to add milk.

The doorbell rang twice. I hurried down the stairs. It was a beautiful bouquet of flowers with the card that read, With all my love, Rhys.

I started to wonder how he was.

He continued to phone every morning and evening, but not this morning, no phone call as yet.

To be fair, I'd been declining all of his calls and text messages. Maybe, just maybe, he hasn't given up on me—I hope not. I intend to give him a call maybe later in the week, because Drake and Renee were having a barbecue this Sunday, and it will be kind of awkward if we don't talk. Don't you think?

Oh, did I mention that Kim phoned the other day? It was a bit weird at first, but we planned on meeting up this Saturday. That should be a lot of fun. She did seem really nice.

I heard that she was in the hospital. I really do hope that she and her baby were okay.

Tuesday morning, I got a text from Renee, reminding me that she'd be meeting me at 3:30 pm at the coffee shop in town, as I was finally going to meet my dad, Aubrey, at last. She offered to go with me.

Well, I was supposed to go with Tamara, but Renee said, "Hell no, I'm going with you."

Well, it's nearly time to meet with my dad, Aubrey. I got a text from Eddie, wishing me luck—so sweet. I hadn't seen him for a few days, as he was working nights, but later, I'd go over to his place.

Renee noticed my dad first. I was so nervous that I forgot his name. I kept shuffling my feet, looking down at the ground. I eventually looked up. He had a nice big afro and was wearing red and blue socks, holding a bunch of flowers.

Then I heard a voice calling out to me, "Tianna."

I looked in the opposite direction, and there he was, my dad wearing a blue coloured jumper, blue jeans and brown shoes.

Renee realised her mistake in pointing out who she thought was my dad, then burst out laughing.

He's not that bad looking, quite tall, and has a beard. He looked as though he was in his late 50s or early 60s.

A smile touched the corners of his mouth and played in the laugh lines behind his brown eyes.

Okay, so let's see what he had to say for himself.

He gave me a hug, and shook Renee's hand. He was so pleased to finally meet me. My eyes began to well up. Renee gave me a tissue.

"Don't cry, Tianna, I have lots to tell you, and I want to get to know you."

"Sorry, I'm just a little overwhelmed," I replied, staring up at him with my chin trembling.

We walked together, side-by-side, with Renee trailing a few feet behind us, until we went into a coffee shop that I hadn't noticed before, and ordered lunch.

He had a charming smile, as he sat opposite me, talking and sipping on his coffee. Then he nibbled on his chicken salad sandwich, and abruptly stopped, realising he was in the company of Renee and me.

My good friend Renee rolled her eyes, leaned in with a furrowed brow, and whispered, "Really, he seems more interested in his sandwich than talking to you."

"Hush, Renee, maybe he's hungry and rushed out to meet with me without having anything to eat first," I replied.

Only for my friend to reply swiftly, "Really? He doesn't exactly look as though he skips meals for anybody."

Aubrey glanced up, while brushing the crumbs from his jumper, to find Renee watching him with a masked emotion.

After an awkward moment, he opened his mouth to speak, but was immediately interrupted by a waiter, who asked if everything was okay with the service.

Aubrey asked if I was in contact with my birth mum.

I shook my head and replied, "No."

For quite some time, his solemn gaze roved over my face as Renee handed me yet another tissue. I felt the awkward silence. I didn't know what to say, so

Renee told him that my birth mother had refused all contact with me, but I recently made contact with her daughter, Sabrina, my half-sister.

A little stunned, he began telling me about her, and recalled her being such a lovely lady, warm natured, just a beautiful person, and couldn't think of an explanation as to why, she would refuse to meet with me, after all these years.

Aubrey said that I could ask him anything, and that he'd answer all of my questions. But before I knew it, I became very emotional, and couldn't speak anymore, so my good friend Renee—she knows me all too well—asked the most important question of all: who is my mother, and what is her name?

Aubrey smiled and told me about my mother. First, he told me that her name is Jessica, and that he first met her when she had some renovation done on her house. He was one of the workmen.

He never knew that she was married, at first, because his boss at the time, always dealt with her.

The affair lasted about four years; he knew she wouldn't leave her husband, but just couldn't give her up, until she became pregnant with me.

Her husband only found out about their affair because I was born of mixed-race, and they decided to give me up, without discussing it with him first.

"I had no idea where to find you. She refused to see me, and her husband told her to sever all ties with me, or she'll be sorry," he said.

"Tianna, love, I'm so sorry that it's taken 30 years for us to finally find each other, but now that we have, unless you have any objections, I'd like to be part of your life."

He went on to tell me that he was married to a lovely lady called Martha, and I have three brothers and a sister. Also, that when I am ready, they were all waiting to meet up with me.

I turned to look at my best friend, Renee, and she was in floods of tears, like me. She held my hand and told me how happy she was that I had found a part of my missing family.

We sat there chatting for a few hours, getting to know each other a little. He suggested, there was no rush; when I'm ready, we'd just go at my pace.

"Let me know when you're ready," he said.

Then I could go to his house for dinner, and I could bring my friend, Renee, or whoever I chose; a special guy in my life—anyone. I just had to let him know.

When he left, Renee asked what I thought about him, and did I think he was someone whom I could get along with.

After Renee's first impression of my dad, believing that a chicken sandwich was more important than me. He explained that he had diabetes. I told her that it was early days, but when I do go to his house for dinner, she'd be coming with me.

"Now that's out of the way, what about Rhys," Renee asked with a broadened smile.

I managed a smile, too overwhelmed by my emotions to speak. I shrugged, wiping the tears from my eyes.

Eventually, after a few moments to compose myself, my lips quivered as I tried my hardest not to cry. I told her that I knew how much she and her husband liked Rhys, but let's wait until Sunday, at the barbecue, maybe he was dating someone else, I told Renee.

Of course, she shook her head and said, "I don't think so, Tianna, he wants you, only you."

For a moment, we both stared at each other in silence until I heard my phone ringing.

Oh my God! Meeting up with my dad, and Renee asking me about Rhys, I'd completely forgotten that I had arranged to meet up with Eddie.

Renee had a look of complete disappointment on her face, and said, "Girl, you better not have had sex with that guy, Eddie, yuck. Have you? Have you?" she kept asking, and asking, until she was out of breath.

"No, Renee, I haven't."

"Good, keep your legs closed, girl," she said, and laughed.

Wednesday morning, opening my sleepy eyes, I yawned, and had a good stretch, then realised, some strange man's arm was around my waist, with a somewhat tight grip.

"Help," I yelled.

Oh fudge, Eddie's in my bed, Oh my God.

He opened one of his eyes, then grinned at me. He wrapped his arms around me and pulled me into his big, strong body. I lay there next to him in deep thought. I couldn't remember if we did it.

So, I dared to lift the sheets and take a peek to see if we were both naked.

Oh my God. Eddie opened both his eyes and asked if I wanted more of him. I pulled the sheets to cover myself, but he smiled and said, after last night, there was no need to be shy anymore.

I closed my eyes, crossed my legs, and thought, 'Shit, what have I done.'

Staring at me, as though he couldn't get enough of me, you know what I mean, with his naked dark body pressed up close to mine, he started to stroke my face, then kissed me gently.

He blew his warm breath against my neck, he kissed me, ever so passionately, then he bit me gently on my lower lip, and stuck his tongue down my throat.

His scent drove my body wild, the mix of sweat, darkness and man. He placed his hand between my inner thighs, then started to caress me there.

"Open your legs," he whispered softly into my earlobe, but I had to stop him.

I rolled over and sat up, but he stopped me with a hand on my upper arm, pulling me back close to him. His concerned gaze took in my face.

"What's wrong? Don't you want to feel me inside of you again?" His deep voice sounded so good.

Okay, so now I was a bit confused about what Eddie had just said, because although we were naked, I'm not convinced that we did anything. I asked if we had done it last night.

He replied, laughing, "Are you serious, Tianna? You were begging me for more."

I pulled the sheets over my head again, because seriously, I couldn't remember any of it. I was feeling a bit embarrassed right now, if the truth were to be told.

"Tianna, Tianna, look at me, I'm just messing with you, you weren't ready to give yourself to me. As soon as I touched you, I knew," he replied, trailing his hand down my arm.

A sense of release came all over my body when Eddie said that.

Don't get me wrong, I like Eddie, but my heart belonged to Rhys, if I'm being totally honest with myself.

Maybe I should stop whatever this was before we end up having sex.

"Eddie," I said, trying to control the emotion in my voice.

He looked at me with his beautiful brown eyes and said, "It's okay, Tianna, you don't have to explain. It was fun while it lasted. I can tell your heart is somewhere else."

Thursday evening. Myself, Renee, Nyomi, and Kayleigh went to Melani's house, just to check in and see how she was doing.

Her baby bump had been getting bigger since the last time we all saw her. Her husband, Terrell, decided to go to the pub with Drake, Deshawn, and Treyvon, just to give us, ladies, some girlie time to ourselves.

We had such fun. All of us curled up on the sofa, eating popcorn, then we ordered pizza, and yes, my favourite ice cream—cookies and cream flavour.

We all laughed, cried and laughed some more. Okay, so why were we laughing, and why were we crying? Because I told them that, I woke up naked next to Officer Eddie this morning.

After Renee's jaw hit the floor, remembering our conversation the night before, she asked if I was completely sure that I hadn't actually done it with Eddie. Everyone except Kayleigh turned in my direction, waiting for my answer, with their eyes firmly on my lips, in case they happened to blink, and miss my lips moving.

I replied, "He assured me that we hadn't done it."

They all burst out laughing. Kayleigh eventually turned her head to face me, rolled her eyes, and shook her head.

"Do you believe him? He's a big, bad cop." Melani laughed, unable to contain the emotion bubbling within her.

"There's absolutely no reason to doubt what he said," I replied, as I sat there poking at a piece of leftover cherry pie, from the night before.

They all looked at me, with different expressions on their faces, and one by one, started laughing out loud.

"He's a police officer, for crying out loud," I told them.

But saying that, it put even more fuel on the fire, and made them all laugh even more than they already were.

I held my head in my hands and burst into tears.

Kayleigh rushed over, put her arms around me, and said they were only teasing me.

"Of course, Eddie wouldn't have taken advantage of you, not in the slightest," she said.

I told them how he asked me to open my legs, so he could have sex with me.

"Okay, girl, so pleased you kept the legs closed," Renee said, staring at me.

"Yeah, I'm proud too, girl, but after seeing a photo of Eddie, I'm sorry, I wouldn't have kept my legs closed for too long," Nyomi replied, smiling, then dropped her cherry pie on the floor.

"That's because you have no shame," replied Melani, jokingly.

We were all friends and anything goes. We say what we think, what you definitely don't want to hear, that's just how we are, good friends.

Friday morning, Mr Kitty, oh, he was purring. He loved it when I stroked him under his chin. I was looking through the window, the birds were not singing this morning. It was actually pouring with rain. Oh fudge, I'd be late for work again.

My dad, Aubrey, texted me. We were yet to meet up again. I haven't forgotten.

It's been a very busy week. I was meeting Kim tomorrow. That should be interesting. She looked as though we'd have a lot of fun together.

I'm thinking if I should invite Tamara tomorrow, when I meet up with Kim. Maybe not a good idea.

The whole idea of being friends with Kim was Rhys' idea, and we were not even together any more. But I hope when I see him on Sunday, that would definitely change.

I've really missed him. I kid you not. Yeah, yeah, yeah, my fling with Eddie, you're not going to let me forget about him, are you? Mr Kitty, I really hoped that Rhys had missed me too.

"What do you think, should I phone, or just wait until Sunday? Mr Kitty, Mr Kitty, here kitty…kitty, come here, I'm speaking to you."

Hmm, I think I'd wait. You know what they say, absence makes the heart grow fonder, or something like that.

Later that day, Officer Eddie phoned, just to check if I'm okay. He told me if I ever felt like having fun, I could give him a call. He also told me that he had a quiet word with Leah, Rhys' ex-wife, and she won't be bothering me anymore. If she does, I have to let him know. Also, he hoped my relationship with Rhys would get back on track. I thanked him for the lovely few weeks that we had fun, and we should definitely stay in touch.

He was silent for a moment and said, "If things work out with Rhys, that it wouldn't be such a good idea to remain friends, because I would definitely want more from you than you would be willing to give me."

He wished me good luck and every happiness that I deserved. But to remember, he's only a phone call away, if it doesn't work out with Rhys.

Saturday. "Hmm…what should I wear, Mr Kitty? I'm meeting up with Kim today. The blue dress, or red? Good choice, Mr Kitty, I thought so too."

Let me have a good look in the mirror. Yes, my hair, okay. My dress, perfect. Although Kim was pregnant, she still looked good, no doubt about that.

When I got to the wine bar, Kim was already there waiting for me. We gave each other a hug and a welcoming smile.

"Don't you look lovely?"

"What this old dress," I replied, knowing that I chose this dress just to upstage her.

She thanked me for meeting up with her. I asked her how her pregnancy was going and how Alex and her kids were doing.

She took out her phone and showed me photos of Mason and Maya.

"They look absolutely adorable."

"I think so too."

She smiled, then tucked her phone away into her handbag. You could see how much Mason looked like her husband.

Kim asked how I was, and that she had heard about me finding my biological dad, Aubrey.

My intent gaze was inquisitive, my eyebrows raised in a silent question. How did she know that I had been in contact with my biological dad?

The way she stared deep into my eyes, she knew what I was thinking. Her eyes pleaded for understanding. She was never going to give Rhys up. Not for me, not even for her husband, and yet here we were, sitting across a table, smiling at each other, as though we were friends.

"Yes, at last, if only my biological mother can be found, wherever the hell she's hiding," I replied.

Then only realised that I had said it out loud, after the look of pity on Kim's face, was more than I could bear.

I ordered a glass of wine, and Kim had orange juice.

She then took a ginger biscuit from her handbag and started to nibble on it.

The whole afternoon was surprisingly pleasant. I really liked Kim. I'm so pleased that Rhys asked us to become friends. I was thinking that she'd fit in so perfectly with the rest of my friends. What do you all think? Although, I knew deep down her true feelings for Rhys.

We carried on chatting for a little while longer, then suddenly Kim's whole demeanour changed.

Without speaking, she went to the bar and ordered me a large glass of red wine.

"Thanks, Kim."

"Don't thank me just yet."

I wondered what the hell she was talking about as she sat down and started to shift uncomfortably in her chair.

She gave me a long, hard stare and said, "I heard that you and Rhys have broken up."

"Really, and where did you hear that from?"

My heart felt like it had stopped.

So, now I'm baffled as to how the conversation suddenly took a nosedive. I was about to deny the fact that she knew every last detail of my non-existent relationship with Rhys.

But she put a finger to my lips, then said, "If you want Rhys back, because if you do, if you're really sure, then tell me now, because I want him back, and I know, that you know, when he comes to me, you'll never get him back."

'What the hell did she just say?'

I was just taken aback by what Kim had just told me, upset at what was being said, emotions crossed my face quickly, and my whole body was shaking with fear. I just stared back at her. I was totally gobsmacked to say the least. My tears mingled with the wine in my glass, a cold feeling suddenly gripped my throat, and strangled the air from my lungs. I continued to sit there, listening, hoping what I was hearing wasn't true.

My chin trembled, and suddenly I cursed and blurted, "What about Alex?"

She looked at me, laughed, and spoke, "What about Alex? I stopped loving him a long time ago. My husband's lies were the most beautiful lies that I have ever heard," she said, sipping on her orange juice, staring at me.

She said that she realised her mistake ages ago, and was ready to give up her husband and move in with Rhys, taking her children, Mason and Maya, with her. And that would teach him for cheating on her, and for all the pain and hurt he caused her over the past five years.

"Nobody deserves misery, but it's my husband's turn now."

"Where's your compassion?"

"Nowhere…can my husband get to it."

Then she went on to say that now she and Rhys were having their own baby, their family would be complete.

Her words caused nothing but rage to boil within me. With a loud roar of anger and tears burning my eyes, I got up and slapped Kim across the face. I know that I shouldn't have done it, as she's pregnant, but I'm not going to let her take Rhys from me. No way, no flipping way.

After a hard slap across the face, I half expected her to get up and walk away, or to at least hit me back.

But no, she sat there, and continued on, as if what just happened—never did. Her cheek was all red, as tears tumbled down, and her smile was gone. I slightly turned my head to see my reflection in a mirror on the wall.

My mascara ran in muddy little rivulets down my cheeks, and my eyes were as red as a three-day drunk.

We're both visibly upset by now, but Kim was determined to carry on with her story.

She went on to say that, when Maya was only two or three months old, she decided to leave her husband, but changed her mind. But now, she had realised her mistake, and was ready to give up Alex, and move in with Rhys and take her children with her. Something she said already, so why repeat that fact?

She just kept repeating every word, as though it was rehearsed.

After just having an emotional conversation with Kim, I decided that I loved Rhys. And no matter what, I wasn't going to let her take him from me.

So, I apologised to Kim for slapping her in the face, because I knew if I didn't, she'll probably make up some sob story to Rhys.

She accepted my apology, hugged me and said that she was really sorry. I covered my face with my hands and cried.

We both cried. What the hell, we both wanted Rhys. I knew deep in my heart that Rhys would choose her any day over me.

I left her at the wine bar, just staring at me. She just smiled and waved, with her effort earning a blank stare from me, as all I could think about, at that precise time, was hearing those three words come out of Rhys' mouth, *I choose Kim.*

But I had to go straight to Rhys' house, it was now, or never, to declare my love to him, before Kim, that bitch did.

Although the heavy rain was holding off, there was a feeling it was only a matter of time, before the full fury hit. I hailed a taxi from outside of the wine bar. I sat quietly in the back of the cab, the driver made light conversation.

"I'm not joking, I'm talking sense," he said.

But I had no clue what he was talking about. All I could concentrate on was what to say to Rhys, as I heard the echo of my heart beating faster and faster.

The rain began, light at first, then drummed wildly on the roof of the taxi.

10 minutes later, the cab pulled up opposite Rhys' house. I opened the cab door and stepped straight into a massive puddle of swirling water, right over my high heels.

I took a deep breath, composed myself, and pressed the doorbell of his house.

Rhys

It's been one week since I spoke with Kim, and I just happened to see Kyla with my ex-wife. I haven't spoken to Kyla about her betrayal. I've had other priorities to deal with, like getting Tianna back.

Kim promised to help me. I've no idea what she was planning.

Every day, I checked my phone for that smiley face she promised me.

Every morning and every evening, I was sending Tianna a text or giving her a call. But to date, she has declined all of my calls.

My last hope was Kim and her plan to help me. If I did manage to win her heart back, I'd never let her go.

Kim was one of the most important women in my life. Our friendship, that's what it is, just two friends, whose feelings linger.

She had given me her blessing to give Tianna all the love that I held for her. If that's what it's going to take to show Tianna that it's she who I want to be with, then that's what I'd had to do.

I was just about to go into the kitchen, and there it was, the smiley face text from Kim that she had promised me.

Every muscle of my face was now quivering with nervous excitement. My eyes, in which the fire of life had seemed extinguished, now flashed with a brilliant light.

I gave Kim a quick call to say thanks. She told me not to waste time speaking to her, and she was one hundred per cent sure, Tianna was on her way over to my house.

I thanked Kim for whatever she had done. She said to make sure, now Tianna's back in my life, to keep hold of her.

"Rhys, you know what this means, our friendship as we know it, it's truly over. You do know that right?"

"I know, Kim."

"Love you, take care of yourself, and I'll just keep in touch, to let you know when I've had our baby."

"Kim, I will always love you, even if it's just one per cent," I joked, even though I meant every word.

We both laughed. Kim hung up before I had the chance to end the call.

Just as the call ended, the doorbell rang, and there she was—Tianna, on my doorstep.

Her hair fell softly around her face as she gazed up at me with lips parted. Her face was flushed.

Her eyes were red from crying, she held her arms out, lifted her lips to my ear, and through tears whispered, "Hold me tight, never let me go."

I closed my eyes and did as she asked. I held her tight with the intention of never letting her go again.

She wrapped both her arms around my shoulders and kissed me. I responded to her kiss, savouring the sweet taste and softness of her warm lips.

"Rhys, I love you so much. I'm so sorry that I left you, but I'm back now, if you'll have me," she said with a smile in her eyes.

I told Tianna how much I loved her, and nothing, or no one, would ever come between us again.

She looked at me with her beautiful blue eyes and asked, "What about Kim? I know she loves you and wants you back."

I smiled at her and reassured her that not even Kim would come between us. Tianna asked me to make that promise, that no one, absolutely no one, including Kim, would destroy what love we have for each other.

So, I went down on one knee, made that promise, and asked Tianna to marry me. She looked down at me, covered her face with her hands and cried. We were both a little emotional at the time.

A few minutes later, she nodded and said, "Yes."

Tianna flung herself into my arms, pulling my face down to spread kisses across my face. We kissed, our bodies pressed together, our arms around each other.

Now that I had the love of my life back in my arms, I needed to be honest with her.

We started walking along the hallway, towards the living room. She slipped her hand through my extended elbow and smiled up at me.

Pulling out a chair, Tianna's movement gave me a peek of the swells of her breasts as she bent.

She sat down, and I took her hand in mine. I needed to be completely honest with her, no matter the outcome.

"Tianna, you've already said yes to marry me, but I want to confess something to you. Don't get mad or angry…just listen, because I have never lied to you, and I'm not about to start now."

I told Tianna what Kim had done to get her to come back to me. She wasn't angry or mad with either Kim or me, but said how she felt terrible now, for slapping Kim in the face, very hard.

At first, being so honest silenced her.

"At least, you're being honest about it, babe," she said, staring me in the eyes.

"Kim is a wonderful friend to you, Rhys, if she was willing to go as far as she did, to convince me she wanted you back, and it worked. I really believed her. But what about her husband, when he finds out what she did, won't he be angry with her?"

"That's one thing about Kim; she always discusses anything that concerns me with her husband. You know Alex welcomes any plan, just so he can get rid of me. Once he heard what she was planning to do, he was up for it. That's how badly he wants me away from his wife."

So, we both laughed.

"One more thing, Tianna, Kim has promised to only stay in contact with the both of us because of the baby."

Tianna smiled and said that everything would now be okay and that she understood. We would have to be in contact with Kim and Alex because of the baby.

"So, babe, where were we in our relationship, can you remember? Because I've missed holding you so close to me."

"Rhys, you are my heartbeat."

Tianna held my hand, and we went up the stairs to my bedroom.

"Oh, Rhys," she kept calling my name, as I kissed her softly on her neck.

"Close your eyes, I'm going to take you on a ride of your life," I whispered softly, breathing in her sweet scent.

She giggled nervously as my warm fingers worked at the buttons on her top. Tianna blushed and laughed.

"So, babe, this was your plan all along, to get me up to your bedroom, and have your way with me," she said, laughing.

Tianna

Rhys held me in his arms. "Close your eyes," he whispered softly.

He began to kiss me on my neck, slowly moving to my lips.

Rhys tugged at my lips, then gently bit me. My heart rate started to elevate, and my pulse was pounding. My body was tingling from his tease as he undressed me.

He pressed his lips softly against mine, then touched my lips with his tongue. Rhys just loved to kiss with his tongue, and slowly put his tongue into my mouth.

"Oh, Rhys…oh, Rhys," I kept whispering his name.

He told me to relax and to enjoy the pleasure he was about to give me.

A burst of need washed over me as my body responded to his scent. His gaze was trained on me with an intensity that made my body feel warm from the inside out.

My heart sang as I realised I hadn't lost him after all, my body echoed the desire on his face.

Rhys picked me up, carried me to his king-size bed, which had white silk sheets. He gently put me down onto his bed and slowly undressed me.

His hands moved over my body possessively. The feel of his warm skin against mine, Rhys' scent and touch overwhelmed me, while his hot kisses set fire to a desire stronger than any I've ever experienced. I closed my eyes at the sensation of his lips, hot mouth, and rough stubble that teased my sensitive skin.

Rhys' lips teased mine. His mouth opened so I could taste him once more. Lip to lip, deep kissing for five minutes.

I began to lick my lips in anticipation of what was to come next. I slipped my arms around his neck and snuggled against his warm chest, as he started to caress my breasts with his tongue. Then he started sucking my nipples, moving slowly to my stomach, my inner thighs. Then, wow, oh, Rhys, the pleasure that filled my body was out of this world.

He licked and sucked my clit, until I come in his mouth. I screamed out, then started to laugh. He whispered in my ear that was his love, which he was giving to me funny?

He put his arms around my waist and rolled us, so I was on top of him.

"Tianna, tease me until I am begging for it."

Oh God, did I give him all of my love? He moved the hair from my face, so he could get a good look at my facial expression.

I position myself on him, moving my hips in sync with him. Oh my God. I kept calling his name.

In fact, I screamed his name, to which he replied, "I know my own name, babe," then giggled, and said, "Tianna, you turn me on, my dick is so hard."

Rhys told me how he loved the way I make love to him.

He held me around my waist, then passionately ran his fingers against my back. He just stared and listened as my body thrummed with desire for him.

Then whispered softly in my ear, "I love it when you're on top."

Rhys, oh my God, he said that he liked it when I took control, and I knew where and how to touch his body.

He wasn't finished with the love-making just yet. He rolled us again and showed me all that I had missed when we were apart.

He eased into me, throbbing, going in deep. Oh God, I loved it when he first slid into me.

"Harder, oh God, Rhys, don't stop. fuck me hard," I whispered in his ear, my heartbeat doubled, as a wave of passion surged over me.

After a night of passionate love-making, we held each other tight for most of the night.

He kept staring at me, with those beautiful green eyes, while gently stroking my stomach, then he kissed me on my neck.

He eventually said that we had better get some sleep before going to the barbecue tomorrow. I completely forgot about that.

Sunday morning, I glanced over to where Rhys should be, but there was no sight of him, just an empty bed space.

His bedroom door suddenly swung open as he held two grey coffee cups in his hands.

"Morning, beautiful," he said, with a smile on his face.

"You're not so bad yourself," I replied, stretching my arm and yawning, as I leaned forward to take the cup of coffee from his hand.

"I guess we'd better get up and get ready for the barbecue, but I'd have to pop by my house to get ready, and feed Mr Kitty," I said, still yawning.

On the way to my house, I told Rhys all about meeting up with my dad, Aubrey, and that he'd invited me to meet the rest of his family.

Rhys was so happy for me. So, I thought I would invite him along as well, to meet up with my brothers and sister.

I was enjoying just being with Rhys, as we were driving to Renee and Drake's house, when I realised that we were heading in the wrong direction.

"Where are we going, babe? Haven't you passed their road, two blocks away?" I asked, turning my head as he carried on driving in the wrong direction.

"If we hurry, we'll just make it in time, before they close," Rhys said.

Before I had a chance to respond, I noticed that we had parked outside a very expensive jewellery shop.

"I can't introduce you as my very beautiful fiancé without an engagement ring. That wouldn't be right," he said.

My heart fluttered at his words, and I grew excited about him wanting everyone to know that we'd become engaged.

Rhys, oops, my fiancé told me to choose whichever engagement ring I liked. So, I chose a cushion-cut halo style diamond ring, with an eye-watering price tag.

He looked at me, smiled and said, "Tianna, you deserve the best of everything."

I lifted my head and gazed up into his eyes. This time, my heart and stomach both fluttered. A smile flickered across his face and turned into a laugh.

"Do you really think that we could turn up at the barbecue and I introduce you as my fiancé with no ring? No way, my man Drake would seriously run me out of town," he said, laughing.

We arrived at the barbecue, half an hour late, holding hands. All loved up.

Okay, so everyone was staring at us. We could tell by their stares that they were all expecting big news.

Melani was rubbing her baby bump, looking at me very suspiciously.

I shook my head, "No, I'm not pregnant, we're engaged."

"Oh my God, girlfriend," said all the girls.

Renee stepped forward, kissed me on my cheek, hugged me and said, "Tianna, I'm so pleased for you."

"About time, my man, what took you so long?" Drake said and fist bumped Rhys.

The rest of the guys shook Rhys' hand, and someone yelled at him, "Welcome to hell. Only messing, bro."

The guys took Rhys to one side to tell him the wife jokes, but having been married before, he'd probably heard them all.

My girlfriends all wanted to have a look at my very expensive engagement ring.

"Oh, wow," they all said.

Kayleigh her eyes started to water because she knew the hefty price tag.

Nyomi, holding my hand and staring at my ring, said, "Rhys must love you, girl, that ring is, what, nearly four thousand pounds, easy."

All the girls wanted to know, when Rhys and I had made up, and did we have making up sex, and it was breathtaking. I couldn't help but laugh.

"I'm so happy right now, you have no idea," I said, smiling down at my engagement ring.

Hakeem made the rum punch and brought over a pitcher, some barbecue prawns, and jerk chicken with mac and cheese.

Renee and Drake's barbecue suddenly turned into Rhys and mine's engagement party.

How fitting. Drakes had a very, hmm, what should I say, colourful playlist, this song started to play, Sativa by Jhene Aiko ft Rae Sremmurd. Okay, so everyone got up and started dancing. We girls stripped off to our bras and knickers, except for Melani, who was pregnant, and we went into the hot tub.

Oh boy, what an afternoon we were having. We drank champagne, eating fresh, sweet, ever so sweet strawberries, and cashew nuts, silly me, fresh cream.

Oh, the champagne was fizzy, and went straight up my nose, causing me to sneeze, then giggle uncontrollably. I can't remember who brought us another bottle over, the discreet popping noise, as the bottle opened, then a cracking fizzing sound.

Yeah, we all screamed. Because by now, we girls were totally out of it, splashing around in the hot tub, being silly, totally silly, except Melani.

She looked really uncomfortable, with her baby bump as she shifted side to side on her chair.

She sat on an oversized armchair—which was especially brought outside for her—curling her legs beneath her, as she drank a glass of fresh lemonade. Melani watched on as we made fools of ourselves in the hot tub, splashing water at each other.

Then we played pass the bottle, a game where you have to pass the bottle without using your hands.

I shouted over at her, "Melani, why don't you come and join us?"

She raised the glass of lemonade to her lips, laughed, then replied, "As a matter of fact, I'm enjoying just sitting here, watching you make fools of yourselves."

I have no idea what was going on, but all the guys, yes, all the guys stripped to their boxers and started singing You by Lloyd ft Lil Wayne.

You should have seen my fiancé, Rhys. Oh yes, he was singing his heart out to me. Although he had already proposed to me, he wanted to do something more fitting and proposed again, but with the help of his friends' singing.

We girls definitely had too much to drink, because we responded by dancing to U My Everything, by Sexyy Red ft Drake. Well, except for Melani, as she was getting moody. No, sorry…tired.

Okay, so now, I'm in the party mood. Then, Promise by Ciara started to play. I had to give my fiancé a dance to remember. Oh boy, then all the girls joined in. What a night, oh boy.

The atmosphere was just buzzing, it started to get dark, then the garden lights magically turned on by themselves. Well, that's what it appeared to do, but in reality, Renee turned the lights on.

All of us girls were all loved up with our men. Rhys and I, what can I say? The love that we had from this day forward would not be broken. I promise you that.

Rhys and I decided to sing a duet. This was our favourite song, but first let me take you back a few months, to the day when Rhys and I first met, and that first dance we had. Oh boy, that first dance. Here we go. This was how the magic first started.

Remember Renee and Drake's wedding, when Rhys finally came back to me, and we started to dance. Well, let me tell you that the first slow dance we had was to Slow Down by Skip Marley and H.E.R.

The way he held me in his arms, and with this song playing, our bodies just swaying in sync to the music. I knew from that moment, I wanted him in my life forever.

If you listen to the lyrics of this song, it was totally appropriate for us both at that precise moment in time.

When we sang our duet at the barbecue, all eyes were on us. Everyone, you should have seen our friends; they were all basically in tears. They all felt the love between Rhys and me. One hundred per cent pure love.

Melani, being pregnant, was feeling tired, so her husband, Terrell, decided to take her home.

As for the rest of us, we partied into the early hours of the morning. I thanked Renee and Drake for such a wonderful evening. It was the best barbecue/engagement party ever.

Renee hugged and kissed me and whispered, "Hold onto him with both arms, girlfriend."

"I intend on holding onto him, girlfriend," I replied, as my eyes welled up with tears, happy tears.

Renee smiled as Rhys' strong arms slipped around my waist, drawing me back against his muscular body.

"Ready, babe?" he asked, as I waved goodnight to Drake.

The night air became chilly on my bare shoulders as I snuggled into Rhys' arms, and we walked the short distance to his parked car.

At six in the morning, it was a little bit dark. I turned and looked to see my future husband, Rhys. He was just staring at me.

"Morning, beautiful," he whispered, stroking my naked body.

"Morning, my handsome fiancé," I replied, then kissed him on his lips.

As I got out of bed, he pulled me back to bed, and we made love several times that morning.

I listened to the rain as it beat on the window. I eventually got out of bed. As I looked through the window, it was raining sideways. I noticed a rainbow. The sun struggled to pierce through the dark clouds above, while the leaves on the trees seemed to engage in a whimsical dance, swaying playfully in the breeze.

"Babe, come and have a look. Come and see the rainbow in the sky."

We looked through the window and saw the beautiful rainbow in the sky.

Rhys turned and gave me a tight hug and said, "Seeing a rainbow is good luck. This will be a new chapter in our lives—for both of us."

Aubrey

My name is Aubrey Campbell. I am Tianna's biological dad. I've invited her and Renee to my house for dinner and to meet the rest of her family.

Tianna has since let me know that she had rekindled her relationship with her boyfriend, Rhys, and she would be bringing him to dinner instead of Renee. I told her that Renee is more than welcome to come along, as well.

She asked if it was okay, if Renee came along with her husband, Drake? I told Tianna, the more the merrier.

We decided to all meet up on Saturday.

I'd like to tell you a little bit about myself and my relationship with Tianna's mum, Jessica.

About 30 odd years ago, I can't seem to remember how many years ago now. The company that I'd worked for were doing renovation on a house in Muswell Hill, north London. I'm from Camberwell in south London. Anyway, the lady of the house was Jessica. My boss always spoke to her about what work she wanted to do on the house. I just assumed she never had a husband, only a couple of children, Sam and Sabrina.

She always offered us workmen cups of tea and biscuits.

She would often have a little chat with us when we took our tea break.

After several days into the renovations, my workmate phoned in sick, so I went to Jessica's house that day, on my own.

That's when our relationship started to blossom. I just took the liberty of asking her out for a meal, which she said yes to, after she initially raised her eyebrows, and then laughed.

That was it. I was hooked on her, then found out a few months later that there was actually a Mr Stewart, when he decided to come home early from work one afternoon.

That was a bloody shock, I can tell you. He was standing there, as I and his misses were kissing in the kitchen.

My warm hands caressed their way up her back and around to cradle her tiny breast. Jessica snuggled closer to me, delighting in the way my hands gently caressed her, sending tingling sensations over her body.

While gazing into my eyes, she whispered softly, "Oh, Aubrey, your masculine smell, the way your big hands caress me."

Her husband's jaw dropped to the kitchen floor, his face flamed, and his anger burned through him.

Jessica pulled away from me, insisting that I had taken advantage of her kindness.

The look of sheer fury on her husband's face replaced her shocked look with fear. Mr Stewart lunged forward. I assumed he wanted to grab his wife from my grasp, even though she had removed her arms from around my waist.

Fear and panic bubble within her when her husband told me to take my filthy black hands off his wife.

Maybe it was anger that prompted him to make the remarks.

He never apologised, only cursed some more, as her embarrassment quickly turned to anger.

Like I said, it was about 30 years ago.

To my surprise, Jessica didn't want to end the affair. So, we kept it a secret for nearly four more years.

At the time I wasn't married, or in a relationship, so she was always at my flat.

She often told me she was going to leave her husband, Matthew, but changed her mind when she discovered that she was pregnant again.

I did ask Jessica if there was a chance that the baby could be mine, but she convinced me it was impossible, because she was very careful when we had sex.

Anyway, that was that, the end of the discussion, on whether the baby could be mine or not.

We carried on seeing each other, all through her pregnancy. She didn't want our relationship to end because of the baby she was having.

I recall one morning, the early winter wind dried the tears on my face and made my cheeks stiff.

Jessica had a friend phone me to let me know she had the baby. Her friend paused for quite some time. I asked if Jessica and the baby were okay. The friend sounded a bit gobsmacked and hesitated before answering.

She told me there was panic and confusion with Jessica and her husband because the baby girl she just had was of mixed-race, and not white.

That's when I realised the baby was mine.

Jessica stopped all contact with me. I couldn't exactly turn up at her house now. Could I?

I waited for weeks, then months, to hear from Jessica, but she never got in contact with me.

About seven months later, I received a letter from Jessica, explaining how sorry she was about the whole situation. She never meant to shut me out from the discussion about having our baby adopted.

After the shock, I was angry and too upset to think straight. I slammed my hands into the living room glass door. I read the letter several more times, then tore it into tiny pieces, with droplets of blood dripping from my wound.

She went on to explain that her husband was totally horrified when he saw the colour of the baby's skin, dark, not white. He demanded, there and then, to get rid of the kid, or else he'll take their two children, Sam and Sabrina, the house and everything that she had and leave her penniless like she deserved.

They left the baby at the hospital that night, without a second thought.

This is a tragic story, no doubt, a heart-wrenching decision, made by the woman whom I once loved.

The adoption agency found Tianna a new family. I heard that they were wonderful parents to my daughter.

Believe me, I tried for years to get any information that I could to find my daughter, but all inquiries led to a dead end.

Eventually, I had to give up looking. I had no clue where to look, no information that I could give anyone about her whereabouts.

The hospital where Tianna was born denied me any information because I wasn't Jessica's husband.

A few months later, I met Martha, now my wife. She's absolutely a wonderful woman. We had four children, three boys, Aubrey JR, Xavier and Marcel.

Then our daughter. She's the youngest. Her name is Larah.

And finally, after 30 years, I'd found my daughter Tianna. We were a very close family, and everyone is looking forward to welcoming Tianna and her fiancé, Rhys, into our family.

As for her birth mother, Jessica, some years later, I passed by her house, and saw a sold sign in the front garden. So, I have absolutely no knowledge of her whereabouts. That was until recently, when Jessica posted photos of herself at work, outside a nightclub called Dare to Dance, on social media.

Since seeing Jessica on social media, I have learned quite a lot about her.

She had another baby with her husband, Mathew, after having Tianna.

What really shocked me, she only lived two miles away from her daughter, Tianna. I think that their paths must have crossed somewhere, only two miles, what are the chances of that?

I don't have the heart to tell Tianna, not the first time that she was introduced to my wife and her siblings.

But if the conversation comes up, I won't lie to her. It's never a good idea to start a relationship with someone special with a lie.

Rhys

It's a horrible Monday morning. The weather, that is. Nothing was horrible about waking up next to my fiancée, Tianna.

She showed me a rainbow in the sky. We stood there for quite some time staring at it.

The clouds suddenly got dark, and the wind was strong, blowing all the dustbins into the street. But hey, we were engaged. There's no better feeling than that.

Except when I eventually got to work. I was going to call my PA, Kyla, into my office. No, I haven't forgotten to ask her about her friendship with my ex-wife, whom I'd served divorce papers on.

I woke early the next morning and dressed in a navy-blue suit, chosen by my fiancée.

I headed to the office before Kyla, going over in my head exactly what words to say.

I had a few things to do at the office, so I thought I would head there around 7:30.

An hour or so later, from the corner of my eyes, I spotted that Sue was walking along the corridor, holding two cups of tea, heading back to her desk.

"Morning, Sue. When you see Kyla, have her come to my office, please."

Sue eventually gave my message to Kyla, who came to my office, soaking wet, with her coat and umbrella, dripping all over my clean office floor.

"Close the door, Kyla." My expression was sour as hell.

She was all smiles at first, and soon realised that something was very wrong.

So now she was looking at me, as though I'd done something wrong. You know those looks some women give. She crossed her legs, then her arms, and gave me a frown. She then raised her eyebrows. I mean, who exactly was in charge here, me or Kyla?

She opened her mouth and started to speak, "Sue told me you wanted to see me."

A deep furrow ran across my forehead, my dark eyes were pools of emotions. I know this because Kyla jerked her head up after staring at something on the floor and then burst out laughing.

"Yes, Kyla, we need to talk," I said, ignoring her laughter.

I began by asking her how she knew my ex-wife Leah, and why she was giving her all the gossip about my relationship.

"Why would you do that, Kyla?" I asked her, staring directly into her big brown eyes.

She cleared her throat, rolled her eyes and bit her fingernails.

Her thoughts turned dark as her mind wandered over my face and came back to my eyes. At first, she denied knowing Leah, but had to confess when I told her that I'd seen them together.

Her excuse was that, at first, she had no idea that Leah was my ex-wife, until Leah began talking about Kim and then Tianna. So she filled her in on the missing pieces about my relationships.

Some things she made up, and some she just exaggerated. I guess that's what made Leah act so crazy.

"Why would you do that, Kyla?"

She looked up at the ceiling, staring at a spider, and then at the floor, trying to find some lame excuse.

Kyla started cursing and shouting. "Blame your snobby, nosy ex-girlfriend, Kim."

My brows shot up in surprise, and my gaze hardened. I was staring at her, she was staring back at me. Now sitting silent, she glanced up at me from under her brows. I was totally lost for words as to the reason Kyla has given. I think I knew what she was talking about.

For those of you who don't know, to cut a long story short, Kim's husband, Alex, found out he has a mixed-race half-brother, called Casey, because his dad had an affair.

Kim, Alex and I met up with him. I asked Kyla to tag along with me to meet Casey's family.

Kim mistook Kyla for my new girlfriend. God only knows why, Kim would think that. Anyway, they both, what should I say, were acting like crazy, or jealous women that day. But Kyla was only messing with Kim, pretending to be my new girlfriend, because Kim looked down her nose at Kyla, causing tension between them.

So, what did Kyla do to teach Kim a lesson? Boy, oh boy, Kyla went and spilt red wine all over Kim's £950.00 Prada shoes.

Kim insulted Kyla, and that's the reason for Kyla spilling the beans, or so she claimed.

All this grief, over Prada shoes? It's a lot of money for a pair of shoes, but I understand that. Alex bought Kim a new pair.

Anyway, Kyla started to give me a bit of attitude. Sorry, but I had to dismiss her on the spot. But good things come to those who wait.

My loyal employee, Sue, had been with the company for over 25 years, when Leah's dad owned it. I promoted her to be my personal assistant instead of Kyla.

Sue was over the moon when I told her the good news.

She gave me a hug and said, "Rhys, if only I were 10 years younger, you'd be my fiancé." Then she giggled.

As she walked towards my office door, she turned around, winked at me, and blushed, closing the door behind her.

Sabrina

I phoned my sister, well, half-sister, Tianna, this afternoon. She was ecstatic over the phone, to be more precise.

"I've found my biological dad," she kept saying, over and over.

I'm really pleased for her. Really, I am. Now she could finally get to know, well, her dad at least. As for our mum, I was going to try and have a word to get mum to finally meet up with the daughter she gave away, many years ago.

My dad, I mean our dad, has early-stage Alzheimer's; he was diagnosed a few months ago. I think it would be nice for Tianna to meet our dad as well, as he was a wonderful husband and dad, before, well, you know, he had no memory of us all. What do you think? Good idea, yeah, I think so. What harm will it do?

Two days later, I asked Tianna. What did she think of the idea? She's up for it as well. The arrangements were made. I did speak to our mum after a few chosen words were spoken. Eventually, she and my dad, bless him, agreed to meet up with Tianna and her fiancé, Rhys. Well, after they have met with Tianna's dad, Aubrey, first.

Melani

Early this morning, I gave birth to our daughter. My husband, Terrell, was so emotional to say the least when he was asked if he wanted to cut the umbilical cord.

We haven't decided on a name for our daughter yet. But our Godparents, you guessed, it had to be Renee and Drake, and, of course, Tianna and her fiancé, Rhys. By the way, I've heard that they had set a wedding date, but not to spoil it for the happy couple. I'd let them make the announcement.

Oh, by the way, isn't it fantastic news that my good friend was finally going to have the family she so craved all these years?

You know what I mean. Clive and Michelle were her adoptive parents, but what she truly longed for were her biological roots. She was eager to uncover her origins, learn about her birth mother, and understand the reasons behind her adoption. And then there's her dad, Aubrey. He seemed nice, according to Renee.

Anyway, I'd let you get on and read Tianna's story.

Tianna

Today's the day that I meet my family. Well, on my dad's side. I looked through the window, drinking a cup of coffee that my fiancé made. Oh wow, did you hear what I just said? Let me say it again, because it sounded so nice, when said out loud…my fiancé.

We were just waiting for Renee and Drake to arrive before we head off to my dad's house. Ahh, here they were.

Hmm, Drake changed his car to a Mercedes. How lovely! Oh, silly me, a newer model.

Anyway, we decided to all travel in the same car together, after a toss of a coin. Okay, so Rhys won the toss because he cheated.

It was between Drake's Mercedes or Rhys' Audi A8; a very expensive and very stylish car, I may add.

Renee chatted away, while I just listened, as I laughed nervously at one of her many jokes.

She leaned over and whispered, "It's okay to be nervous, babe." Then, she held my hand tightly.

We arrived at my dad's house at the same time as one of his sons, Xavier, my half-brother and his girlfriend.

I must say, they had a beautiful, end-of-terrace four-bed house, with a sunny south-westerly garden.

The house opened into two large porches/entrance halls, which led through into a cosy reception room to the front. Then, a dining room, leading to the modern kitchen. Hmm, very impressive.

My dad sure knew how to remodel a perfect house.

My dad, Aubrey, did the honours of introducing us to my family; first to his wife, Martha, who stood behind him in the doorway.

She was a little different to what I had imagined she'd look like, but still very attractive nevertheless.

Then my three brothers, Aubrey Jr, his wife and son; Marcel and his girlfriend; Xavier and his girlfriend, who we first met at the street door.

Then last, but not least, my half-sister, Larah. She's only 18, at university, studying to become a midwife. She had a friend with her, Marlee, whom she met at university.

Martha gave me a beautiful bouquet of roses, which I found touching. She embraced me, and I began to cry.

This was my family: my biological dad, his wife, and my half-siblings. Yet, they were also strangers.

Rhys took the bottle of wine from my grasp—as I almost dropped it, forgetting that I was holding it—and gave it to my dad.

Then he put his arms around my waist, as we all walked down the hallway, passing family photos on the wall.

I must say, what a lovely family they were to welcome me, Rhys and my friends, Renee and Drake, into their beautiful home.

The day was so perfect. I couldn't have asked for more. I just sat there, staring at Aubrey's family, thinking about something else, but my mind kept coming back to the same thing.

Over the years, I collected questions, but as I sat there, staring at them, they smiled at me. If I am being honest, it made me feel uncomfortable to a degree.

There were only two questions I wanted answered: Why did you leave me, and why didn't you look for me?

Maybe those questions were answered when I first met my dad, yet I can't seem to remember. I had wondered if guilt and regret might overwhelm Aubrey; if I shared my thoughts, would he break down in tears.

Oh, shit, Tianna love, what have I done? The moment, followed by an overwhelming feeling of sadness for him.

Renee, being my friend for the best part of eight years, could sense that complex array of emotions that ran through my mind. She glanced over at me, and smiled that reassuring smile she always gave when she knew how sad I was and how I was feeling on the inside.

She handed me a tissue to dry my eyes and made a funny face, trying to cheer me up. But I'm not sad, not one bit, far from it. My dad spoke just a little bit more about my birth mum.

Not wanting to spoil the evening, we decided to catch up on our own, in a couple of days. He promised to go into more details, and answer any questions that I may have. Oh gosh, meeting everyone and having such a lovely day, silly me, I forgot to ask, one of the most important questions of all.

"What's my birth mother's name?"

I think that I asked already, but I needed to hear it once again.

Rhys

It's been a few days since Tianna and I met her family on her dad's side.

At the moment, she was a bit distraught. She met up with her dad, Aubrey. We all had such a lovely day, meeting all her family.

Fuck, what can I say? Boom, what a shock? Tianna's world came crashing down on her like a ton of displaced bricks.

That's when her whole world just started to crumble and fall apart like a broken biscuit.

Tianna's dad, Aubrey, told her a little bit about her mum, like how they first met, then he said, "Tianna, sweetheart, let me tell you your mother's name. Jessica, her name is Jessica Ann Stewart, and her husband is called Mathew Stewart."

Okay, so no alarm bells rang at that moment. Tianna was finally pleased to know her birth mother's true identity.

So now for boom, boom. Tianna was in a mess over what her dad told her about her mum.

She was too distraught to speak. She nearly bit through her bottom lip. None of this made any sense, yet it had to be true for her to be this upset.

It was a sad truth that Tianna had come face-to-face with her mother Jessica at Dare to Dance, the nightclub where her mum worked for many years, not knowing she was, in fact, her biological mother.

Aubrey happened to show Tianna some photos of Jessica, outside of the nightclub where she so happened to work. It's the nightclub where Tianna and all her friends go to do pole dancing. It was something Tianna loved doing.

Who can forget the pole dance she gave me?

Sorry, I've gone off the story a bit, how rude of me, when my fiancée was so distraught. Where was I? Oh yes. So, Aubrey showed Tianna some photos of Jessica, who happened to be the one and only Jess, the nightclub manager, who doesn't like Tianna, for some odd reason.

Can you imagine how she felt, knowing that her birth mother was a stone's throw away from her, for all those years?

As well as just living 2.6 miles away from each other. What the hell?

This story that I'm telling you did not end there. You're not going to believe me, what do they say, bad news comes in threes, or something like that.

We had just announced the date for our wedding, this autumn, 10 September 2022. Tianna, being upset as she was, said nothing would change that date. However, the bad news just kept coming, thick and fast.

How much more could my beautiful fiancée take? This is where I shall end, what I'm telling you, because as much as I would like to tell you, this is my fiancée, Tianna's story to tell.

Sabrina

I received a phone call from Rhys, my half-sister's fiancé. Well, he was fuming to say the least.

It turned out that Tianna and our mother were no strangers to each other.

From what I understood, Tianna had been going to the nightclub with her friends for about four years, where our mother worked.

And get this, our mum took an instant dislike to Tianna. This day couldn't get any worse.

So, what now? Does Tianna still want to come and meet with Mum and the rest of the family? Or do we just call it quits? What do you suggest, cos I don't bloody know, flipping hell.

Our mum had to sit down and explain to my brothers, Sam and Stevie, who Tianna was.

Stevie got very emotional and refused to speak with our mum. As for Sam, he called our mum a fucking whore, who kept her dirty little secret hidden for years. Both my brothers have cried, more than enough tears, to fill a bathtub.

And the day just gets worse. Now, Mum started crying. Dad, well, he kept asking Mum why she was crying.

He can't help it; he forgot that he'd already asked.

As for me, I'm just sad that it all came to this.

Just who exactly would Tianna be meeting if she did come to our house?

Mum already kind of knew that Sam and Stevie don't want anything to do with Tianna.

"She's not our fucking sister," is what they both said, shouting at the top of their lungs.

Well, Stevie shouted, while Sam punched a hole in the kitchen wall.

Then there's my dad, bless him, he'll forget who she was as soon as she'd introduced to him.

My husband, Micheal, suggested that we invite Tianna and Rhys to our house for dinner instead, to give my brothers a chance to cool down. So that's what I've suggested.

I gathered from Rhys that they have set a wedding date, in a few weeks' time. Can you imagine the atmosphere at that wedding? Well, if we'd all be invited, and actually would all go? As for Sam and Stevie, hell would have to freeze over before they show their faces at our half-sister's wedding, whom they knew absolutely nothing about.

And unfortunately, that's the sad, damn truth, if ever there was one.

Tianna

My fiancé has filled you in on what has been happening over the past few days. The whole situation has got to me, not wanting to get out of bed. I lay there for two days, too emotional to contemplate what life had thrown my way. I hadn't so much as taken a taste of Rhys' home-made, mouth-watering chicken soup, which sat uneaten on the bedside cabinet, until it went cold.

Rhys sat next to me. I leaned forward, burying my head against his chest, wiping my tears, deep in turmoil.

Darkness lingered at the edge of my mind, but refused to take me.

My hands dropped from my eyes to reveal a monster, my mother Jessica, from a nightmare framed against the light, coming from the bedroom.

But like they say, life goes on. I'm so glad that Rhys was here with me, holding my hand. He's been a huge rock for me to lean on. I heard from my sister a few days later, after having a complete meltdown.

Sabrina has been honest and filled me in on the current situation, on her brothers, not wanting anything to do with me, at the moment.

Our mum, Jessica, agreed to meet me when we all go to Sabrina's house for dinner. I'm not sure how I feel at the moment, but I am ready to face whatever misery was heading my way.

The day arrived for my sister, Sabrina's dinner. So, I made the effect, and got out of bed, had a shower, did my makeup, and brushed my hair into a pumped-up curly ponytail.

Rhys sat beside me, resting the cup of coffee in his hand on the dresser.

"You look beautiful, babe. Don't worry, everything will work out fine, you'll see," he whispered softly, then kissed me on my forehead.

My worry of being accepted by my mother faded with his comforting words.

After a quick stop, to buy a bottle of wine, and some flowers, we made the hour-long journey to Sabrina's house. I hesitated then exited the car, pausing at the street door for an instant, as if struggling with myself. I glanced back at Rhys, he smiled at me, and then the street door opened.

Sabrina gave us a warm, welcoming smile, then her husband came darting down the hallway, also smiling, then stared at the bottle of wine in Rhys' hand.

We went through to the living room, and there was Jessica. She sat next to her husband, smiling, but I could tell she was a bag of nerves, like me. I sat down on a brown leather sofa with large cream cushions and looked around the room, using only my eyes. Then slowly, I leaned back into the sofa, staring at our mum.

The day was a pleasant one. Jessica actually apologised for being very rude and not friendly to me at the nightclub.

"Had I known that you were my daughter—" she started to say, but cut her conversation short, as she gazed up at me, chewing her lips.

Sabrina went and sat next to her mum, handing her a handful of tissues, as the tears rolled down her rosy cheeks.

"Don't cry, Mum, you didn't know she was your daughter," Sabrina said, now wiping her tears.

Some time had passed. I counted the seconds in tense silence, waiting for someone to speak.

Well Mathew, Jessica's husband, kept asking who the hell me and Rhys were and why did we make his wife cry. Then he forgot who Jessica was, and wanted a cup of tea.

We sipped our glass of wine in silence, for a few minutes, and I decided to ask Jessica that question, which had haunted me ever since I found out she was, in fact, my mother.

I did ask her why she had taken an instant dislike to me at the club where she work.

She told me that she hadn't the foggiest idea, but would like to make amends, if I would let her.

So, after a few more glasses of wine, we got chatting, and she explained the reason that she had to give me up for adoption.

Her husband, Mathew, although he was at the house, he doesn't remember quite a lot of things, to be honest.

He forgot all our conversation. He often forgot what words he wanted to say, and kept saying that he had misplaced his car keys.

It was really sad to see him this way, because of the lovely stories that Jessica and Sabrina said about him.

He sounded like the father I wished I had growing up, not to say anything bad about my dad, or to disrespect him. I had a wonderful upbringing by my adoptive parents, Clive and Michelle, but Mathew sounded like the perfect dad, every little girl would dream of having.

Now, I knew that Rhys told you a little bit of what was going on, but I did not foresee this in any way, shape, or form.

My mouth dropped open, and disbelief crossed my face as I stared at Rhys while he sank into the sofa, shaking his head.

My sister Sabrina, you know that she did her DNA on the Ancestry website. Well, girl, let me tell you what she kept to herself. Yes, the whole breakdown of the results. Sabrina explained, and finally told the truth, that on her DNA results it confirmed that she was of mixed heritage, 70% British, 5 % Turkish, and I've left the best till last, a whopping 25% South African. Yes, that's right, can you believe that?

So, now she did a little digging to find out who in their family was South African.

Our mum, Jessica, then her husband took the test, and, wait for the drum roll, boom, Sabrina's dad, his grandmother, was the one who was black.

'What the fuck?'

But she was apparently very light in complexion and easily passed as white.

So now, where did that information leave me?

Well, with this new information that my half-sister, Sabrina, kept to herself, I decided to ask my dad, Aubrey, if he wouldn't mind taking a DNA test. What the fuck, he's not my biological dad. Are you confused, because I am?

Rhys suggested that Sabrina's dad should take a paternity test to see if he could possibly be my dad. At first, my mother, Jessica, refused. She got up abruptly from where she was seated and stormed off. Her footsteps thundered down the hallway because her husband, Mathew, was confused and wouldn't understand what was going on. Then, she decided, three minutes later, that it wouldn't actually cause him any harm.

A few anxious weeks went by, and then the e-mail with the results was in.

Rhys handed me my phone. I could tell by the look that quickly appeared on his face. it wasn't the results we were expecting, far from it.

Rhys read it first, as I sat nervously biting my finger nails. I remember it was 7:37, early on a Saturday morning.

Raindrops tapped on the window lightly at first, then drummed on the roof hard.

Boom and boom, frigging hell. Mathew was my biological dad. I'm telling you, when I say that not only did I cry, but I paced the room, ready to burst.

When Rhys phoned Jessica then my sister, my mother and sister cried.

My mother cried the most because she gave me away 30 years ago, not knowing that I belonged to her and her husband.

Then my mum cried some more, because her husband, my real dad, was the one who said to get rid of me.

And now, he would never understand what he did, all those years ago, to his own flesh and blood, because of my skin colour.

Although I was light in complexion, but not light enough to fit into his family at the time. So, he assumed that I must have been conceived by my mother and her black boyfriend, Aubrey. Now I could see where I got my blue eyes from. Yes, Mathew, my biological dad.

That Saturday morning, Rhys and I stared at it, frozen for a while on the bed. My chin trembled as I cried, and the tears tickled down my cheeks.

Rhys placed his hand on his throat as I looked at the expression on his face.

He had widened eyes and raised eyebrows. Then disbelief quickly became raw anger, as the anger flooded his veins.

As for me, Rhys said my words. He described me as having a stammer with pure rage.

I could hold the heartbreak no longer, and fell to the floor, as my anger poured out. I wiped my eyes so much that they were red and swollen. I could hear Rhys' constant sniffing, like he was resisting tears, as he tried staying strong for me.

He sat there on the floor with me as he cradled me in his arms.

Leaning my head back, I looked up at him, wiping the tears from my eyes.

My lips parted, a single word barely left my mouth, when Rhys put his finger to my lips, and said, "Don't, babe, don't torture yourself. You'll never know the real reason why Mathew did what he did. He doesn't even know his wife most days. Don't look to him for any answers. The best advice that I can give you, as your future husband, is to move on and let it go. Otherwise, it will break you."

The phone rang several times, which we both ignored.

We must have fallen asleep, because when I opened my eyes, the sun was shining. The birds were singing, and the sky was replaced with glorious streaks of sunlight and an arched double rainbow.

Kayleigh and Nyomi

Where do we start? We've all heard what has happened to our beautiful friend, Tianna.

Usually in times of real crisis, Renee would be the one to speak for all of us, but not this time.

Renee had known Tianna the longest, and was very distraught and emotional to learn that a wicked and cruel…what shall we call it? We have no idea, but let's just say, evil act for now, has happened to Tianna.

Melani's also very upset, but she had her baby not long ago, so we'd just leave her to recover for now.

Tianna's friend, Tamara, was at her house along with Rhys, trying to comfort her as much as possible.

Tamara has suggested that, although the six of us girls were very close—and in times of our troubles, we all stuck together—she asked us to give Tianna and Rhys a bit of space to overcome this chapter in her life.

We've decided to give them all the space that they needed. We did a whip-round and sent a beautiful bouquet of flowers to let her know that we were all thinking of her.

Tamara did let us all know that they decided to postpone their wedding for seven weeks. The new date would be Saturday, 22 October.

Let's all hope, by then, there would be no more surprises waiting to spoil their big day.

As I understand it, Rhys got his decree absolute two weeks before their first wedding date, so he was cutting it a bit fine and is finally rid of his ex-wife, Leah. I think…No, I know that, Tianna's police man friend, Eddie, hmm, remember him, yeah…he had a quiet word with Leah to stop all her nonsense and leave Tianna the hell alone.

Drake

I'm not really in the talking mood right now, but I'd just say a few words anyway. First, my wife, Renee, in all our years together, I'd never seen her in such a state. Her good friend, Tianna, oh man, what can a brother say, tell me, cos boy, I'd no clue.

Then my man Rhys, he's just as gutted to see his woman so distraught.

How were you going to just chuck out your own flesh and blood, without checking first? I don't even know what to say right now.

It's been a couple of weeks since we all heard about this awful news.

Kayleigh, my wife's friend, suggested that Tianna get some counselling, because, boy, oh boy, how was she going to deal with the mess?

Some people shouldn't have kids, seriously, man.

My man Rhys was going to pass by later. Our good friend, Hakeem, kindly cooked some food for Rhys and Tianna. Thank God for Hakeem and his wife, Waveney.

There was a soft knock at the street door. It must be my man Rhys. He stood at my doorway, puffing on a cigarette, as I stood motionless for a moment and stared. Because this wasn't my friend whom I've known for most of my life. He was smoking a cigarette.

A minute or two went past before any of us spoke.

We fist bumped.

"Good to see you, man. How's, ahh…Tianna, my love, sorry I didn't see you standing there. It's nice to see you both. Come in, Renee will be pleased to see you."

Tianna took a few steps inside the hallway and paused, glancing up the stairs to see my wife staring down at her.

Overcome by her emotions, Tianna burst into tears.

Renee

"Oh, come here, girlfriend. You don't have to talk if you don't want to. Cry, if that's what you feel like doing," I said, with tears in the corner of my eyes.

I put my arms around my best friend and told her to just let it all out. "Scream, shout, yell, at the top of your voice, if that's what you feel like doing, if you have to, just do it."

My best friend, Tianna, had a lonely look in her eyes, just empty like a void, but she's not lonely as she has Rhys and all of us girls.

Tianna handed me a bottle of red wine she was holding, looking at me. Her smile was sad.

This Jessica woman, Tianna's birth mother, and her family had caused nothing but great sadness to our friend. It's so agonising to see her so sad. Truly it is.

My husband made Tianna a cup of coffee and added a touch of brandy.

Tianna only took a sip and put the cup down.

The door knocked again. It was Nyomi and Kayleigh. When Tianna saw them both, standing there, at the living room door, just staring at her, with a sombre expression, she couldn't help but burst into tears.

So now, all four of us girls started crying and hugging each other, because that's what we do.

If you cry, we all cry. If you laugh, trust me, we all laugh.

So now my beautiful best friend was given a tissue by Nyomi to dry her eyes. Tianna suddenly burst out laughing.

Silly Nyomi. She forgot to put her daughter's fallen baby tooth in a jar and accidentally gave Tianna the tissue it was wrapped in to dry her tears.

You really had no idea how pleased we all were to hear the sound of Tianna's laughter. So now we all laughed. Who would've thought that a five-year-old baby's tooth would be the reason for Tianna to start laughing again.

Rhys and my husband came bursting into the living room to see what was going on.

First, it was wailing, unstoppable wailing, by the four of us girls, then it was a roaring sound of laughter, or as my husband and Rhys said, it sounded more like four wounded hyenas.

Jessica, Aka Jess

"I'm so sorry, honey, to have caused you so much pain." I sobbed as my emotions from the week's events broke free.

I collapsed onto my bed crying. My husband was sitting on a chair in the corner of our bedroom, crying with me.

Well, that's what I'd like to say to my daughter, Tianna. But her fiancé, Rhys, asked that I give her a few days to digest what has happened.

I honestly had no idea, no clue, that she could have possibly been my husband's child. Please, believe me, when I say how sorry I am.

If only I could turn the clock back, things would be so different.

I sometimes wondered, if I had not had the affair with Aubrey, what then? What would have happened then?

Surely, my husband and I would have looked into why our baby had such dark skin. Well, she was not that much darker than my other children, to be honest with you.

She was just as beautiful as my other children. She had her dad's blue eyes, just like her brothers and sister.

I suppose with her darker skin tone and her brown hair, okay, she looked a little different from her siblings. They all have mousy brown hair, not much difference really.

But when my husband first saw her, he put two and two together and said, "That kid isn't mine, so get rid of her, or I'll get rid of you."

So, I selfishly did as he asked. Why? Because I had two small children, Sam, who just turned four, and Sabrina.

Sabrina was only a toddler at the time. I had no job, no money—nothing. My husband owned everything that we had.

What should I have done? I know it's just making excuses. I made my choice, and now, I would have to live with the consequences of my actions for the rest of my life.

My sons, Sam and Stevie, haven't spoken to me for weeks. My youngest son, Stevie, found it hard to understand why I would give birth to a baby, then give it away, whether it was my husband's child or not.

My eldest son, Sam, a different kettle of fish. For one, he told me some horrible home truths, just vile and disgusting things came out of his mouth.

No matter what, no son should speak to their mother in such a terrible tone.

But in reality, I guess that I deserved everything he said.

My daughter, Sabrina, basically the only one of my children was the one who did not hate me. Well, Tianna, I have no idea how she was feeling.

Yesterday, Rhys texted me and said that Tianna was up for having a discussion with me. I'm so pleased that she decided to give me a second chance.

Alex Roberts

My name is Alex Roberts. I'm married to Kim. She had an affair with Rhys. Yeah, that dude.

The reason why I am telling you this, well, to put it bluntly, it's kind of a long story, but I'd try and shorten it as best as I can.

Fat chance of that happening, I want to tell my side of the story, however long it would take.

My wife's dad, Leon, was murdered 26 years ago by a man called Mark and also a man called Steve Brooks.

That name should be familiar to some of you; if not, it's Rhys Brooks' dad. That's right, Rhys' dad killed my wife's dad, purely by accident, or so he claimed.

There's also a third man involved in the murder, but his name wasn't disclosed, so I'm not going to tell you for now. Well, because, it's someone close to me.

My wife had no idea about the full story. Well, I'd told her a little bit, but it's not public information. So best leave it that way.

My wife has been informed that Steve Brooks has begun an appeal hearing against his 25-year prison sentence.

It totally came out of the blue. We weren't expecting him to appeal his sentence.

As for the other guy, Mark, we were waiting to hear what he'd do.

Two days ago, Kim phoned Rhys to talk about the whole situation, and his response to my wife was, "It's not a good time to talk at the moment. I'll phone you in a few days."

Well, I'd be damned. What did that dude just say to my wife?

You have no idea how long I've waited for Rhys to stay the hell away from my wife—no idea. I'm not really sure what was going on with him right now.

The way he felt about my wife, for him not to want to talk to her, or meet up with her? Well, he must be sick.

Oh, no, that wouldn't stop that dude. He must be dying. I never thought in a million years I'd live to see the day when Rhys doesn't want to talk with Kim.

Yeah, I'm sitting in my garage, drinking a very expensive bottle of whiskey, smoking a cigar, laughing that hell must have frozen over.

As for my wife, straight away, I told you she had an affair with Rhys. That was totally wrong of me. We weren't actually together when she started dating that fool.

Kim only turned to him for comfort, after he, yes, that dude, he pursued her for months, knowing that she was married to me. I'm to blame because I had an affair with her ex-best friend, Chloe, for five years. The whole time that Kim and I had been together. Foolish of me, I know.

When a man is attracted to a woman, his head goes crazy. Now Chloe and I have two boys together.

Kim has forgiven me. I'd put her through so much, yet she stayed with me. I love my wife more than any words could say. That's why, when we got back together again, I kind of turned a blind eye to her and Rhys still having their, what should I call it, a shag a week; a bit on the side with that dude. Call it what you like. And now she's having that dude's baby.

Having fathered two kids with my wife's best friend was different—trust me on that—than to her having a kid with that moron.

Spin the story, whichever way you want. It was different, in my eyes anyway.

I'm so hurt by the whole situation. I know that I'm not really in a position to judge, because of how long I was with Chloe. But you know, we, men, see things differently from women. We can't handle things like women can.

Even when Rhys started dating his new woman, Tianna, or whatever the hell her name happened to be, he still wanted my wife. Yeah, he did. I did know this dude better than he knew himself.

And now, he won't even return my wife's messages. I know in my heart, it's not his new woman, stopping him from returning Kim's phone calls. So what can it be? I had a good mind to call that fucking dude up, so that he could explain himself. But, hey, why rock the boat, for fuck sakes.

Sipping on some fine whiskey, smoking my cigar, I was sitting with my legs propped up on a cardboard box. I was thinking and smiling to myself. Fuck me, he had finally moved on with his own sad, pathetic life.

Whatever it was, it suited me just fine, as long as it'd stay like that, and he doesn't pop up again, anytime too soon. Well, let's just say, I'd be really pissed.

Oh, for fucks sake, I've spoken too soon.

Falling off my chair, I've only gone and smashed my fine whiskey bottle when it slipped out of my hand.

Why, because my wife yelled out to me. "Babe, Rhys has messaged me and wants to meet up this Saturday."

Where's that bloody dustpan and broom then?

Well, she wasn't going to meet up with that dude on her own, I'd tell you that much, as I sweep up the broken whiskey bottle from the garage floor, cutting my finger in the process. Fuck.

I trusted my wife, as far as I know, she had never lied to me. It's that dude, whom I don't trust.

Do you remember when Kim agreed to meet his new woman? Yeah, how can I forget that day? He was throwing out insults, after insults, and cutting his eyes, all to get me wound up.

But what this dude didn't realise is that I am smarter than him. I'm not falling for his stupid antics. Trying to wind me up, in front of my wife, like that? But I had the upper hand here. I was the one holding all the cards. Yeah, me, Alex Roberts. He'd have to ask me if he could see his own kid. Come on now, don't feel sorry for that bloody idiot. Kim is my wife, not his. And his kid, believe it or not, would be living in my house rent-free.

Okay, okay, for fuck sakes, don't all start hating me all at once. Calm down. I would never deny him access to his own kid.

But just to look the dude in his green eyes, when he has to ask, that alone is justice for me. Cruel, I know.

Don't all take his side, he tried, and failed, I may add, to take my wife from me.

What kind of guy is he, then? Worse than me, I can tell you that much.

I love my wife, one hundred per cent. There's absolutely nothing that I wouldn't do for her.

We have two beautiful children: Mason, he is two, and our daughter, Maya, who turned seven months recently.

We've not long ago, moved into a five-bedroom house in Highgate. Yeah that's right, anything for my wife. It had four large bedrooms and a box room.

I've decided, when my wife would give birth to Rhys', that dude's baby, yeah, the *oops baby*, he's definitely going in that box room.

Ha, ha, ha, come on now, all you haters. I'm only messing with you guys. Would I do such a cruel thing/

Yeah, I love my wife, so I have to love this kid.

This is the house she fell in love with, so this is the house we bought.

We celebrated our third wedding anniversary in July this year, and because I was a total idiot, I was not proud of cheating on my wife. I decided to let her choose her own wedding anniversary gift.

My wife went full on big, and bloody expensive, let me tell you.

Yeah, I had to buy her a BMW 3 series. Yeah, she did ask for the 7 series, like mine, but I told her, she was taking the piss, in a nice way, of course.

Word of advice, fellas, if you're going to cheat, make sure you have a large bank balance and deep pockets.

Since I met Kim, my bank balance has slowly…sorry, I'm not going to embarrass my wife. I'm the moron, my bank balance was doing just fine.

I've slightly gone off topic. I was supposed to be telling you about that dude, Rhys. Well, my wife and I were going to meet up with him tomorrow. This should be fun.

Let's see how far this dude was prepared to try and wind me up this time.

While I've been babbling on, my wife just told me that Rhys explained the reason why he hadn't been so forthcoming in discussing the appeal that his dad had coming up. Apparently, his girlfriend, Tianna, just found out who her birth mother was, and was not doing so well with the information.

So, I'm a decent guy. I'd let him off, just this once, and be civil, for all of 10 seconds. Come on now, you all know me. I'm just kidding.

Yeah, alright, I know that I'm messing with you. A bit of crocodile tears fell from my eyes, but it couldn't be helped.

As long as my wife loves me forever, I don't care what anyone had to say about me. Well, except you guys, and I know for a fact, there were quite a few of you who hated me right now. Especially my wife's aunt.

"Not going to name you, Sandra, oh fuck."

She's not too fond of me, right now. It was her birthday recently, and I sent her a lovely bouquet of flowers and a £100 gift card, yeah, cos I'm generous.

But that's okay, by the time you get to really know me, you'll love me as much as my wife does, if not more. I'm really a decent guy. Only, a bit of an arsehole sometimes, my mates would tell you that. But in all honesty, if I weren't a decent fella, trust me, my wife wouldn't have stayed with me.

Kim

4

Rhys and Tianna finally turned up, about 15 minutes late, to our arranged meeting, to discuss his dad's appeal hearing.

I'm so glad that my husband, Alex, was with me. Although, Tianna knew the story that I'd spun her, about wanting Rhys, was a lie.

You could see that she was a little insecure, having me around him. But soon she settled down, when she saw the look that Alex gave her, to reassure her that I was going nowhere, and I am not some home-wrecker.

Alex and Rhys shook hands. That was a great comfort to Rhys, as I don't think he was quite in the mood to play silly games today.

My husband, on the other hand, just sat there gloating. No…I'm going to take that back. My husband sat there in total silence, just occasionally looking up at the ceiling, with a smirk on his face.

Please, don't hate my husband. I seriously know that he could be an idiot sometimes, rather than being arrogant or inconsiderate. But it's just his ego.

Someone, not quite sure who, described my husband, as a small child, who would rather break his own toys, than let some other kid play with it.

Some people have accused him of being patronising, but these claims are untruths.

I asked Tianna how she was doing, after finally finding out the truth about her parents.

She thanked me for asking, and said that she was doing much better now, with the help and support of Rhys and of all their friends.

I noticed when she called Rhys' name, she gave an affectionate smile each time.

In return, his smile for Tianna was so cute. I guess there were so many things about Tianna that drew him to her, but her captivating smile took the cake.

Enough said. The reason why we were here, meeting up, was to discuss the reason behind Rhys' dad's sudden interest to appeal his 25-year prison sentence.

We ordered coffee and a slice of cheesecake. Well, my husband had cheesecake, not sure why, it's not something he loved, really.

Anyway, we got the conversation going, after a few minutes of awkward staring, then bam, just like that, my blood ran cold.

Oh my God, so now Alex and I were aware of the reason why Rhys' dad suddenly decided to appeal his prison sentence.

It can only be her, Rhys's new girlfriend, Tianna, meddling in things that don't concern her.

I stood up in anger and yelled. "How dare she, how frigging dare she?"

Then turned to Rhys, and gave him a mouthful.

"What the hell, Rhys? Why, why, have you got her meddling in my business, your business? I don't care, it has nothing to do with her."

Rhys looked up at me, his eyebrows lowered and pulled together, and his lips tightened inward.

He was just about to say something when my husband turned to face Rhys, shook his head, and said, "Whatever you're going to say to my wife, please don't. I'm warning you now, mate, I'm not going to sit here and have you, or your woman, disrespect my wife. Do you understand me?"

Then Alex, gently grabbed hold of my hand, and asked me to sit back down.

Rhys' nostril flared outward, and he suddenly had restless movements when Alex spoke to him like that.

Rhys had a bit of stubble on his face. I'd never ever seen him look this way before. His hair was a bit longer, and needed a trim. And as for Tianna's look, her eyeliner was caked on.

I'd never let my husband leave the house looking so grubby, not even if he cheated with a hundred different women. He always leaves the house, smartly dressed with a clean-shaven appearance.

His hair is always in a classic taper haircut. He always looked absolutely handsome, one hundred per cent.

Always, every day, and every second, no way my man would look so damn right unshaven, hair needing a trim, no fringing way, no frigging way, ladies.

Alex could hear Rhys muttering something under his breath as he sat there staring at me with a cold and dark expression on his face. Alex's mood shifted rapidly as he spoke to Rhys, who shook his head, clearly unsettled by my husband's outburst. Just the thought of it left Tianna and Rhys visibly shaken.

"Don't you dare mutter curse words under your breath to my wife, you moron."

My husband sat at the table, like he owned the restaurant. He leaned back in his chair, in a display of relaxed power. Rhys, on the other hand, I gazed into his angry red face, knowing my husband had gone one step too far this time. But I was happy enough to just sit back and watch that smile drop off Tianna's face.

Tianna asked if we could all just calm down a little, so she could explain. Alex told her that her explanation had better be good, because his patience with Rhys, and now her, was about to wear thin.

So now Tianna revealed that a few months ago, Rhys went to visit his dad Steve in prison, and she went with him.

As she worked in social media, she began delving into his case. Things didn't seem to add up.

She then completely took us by surprise and said that Steve told her that a third person was involved in the murder of my dad, but stopped short of revealing the person's identity. Alex and I could only stare at each other.

What the hell has this bloody woman gone and done?

Out of the four of us at that coffee shop, Tianna was the only one right now who didn't know the truth of what happened to my dad.

Did I mention that my husband began to fidget in his chair?

He stood up suddenly, looking back at an utterly confused Tianna, and then sighed and wobbled over to the counter, and bought two more slices of cheesecake. It did little to satisfy whatever thought was going on in his mind.

He got up again, and bought a carrot cake, a lemon slice and a black forest gateau slice, until I eventually told him to stop.

26 years ago, my dad went to buy some takeaway food, he never returned home. That was the last time I ever saw my dad alive. I was about eight or nine years old at the time.

I think now the truth, the whole truth, was about to rear its ugly head, all because of Tianna.

Alex and I decided to tell you, in our own words, the truth as we knew it.

Five years ago, when Alex and I first met, his dad, Carl, wasn't very fond of me.

At first, I thought it was because I was black, but nothing could be further from the truth.

Whenever I visited Alex's parents' house, his dad would always say, "Kim, let's go into the garden."

He always told me to sit on an old, grubby garden bench.

For years that's where I always sat. No one ever questioned him as to why he always told me to sit there.

One sunny afternoon, as usual, Alex and I were at his parents' house, they were having a barbecue, I think. Anyway, my mother-in-law, Lyn, asked me, how come I never spoke about my dad. I began telling Lyn that, as my dad left my mum and me when I was young, I didn't really remember much about him, until the previous week, when Alex and I went to see my mum, and she was showing Alex some old photos of my dad. My mum happened to mention that our son, Mason, looked similar to her husband, Leon, my dad.

I mentioned to Lyn that I had forgotten that my dad had one blue eye and one brown eye.

With that, Alex's dad fell and hit the ground hard, having suffered a massive stroke, then a heart attack. He then died right in front of us.

After the funeral, a man approached Alex, saying he was a friend of his late dad. He introduced himself as Mark, the other guy in prison, for murdering my dad.

Mark explained to my husband that my dad was murdered by accident, having been in the wrong place, at the wrong time, simply a case of mistaken identity.

There were three men at the time of my dad's murder, but only two were ever convicted of murder.

The third person responsible for killing my dad, it broke my heart to say it out loud, but it was Carl Roberts, that's right, my father-in-law, my husband's dad. He actually threw that punch that caused my dad to fall and hit his head on the pavement and die instantly.

Why did he throw that fatal punch? All because of the love of a woman with whom he was having an affair.

Having had too much to drink, he mistook my dad for the woman's husband and confronted him for taking the love of his life away from him.

Apparently, Carl and this lady were planning on running away together until her husband found out and put a stop to their affair, and that is why my dad was killed, being mistaken for this lady's husband.

Alex and I have been through hell and back over the past five years.

When all of this happened, with Alex's dad killing my dad. Alex kept it to himself for a while, then he eventually told me.

In his mind, he didn't want to cause me further pain, of not knowing what really happened to my dad. My husband thought it was better to have me think that my dad was still alive, out there somewhere, rather than dead.

The thing was, with my husband, that he always did the wrong things for the right reason.

But this was going to be a big but. Eventually, Alex came clean and told me about my dad because, remember, at the beginning of my story, how I told you that, whenever I went to Alex's parents' house, Carl, my father-in-law, always had me sit outside on the grubby old garden bench.

Well, for 24 years, he had my dad buried under that bench. That's right, the very bench he had me sit on for nearly four years.

He's dead, my father-in-law, and we will never know the true reason behind his thinking and why he did that.

Before you jump to any conclusions and have your own opinions as to the real reason why, let me tell you. As you were aware, my husband, Alex, is white and I am black.

The woman that Carl was having an affair with and yes, fathered a child with, was black.

This was the reason why my husband has a half-brother, who was of mixed-race, called Casey.

And now, because of Tianna's unintentional meddling, the truth came out about my father-in-law, being the one to have murdered my dad, Leon.

So many people were going to get hurt, including my mum, Alex's mum, and his brother and sister.

Carl died and took the truth with him. I am sorry, really sorry, that Rhys' dad took the blame for the murder, but the truth was Steve and Mark took hush money from Carl, one hundred and fifty thousand pounds each, to keep quiet about the murder. Now, they want to talk, seriously?

When Alex's dad, Carl, died, he owned an impressive two hundred properties, which were divided into one third share between him, his brother and sister. I suppose he must have sold a house to gain funds to give the money to Steve and Mark.

The unbreakable love that Rhys and I once had was all destroyed by Tianna. Drake once described our love for each other as glue. But that's sadly all gone now. We hardly ever talk or text like we used to.

The baby that I am having for Rhys, my husband and I, were seriously thinking of having him adopted, and sever all ties with Rhys. Horrible, I know. Alex always told me what kind of person Rhys was, but I never wanted to believe it, because of how I felt about him.

I never thought in a million years I'd ever grow pure hatred for Rhys, but in all honesty, I have. Rhys, having betrayed my love the way he had, I can't, in all honesty, destroy my marriage with Alex by having this baby, knowing full well, that my husband was hurting so much.

This baby, I hope, would be given to a wonderful couple who would give him the love he deserves.

Now I see why Alex hated Rhys so much. Yes, I see it now. It was there all along.

Alex always told me. "You wait, one day Rhys will find someone new to love, and he won't love you anymore."

Guess I should have listened to my husband.

The one per cent he promised to hold onto for me, he lied, and gave it all to Tianna. I blame myself for that, as I was the one who told him to give his love, that he has for me, to Tianna, never once thinking he would actually give it all to her.

As for me, I never lied to Rhys. I held on to 50 per cent love for him and 50 for my husband.

Even though I wouldn't dream of ever leaving my husband for Rhys, my love for Rhys, in the end, had no meaning to him.

It's my fault, as I've already said, I was the one who told him to give all his love to Tianna. He did just that, but unlike me, I still found a way to love him.

They'll be getting married soon and have their own children. I felt a deep certainty in my heart: as Rhys poured all his love into Tianna and turned his back on me, he would inevitably forget about the child I am expecting.

Tianna would never love any child of mine. I could see it in her eyes.

As this story isn't about Alex and me, we decided to bow out gracefully and let Rhys and Tianna continue on their journey with their love story. Even though it hurt me to say it out loud. I wish them both, all the best. Really, I do.

Whatever happened with Steve and Mark, if their appeal is successful, we'd all have to wait and see.

We have taken the decision to not attend their wedding, as there was too much animosity between Alex and Rhys.

As for my friendship with Tianna, sadly, I no longer wish to remain friends with her. How can I after all her meddling?

I hope, one day that Rhys and I can become good friends, like we always were. But until that day, Alex and I bid you all farewell.

Drake

Rhys, my man, I've been telling him for a while to give all his love to Tianna and forget about Kim.

But Rhys, I can honestly say, he is an idiot. I mean, I knew that Tianna is his fiancée, but look what Kim did to help him get Tianna back.

Once upon a time, I remember describing his and Kim's love for each other as glue. Every time Kim's name was mentioned, his face lit up like a ray of sunshine. Seriously, what happened, bruv?

Has Tianna turned him against Kim? What, tell me, cos I can't understand what his playing at.

To actually diss her like that, come on, that isn't right, my man.

I know her husband would be glad to see the back of you. But Kim, what has she done to Rhys for him to treat her like this?

What about the baby you had with her, your son, remember him? My man, what's going to happen to your son when he's born? Are you going to eventually diss him too?

I remember when Rhys first laid eyes on Kim, he said, "Kim waltz into my heart, and now, I can't get her out."

I'm your good friend, and I am telling you straight up, no lies, no beating around the bush, bruv, seriously bruv, man up, and whatever it is that you and Kim have fallen out about. Please, bruv, kiss and make up. I love my wife, Renee, to death. But if I had a woman expecting my child, sorry, but no woman could drive a wedge between me and my baby mama. No man, that won't happen.

Look, I know Rhys wouldn't want to hear this right now, but it had to be said, whether he or his woman, Tianna, liked it or not.

I've been friends with my man Rhys since the first day of secondary school. That's like 23 years. Seriously, what can I say? He has changed.

Not sure if it was Kim, Tianna, or even his ex-wife, Leah. But my man, Rhys, is not the same guy I met all those years ago. Well, I'm not the same guy either, but Rhys, he was always one of those genuine guys when it came to ladies' feelings. I guess that all changed when it came to Kim, breaking his heart.

He said hurt or be hurt. What kind of nonsense is that, my man?

Just out of curiosity, here's a quick question for you, if you wish to answer.

"Would you rather be the cheater, or cheated on?"

You know what, this is the type of shit Alex would love. You all hate my man, Rhys, and started to like Alex instead. Well, hell no, please, don't start to like Alex. He's a dickhead.

One thing about Kim. She insisted that her husband is nice. Well, for such a nice guy, he can sure act like a bad guy. He's a loser, and a fucking moron. Err, excuse me, sorry about my language. What I meant to say was, Alex is not nice, trust me.

Tianna

What a hell of a few weeks it's been, let me tell you. I've no idea what the hell was going on with Rhys, Alex and Kim.

But what I do know is that I offered Steve some help in his appeal and all hell broke loose.

I had no idea that I'd be opening up a can of worms, but it's too late to zip it in its bud now. The damage and hurt have already been done.

I've tried to apologise to Kim for all the hurt I have obviously caused her.

But my priority was to my fiancé, Rhys, and helping his dad to be freed from the nightmare he finds himself in.

But first, I agreed to speak with my birth mother, Jessica. Just the two of us.

So, we'll meet up for coffee in about one hour's time, Oh fudge, I'm running late.

Okay, so I'm not the only one who was late. I chose a table near the window, you know me, always looking out the window.

Suddenly, I had a churning feeling in my stomach, my heart began to thump, and I became really restless, unable to sit still. I tried counting from one to five when that didn't work, I tried to breathe as slowly as I could.

Closing my eyes, too nervous to look at the woman approaching me, I closed my eyes, then opened them to take a peek, then shoved my phone into my handbag with shaking hands.

There she was. Oh my God, I almost called her mum instead of Jessica. What was I thinking?

Hmm, she looked quite nice in a lovely floral dress, sling-back sandals with bright red nail varnish on her toes.

Her hair was wavy brown with highlights, and looked as though she had recently been to the hairdresser. I guess she was making an effort.

"Hi, Tianna," she said, smiling.

I stood up and gave her a hug.

"Thanks for agreeing to meet me."

She gently broke the embrace and stepped away, still smiling at me. I looked at my birth mother. She looked genuinely sorry for all the hurt and pain she had caused me.

So, I decided, then and there, to give her a chance, and get to know her instead of having hatred and being resentful.

My mother surprised me, I've got to hand it to her. She is quite a lovely lady.

We ordered our coffee and cakes. Like me, she is also quite partial, to a bit of carrot cake and cappuccino.

She showed me photos of my brothers and sister when they were young. Also, photos of my dad, Mathew, he was very handsome when he was younger.

Sam, my oldest brother, look just like Matthew. I noticed, as I looked at the photos, that my mum smiled at me with pure love in her heart.

"Tianna, sweetheart, I want to show you something."

She opened her handbag and removed a carefully folded handkerchief. It contained a pink baby hat, tiny knitted pink booties and two hospital name tags.

Jessica went on to tell me that she didn't want to give me up and had hoped that one day, I would come looking for her. So, in anticipation of that day, she kept these things for me, in the hope that I would one day know that she hadn't forgotten about me.

When she presented me with these baby items, a sense of sadness and joy filled my whole body. We leaned into each other and had a long-awaited mother-daughter hug.

She smelled so nice, as a mother should. I can't really explain it. But here she is, my birth mother, whom I'd been looking for since I was 18 years old.

She held my hand, I cried, and a single tear fell onto her hand.

She started to say something, but just bit her lip and began to cry instead.

After about 10 minutes or so, she noticed my very expensive engagement ring.

"He must love you, Tianna. I'm so happy for you both."

"Yes, he does love me."

She asked a few questions about Rhys, you know, how we met, stuff like that, and said she hope he makes me very happy.

My birth mother had one more surprise for me. Apparently, before her dad died, nearly seven years ago, in his will, he left some money for her, and she decided to divide it equally between her three children.

My mum changed her mind, and divided the money into four, not three; she included me, and gave me a large crumpled white envelope, with 70 thousand pounds, stuffed inside.

I was stunned. I just sat there shaking in complete shock.

I felt so overwhelmed, then burst into floods of tears, then counted the money. Well, wouldn't you?

"I never forgot about you, sweetheart. I know this money won't replace the family that you should have grown up in, but I hope it can offer some sort of comfort, knowing that I never, ever forgot about you," she said, her voice all emotional.

"Mum."

"Hush, it's okay, sweetheart."

Rhys

Woah, so I would just like to clarify something that Kim has told you. Yes, I did promise to save one per cent of my love for her. But as you and I all know, Kim has told me, several times in fact, that she will never leave her husband.

I would always have a special place in my heart for Kim, but unfortunately, she now doesn't believe me. It's nothing more than a fucked-up tragedy.

Remember, she was the one who told me to give whatever love I have for her to Tianna. Yes, I did promise to reserve one per cent of my love for her, in case I needed to find my way back to her, but come on, be reasonable. I have to give Tianna one hundred per cent of my love.

Tianna knew how I felt about Kim, and for that reason, I had to prove to Tianna that she deserves my full love and attention, not some, but all.

What Kim and Alex have you know as well as I do, Alex would never leave Kim, no matter what, and vice versa. He's making amends for all the hurt he'd ever caused her.

Tianna's my fiancée now. I have to give her all my love, one hundred per cent, to prove that there is no more Kim and I. It's only reasonable.

As for the appeal hearing for my dad, yes, it was Tianna's idea, but why should my dad serve 25 years for a murder he didn't actually commit?

Yeah, okay, he took the hush money, what can I say?

Remember, it was actually Alex's dad, Carl, who threw that fatal punch, not my dad. Only Carl is dead, the one who did need to face the consequences of that terrible night.

As for Alex, yeah, that fool, he took no responsibility for lying to Kim about what happened to her dad.

Just in case you didn't know, Kim confided in me about what Alex had told her.

As for me, I never told a soul. That's how much love I had for her.

Sadly, our friendship, the love we once had, it's all gone. Yeah, I'm gutted, but what can I say!

I had a lot of love to give to Kim, but she didn't want to take a chance on me. Why? Because she'd been with Alex for more than two years by the time we met.

As for me, we only knew each other for a few months. So, I can see why she wouldn't take the risk. You all know me by now. When I love you, I give one hundred per cent, and that's what I offered Kim. But she chose to be with Alex, the idiot. So here we both were, and the love that became unstuck.

The only regret that I had was knowing that our friendship is no more.

Aubrey

This is a sad story, if ever there was one. What can I say? Tianna and Rhys came to see me a few weeks ago. I'm both saddened and shocked to learn that I'm not Tianna's biological dad.

It broke my heart to see her and Rhys so distraught, and to now find out that Jessica's husband, Mathew, is her dad. Wow, that must hurt.

I really don't have any words that might make the pain, that Tianna was feeling right now, go away.

How does anyone come back, from this information, and stay strong. It, beggars' belief, it really does.

Tianna introduced me to her adoptive parents, Clive and Mitchelle. They were really nice. They're really upset too, everyone's upset, but you can't change what's happened.

Tianna is getting married in about three weeks.

We're all looking forward to the happy couple getting married.

As I understand it, I was going to walk Tianna down the aisle. Clive and I came to some sort of understanding. That was before we knew Mathew was her dad.

But the arrangement has changed. From what I've been told, Mathew, her biological dad, was supposed to walk her down the aisle, but his Alzheimer's has progressed a bit more, and he was now in a wheelchair.

So, it's going to be Clive doing the honours. I'm just glad that the wedding is still going ahead after being postponed once before.

My daughter, Larah, is one of the seven bridesmaids, as well as Tianna's sister Sabrina.

My wife, Martha and I, have gifted them their honeymoon to the Seychelles.

Two weeks in the sun, I hope that everything goes well for them on their big day.

Renee and Tamara

Our dear friend, Tianna, is getting married in two weeks. We, girls, got a little surprise for her. We have only gone and organised a yoga class with a difference.

"Hmm, what the hell, Tamara?"

"Apparently, you can have a yoga workout with kittens or puppies. Since Tianna loves cats, I've booked us in with the kittens."

"Oh boy, Tamara, you're insane, really you are. It's a good job that I'm her maid of honour. I've booked a group of hot, sexy men, dressed as police officers, and her mum Jessica has said that we can have the hen do at her club, free of charge, of course."

"Now you're talking, girl. When are these sexy police officers going to perform their sexy dance, Renee?"

"Tomorrow night. We just have to get Tianna to the club on time."

"Well, I don't know about you, Renee, but I can't wait for tomorrow night."

"Oh, yes, before I forget, Nyomi has organised all of our outfits, apparently, we've all got to dress the same, even Tianna, but, of course, her being the bride, she gets to wear a different colour." Renee laughed, almost choking on a biscuit.

"Oh, please, tell me you didn't just say that Nyomi organised our outfits. Oh God, help us all," replied Tamara, eyes wide open, hands on her hips, as she made a face.

"Don't be like that, Tamara, just grin, and bear it, ha, ha, ha, see I'm laughing, and I haven't even seen what we're going to wear yet," Renee replied, wiping biscuit crumbs from her lips.

"Tomorrow is going to be one hell of a night, judging by our outfits, that we have yet to see."

"Well, going by past experience, let me tell you what we all had to wear at Renee's hen do." I turned my head and giggled to myself.

Okay, so Renee has just told me, if I dare utter a single word to you, she's going to kill me. So, let's just have fun with what we're going to wear tomorrow night.

Shh, at Renee's hen do we all had to dress up as Where's Wally, remember him, but of course, you didn't hear it from me.

Tianna

I'm so excited, yet nervous, but at the same time, my heart was singing for joy this morning.

My friends organised my hen do. In the afternoon, we went to do yoga with kittens. Wow, I really enjoyed. It was such a wonderful afternoon.

"Did you know, kittens will play-fight with one another, and also with you, if you allow it," Nyomi said, staring at Renee's hands.

"Well, it certainly is a little too frigging late for that information, I mean, girl, look at my hands," replied Renee.

Then tonight, it's going to be when the real hen party starts.

Unfortunately, Larah, one of the bridesmaids, too young for this kind of entertainment. Over 21s only. My mum, Jessica, was reluctant to sneak her in.

Outside my house, beyond the gate, a car horn sounded, drawing my attention to our surprise means of transport.

Grabbing our handbags and coats, we hurried down the hallway, and I opened the street door.

We paused, gazing down at the guy, stood by his vehicle.

"Damn, he is hot, flipping handsome, and cute," Nyomi said, unable to take her eyes off him.

I think he felt flattered, as he caught her staring, and smiled back.

Anyway, swiftly moving on, my friends, all five of them, suddenly, their movements changed to a sort of jumping, up-and-down movement, when they saw the limousine. Melani and Nyomi were taking selfies with the driver, who so happened to be a gorgeous guy with a man bun. Yes, I noticed too, dare I say it.

Renee told them to calm the hell down, and to stop acting like silly school girls with a crush.

I tossed my head back to stare up as the sky began to dim. I was so happy, adrenaline was speeding the power's flow through me. All I could think about was being Mrs Brooks, very soon.

The driver took the scenic route, adding an extra 12 minutes to our journey, which I didn't mind.

Eventually, arrived in the limousine, outside the entrance to Dare to Dance, courtesy of my ever-so-generous fiancé, Rhys.

We were given the red-carpet treatment, being treated like A-list celebrities. A sexy guy wearing nothing but pink boxers and a bow tie handed us a glass of champagne. I couldn't help it, and dared to stare, where my eyes had no business staring. I felt my cheeks blush scarlet, and I stumbled over my words.

"Hi, gorgeous," he said, as I took the glass of champagne from his big hands.

The venue was decorated with *she said yes*, balloons in pink and white.

There was a hen party photo booth, with the words, *almost Mrs Brooks*, written in large letters.

"Oh wow, this is so amazing. Thank you so much, you guys," I said, hugging my friends.

I almost ruined Kayleigh's hairstyle, which she claims to have paid rather a large sum of money to have done, hmm.

We quickly transitioned into our next adventure, all dressed up as our husbands or boyfriends. Nyomi took it a step further by insisting that we embody a gangster look as well. I was not really sure where she got her ideas from, but I'm fine with wearing my future husband's clothes.

Now, the moment we've all been waiting patiently for. Yes, you guessed it. The boys in blue panther, dressed as police officers, seriously? It's a full house tonight, but we, girls, were all seated in the front row, near the stage, all hot and flustered, at the thought of being so close to these sex on legs guys.

"Somebody pass me a fan because I definitely needed to cool down," I shamelessly shouted to my friends, but they were all eyes peeled at the stage.

They came out all dressed as police officers. Oh my God, every single woman was screaming. They all danced provocatively, moving their bodies to the music. Holding their truncheon, and doing something that I can't really describe.

"What the hell, he's stripping off already? Oh my God, what the frigging hell."

Do you know what, I'm screaming, and closing my eyes, at the same time. I can't look. I can't look. My heart rate has jumped to a new all-time high.

I was taking a peek, with one hand, covering my eyes. What's he doing?

He was sitting on a lady's lap, moving his body in a seductive manner, which I'm guessing, his scent drove her body wild, the mix of sweat, darkness, and man.

Well, from where I was seated, that's the jealous opinion I have.

With all the screaming going on, I wasn't quite sure if what I heard was correct.

The lap dance guy started shouting to the crowd, "Where's Tianna, the bride-to-be?"

Everyone shouted, "Over there."

They pointed in my direction.

Let me tell you, this police officer had a mask on. He performed a very dirty dance in front of me, then sat on my lap, and oh my goodness, he's a very big boy. If you know what I mean.

Oh my, did he whine his body against mine. He started to strip off his uniform, very slowly.

Then he took my hand and put it somewhere, I really shouldn't say out loud.

He kept staring at me, as though he knew me.

"Tianna, Tianna," he kept saying over and over.

He slowly started to take his clothes off. So now, he only had his mask and helmet on.

His chocolate skin body was so muscular. His movements were so familiar. Oh my, oh fudge, what a physique this officer had. Dare I say it?

He kissed me softly on my lips. His warm breath on my neck, as he breathed my scent in deeply.

Just thinking about him made my body heat up and my heart flipped.

Then he gave me a red rose. I have no idea where this rose was before he gave it to me, but I took it anyway.

He kept saying, "Tianna, Tianna."

And what the hell, I kid you not, the police officer removed his helmet and mask.

"Frigging hell," I screamed out, and then laughed.

"Eddie, what the hell are you doing here?" I asked, blushing.

I'm sure you all remember my fling with Eddie, the police officer. Well, someone thought it would be such fun to get Eddie to perform that lap dance. Ha, ha, ha, how hilarious.

But whoever you were, wow, I did enjoy it so much. It got me wondering what the sex would have been like if I had done it with Eddie the officer. Oh well, that ship has long sailed, sadly.

Eddie gave me a hug and wished me all the happiness that I deserve.

"Oh well, Eddie," I said, laughing, and somehow trying to get over the shock. "It was nice to see you, a lot of you."

Okay, so I couldn't resist that joke.

"Tianna, Tianna, let's commit the perfect crime together. I will steal your heart, and you can steal mine. What do you say?"

"You're so sweet, Eddie, but my answer is…maybe."

15 minutes later, it was time for us girls to have our own private party in one of the VIP booths upstairs.

The cocktails were just coming thick and fast all evening. We were having such fun. Then we noticed a game called Truth or Dare lying on the table. It's a hen scratch card game.

Everyone had to write some truths and dares, cover them with a scratch to reveal stickers. So, let the fun begin.

It was all going just fine. We, girls, we knew how to have fun. If you cry, we all cry. If you laugh, we all laugh.

That's until Renee happened to scratch and reveal a truth.

I'm sorry, Renee, but I had sex with your husband, Drake.

What the hell, what the frigging hell.

My best friend Renee, she went full on crazy, she kept shouting, "Which one of you, bitches, slept with my husband."

Because Renee and all of us girls had too much to drink, when she got up, she fell back down sideways, bounced off the smooth pink velvet chair, and rolled somehow face-first into my party cake.

Okay, I know that we shouldn't have laughed, but we did, because, well, because she looked absolutely ridiculous. Remember, we were wearing our husbands' clothes. Her husband, Drake, what can I say, he's more than six feet tall, and well-built.

So, can you imagine how silly she looked in her husband's trousers? And she had on six-inch heels to compensate for the length of his trousers. Oh well, she wasn't the only one looking ridiculous that evening. It was just supposed to be a bit of harmless fun.

Anyway, Renee was lying on the floor with my party cake on top of her. We were all laughing, and okay, now we've all stopped laughing, because, well, I'm not sure why we were all laughing.

Melani, oh dear, you can always count on her to indulge in the cake first. And what a cake it was! Picture this: a golden sponge adorned with luscious strawberry jam and whipped cream; it's reminiscent of a Victoria sponge but with a touch of sophistication. I believe they refer to it as a naked cake.

My friend, Melani, was eating the cake, which Renee is covered in, remember now, that Renee is on the floor.

Melani, took her finger to scoop up the buttercream icing, licking and sucking her finger. So, we all started to do the same thing, licked the buttercream off our fingers and ate the cake, until it was finished.

The cake, in all honesty, was too delicious for words. Then we all started to laugh again. Well, except for Renee.

Renee, I think she remembered something. She started to cry. Her mascara started to run down her face.

As she wiped away her tears, her false eyelashes came off in her hand. Oh dear.

"Don't cry, Renee," I said, kneeling down beside her.

We're all friends, and I promise you, I'd get to the bottom of who wrote that truth or dare.

She hugged me and whispered that she already knew that it was Kayleigh.

Renee continued lying on the floor with cake all over her face.

There was cake in her hair, falling off her eyelashes as she lay there with a glum expression on her face. And not forgetting the sad little pout on her lips.

Kayleigh

I have a confession to make. You see, I've known my good friend Renee's husband from secondary school. He obviously doesn't remember me. Why would he?

He was several years above me. I'm not sure if you're aware, at our school, Drake and his friend, Rhys, no girls would go on a date with either of them.

The older girls, whenever they used to see the two walking down the corridors, would turn around, run and hide from them.

We, younger girls, we'd just stand in the corridor, laughing at those two silly boys.

Drake was tall like a giant, around six feet, and only 15 and a half years old, well-built and had a spotty face.

Rhys was some skinny arse kid, who wore thick-rimmed glasses and had braces. We nicknamed him ugly Rhys, for obvious reasons, he was ugly as fuck.

Drake and Rhys both wanted a girlfriend so badly, they ended up going to the gym and changed their body shape. Look at their physique now.

And fast forward a few years, they're both *drop-dead gorgeous*, and my heart beats really fast.

I'd let you in on a little secret. I started to feel short of breath every time I saw them both. But Drake's with Renee, and Rhys, omg Rhys, he's with Tianna now, oh well.

The realisation came slowly and too late, to think that one day, they'd actually cause me to have such…Well, I'm trying my hardest to explain my feelings towards Drake. That's why, when the opportunity presented itself, at the swinger's party, and Drake was there, well.

His presence was intense but calming, almost to the point. I had the urge to lean against his muscular body and let his hands roam my body.

He gripped me from behind and pulled me closer to him. We made love, in fact, several times that night, including in the hot tub, on the kitchen table, against the kitchen sink, and in front of a rather large mirror, in one of the many bedrooms.

But regret sat in my stomach for a long time now.

As for Drake, the regret in his dark eyes made him want to confess to his wife, the minute he realised I and she were friends, but I persuaded him otherwise.

Can you picture in your mind her hands around my throat, if she knew that I've tasted her husband?

Omg, his big... Anyway, that was years ago now. No need to drag up the past, maybe I should shut up about the whole thing between Drake and me. You know, loose lips sink ships.

Anyway, where was I? Drake cut off his dreadlocks, my goodness, his chocolate brown skin, his wavy cut hairstyle, and he had a well-trimmed goatee beard; what a huge transformation, let me tell you.

He was almost unrecognisable, as well as Rhys, and those beautiful green/hazel eyes.

I met Renee, about four years ago at a swingers' party. After a while, she stopped going, but I guess her husband, Drake, continued, and that's when it happened, the magic.

He lit every part of my body with fire and ecstasy. A few months later, she invited me over to her house for lunch.

I was so shocked when she introduced me to her husband. I seriously didn't know where to look. I felt the awkward silence between Drake and me. I didn't know what to say, apart from *hello*. I hadn't seen him since that night we had sex.

What was going on in his mind, I honestly couldn't say, but Drake's jaw dropped a mile when he saw me standing before him.

Well, I just couldn't believe he was the same old Drake whom all the girls at school ran and hid from.

I'm so sorry, when I saw him at that swingers party, well, quite a while ago now, maybe two or three years ago, I just had to have him.

Lucky for me, that's the rule of the game. You can choose who to have sex with, otherwise, it's a no, no.

As for Nyomi, I introduced her. We've all stopped going now, as Renee said it's foolish to keep on going because eventually someone was going to get hurt.

"Unfaithful lovers, betrayed by friends, sooner or later, it all has to end." Renee's words, not mine.

Tianna

The days were just going so quickly. Rhys and I would be getting married next week.

Everything has been arranged: the caterers, flowers, the photographer. I'm so nervous, as well as happy.

Truth be told, I wanted my biological dad, Mathew, to walk me down the aisle. But unfortunately, he's now in a wheelchair. So, my adoptive dad, Clive, has agreed to do it instead.

Oh, well, never mind, because that was the original plan anyway. Well, sort of, then it was going to be Aubrey. Anyway, it's my adoptive dad now, walking me down the aisle.

Rhys and his mates went to Amsterdam last weekend. Hmm…should I be worried? No, I trust Rhys one hundred per cent.

As our wedding is not too far away, Rhys went to stay with Drake and Renee until after the wedding. Anyway, my good friend, Tamara, was with me at Rhys' house.

Well, I should really say Rhys, and my house, yep, that sounded about right, yes, I'm going to be the next Mrs Brooks.

I went for my dress fitting yesterday. Hmm, I've gained a little weight around my waist.

I chose a plain sleeveless dress. The fabric has a stretch crepe with a V-neck and a sweep/brush train. I was gifted a striking and dazzling tiara in rhodium-plated finish, encrusted with cut crystals. Courtesy of my mum, Jessica.

As we waited for our wedding day, Rhys' dad has been given a date for his appeal hearing, in three days' time. I'm not looking forward to this, nor was Rhys. I can tell you that much.

Because of the last encounter that we had with Kim and Alex, we were not sure if they were going to attend the hearing or our wedding.

To be honest, Alex was like a cat that freaked out during a thunderstorm, no offence intended.

But I am under the impression that Alex was more of an enormous lion. He had the eyes of a tiger, the heart of a lion, yet, he's a flipping arsehole.

I hope, if they did attend our wedding or the hearing, we can at least be civil to each other.

Seems like I've spoken too soon, they've sent back their RSVP. Unfortunately, they have decided not to attend our wedding next weekend.

I know that Rhys was gutted to have fallen out with Kim. As for me, okay, so you've just realised that. I secretly smiled. Hell, yes, you bet that I am. I'm not sorry, come on, honestly, what kind of flipping relationship did those two have anyway? I'm glad it was finally over.

I get to have Rhys all to myself, without him giving or keeping the one per cent of his love for her. I mean, seriously, who the hell did she think she was? Oh yes, he told me all about that promise he made to Kim, which, in my opinion, was unrealistic, don't you think?

There's no way that husband of mine was going to hold onto anything for Kim, even if she was going to be his baby mama, that's just how I feel right now.

You may think it's a bit harsh, poor Kim, but really, she had her husband. Why can't I have mine?

Come on, don't look at me like that. I'm just being brutally honest.

Luckily for me, I can spill my guts to you, honest to God, I can!

"Anyway, what I've just said is between you, and me, right, Mr Kitty? So don't tell anyone, or no treats for you for a month, make that two months."

Tamara just got in from work, and has my favourite ice cream—cookies and cream.

It's a bit chilly for ice cream, being in October, she was nice enough to buy some. So, I'd have a couple of scoops.

Oops, I've just dropped my phone onto the floor, as it started to ring. It's Renee, she decided to stay with me and Tamara and let Drake and Rhys have some guys' time alone, before our wedding.

It's a rainy day today. The sky's dark, and the leaves started falling off the trees. The birds weren't singing their beautiful love songs in the mornings anymore. I looked through the window nervously, drinking my coffee and eating a bit of toast. I waited patiently for Rhys to arrive. He'd pick me up on the way to his dad's appeal hearing.

Finally, his black Audi pulled up outside, and I watched him get out of his car, dropping his phone to the ground. Ayesha, his overly friendly neighbour, ran from across the road, bent down, exposing her lean figure, her face close to his, and began to whisper something, hmm.

I gave him a big hug and a kiss on his lips. His face engaged in a smile that created little wrinkles around his eyes and grooves in his cheeks. Rhys then said how nervous he was feeling.

He looked fine to me, standing there in his navy-blue suit, but then again, his tone did sound nervous when he spoke.

An hour later, we arrived outside the court building. Rhys' body shook from the inside out before he stepped a foot inside.

His mum, Marcia, and his twin brothers, Lewis and Kyle waited patiently for us to arrive before going inside.

I thought for a second that Kim and Alex weren't here, but they were already seated inside courtroom number nine.

We entered the courtroom. Kim and Alex turned around, looked at Rhys and me, and gave an awkward half smile. But that was all, no hello, nothing. Which, to be honest, suited me just fine.

After the hearing, I could tell that Rhys wanted desperately to speak with Kim. He stood there just staring at her, his green eyes followed her.

But Alex was holding her hand, and he guided her away from us both.

Rhys just stood there, staring at Kim, his soon-to-be baby mama, with pure undeserved pain in his heart.

What could I have done to soothe that pain, the pain he so badly felt?

No words could have comforted Rhys. It broke my heart to see him like that. I put my arms around him, and he leaned towards me, resting his head onto my shoulder.

I reassured Rhys that I'm sure Kim would see sense and speak to him soon, and reminded Rhys why we were at court today.

He agreed with me and said that he should concentrate on his dad and our wedding in two days' time. I mean, how much more can I take, my future husband loving a woman who obviously doesn't love him anymore? I guess in a way, it was a relief, and yet, it was sad to see Rhys so broken. I'm thinking it was never more than lust, well, on Kim's part.

Her presence was quite overwhelming. My body reacted with both horror and fear, so strongly that it made my head spin. I gazed up to look at my fiancé, his upper lip swelling as his teeth grew stimulated by lust for her. I turned to face Kim. Her smile was as cunning as ever. The glow of lust in her eyes as she stared back at my fiancé.

The emotional side of me wanted to slap Rhys' face so hard, but what would that have achieved? Nothing, that's what.

And even if that happened, I'm guessing Kim would have darted over to see if Rhys was okay, with her husband no doubt following swiftly behind her.

The day before our wedding, there was a knock at the street door. It was the postman. He was holding a small parcel addressed to me.

"I don't recall ordering anything," I told Tamara, staring down at the parcel in my hand.

She took the parcel from me and opened it on my behalf.

Okay, so this is very weird. It was from Kim and Alex.

A personalised wedding good luck horseshoe. There was also a card inside which read,

'Wedding wishes for the bride and groom, wishing you both a wonderful wedding and life together. May you enjoy the love and happiness of each other. Together you are stronger than apart, and together, you have found true love.'

"Omg," Tamara said out loud.

As for me, I could feel the tears trickle down my cheeks as Renee held me, just before I started to cry out loud.

Although, they have chosen not to attend our wedding, I thought it to be a lovely gesture; them sending the gift. And I knew for certain, it would be a small comfort to Rhys.

And now, when Tamara and Renee were both asleep, I'd go and talk to Mr Kitty, and take back every horrible thing that I have ever said about Kim. Oh fudge.

Rhys

Our wedding day was approaching fast. My friends and I went to Amsterdam for my stag do.

We ended up slap bang in the middle of Rembrandtplein, which had to be Amsterdam's answer to Times Square.

What a weekend we all had! I won't reveal the name of the club, but let me tell you, this is truly the ultimate dream for any clubber. Picture multiple floors filled with booming music, dazzling strobe lighting, and an incredible smoke machine. It was almost like being in an Ibiza mega club vibe.

There was a beer garden, with a terrace, and oh yes, of course, it was fancy dress. And no, we didn't dress up as our wives or girlfriends. We chose to dress up as Willy Man, the superhero.

On our last night, we did a bit of sightseeing, then headed to De Wallen. The Red-Light District. It's a pretty X-X-rated area, and certainly not for the faint-hearted.

Eventually, we headed to the bar, what the…oh man, this bar, I can't tell my fiancée about. All I'm willing to tell you was that it's named after a yellow fruit.

It's a regular erotic bar in the area, and you are served your drinks by scantily clad, attractive women.

They do some sort of tricks with a banana, but I wasn't looking, so I can't tell you much. What I could tell you, is that, all of us, yes, all of us guys including me, had a lap dance…fuck. Come on now, you can't come to this sort of club and leave without a lap dance. I mean, none of us came just to enjoy the scenery.

What a night we all had. We've all agreed, what happened in Amsterdam, stays in Amsterdam.

A few days after returning from Amsterdam, it was my dad's appeal hearing. I'm staying at Drake's house before my wedding. Renee and Tamara are staying with Tianna, at my house.

I've been tossing and turning in my sleep for most of the night. I miss waking up to Tianna every morning.

Her beautiful smile, her sweet scent, that kiss first thing in the morning, what more can a guy ask for?

I kept checking my watch to see if it was time to leave out to pick Tianna up, as she'd attend the court hearing with me.

When we arrived at court, my mum was already there with my brothers. I haven't seen Alex or Kim yet. Maybe, they have changed their minds about attending.

My brother, Lewis, opened the door to courtroom number nine, and held the door for us to go in, and there were Kim and Alex sitting at the front with a guy. I'm not quite sure who he was.

Alex and the guy both glanced over their shoulders, but Kim held her head slightly, looking to her left in a daze. I'm not really sure what she was staring at.

The hearing got underway. I assumed that my dad would be in court, but he wasn't. A few statements were made, that's when I could see Kim. I could only describe it as when you cry silent tears.

Alex put his arm around her shoulder, the guy that they were with whispered into Kim's ear. That's when she turned her head and smiled at him.

Tianna held my hand and started to gently rub her thumb along my hand. Just doing that little gesture calmed my nervousness.

Before we knew it, the hearing was over. I'm not really sure what just happened. Well, because my thoughts were with Kim, and how she felt right about now.

I was sure that after the hearing, I'd get to speak with both her and Alex. But no, she left the courthouse crying, after hearing what was said about that fateful night her dad was murdered.

Alex stood staring, shaking his head, his jaw tightened, and his eyes turned cold.

He obviously knew, that I wished I could have spoken to his wife, but he wasn't having any of it. Not today, not tomorrow, not ever.

Tianna and I would be getting married in a couple of days, and the mood with everyone was a bit low. That's what I should have been concentrating on. However, I found myself thinking about Kim every waking moment of the day.

My mum suggested we all go back to her house, order a takeaway, and have a few drinks to lighten the mood. I didn't really know how my mum copes without her husband, my dad. Really, I don't.

My brother, Kyle, I've just spoken with him about our mum. He's just told me, mum cried herself to sleep every night since dad has been sent to prison, but hopefully, he'd be coming home soon.

I took Tianna home, our home, she's soon-to-be Mrs Brooks. I held her tight around her waist. How I wish that we could spend the night together. Looks like she was thinking the same thing.

"Tell me why we agreed to spend one week apart from each other?" she asked, gazing up into my eyes, then she drew a big breath.

I guess you could say her friends got the message and decided to leave for the night and came back in the morning.

We went straight to the spare bedroom, where I had Tianna's pole…oh yes, remember her pole, well, it's here at my house.

"Err, excuse me, babe, our house," she said, laughing.

"Of course, babe."

Oh boy, did she perform a pole dance for me. How she wrapped her body around that pole, and did all those movements, wow.

Tianna did something called the aerial invert, boy, oh boy. Then an angle hang, but my favourite was the overspilt. She drove me crazy with all those moves. I'm telling you now that night, the sex was what some would call intense love-making.

"Morning, beautiful, I'm still thinking about last night," I said, smiling, then kissed her on the lips softly.

My fingers caressed her palm warmly, then I brushed the hair away from her cheek, and kissed her once more.

My fiancée blushed, she's gone all red in her face.

"Don't be shy, you'll soon be my wife," I whispered.

But she's gone, and put the pillow over her face to hide the fact that she's a little shy.

Removing the pillow, I kissed her again, she smiled. Moving closer to her, my fingers sliding up her arms,

I whisper, "Love you."

Lacing my fingers through hers, my palms touched hers, so warm, and exciting. Tianna soon forgot about being shy, and her fingers slid across my smooth muscles, and up to my neck, drawing my mouth down harder onto hers, than ran her fingers through my hair.

"Tianna, you'll soon be my wife," I whispered again.

This time she just giggled, and couldn't look me in the eyes, for all of six minutes, or was it six seconds?

Anyway, she's okay now. I caressed her between her thighs, how she loved when I touched her there. I move my hands all the way up to feel her. She looked at me with her beautiful blue eyes. I can see by the look on her face that she was enjoying every touch that I made.

I kissed her gently on her lips, her neck, and left a trail of hot kisses to her breast. Tianna groaned softly, calling my name.

My hand is still caressing her inner thighs.

"Oh God, I love it when you're so wet," I whisper softly in her ear.

She pulled me closer to her. She wanted me, oh yes, she wanted me to make love to her, but first, I had to show my future wife how much I appreciated her pole dancing, and do something that she really enjoys.

I have to tell you this. Oh man, my fiancée love when I go down on her. She loved when I put my head there, in between her thighs, licking and sucking.

She held my head there, enjoying the sensation my mouth was giving her. Just to hear her scream out my name, oh man, Tianna, she's some sexy lady. I love everything about her, except when she snores, it is deafening. I feel so privileged to have her heart.

Tianna is everything I've dreamed of, and more.

She's the first and last thing on my mind every day. I can honestly say that she completes me, and my heart would be empty without her.

A few days ago, I made Tianna cry, it was tears of joy. Why did she cry? Because I told her my sole mission would be finding ways to make her happy and excited.

My happiness is, after all, now tied to hers.

For a few seconds, we gazed silently into one another's eyes. She bit her lips to keep them from quivering, then the tears rolled down her cheeks.

My hands slid up her arms, gently caressing her shoulders, then she burst out crying.

Without a word, she slipped into my arms, then whispered, "I love you so much, Rhys."

What can I say, got to keep the future Mrs Brooks happy.

This morning, she cried again when I gave her a small jewellery box. She opened it. Inside was a white gold diamond cluster pendant, something new, for her to wear on our wedding day.

She looked at me, with pure love in her eyes, and said, "Rhys, I'm so addicted to you. I want to tell the world how I feel about you." She started to giggle and thanked me for the pendant, kissing me softly on my lips.

Her love and joy bubbled up from within, and she could not hold it in any longer. What the hell, I think I've been watching too many romance movies since being with Tianna.

She had me all loved up, until I was talking words that I haven't spoken before.

Steve Brooks

My name is Steve Brooks. Some of you may know that Rhys is my son. I'm currently in prison, serving a 25-year sentence, for a murder that I didn't commit. Although me and a fella called Mark were there.

My solicitor has informed me, the hearing yesterday went well and was looking good. So, fingers crossed, I'm looking to be home by Christmas.

I was given a letter from Mark, the other guy, also in prison for the same murder. Apparently, he has only three to six months left, as he's dying, but he did not say what his condition was.

Anyway, he has taken full responsibility for killing Leon, letting me off the hook, and taking all the blame.

I haven't asked him to do this, as we can both fight to be freed. But he has declined to fight the charges against him, and wished for me to get back to my family.

I've known Mark for years, and this is the sort of thing that he'd always do for his mates.

Unfortunately, I will miss my eldest son's wedding tomorrow to his lovely girlfriend, Tianna.

Not long ago, my son told me that he had started a relationship with Kim Roberts. You know, the daughter of the man I've been convicted of killing. I told him then that it wasn't such a good idea, considering the situation that I was currently in.

"Are you fucking kidding me," I yelled, dropping a very expensive glass of whiskey to the floor.

Which I quite rightly told him to fucking pick up.

But my son wouldn't listen.

"Dad," he said, as he dared to look me straight in the eyes. "I love her so much, she makes me happy when we're together."

I told my son it was a love affair that wasn't meant to be.

Apart from me being charged with her dad's murder, my son has told me she was having his baby.

Fucking hell, what an idiot. My wife and me have raised him better than that, apparently not.

What a predicament that my son found himself in; it's like watching a car crash in slow motion.

Kim was married at the time. Although I understand she was separated from her husband, nevertheless, it was still a bad idea to get involved with her.

But I guessed the heart wants what the heart wants.

Now my son told me that they were not even on speaking terms anymore, because of his fiancée, Tianna's, meddling in my case.

I would like to clear something up, so as not to let Tianna take all the blame.

Tianna had a friend called Renee, yeah, I'm sure you've all heard of her. She's quite a feisty little thing.

She's a prison warden here at my prison, only, I didn't know at the time that they knew each other, until Tianna came to visit me with Rhys.

Renee, so happened to be on duty that afternoon, and that's how all this appeal hearing started.

Renee doesn't mess about or beat around the bush.

She encouraged my son and Tianna to get the appeal case going that's when Tianna started the process.

As for Kim and her family, especially her mum, Denise, I know all of this was going to hurt them. I understand that Denise did not attend my appeal hearing. I guess it would be too much for her to listen to.

And I'm also guessing that everyone wanted to know about the money.

Yeah, I took it. It seemed like a good idea at the time. One hundred and fifty thousand pounds was what Carl handed me in a brown envelope. I paid off the mortgage and put the rest into my son's university funds. I'm not proud, but no fucking way, do I regret taking the money, hell no.

One more thing, everyone wanted to know, how did Leon's body get to be buried under the bench in Carl's garden?

Well, I'm not that stupid. If I do tell you, just before the outcome of my hearing, I'm likely to rot in jail.

Tianna

Morning, Mr Kitty. Do you know what day it is today? Yes, that's right, my and Rhys' wedding day, oh Mr Kitty, I'm getting married, to a wonderful man in a few hours' time.

My friends Renee and Tamara are here with me.

We've just had our breakfast. Well, I only had a bit of toast and a sip of coffee, as I'm too nervous to eat anything.

I looked through the window, the sky was still dark and peaceful.

The hairdresser would be arriving soon, to do our hair and makeup, any moment now. Renee has told me to relax, as she can see how nervous I was getting. So, Tamara put on her playlist, with some relaxing tunes playing.

The doorbell rang. It was a beautiful bouquet of flowers, there was a card, it read,

'To my beautiful future wife, I can't wait to marry you. Love, your future husband.'

Renee and Tamara both said, "Aww," at the same time, smiling.

My dad, Clive, arrived.

"Not long to go now, Daddy."

Staring up into his eyes, he was smiling down, with a tear in his eye.

The bridesmaids have all arrived, and oh my gosh, I'm so over excited, if that's the right word, my wedding car has just arrived, my heart gave a little flutter.

My friends, Renee and Tamara, both have tears in their eyes. They told me not to cry, as I'd ruin my makeup.

My dad, Clive, has just told me how beautiful I look and that Rhys is a very, very lucky young man to have such a beautiful young lady like me for his wife.

We arrived at the church almost 15 minutes late. That's because Mr Kitty decided he wanted to go into the garden, at the very last minute, and had Renee chasing after him for nearly 10 minutes.

I walked down the aisle, holding onto my dad's arm. I can see Rhys and Drake both were staring at me, but it's Rhys whom I stared back at. He looked so handsome standing there in his Tuxedo.

Rhys held my hand, I gazed up at his face, we both smiled, and made our amazing wedding vows, and promises to each other.

We're finally married. I'm now Mrs Tianna Brooks, what a wonderful feeling it has. Rhys told me how much he loves me and would do so forever. I replied by telling him how much I loved him, more than any words could ever say.

At our reception, our first dance as husband and wife was to I Care 4 U by Aaliyah. To tell you the truth, some people have commented that this song was a dig at Kim. Yeah, whatever.

Well, it really doesn't matter, because she didn't attend our wedding, anyway.

What matters is that Rhys and I are married now. I love him, and he love me.

All of our family and friends were at our wedding. my biological dad, Mathew, looked very smart and handsome. It broke my heart, though, to see him in a wheelchair.

My mum Jessica's here, as well as my sister, Sabrina and her family.

And who would have guessed that my two brothers, Sam and Stevie, also came with their families. And the family that I thought I was part of, how can I forget my almost dad, Aubrey, and his family.

Our wedding was the best thing that has happened to us in a long time. Both Rhys and I deserved happiness in our lives. Don't you think?

Rhys' mum, Marcia, and my adopted mum, Michelle, seemed to have hit it off straight away.

Then there's my real mum, Jessica and Aubrey's wife, Martha. Oh boy, I'm getting really confused as to who is who. Aren't you?

My husband and I booked two nights at a hotel by the River Thames, in London, before going to the Seychelles, on our honeymoon.

Don't worry, we've left Mr Kitty in good hands. Hopefully, he won't be too upset when we get back, he did hate me leaving him for too long. But we've left him lots of treats and promised to buy him a new cat climbing frame.

We've just arrived at our four-star hotel by the riverbank. It's a one-bedroom suite with a balcony.

The room had a super king-size bed and a rather large window.

Fresh flowers, a bottle of very expensive champagne, and a small box of chocolates, wrapped with a beautiful red ribbon, with a pretty little bow, and a card that read,

'Congratulations on your wedding, Mr and Mrs Brooks.'

Our first night as husband and wife, we had room service, but who could eat, certainly not me, when I knew how much my husband, yes, my husband, wanted to make love to me.

"Come to me, Mrs Brooks," he whispered softly.

I certainly didn't hesitate in moving swiftly to my husband's embrace.

And yet, there was a flutter of nervous giggles. He held me tightly in his arms, his kiss was so full of passion, long, almost a breathless smooch.

Soft romantic music played in the background, as we danced slowly and gazed affectionately into each other's eyes.

Our fingers interlock, his tight embrace, our arms around each other.

He whispered in my ear, "I love you, truly love you."

My husband leaned in and cupped the sides of my face with his soft hands.

Rhys' lips met mine, which had a taste of sexy sweetness. His lips moved across my cheek and down my neck with soft, caressing kisses.

He slid my dress free, his warm hands moving over my naked body possessively, then he lifted me and carried me to the bed.

Rhys' gaze lingered then went over my body, my body entwined with his. I breathed his scent in, as I leaned into his muscular body.

Rhys licked my stomach and said he liked the way I tasted.

I groaned softly and whispered his name, "Rhys, don't stop, please don't stop."

My husband's scent and touch overwhelmed me, yet his hot kisses set fire to a desire stronger than any I'd ever experienced.

The way I'm feeling right now, butterflies, butterflies, and even more butterflies, in my stomach. My husband started to caress my breast, and planted soft kisses on my neck, leaving a trail of hot kisses along my collarbone to my stomach.

He slid his hand between my inner thighs, and slowly raises his hand, and caresses me there, again I tell him.

"Don't stop, oh God, Rhys, don't stop."

He kissed me and put his tongue into my open mouth.

He raised both my arms above my head, and whispered sweet love songs into my ear, his words were so breathless.

"Tell me how you're feeling?" he asked.

All I could do was to give out a soft moan and groan.

His strong arms slipped around my waist, as I slid my arms around his neck, and pressed our bodies closer together, completely surrendering to his arms that surrounded me.

My body sparked with desire, my inner sex-kitten, "Mee-oow!"

Oh fudge, did I really think that out loud?

"Oh, Rhys," I moan softly.

I felt him, all of him pressed against me. I didn't want him to stop.

We moved our bodies against each other in sync to the sound of the music playing in the background. I Love You by JaMelody. I didn't want this night of love-making to end, our first night as husband and wife.

Rhys put his arms around my waist and rolled us until I was on top.

He whispered as he kissed my neck, then took in my sweet scent. "Show your husband what you have to offer me, you little sex-kitten," he said, and laughed.

"Opps, you heard me then, babe."

"Every word."

Boy, did I give my husband the love that he deserved. That night, the chemistry was more than crazy.

He moaned and groaned, calling my name. "Oh Tianna, sexy Tianna," he whispered, ever so softly.

He gently moved the hair from my face, so he could get a good look at me. He held onto my waist, squeezing my bottom at times, and caressed my breast.

Then, he rolled us again, hmm, like rolling a dice.

Where was I...oh yes, my husband raised both my legs, onto his shoulders, and went deep inside of me. I screamed out with pure pleasure, but Rhys asked if he was hurting me.

"No, oh no, don't stop, keep going, keep going," I moaned.

Oh boy, that was some marathon.

Afterwards, he lay on his side, with his body pressed close to mine, stroking my hair and face, then he kissed me and whispered, "Je t'aime." I love you.

The desire lighting my body was hot and aching, as if my body innately knew how well he'd satisfied me. I ran my hand over his perfect body, marvelling at the smooth skin stretched over his solid muscle.

He smiled at me. I smiled back. I could see, one hundred per cent love, that he had for me.

So, I picked up the courage, and said it back in French, although not as perfect as his accent, but I said it, "Je t'aime."

He only laughed, and then started to wipe the tears from his eyes. He laughed, not at me, but with me. Although I said the words correctly, the accent just wasn't there.

"Don't worry, Mrs Brooks," he said, as he continued laughing. "I will teach you to have the perfect French accent like mine."

"That's why I love you so much," I said, smiling.

Tamara

Wow, what a lovely wedding my good friend, Tianna, had yesterday. Rhys is such an amazing guy.

Those two were truly meant to be together. Tianna has finally met her Prince Charming, and I'm so happy for her.

I can tell, just by the way he looked at her, with those beautiful green eyes, how much he's in love with her.

There isn't anything that he wouldn't do for her, and get this, he's even finally given Tianna all of his love that he was holding onto for his ex-Kim.

We all know how much he loved her, and now she's expecting his baby.

I don't know Kim personally, but from what I've heard about her, you know, from the odd gossip here and there, everyone said she's such a nice lady.

However, she did herself a favour and stayed with her husband.

So, now, my friend, Tianna can have Rhys. Well, she had him, because they got married yesterday.

Anyway, if you don't mind, while Tianna and Rhys are away on their honeymoon to the Seychelles, I would like to tell you all, just a little bit, about my background story.

As you all know, I, too, was adopted as a child. But unlike Tianna, I've always known who my birth mother was.

When I was about three or four years old, my biological mother became ill. I think it's because of my biological dad.

He would come home drunk every night and beat her until she was black and blue.

There were six of us children, and all under the age of 10. I had three older siblings and two younger; the youngest, my brother, was only a baby. I'm not really sure how old he was.

Anyway, social services got involved because, I found out years later, a neighbour reported my dad; they got fed up of hearing my dad repeatedly beating my mum up, and her cries for help.

We all got taken into care, we were all separated into six different foster homes, which really wasn't fair.

Eventually, my two youngest siblings, social services, found a home, so they could be together, but myself and my three sisters, never got to see each other much while growing up.

The only good thing was, the social worker always arranged a visit for me to see my mum, as for my dad, he divorced my mum and remarried. As to his whereabouts, I have no idea.

Now for a happy ending to my story. About two years ago, I had a problem with the electrics in my house. So, I phoned an electrician, he came highly recommended.

A few hours later, the doorbell demanded my attention. I open the door, and there he was, my future happiness, just standing there.

Oh my God, he stood there in his navy-blue uniform, holding his tool bag, cool as a cucumber, may I add, oh yes.

He had the most amazing eye colour, blue/greyish, that I have ever seen. I mean, I was just lost for words when I saw him standing there.

He looked at me, I looked straight back at him, and I fell instantly in love with him. His hair was blond, he was clean-shaven, with the most beautiful smile you could ask for. His name is Dean, and we've been together ever since.

Eight months later, we moved into our home that we live in now. We are very happy, and hopefully one day soon, I'd be the one getting married.

As for me, I'd never told you what I look like. Well, I'm a black lady. I have a short cut hair style; I believe it's called a straight layered pixie cut.

Dean told me that I also have a beautiful smile. When I smile, you can see my dimples on my cheeks.

Dean's also a good guy. He was a bit cautious when we first met, as he'd never dated a woman of colour before, but hey, he loves me for who I am, not the colour of my skin.

And to be honest, I've never dated outside of my race before, so it was a new experience for us both.

I've met his family and his friends, and they have welcomed me into their homes. Likewise with my family and friends.

Well, you've met all of my crazy friends; they're my friends, and I also call them my family.

Dean's parents they've told me to call them Mum and Dad, as they know my background, and want me to feel comfortable within their family, even though we're not married yet. I'm like the daughter they never had.

Dean has four brothers, no sisters, unfortunately, so you can say I fit right into their family. Lucky for me, I guess.

Drake

My man Rhys had finally put a ring on Tianna's finger. I'm pleased for the happy couple.

He texted me from the airport, before they boarded the plane for the Seychelles. Tianna was worried about Mr Kitty. I told him not to worry about the cat, he was sitting on Renee's lap and purring.

"Just enjoy your wife and your honeymoon," I said.

But let's get serious for a moment. It was a nice wedding; however, I wasn't too excited about their choice of the first dance song.

Boy, Rhys needs to reel in Tianna, and do it quickly. That song, if you listen to the lyrics, it's a sure dig at Kim. I can't believe that Rhys would actually play that tune. what's wrong with the brother these days?

Almost, yeah, almost everyone who knows the situation that Rhys found himself in with Kim was gossiping about the lyrics to that song. I mean everyone.

Boy, I haven't got a clue what was going on, but it certainly needed nipping in the bud before Kim has his baby. Because what's going to happen then?

Anyway, when he gets back, we're definitely going to have words.

This bloody cat, man, it's doing my head in. The damn cat meowing all through the night. What's its name, Mr what, frigging puss. Mr Kitty, is that its name? What kind of a silly name is that, then?

The cat meowing to come into our bed, no, no, no, I'm not having any of that.

Tianna gave us a big box of treats, the cat looked at me as if it were in charge of me, staring at me, with its big, scary eyes, woah.

Do you want to hear a joke? This morning I'm in the kitchen, making coffee.

What did Mr Kitty do? Yeah, this cat knows tricks. Mr Kitty started to move his food bowl, with his paw, over to where I was standing, no word of a lie.

Then he looked up at me and stared down at the empty food bowl. What does that mean? He's telling me he's hungry.

Boy, all I could do was laugh and feed him, of course.

Renee googled why; Mr Kitty wants to sleep in our bed with us. Apparently, it's because he thinks it's his bed, and he's a little too spoiled.

Well, Mr Kitty seemed to be a happy cat, so I will have to give him back the way Tianna left him. So Mr Kitty, puss, puss, puss, come for your treats.

Rhys

We've just got back from a lovely two-week honeymoon in the Seychelles. My wife is happy, I'm happy, everybody is happy, except Mr Kitty. He's very upset with Tianna for leaving him for so long.

Drake told me that Mr Kitty was as good as gold. He never caused any problems, and he slept in his own bed. I'm pleased, because I know that he sometimes can jump up onto the bed, without you noticing.

Drake reassured me, Mr Kitty slept in his own bed.

Today, we received an invitation through the post to Casey's 30th birthday party. Well, in case you didn't know, he's Alex's half-brother.

I suppose Alex and Kim will be there. Well, of course, they'll be there. I'm kind of looking forward to seeing Kim, only to ask how she and my baby were doing.

I had Drake on my back, about our wedding day's first dance. Yeah, I guess it was a little insensitive for my wife to have chosen that song for us to dance to.

However, Kim and Alex chose not to attend our wedding. Looking back, my wife shouldn't have played it.

This afternoon, my wife was catching up with her friends. I was thinking about phoning Kim.

Us not talking like we used to, it's not what I wanted; it's killing me. Maybe I would give her a phone call, because it will look bad, at the birthday party, if half the guests weren't talking to each other.

Well, it went better than I had hoped for, she is doing okay. Kim saw the midwife a few days ago, now that she is 34 weeks, not long now, until she'd give birth.

She told me that, she had a couple of black and white images of the baby, and asked, if I would like one.

I asked Kim, if she would like to meet up for coffee, you know, just so she can give me the photo, that's all.

I've still got a few days off until I go back to work, so, why not meet up with her.

And yes, I did tell my wife, she had that look in her eyes, that said, *what the fuck are you playing at*. I did ask my wife if she wanted to tag along, but she just rolled her eyes and walked off in a huff. What am I supposed to do.

I met up with Kim the next day, she looked so radiant.

Her hair was slicked back, with a side-swept bang. Tianna occasionally does her hair in the same style. I won't lie, Kim looked gorgeous.

I gave her a little cheeky kiss on her lips, I know I shouldn't have done it. She blushed, then looked over my shoulder. I guess that I took her by surprise doing that.

The baby started kicking, so she let me feel her tummy.

That's our son, and I can feel him kicking. He'd definitely be a footballer when he grows up.

I've just realised that her soft hand, is on my hand, while I was feeling the baby kicking.

Fuck, we're staring at each other now. I could tell by the way her eyes welled up that she was missing me. But what can we do? It's too late, it's bloody too late, Kim.

I gave her a tissue, she thanked me, and said she just gets emotional sometimes for no reason, and said that it's her hormones.

But was it, or was she missing me? To be sure, I knew I'm playing with fire here. I held her hand, and she gave my hand a tight squeeze.

Kim then told me that she and Alex have agreed that I can name my son.

But Alex would be adding his middle name to whatever name I chose. There's always a catch with that dude, but at least I get a say in my son's name.

However, she did let slip that they had spoken about having the baby adopted, which really upset me.

I made a little joke, and told Kim that I had hoped my son would have green eyes like me, but that didn't go down too well.

"Oh please, for God's sake, Rhys," she said, rolling her eyes.

But then looked at me, and giggled.

I only went, and asked her if I could see her again, she said yes, then asked if Tianna and I were going to Casey's birthday party next week.

She kept staring at me, then said she had to leave, to pick Mason up from the nursery and Maya from her mother-in-law.

I walked her to her car. Yes, the BMW that her husband had to buy her, for all the cheating that he had done. I got to hand it to Alex. It's a very nice car. It must have cost him a fortune, but I guess Kim's worth every penny, no doubt.

As for me, yet again, I didn't want to let her walk away from me, just seeing her today, and especially that she's having my son, right now, my emotions were playing up.

I've just got married to Tianna, yet, seeing Kim, bloody hell, I'm lost. I'm drowning in love for her, and I know she was feeling the same way.

But for now, let's just say, for now, I'd keep my thoughts to myself.

When I got home, Tianna wasn't that pleased with me seeing Kim. But she understands that I have to maintain some sort of relationship with her and Alex because of the baby. After all, I want to be in my son's life.

We went to Tianna's parents' house for lunch, Clive and Mitchell, well, it is Sunday, and she still regarded them as her mum and dad.

This whole drama about who her parents were was getting rather confusing. I am pleased for my wife, she can finally fit the missing pieces to the jigsaw puzzle.

It's Sunday evening, and boy, my wife has promised me something special before we go to sleep.

My head was spinning right about now, my wife, she's one hell of a sexy lady. Boy oh boy, I can't wait.

My wife taken me by my hand, and we've gone up to our bedroom. The lights were dimmed, there was a sweet-smelling candle burning.

Then I see a chair in the corner of the room, she told me to sit on our bed. Tianna drove me wild. Let me tell you, guys, what my sexy, beautiful wife performed for me.

Do you know a particular song, not going to name it, but my wife performed it just as well.

Tianna, my God, she was rocking her body, she was tilting her bum on that chair, jiggling her body. My God.

She opened, then closed those beautiful legs of hers, just teasing me, giving me a peek of what was to come next.

She rested her hands on those thighs of hers then took her hand, and opened her legs to reveal. Oh boy, no knickers.

Boy, she just let it go and channelled her inner diva self. And did I say what she was wearing, or not wearing?

Fuck, I'm gasping for breath right now. Boy, I'm telling you, I'm so horny right now. I took my wife straight to bed, and I buried my face between her thighs, then she wrapped her legs around my head.

My wife screamed my name. "Rhys, oh babe, I love what you're doing to me right now. Oh God, Rhys, don't stop, don't stop."

I just kept licking my wife until she, well, you know what, I'm not going to spell it out for you.

She then performed a lap dance to remember. Shall I say, it took me back to when I was in Amsterdam. Oops, I shouldn't have said it out loud.

This is how guys get themselves into trouble, let me just tell you. What's that saying, loose lips, sink ships. Anyway, enough said about that.

Next Saturday is Casey's 30th birthday party. I'm looking forward to going, especially to see Kim. I'm not going to sit here and lie.

Don't worry, I'm not thinking of starting any kind of relationship with her. After all, I've just married my beautiful wife, and she's my priority right now.

But first, my wife and I were just visiting my dad in prison before going to Drake and Renee's house. He said that he has some good news to tell us. Looks like my dad won his appeal, and hopefully would be out of prison by Christmas.

As Tianna and I were about to leave for Drake and Renee's house, Kim phoned. She wanted to let me know that she was informed, just a while ago, that Mark, the other guy in prison for murdering her dad, died early this morning.

Well, that's a big shock to the system. I know that my dad said he was ill, but I wasn't expecting him to die suddenly.

An hour later, I arrived at my mate, Drake' house, and all hell had broken loose. Apparently, someone has sent his wife death threats.

She works at a prison, but I can't think of anyone who would do such a thing.

Renee's a tough cookie usually, but this made her mad, as well as cry.

Drake was fuming, he swore he was going to kill whoever was responsible for threatening his wife when he hunted them down.

Drake was so angry, and who could blame him? I tried to calm him down.

"Bruv, come on, come outside, and have a cigarette and calm down."

He's pacing back and forth, the length of his garden, swearing and cursing, vowing vengeance, then he yelled back.

"Bruv, calm down, calm down, you mad. No one is threatening my wife, and gets off so lightly."

I stood watching, as his body rippled with anger, his face was livid, the veins standing out of his neck.

You know what, if someone threatened my wife, I'd probably be doing the same thing as Drake right now.

Seriously, I can't blame the brother, it could be anyone, but who?

Tianna is shaken up, by the whole experience, to say the least. My wife and Renee both went into the bathroom, crying.

You got to be fucking shitting me, Tianna's phone also pinged, she received a death threat. What the fuck, who is this person?

We thought about it, if they both received death threats, it's got to be from the same person, right? It has to be.

There was nothing we could do, except report it to the police, to find out who's been sending the message. So we decided to attend Casey's birthday party, even though I knew how distressed my wife was.

The evening of the birthday party, there were lots of friends and family. My mum was here, also my twin brothers and their partners.

The venue was a beautifully decorated room with high ceilings and an enormous chandelier.

Each table had a large flower display in the centre. Sorry, I'm telling you what the venue looks like, that's something my wife would tell you. So, I got to let you all know, she's the one telling me what to say.

She nudged me and said how beautiful the venue was.

You know me, as long as there's plenty to eat, and the drinks keep flowing, to tell you the truth, I'm not really fussed about all this looking good venue stuff.

Anyway, we've been here for about 45 minutes, and I can't see Kim or Alex. There were a couple of tables with empty seats. My wife kept asking me, who was I hoping to see, walk through the door.

She's no fool. She knew who I was looking for, but wanted me to say it out loud. Tianna looked at me, rolled her eyes, and tutted.

She caught her breath and sat up sharply, instinctively searching the sea of faces, then pointed in the opposite direction of the venue door, and pointed to Alex and Kim. Literally just two tables away from where we are seated.

"Rhys, if only you had said you were looking for Kim, I would have put you out of your misery. She's been here all along before us. Look how she's been staring at you all evening; she has no shame. She just watches you, and her husband is sitting next to her, letting her do whatever the hell she likes."

What can I say to my wife? I turned around to see Kim staring, but believe me, when I tell you this, it was not me whom Kim was staring at.

My mum, Marcia, that's who Kim had been staring at. Boy, I'm laughing inside…hmm, that doesn't sound right.

My mum really liked Kim. She thought that we had a future together, but sadly, it wasn't to be.

My mum's the one who started to stare at Kim first, as I found out later that evening. She did not conceal her vexation and disappointment at Kim sitting there with her husband, yet expecting my baby. I suppose it wasn't really warranted. I had to plead with my mum not to look at Kim in that way.

What the hell was going on in my mum's mind, I couldn't say, but my wife's jaw dropped a mile when my mum kept talking about me and Kim this, and me and Kim that.

My wife's blue eyes, were boring into my soul, searching, demanding answers to questions that were not spoken.

Mum started to roll her eyes, then leaned over towards me, not even bothering to whisper, and asked, "When is the baby due?"

As my wife sat in complete silence, sipping a glass of red wine, staring at me, then Kim.

I must have sat there for at least an hour, with all eyes on me at the table.

My wife's fixed gaze on me to…say something to your mum, she's upsetting me by talking about Kim, for the entire evening.

My mum's eyes fixed on me, she's probably thinking, *look at Kim, sitting over there with her Alex, yet, she dares to stare at you, she has no flipping shame.* And yes, I did enjoy Kim staring at me, only, she wasn't. She was, in fact, staring at my mum, or that's what I keep telling myself, for my wife's sake.

I'm feeling anxious right now. So, I decided to go outside the venue for a breath of fresh air. And there she was, as if she knew I'd be coming outside.

Kim was looking beautiful as ever, with her baby bump, my son—our son.

Of course, I went straight over to her. Come on now, wouldn't you? No, you sure now. Yeah right, I don't believe a word that any of you are saying.

"Rhys," she said quietly, "can we talk?"

Smiling at her beautiful face, I told her that she could talk to me about anything. I held her hand, she smiled, and gave my hand a tight squeeze. I loved when she always held my hand, and squeezed it, just like old times.

I couldn't help myself, and put my arms around her baby bump. She, in turn, leaned towards me and rested her head on my chest.

Kim smelled so sweet as usual. I rubbed my face against her soft cheeks, she moved her face slightly, and before we knew it, we shared a kiss.

Oh fuck, I put my tongue into her mouth. She held me so tight, what should I have done, pull away from her? No, that isn't going to happen.

"Rhys," she whispered my name.

Just hearing her voice alone, just saying my name. Oh man, I just couldn't tear myself away from her. But she was calling my name for a different reason.

You see, Kim spotted Tianna coming out of the venue, obviously looking for me. And that's the only reason why I had to pull myself away from her.

Tianna came straight over, okay, now this is true. My wife came out of the venue looking for me, and Alex was straight behind her.

If you saw the look on both of their faces. Ever heard the expression, if looks could kill. Alex's face was angry and red, becoming very hostile the closer he got.

My wife, her march turned into a stroll, wiping away angry tears.

My wife was just about to confront Kim, but her husband, Alex, that dude, he's a swift mover, grabbed Kim so quick, out of harm's way.

Now the dude was asking me, what the fuck, was I doing with his wife. He stood right up close, in my face.

He yelled at me, "She might be having your fucking kid, but she's still my fucking wife, so, do yourself a favour, and piss off, you fucking moron."

Sorry, but I just laughed in this dude's face.

Kim looked at me, shook her head and whispered, "Rhys, don't."

This dude, he thought that he was going to get the better of me, and gave me a sucker punch. But as I stand here before you, no way he was getting the upper hand this time.

The idiot, lunged towards me, yeah that's right to punch my lights out, but I was too quick for the fool.

Unfortunately, Kim somehow got in the way and ended up on the pavement. It was just a quick reflex, on my part, I held my hand out to break her fall, and that stupid dude, she called her husband, pushed me away.

That's how she ended up on the cold pavement, seriously, man. That dude she calls a husband is such an idiot. What the hell does Kim see in him?

So, now the fool is lifting her from the ground, and she buried her face in her idiot husband's chest, sobbing.

A few minutes later, some of the other party guests started to come outside and wanted to know what was going on.

Everyone's asking that stupid dude, the reason why, his wife was crying.

An ambulance was called, but she's okay and didn't need any hospital treatment, thankfully.

Anyway, everyone went back inside to enjoy Casey's 30th birthday party. I mean, that's the reason we all came here, right?

Clive

My name is Clive. I'm Tianna's dad, well, adopted dad, she was raised by my wife, Michelle and me since she was three days old.

The reason I decided to speak is, this afternoon, I received a distressing phone call from my daughter.

She told me that she and her friend, Renee, have both been sent death threats via text message.

How can anyone be that cruel? I know my daughter has a heart of gold and wouldn't deliberately hurt anyone.

She also told me that last night, she and her husband went to Casey's birthday party, and there was a confrontation between Rhys and Alex, Casey's half-brother.

I'm not really sure what the problem was between those two, but I think it has something to do with Alex's wife, Kim.

Tianna told me that she believes Rhys was still in love with Kim, although he denied this.

When it comes to Kim, my daughter knows deep down in her heart that Rhys would choose Kim every time. I told my daughter not to be silly, and that Rhys loves her one hundred per cent.

But she went silent for a few seconds before responding to my words of comfort.

"He doesn't love me like I want him to, Daddy, because of her," she sobbed.

I told my beautiful daughter, "Rhys does love you; he married you and declared his love to you in front of friends and family."

But my daughter wants an answer that I can't give her.

"Daddy," she sobbed, "I love my husband, more than any words could say. He does make me feel special, in every way possible, the things he does for me, he gives me his undivided attention."

So, I had to ask my daughter, if that statement is true, then why put any doubt in her mind?

She went on to tell me that the way Rhys was looking at Kim yesterday, and any time that he laid eyes on her, she sees the love he had in his heart for her, even though he swore that he had given my daughter all of his love.

I had to give my daughter a good talking to, and let her know that her mother and I, have been married for many years, some good and some bad. But we never go looking for problems in our marriage that aren't there.

"So, please, sweetheart, don't create any with your husband. Sweetheart, he's your husband, not this lady called Kim's husband, yes, honey, yours. Do yourself a favour, and talk to him, that's the only way you're going to get to the truth."

As I was speaking with my daughter, I could definitely hear crying, but I had to tell my daughter that she'd been bawling for 35 minutes, and it was time to stop. Cruel, I know. Crying wasn't going to get her anywhere in life.

"Tianna, sweetheart, it's time to hang up the phone and talk with your husband."

All I could hear was sniff, sniff.

Then she sobbed, "Yes, Daddy."

Then hung up the phone before I had a chance to say goodbye to her.

Tianna

It's early on a Monday morning, the air is chilly and still. It was still dark outside as I looked through the window.

My neighbour, Sally-Anne, looked up at me and gave me a wave before getting into her car.

Rhys brought me a cup of coffee and gave me a kiss on my forehead. I gave him a smile, and he smiled back with those beautiful green eyes.

He then gives me a jewellery box, inside was a diamond-cut bracelet.

"For a beautiful lady, who happens to be my wife," he said, smiling.

"Oh, Rhys," I said, as I let out a little gasp, and clutched my husband's hand.

How can I have any possible doubt that he truly loves me?

He went to take the cup from me, but it fell out of my hand onto the floor.

"Don't worry, I'll clean it up."

I watched as my husband as he cleaned up the coffee spilt onto the floor. Why do I doubt the love he has for me?

But I needed to know the truth, so I asked him. This is what he told me.

"Babe, why doubt the love that I have for you. I married you. I fought for this love, remember, I fought to win you back. Don't destroy what we have. I love you, and only you. Kim is having my son, I can't change that, and I'm being honest, if I could go back in time, I wouldn't change a thing."

"I'm sorry if that's not what you want to hear, I'm sorry, Tianna, but it's the truth. You know that I would never leave you, you do know that, right?" he said, standing next to me.

He held my hand, then wrapped his arms around my waist.

The tears slowly rolled down my face. I believed every word that he said, but…if he could go back in time, why not change the fact that Kim was having his child, why not change that?

I held onto my husband, raising both my arms around his neck loosely, looking deep into his eyes.

He whispered into my earlobes, "I love you, only you."

We held each other, then our bodies started to sway from side to side. I closed my eyes, I thought to myself, whatever it is, that he feels for Kim, he's my husband, he married me, and she can't have him. But I can't shake out of my mind; Kim, how she melted, in my husband's embrace, returning his hungry kiss.

I'd Rather Go Blind by Beyonce.

I'm just taking a few moments to hold onto my husband, the smell of his cologne, his soft hands around my waist, the way he kissed me.

He's holding me so tight that I can literally feel his heartbeat; that's how close we were.

He cupped my face, looked me in my eyes, and kissed me softly onto my lips. I respond by putting my tongue into his mouth. I didn't know, that it was physically possible for him to hold me even tighter than he had been holding me, but it felt so good to be held so tight.

"My God, Tianna, don't ever doubt my love for you."

"I'm sorry."

"Never doubt me, I will never lie to you, surely you should know this by now," he said, as we stood gazing into each other's eyes.

I was so lost in the moment that I didn't hear my phone ringing. I eventually tore myself away from my husband and answered.

It was Renee. She told me that the police had informed her that they cannot trace the death threats on her phone because whoever sent the message did so on a burner phone.

"Oh my God, Renee, so whoever is sending us death threats is using a cheap phone that you can discard when they no longer need it, flipping hell," I said, shaking nervously.

"This way they will never be caught, they can just keep sending messages, or even kill us," replied Renee, upset and angry.

I felt sick to my stomach. Really, I did. Whoever it is, they could be watching the house, watching me, watching my every move.

Steve Brooks

Fuck me, hello people, I am finally free from that shit hole of a prison. Thank you, your majesty's service. I'm free from this hell of a nightmare. What a waste of one year of my life. Can't ever get that back.

I'm just waiting for my wife, Marcia, and my son, Rhys, to pick me up. At least, I get to spend Christmas with my family.

Today is, damn, what day is it. Inside, every day is the same. Same shit, every flipping day.

Oh God, there's my wife.

"I've missed you so much, hun."

"I've missed you too, babe."

"Oh, hun, I'm home, I'm never leaving you again, not if I can help it." I held my wife tightly around her waist, as a single tear trickled down my left cheek.

My wife started crying tears of joy. I held her even tighter, and told her not to cry, as I'm home for good now.

I gave Rhys a big, old bear hug. His eyes welled up, as did mine. We both tried not to cry in front of his mum, you know, it's a man thing.

"Dad, I knew you'd be home for Christmas."

"Looks like—"

Before I even got the chance to respond, I looked down the road, as I could hear the roaring noise from a car. I knew that sound only too well. Yes, it's my sons Lewis and Kyle.

"It's good to see you both," I said, hugging each of them.

It will be Christmas in four days' time. I'm so glad to be home where I belong.

It's shameful that my good friend, Mark, had to die in prison. He, of all people, did not deserve to die like that, especially in prison, with no family around him. No man deserves to die like that.

Me and a few of his mates, we're going to pay and give him the funeral that he so rightly deserves.

Mark's one of those genuine blokes, he definitely wasn't no criminal. RIP, my friend.

Now, I am a free man, I'd like to confess my sins. You know what happened to Kim's dad, Leon. Well, Mark did run away sharpest the little shit. As for Carl, he shouted at passing cars to get help for Leon.

He jumped up and down waving his right hand, half drunk, shoeless, scared shitless and wearing a silly hat.

That would explain why no one stopped. What Carl never knew at the time, because I never confessed, when he turned his back, yelling for help, I kicked the shit out of Leon. I was the one who suggested Carl cough up some cash to keep me and Mark quiet.

The stupid idiot, thinking he had killed Leon, seeing his lifeless body just lying on the pavement, feeling all guilty, paid the money. What a fucking plonker.

With that much cash, I paid off my mortgage and some debts, which I kept hidden from my wife.

Am I sorry, absolutely not. I lived a mortgage free life, and paid for my son's university, enough said.

Moving on because I am a heartless fucker.

It's two days before Christmas, and Kim agreed to meet with me. I'm really sorry for all the pain she and her mum, Denise, had been put through. I did apologise to Kim, she stood staring up at the dark, starry sky, for a time, attempting to push away the torment which had gripped her completely.

But the look on her face said it all. Kim's face was like, *you murdered my dad*.

Yeah, okay, what a boring story…you must think I'm a right nasty fucker.

Then there's Alex, her husband, and his mum, Lyn, who was married to Carl. My mate, who got me into this trouble in the first place.

But sadly, he died, and now here we all are, it's like picking up the pieces from a shattered glass.

Kim's a lovely lady. I first met her a while back, when she was dating my son, Rhys. I liked her then, and I still like her now.

But unfortunately, she chose to go back to Alex, the moron, which is a shame.

As I've said, she is a lovely lady. I remember the first time my son brought her over to the house. We were having a barbecue, as I recall. I gave her an undercooked sausage, which my son hastily grabbed from her hand, and chucked it back on the grill.

She smiled sweetly up at me, but I could tell Kim's heart was full of trouble. That trouble was her husband, Alex. She's no Bonnie, but from what I heard, he's definitely a Clyde.

Rhys told me she's having his baby, what a mess. Although I liked Kim, when I found out who her dad was, I told my son to end the relationship, but he refused.

He confided in me that he still loved Kim. What the fuck?

I've told him many times to give up on her ever being with him. But he still insisted that one day, they'd be together, yeah, and pigs will fly.

And now that there's a baby on the way, he's more determined to have her.

Hmm, I hear you, what about his wife, Tianna? He swears to me that he loves her, but Kim, he wants her, and only her. What a total screw up, don't you think.

This is not how I've raised my boys to behave, believe me. You don't mess about with another man's wife, but I guess the heart wants what the heart wants.

Like I've said, I've arranged to meet up with Kim, and her husband came along too.

Looks like Alex doesn't let her out of his sight.

He's no fool. He definitely knew that my son wants her back. From what I understand, my son and Alex don't see eye to eye. They've had a few punch-ups recently, one of those being at Casey's birthday party.

What I do know about my son, he'd never give up until Kim is his.

But where does that leave his wife, Tianna? She's also a lovely lady and doesn't deserve to be messed about.

So, like I've said, I met with Kim and Alex in a coffee shop, Alex's idea, not mine. I apologised for what happened to her dad, and the way he had died, and they both accepted my apology.

Yeah, I know, I've got no flipping shame. I had hoped that we could all move forward and be civil to one another, that includes both Rhys and Alex, but unfortunately, I can't see that happening anytime soon.

I suggested to Kim and Alex to come over to my house on Boxing Day for dinner, and to invite Denise, Kim's mum and Lyn, Alex's mummy.

But before Kim could reply, Alex jumped to his feet, and yelled, "Are you out of your fucking mind."

Kim pulled at her husband's shirt sleeve, shook her head, then calmly asked him to sit back down.

"Not happening, mate," Alex said, with his face turning 100 shades of red.

I explained to Alex that it's about building bridges, not a wall. I told him, if we were to all move forward…but he cursed under his breath, and rolled his eyes, still saying, "Not going to happen, anytime soon, mate."

Kim looked at Alex, as though he shouldn't really be answering for her, but she said nothing. Instead chose to sip her coffee, and nibble on a shortbread biscuit, smiling to herself at some amusing thought.

Changing the subject, I asked Kim how her pregnancy was going.

First, she looked at her husband, blushed and continued to nibble on her biscuit, as he glared at me. His cheeks flushed, as though I shouldn't have asked.

Alex then gave a glum shrug of the shoulders, Yeah, okay, for a moment I forgot who the father was. Yeah, my stupid son, Rhys.

After an awkward few minutes, she told me that the baby was due in 12 days.

"I can't wait to meet my baby son," she whispered.

That's when her husband looked at her, and his chin dipping to his chest, his facial expression was one of a chef whose souffle had just collapsed.

I guess you could say he was not happy about his wife having a baby for my son. Well, what man would be happy with their wife having another man's child?

My wife wanted to be involved in the baby's life, as well as myself. I know that Rhys chose his son's name. Hmm, what did he? Say again?

Alex kindly reminded me and let me know that the baby would also have his middle name and surname. Mikel Lyndsay Jordan Roberts. What a bloody mouthful.

The name Jordan Roberts, that's Alex's middle, and surname, guess he got the last laugh.

Now, swiftly changing the subject again, because these two fools were doing my bloody head in.

It's sad that some monster decided to send Tianna death threats, all because I've been released from prison.

Not only her, but her best friend, Renee, who is a prison guard at the prison where I was.

I've got my suspicions, but you know what, I believe that you're innocent, until proven guilty. So, I won't call that little shit, Alex's name, oh fuck.

Well, now it's out there. Yeah, judging by his demeanour, I'm one hundred and ten per cent sure, it's that bloody idiot.

But as of yet, I really don't have any proof. The smart bastard had used a burner phone. But you know what, I've met some right shits inside, I'd have that bastard taken care of. You mark my words.

If my son weren't married to Tianna, I'd have Alex disappear, preferably six feet under, like his daddy Carl.

Then Rhys could be happy with Kim. Oops, did I just say that out loud?

Oh, flipping hell, listen to me babbling on. I've just been released from prison. I'm not planning on going back anytime soon.

I'd really appreciate it if no one mentioned to Alex that I've cottoned onto him, especially you, Rhys.

The pathetic little shit, won't see what's coming to him.

What the hell. I had it all planned. But my son informed me, if I dare lay a finger on Alex and Kim finds out, she'll never forgive us and he'd lose any chance of them being a couple.

Fuck Alex, that stupid idiot. I'd only go, and get someone else to fuck him up, enough said.

Rhys

We all had a lovely Christmas, and New Year. Having my dad home, what more could you ask for. My mum was happy that her husband is home at last. Who can get used to an empty bed space, when the love of your life has been sleeping there for over 35 years.

So, now, my phone was ringing, like there's no tomorrow. It's that dude Alex. What the hell does he want?

All I heard him say at first was:

"If I didn't have a pregnant wife, practically begging me, I wouldn't even be making this phone call, believe me, Rhys, even though it's your kid," he blurted out, his voice getting frustrated by the minute.

Oh God, Kim has gone to hospital. She's in labour. Oh God, she's having my son.

Alex has warned me not to come to the hospital. He can't stop me. Kim might be his wife, but she's having my son.

30 minutes later, I arrived at the maternity ward. Obviously, they didn't let me in or tell me any information because I'm not her husband.

My wife did ask me to show Alex some respect and not to go. I looked at my wife, she began to cry. Something she's been doing a lot of lately.

She forgot she was holding a bottle of perfume that my mum had given her as a Christmas present. It dropped out of her hand, probably because I stood there, like some idiot, begging my wife to let me go to the hospital.

"Kim's having my baby. I promise you, it will be the first and last time that I do something you're totally against."

Then turned my back on her and ran out of the house, slamming the street door shut before she even had the chance to answer.

I waited for about two hours in the hospital waiting room, and finally Kim phoned. She asked me to come onto the ward to see my son.

When I got there, that dude Alex was holding my son, as if he was the daddy.

He stood there, watching me, watching him, holding my son.

So, what does he do next? Yeah, he started cradling my son, rocking him side to side, and kissed him on his forehead. All the while, giving me a look of contempt. I could do nothing, but concede to that arsehole.

I asked Kim how she was doing. She smiled, and said that she was okay. Then told Alex to give my son to me to hold.

He didn't like the thought of being told to let me hold my own baby. But that's exactly what I did.

He's so tiny. Kim told me he weighed 7 lb 6 oz. I just held him for ages, he's so small and beautiful. He's my son.

Anyway, that dude started getting restless. I knew that he wanted me to leave already, but I'm not going anywhere.

Alex then decided to leave the room for a few minutes. I sat next to Kim on her hospital bed.

We both stared at our son, then at each other. I had to, I'm sorry, I just had to let Kim know how I was feeling about her.

She looked at me and said, "Shush, not here, Alex will hear you."

I told Kim, as soon as possible, that we needed to discuss our future together. But she just stared at me.

"Kim, let's just do it, pack your bags, get your kids, and let's just go."

"Are you crazy, Rhys?" she said, now whispering, so Alex couldn't overhear us.

"Kim, don't you love me?"

"Rhys, you just married Tianna. What about your wife?"

I shook my head, I can't believe that Kim was thinking about Tianna, what about her own happiness? I know deep down that she wanted to be with me, so why hold onto Alex, why?

"Look at our son, Kim, think about him."

Kim bit her lip, but didn't acknowledge anything that was said to her.

"We have about 20 seconds, Kim. Decide now, before Alex comes back into the room. Please, Kim," I begged her.

I would have gone down on bending knees, if Alex hadn't been standing watching us.

But of course, she never did give me an answer to my question.

In fact, she only stared at me and said, "Rhys, don't beg, it's pathetic."

Moments later, Alex walked back into the room, his gaze shifting from Kim, then to me.

His whole demeanour suddenly changed, and darkness engulfed me as I felt the full fury of his built-up anger towards me.

He had the nerve to ask me whether my wife wasn't expecting me to be home by now, instead of hanging around maternity wards, where I'm clearly not wanted.

He stood there with a big smirk on his face, so I gave him a sucker punch.

Only this time, I was full of rage, and he felt the full force of my frustration and anger.

He fell to the ground in obvious pain. He lay there, in the foetal position, like the fool that he is.

Kim started screaming, and told me to, get the fuck out. I tried to explain that I was sorry for hitting Alex, but she wasn't ready to listen to my apology.

"Get out, get the fuck out, Rhys," she yelled.

I tried to make amends by offering Alex my hand, but he got up and turned around and started to throw punches, left, right and centre.

So, now we were having a man-to-man fist fight in front of Kim and my son.

Security was quickly called to break up our fight.

We were both escorted off the hospital grounds. I can't believe that, me of all people, would stoop that low, and have a fist fight.

Both of us were black and blue. As for Alex, he came off worse than I. I think he ended up with a broken nose, split lip, and a cut above his left eye.

There was blood all over his white shirt, and a rip in his armpit.

We stood there, I in complete shock, watching each other, trying to suss out our next move. Alex broke the silence and told…actually yelled at me, if I came near his wife again, that he promised to rip me apart next time. I yelled back at him, wiping the blood from my cut, a little surprise at the amount of blood dripping from my wound.

"You're the fool who phoned me up and invited me to the hospital, remember?"

"Yeah, big fucking mistake."

He didn't for one second like my attitude and swung at me with a closed fist.

He somehow missed. I laughed at him when he slipped and fell onto the wet pavement, splitting his trousers.

Right now, I'm not being a gentleman, just an arsehole. I knew it. Alex knew it. Kim knew it. Even my wife, whom I stupidly left at home crying, knew it.

Fuck, I've just noticed the blood on my trousers.

Alex, that dude, saw me trying to wipe the blood off, then shouted, "Yeah go home, and explain that to your wife, you fucking moron."

Then he sped off at high speed from the hospital car park.

I really don't know how I'm going to go home and explain what happened to my wife, really. I don't. I sat in my car, for a long, long time, feeling like the biggest arsehole ever. My heart raced as I sat there, watching shadows sway to the rhythm of a gentle breeze drifting through my open car window. In that moment, I found myself weaving one lie after another to tell my wife.

Eventually, I took a cigarette out from the glove compartment, lit it, and sat there smoking until my phone rang, not once, but several times.

Steve Brooks

Well, I'll be damned. What the fuck, it actually wasn't Alex, who's been sending Tianna, and Renee the death threats. I completely overlooked this person.

Well, it all makes total sense now, when you think about it. Guess you all had your own theories on who it could be.

Blaming Alex was the obvious choice, but who would've thought it was Kim's mum, Denise?

Not in a million years did I see that coming. She was conniving, I give her that. She had us all fooled.

She blamed them for getting me out of prison. What can I say, I'm sorry, that's about it.

When your soul is black, even when the sun shines, you still see darkness.

Guess everyone wanted to know how I managed to suss her out. Sorry, but if I tell you, I'd have to kill you and bury you in Carl's garden. Woah, let's just leave it at that for now.

Now, I hear my son, Rhys, has gone and got himself into trouble, bloody idiots, the pair of them. Fancy fighting for Kim in the hospital ward, especially when she's just given birth.

Son, have I taught you nothing? If it's Kim whom you really want, you're bloody going about it in the wrong way.

I've told my son, don't he dare go home, in that state, to his wife, unless he wants her to kick him out.

He's told me that he knows better than to go home looking all beaten up.

So, he went to Drake's house, for a couple of hours, to cool down, and come up with some cock and bull story to tell his wife.

Just so you know, my son didn't say cock and bull story, it was my chosen words.

His mum would be very disappointed with her son's recent behaviour. I'm not sure, to tell you the truth, why all of a sudden, he was acting this way. Well, that's not strictly true; it's got to do with Kim.

What the love of a woman can do to some men.

Rhys wants what, clearly, he can't have, which in turn was driving him nuts. I only hope that Alex doesn't press assault charges against my son.

Drake

Late last night, my man, Rhys, was here. What the fuck was he playing at, fighting with Alex at the hospital in front of Kim.

Boy oh, boy. He just couldn't go home to his wife looking all bruised and battered. That night, Alex gave Rhys a good kicking, let me tell you.

I asked Renee to clean him up, as best she could.

Then, fucking hell, man, I had to spin my wife, some bull shit story, as to why, he was looking all beaten up.

Do you think for one minute, if I told my wife the truth, who and why my man Rhys was fighting, that she'd help? Not in a million years. Tianna is her good friend, and to know that her husband was fighting over Kim, knowing my wife, she'd have beaten Rhys up, as well.

Why, Rhys, why? What's going on in that head of yours?

Whatever this was right now, I can only see it going down, one of two ways.

Either Rhys would continue with his marriage to Tianna, or cut her loose, before he really hurts her, if he hasn't already. Then he can keep pursuing Kim until she changes her mind. I really can't see that happening anytime soon.

My wife has just spoken to her good friend, Tianna, and she was asking me to talk with her and wants the truth about what really happened to her husband.

My man, Rhys and I, you know that we go way back. We've always helped each other out of hot water. As far back as I can remember, Rhys never lied, not to me, or any woman he's been in a relationship with.

But this, what is happening with the brother? I'm lost for words. I can't put my head around why, well, I know why, really, but Rhys' just messed up, with his feelings for Kim.

I'm not sure how I'd ever look Tianna in her eyes, knowing that her husband, my good friend, was in love with another woman.

You know what, before I open my mouth to his wife, I'd better phone the brother to get our stories straight.

Rhys's not thinking straight, the bull shit story he wanted me to spin to his wife. I might as well tell her that I beat him up.

You ever heard the expression, liars getting caught in their lies. I'd say no more.

Tianna

Heart of a Woman by Summer Walker.

My husband received a phone call from Alex early this morning. I think about 1:26 am. Kim was in labour.

This is it, the day that I've been dreading for months, literally.

He looked at me and smiled as I held his hand and felt it slipping away from my grasp.

"Don't worry, babe, I'll be back soon, love you," he said, before running down the stairs and slamming the street door shut.

This is the truth. My husband right now didn't know whether he was coming or going. So, may tell a different version, the way he saw that day unfold.

I lay in bed thinking and all sorts of thoughts crossed my mind. When my husband lay eyes on his son, would he still want me, or Kim and their baby?

Mr Kitty has just jumped up onto our bed. No, I'm not going to tell him to jump back down. He's the only thing comforting me right now.

Me and Mr Kitty are cuddling up right now, and of course, he's purring, like he always does.

It's almost 7:24 am. I'm taking a peek through the window. My husband still hasn't come home yet from the hospital.

I immediately knew that it was going to be a cold morning, as I could see fog covering the houses across the street.

For a moment, I thought about going back to bed and waiting for my husband to come home. But in the end, I decided to get up and go to work.

I sip my coffee as I continue to look through the window, waiting for Rhys to come home to me.

Meow, said Mr Kitty. Oh gosh, I'm going to be late for work again.

40 minutes or so later, Martin, my boss, was looking in my direction.

He stared at the clock on the office wall, then gave a tutt, and said, "Young lady, my office, now. Why are you always late, your mind is somewhere else lately."

He dived his biscuit into the cup of tea, as I watched half of the biscuit disappear into the bottom of the cup.

He leaned over his desk, which was full of empty biscuit packets, grabbed a teaspoon to retrieve the biscuit from the bottom of his cup.

I apologised to my boss, and was just about to give him an answer that I made up on the spot, when Rhys phoned.

He apologised for not coming home sooner, and said that he wanted to spend a little bit more time with his son, but then had a car accident on the way home. So, he had to phone Drake for help. I asked if he was okay and should I leave work early, and be with him? But he told me not to, and I'd see him when I get home.

Later, when I arrived home and saw his bruised and battered body, I really wanted to scream and cry out loud, but he told me not to, as he was fine.

"Oh my God, Rhys, what happened to you?"

"I'm fine. I'm okay, babe."

My hands trembled as I reached out to touch the cut above his right eye, then the cut across his nose.

He took my hand in his and kissed my forehead. My husband of less than two months stood there, looking directly into my eyes, as I cried, and lied to my face.

Do you know what he told me? After seeing his son, he was just so overwhelmed that when he got into his car, he just drove off, without looking, and hit some guy's car.

He did stop and apologise, but the guy was too angry to listen, then just hit him for no good reason. So, he had to defend himself.

But as soon as he threw the first punch, the guy's friend joined in, that is why he was so battered.

I almost believed him. But remember, I told you that Aubrey, who I thought was my dad, well, turned out he isn't. Anyway, his daughter Larah was at university training to become a midwife.

Well, it so happened that she done a three-week placement on the labour ward. She didn't help to deliver Kim's baby, but there were rumours going around about two men fighting on the labour ward over a lady. And the description of the two men fighting was, of course, none other than my husband and Alex.

This lie that my husband has spun me, where is it all coming from? He's never lied to me in the past, so what has changed?

Even if he knows that what he had to tell me would hurt, he'll tell me, no lies, straight up brutal honesty. But now, I'm at a loss as to why all the lies, why now.

It was the moment, I realised my nightmare was beginning, but I needed to phone Drake. Hopefully, he hasn't turned into a liar as well, overnight.

10 minutes or so later, I composed myself, stopped crying and made that call.

In fact, I phoned Drake several times, each time hanging up, before he answered the call.

And just like I thought, he confirmed that the story, that my husband was telling me was the God's truth.

So, now, I have two lying husbands to deal with, Renee's and mine.

Is my marriage over, before it has really begun? I'm really tempted to phone Kim, but as you know, she recently had her baby. But I'm sorry, fuck her, I'm phoning that bitch.

So, no one is decent enough to be honest and tell me the truth.

As for Kim that bitch, according to her, she was in the bathroom. So, she doesn't know exactly what happened between her husband and Rhys.

But what she did tell me is that Alex was taking out an injunction against my husband, and I'm lucky that her husband was not pressing assault charges as well.

So, as mad as I was, I had to ask, "What about Rhys seeing his baby?"

That lying bitch told me, "Oh, I won't stop Rhys from seeing our son."

Hmm, she's playing with fire. Don't you think?

Her husband had a fight with my husband, and yet, she's there defending Rhys. What kind of a hard face bitch is she? Oh, I've just answered my own question.

Let's get down to business. So, I had to ask that two-faced liar, what her intentions were and did she want my husband?

That bitch told me, "Yes, girl, I want your husband, he was only on loan to you, you're just a placeholder girl, a good short-term girlfriend, until I'm ready to take him back. Oh, and another thing, you're so desperate that you pursued Rhys to lock him down."

Woah, the lying two-faced home-wrecker. Wow, she also let me know that they never actually broke up, and this whole time, they had been carrying on with their affair behind my back.

She was quick to let me know that they had made love in my bed, on my sofa, and in my husband's car.

What a fucking lying two-faced, bitch, she is.

"What if I fucked your husband," I asked her.

Do you know, I could hear her laughing at the other end of the phone line.

Okay, so I let her have her fun, laughing at me, then she said, "My husband? He would never go with a bitch like you, so get over yourself."

I slammed the phone down, collapsed on the bed, and started to cry.

A little voice deep inside cried that if I didn't fight for my husband, then I would have let Kim win. But I needed to know the truth, regardless, whether it hurt or not.

I didn't plan on drinking a half bottle of red wine, but that's what I found myself doing, to pick up the courage to ask my husband to tell me the truth.

So, now it's time to question my husband again. Only this time, he'd better come up with a different story.

I stood looking up at him, only inches between us.

"Rhys, I'm only going to ask you one more time, what happened. If you lie, then we're over. So, you need to tell me the truth about your relationship with Kim."

My husband looked at me, held my hand, placing it against his chest, and said, "Babe, when have I ever lied to you? I've told you what happened, it's the God's honest truth. And as for Kim, there is no me and Kim. I think she's jealous. Remember, jealousy is a powerful emotion."

His voice had an annoyed edge to it. He held me in his arms, looked me deep into my eyes, and kissed me so tenderly on my lips.

"I promise you, babe, there is no Kim and me," he insisted.

I heard a voice whispering in my ear, "Your husband took a test, the results are back. As predicted, he's pathetic."

My husband watched the tears, starting to run down my face, as he stood there looking into my eyes, lying to me.

So, I told him what Kim had said to me. He was taken aback, with his eyebrows raised. He was rendered speechless, with a look of shock on his face. A silence grew between us.

"Babe, what the hell are you talking about? Kim is just messing with you. Don't listen to her. She's angry that you and Renee helped my dad get out of prison, that's all. Please, Tianna. And as for me and Kim, still having an affair, why would you believe her over your own husband?"

The sincerity now in his voice brought more tears to my eyes. My husband's eyes clouded with belated concern, and his voice lost its edge. Why, on God's Earth, would I believe Kim over him? I'd answer that, shall I?

Before he answered my question, he looked down, not able to face me, then covered his face with his hand, finally closing his eyes.

He got angry and defensive, his overblown reaction due to fear of being caught in his lie. He tried and failed, I should point out, to keep the spotlight off his lies.

Every time I asked him a question, he replied, "As far as I recall, or, if you really think about it." Then bit his lip.

So, I dared to look directly in his eyes, told him that I believed her, because every word that came out of his mouth had been a lie so far.

He told me that it wasn't true, and he has never lied to me.

So, I gave my husband an ultimatum to tell me the truth now, or it's over.

My cheating husband stood there gazing into my eyes, cool as a cucumber, and told me what I wanted to know, the truth this time.

"My God, Rhys, what the hell?" I cried my eyes out, no, I was bawling.

I cried, I screamed, I slapped my husband across the face.

That bitch was telling the truth, they never ended their affair, this whole time, they have been carrying on behind my back.

"I want to die, Rhys, I want to die. Do you hear me?" I screamed, hitting him in his chest, over and over again.

Grabbing my arm, then pulling me close to him, he said how sorry he was, and to forgive him.

He begged me not to leave him. But I asked him, why should I stay, if it's Kim that he wanted?

He stood there, with his bare faced lie, as he told me, "I don't want Kim, I want you."

My cheating husband, actually went down on his knees, and asked me not to leave him. What an act. I told him to, fuck off, but he held onto me.

"Rhys, fuck off, and let me go," I shouted, trying to remove his tight grip from my arm.

So, now what, my husband was down on his knees, begging me not to leave him.

"Why should I stay, give me just one reason why I should stay, just one. Yeah, I have one reason. I'm pregnant. Rhys, I'm pregnant. Do you hear me, I'm your wife I'm going to have your baby." I said, sobbing like a child.

He got up from the floor, where he had knelt down, and hugged me.

"We're having a baby," he said, all emotional.

"Oh, Tianna, I love you so much, please forgive me, don't tear our family apart, please, Tianna. I'm so sorry, I'm a total idiot," he sobbed, with tears all welled up in his eyes.

It shouldn't have, but the emotion was so strong, that, it brought tears to my eyes, yet again, although I was as mad as hell.

I agree, my husband is an idiot, but I love him, and I'm not prepared to let Kim take him from me.

No matter how hard she tries I'd try harder to keep him here with me.

Rhys kissed my stomach, and said, "There's a mini me inside there."

I held onto my husband, knowing that, although I'm going to have his baby, he's still in love with Kim, and she can, at some point, take him from me. But for now, he's my husband, and I'm going to make him love me more.

If Kim wanted to lower herself, play dirty, and try to destroy my marriage, then let the games begin.

So, against my better judgement, without discussing it with my friend, Tamara first, I stupidly phoned Kim's husband to tell him about his wife, and my husband sleeping together and that their affair never ended.

I was completely knocked for six, struck dumb, is a more appropriate word to use. Alex told me that he knew all about my husband, and his wife fucking each other, as he sometimes joined in.

His exact words were, "I like to watch your husband fuck my wife."

He actually said, what a turn on it was for him, then he yelled, "It's time to fuck shit up."

What the hell was going on? This was certainly not the response that I had hoped for. I'm not even bothering to respond to Alex's remarks, he'd never watch my husband fuck his wife.

My good friend, Tamara happened to phone me, shortly after I spoke with Alex. So, I told her about the conversation between Alex and me. I definitely heard when she gasped.

Reeling and in shock, I asked, "Do you really think that they are having a threesome."

At first, she was silent for a few seconds then, the answer came to her in a blinding flash.

"Tianna, think about it, do you really think, Kim's husband would turn a blind eye to her having an affair with Rhys, let alone join in on them having sex. My God, girl, it definitely sounds like they are both playing you."

"Maybe they are, but why, I can't possibly think of anything that I've done, for them to hate me, like they do," I sobbed to Tamara.

Rhys was right, it was me who encouraged Steve to appeal his sentence. Oh my God. Before I came along and suggested it to him and Rhys, he was quite happy to sit in prison for 25 years and rot.

I'm so pleased, that I spoke with my good friend. Tamara. Like I've always said, she is level-headed, what she has just said, makes total sense to me.

Drying my eyes, with my husband's favourite t-shirt, I realised I've been made a fool of by Kim and Alex.

My God, I almost believed Kim. Why would I disbelieve my husband? He has never, like he has said, lied to me.

I seriously have some making up to do to my husband. Although I asked Rhys to tell me the truth, I thought that he was lying, until Tamara suggested to think carefully about what Kim and Alex both said.

Rhys did say that, although he still had feelings for Kim, he would never act on them.

"I'm yours," he said.

Stroking my face, he kissed me, then bit my top lip softly. I did ask him why he spun me a pack of lies about still having an affair with Kim. His answer, because it was what, I wanted to hear.

Rhys and I have decided to put this whole saga of, he said, she said, behind us.

We're going to have a well-deserved, romantic evening together.

We had a gourmet meal at a rooftop bar, and restaurant, with a panoramic view on the 10th floor, overlooking the city. I stood looking through the window, with my husband standing behind me, with his arms tightly around my waist.

Breathing in my scent, he whispered in my ear, "I love you, Tianna Brooks."

Afterwards, we went for a stroll along the Thames Embankment. It was such a lovely evening, my husband and I, walking hand-in-hand, gazing up at the stars above.

"Babe, never, ever, doubt, the love that I have for you."

"How could I ever doubt you, Rhys, my husband, the man that I promised, to love for eternity."

He put his arms around me, then moved the hair from my face, to reveal my smile. The smile that says a thousand times over, I love you, Rhys Brooks.

As I snuggled up close to my husband, he got a text message from Kim, which read, "Babe, we need to talk."

Stunned, I was silent, staring at his phone in his hand, trying to digest her text message.

Silence followed, and I wondered if my paranoia had cause me to imagine it. His eyes shone and his lips twitched, as if he were smiling to himself, at some amusing thought, then shoved his phone back into his pocket.

He gazed down at me, smiled through the anguish his eyes betrayed and spoke, "Do you know how much I love you?"

"I love you too."

Those eight words revealed why I chose to keep smiling in the worst of circumstances.